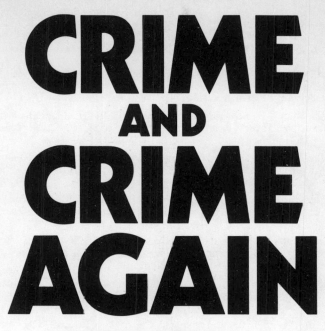

CRIME
AND
CRIME
AGAIN

Mystery Stories
by the World's Great Writers,
Including Joyce Carol Oates,
Arthur Miller, Norman Mailer,
and P.G. Wodehouse

Edited by

Bill Pronzini, Barry N. Malzberg,

and Martin H. Greenberg

Originally published as *Mystery in the Mainstream*

BONANZA BOOKS
NEW YORK

Originally published as *Mystery in the Mainstream*

Copyright © 1986 by Bill Pronzini, Barry N. Malzberg, and Martin H. Greenberg
All rights reserved.

This 1990 edition is published by Bonanza Books, distributed by Outlet Book Company, Inc., a Random House Company, 225 Park Avenue South, New York, New York 10003, by arrangement with William Morrow & Company, Inc.

Printed and bound in the United States of America

Library of Congress Cataloging-in-Publication Data
Mystery in the mainstream.
    Crime and crime again : unexpected mystery stories by the world's great writers.../ edited by Bill Pronzini, Barry N. Malzberg & Martin H. Greenberg.
        p.   cm.
    "Originally published as Mystery in the mainstream."
    ISBN 0-517-01758-X
    1. Detective and mystery stories.   I. Pronzini, Bill.
II. Malzberg, Barry N.   III. Greenberg, Martin Harry.   IV. Title.
PN6120.95.D45M9 1990   90-47812
808.83'872—dc20   CIP

Book design by Jaye Zimet

8 7 6 5 4 3 2 1

CONTENTS

INTRODUCTION

The renowned mystery writer, editor, and scholar of the criminous short story, Ellery Queen, once wrote: "Few people realize—few critics, too—that nearly every world-famous author, throughout the entire history of literature, has tried his hand at writing the detective or crime story." And yet the essential fact is an obvious one when you consider literary history from a thematic point of view.

Think of any important author, past or present, and that author will have produced at least one work with a criminous theme. Homer? The *Iliad* is a story about a kidnapping. Chaucer? More than one of the Canterbury Tales is about crime—"The Pardoner's Tale," for instance. Shakespeare? *Macbeth* is a pure murder story, and murder and violence are prominent features of several of the Bard's other plays. Sir Walter Scott? "The Two Drovers" is both a tale of homicide and a trial story. Honoré de Balzac? Many of his ninety-plus novels deal with crime and criminals, including *The Human Comedy.* Victor Hugo's *Les Misérables* and Dostoevski's *Crime and Punishment* are each brilliant psychological crime studies. Joseph Conrad's *The Secret Agent* is a tale of intrigue and espionage. Mark Twain's "The Stolen White Elephant" and "Tom Sawyer, Detective" are delightfully humorous detective stories.

Some mainstream writers have, in fact, made major, even seminal contributions to the development of the mystery genre. Edgar Allan Poe is often referred to as the "father of the mystery story"; in but five tales he anticipated every major plot device associated with the form. "The Murders in the Rue Morgue" is the first locked-room enigma; "The Mystery of Marie Roget" is the first psychological detective story; "The Gold-Bug" is both the first cipher story and a masterpiece of deductive analysis; "The Purloined Letter" combines the secret-agent story with pure ratiocination; and "Thou Art the Man" utilizes such now-standard ploys as false clues, ballistics, and the least likely person as the guilty party. Charles Dickens, in his unfinished and posthumously published *The Mystery of Edwin Drood*, provided an unsolved mystery that has tantalized readers and scholars for well over a century. Wilkie Collins's *The Moonstone* and *The Woman in White* are oft-imitated giants of the Gothic crime novel whose complex plots anticipate such other modern genre staples as red herrings and cliffhanger chapter endings.

In this century no short story has been more often impersonated in style and substance, especially by crime writers, than Hemingway's account of two professional assassins on a mission in a small town, "The Killers." Arguably, it is the finest of all of Hemingway's short fiction. The same is true of William Faulkner's terrifying "A Rose for Emily." In the novel form, Hemingway's *To Have and Have Not* has had a great deal of stylistic and thematic influence on the traditional crime story. And to an even greater extent, so has James M. Cain's elemental narrative of sex and violence, *The Postman Always Rings Twice*.

Not only do mainstream writers often choose to write literary stories about crime, occasionally they choose to write traditional mystery stories (or what they consider to be traditional mystery stories) under their own names or, more often, under pseudonyms. None other than the creator of Sherlock Holmes, Sir Arthur Conan Doyle, considered himself a literary writer and his historical novels and works on spiritualism far more important than his detective fiction. Graham Greene prefers to label such outstanding crime and espionage novels as *Orient Express, This Gun for Hire, Ministry of Fear,* and *Brighton Rock* as "entertainments" to differentiate them from his more "serious" works. William Faulkner's "Uncle" Gavin Stevens, Yoknapatawpha County attorney and sleuth, investigates a variety of crimes in the six mystery stories that comprise the 1949 collection *Knight's Gambit* (as well as the murder in the mainstream novel, *Intruder in the Dust*). In the early 1950s Gore Vidal wrote three straightforward (and unfortunately less than memorable) detective novels as by Edgar Box: *Death in the Fifth Position, Death Before Bedtime,* and *Death Likes It Hot.* And over the past thirty years Evan Hunter, author of such acclaimed novels as *The Blackboard Jungle* and *Last Summer,* has made a second "name" for himself—that of Ed McBain—with his 87th Precinct series of police procedurals.

Whatever the type of crime story mainstream writers choose to write, they generally do it well—even when, in the words of Ellery Queen, they "stoop to conquer." For as another renowned mystery novelist, Donald E. Westlake, has written, "writers of substance tend to write stories of substance no matter what the story category. Great writers, when they write mystery stories, write great mystery stories."

The entries in this anthology are great mystery stories. They are also relatively little-known mystery stories. No good purpose would have been served in reprinting yet again such familiar tales as "The Stolen White Elephant," "The Killers," and "A Rose for Emily"; the rationale behind *Crime and Crime Again* was to gather together a selection of *un*familiar, entertaining, and thought-provoking stories by some of the most influential writers of the past 150 years, from Nathaniel Hawthorne to Norman Mailer.

It has been our pleasure to select these stories; your pleasure lies ahead. By all means proceed with dispatch.

—BILL PRONZINI, MARTIN
H. GREENBERG, and
BARRY N. MALZBERG

Nathaniel Hawthorne (1804–1864) was the first American writer to explore the dark side of human nature. Born in Salem, Massachusetts, of an old New England family, Hawthorne began writing while at Bowdoin College and spent the decade following his graduation developing the skills that would make him a major figure in American literature. His dream to write full-time was frustrated by economic realities, but he nevertheless produced some of the most important work of the mid-nineteenth century—the story collections Twice-Told Tales *(1837),* Mosses from an Old Manse *(1846), and* The Snow-Image and Other Tales *(1851); and the novels* The Scarlet Letter *(1851), a major thematic contribution to the development of the crime story in the United States, and* The House of the Seven Gables *(1851). "The Birthmark" is Hawthorne at his darkest and most powerful.*

THE BIRTHMARK
Nathaniel Hawthorne

In the latter part of the last century there lived a man of science, an eminent proficient in every branch of natural philosophy, who not long before our story opens had made experience of a spiritual affinity more attractive than any chemical one. He had left his laboratory to the case of an assistant, cleared his fine countenance from the furnace smoke, washed the stain of acid from his fingers, and persuaded a beautiful woman to become his wife. In those days when the comparatively recent discovery of electricity and other kindred mysteries of Nature seemed to open paths into the region of miracle, it was not unusual for the love of science to rival the love of woman in its depth and absorbing energy. The higher intellect, the imagination, the spirit, and even the heart might all find their congenial aliment in pursuits which, as some of their ardent votaries believed, would ascend from one step of powerful intelligence to another, until the philosopher should lay his hand on the secret of creative force and perhaps make new worlds for himself. We know not whether Aylmer possessed this degree of faith in man's ultimate control over Nature. He had devoted himself, however, too unreservedly to scientific studies ever to be weaned from them by any second passion. His love for his young wife might prove the stronger of the two; but it could only be by intertwining itself with his love of science, and uniting the strength of the latter to his own.

Such a union accordingly took place, and was attended with truly remarkable consequences and a deeply impressive moral. One day, very soon after their marriage, Aylmer sat gazing at his wife with a trouble in his countenance that grew stronger until he spoke.

"Georgiana," said he, "has it never occurred to you that the mark upon your cheek might be removed?"

"No, indeed," said she, smiling; but perceiving the seriousness of his manner, she blushed deeply. "To tell you the truth it has been so often called a charm that I was simple enough to imagine it might be so."

"Ah, upon another face perhaps it might," replied her husband; "but never on yours. No, dearest Georgiana, you came so nearly perfect from the hand of Nature that this slightest possible defect, which we hesitate whether to term a defect or a beauty, shocks me, as being the visible mark of earthly imperfection."

"Shocks you, my husband!" cried Georgiana, deeply hurt; at first reddening with momentary anger, but then bursting into tears. "Then why did you take me from my mother's side? You cannot love what shocks you!"

To explain this conversation it must be mentioned that in the center of Georgiana's left cheek there was a singular mark, deeply interwoven, as it were, with the texture and substance of her face. In the usual state of her complexion—a healthy though delicate bloom—the mark wore a tint of deeper crimson, which imperfectly defined its shape amid the surrounding rosiness. When she blushed it gradually became more indistinct, and finally vanished amid the triumphant rush of blood that bathed the whole cheek with its brilliant glow. But if any shifting motion caused her to turn pale there was the mark again, a crimson stain upon the snow, in what Aylmer sometimes deemed an almost fearful distinctness. Its shape bore not a little similarity to the human hand, though of the smallest pygmy size. Georgiana's lovers were wont to say that some fairy at her birth hour had laid her tiny hand upon the infant's cheek, and left this impress there in token of the magic endowments that were to give her such sway over all hearts. Many a desperate swain would have risked life for the privilege of pressing his lips to the mysterious hand. It must not be concealed, however, that the impression wrought by this fairy sign manual varied exceedingly, according to the difference of temperament in the beholders. Some fastidious persons—but they were exclusively of her own sex—affirmed that the bloody hand, as they chose to call it, quite destroyed the effect of Georgiana's beauty, and rendered her countenance even hideous. But it would be as reasonable to say that one of those small blue stains which sometimes occur in the purest statuary marble would convert the Eve of Powers to a monster. Masculine observers, if the birthmark did not heighten their admiration, contented themselves with wishing it away, that the world might possess one living specimen of ideal loveliness without the semblance of a flaw. After his marriage—for he thought little or nothing of the matter before—Aylmer discovered that this was the case with himself.

Had she been less beautiful—if Envy's self could have found aught else to sneer at—he might have felt his affection heightened by the prettiness of this mimic hand, now vaguely portrayed, now lost, now stealing forth again and glimmering to and fro with every pulse of emotion that throbbed within her heart; but seeing her otherwise so perfect, he found this one defect grow more and more intolerable with every moment of their united lives. It was the fatal flaw of humanity which Nature, in one shape or another, stamps ineffaceably on all her productions, either to imply that they are temporary and finite, or that their perfection must be wrought by toil and pain. The crimson hand expressed the ineludible gripe in which mortality clutches the highest and purest of earthly mold, degrading them into kindred with the lowest, and even with the very brutes, like whom their visible frames return to dust. In this manner, selecting it as the symbol of his wife's liability to sin, sorrow, decay, and death, Aylmer's somber imagination was not long in rendering the birthmark a frightful object, causing him more trouble and horror than ever Georgiana's beauty, whether of soul or sense, had given him delight.

At all the seasons which should have been their happiest, he invariably and without intending it, nay, in spite of a purpose to the contrary, reverted to this one disastrous topic. Trifling as it at first appeared, it so connected itself with innumerable trains of thought and modes of feeling that it became the central point of all. With the morning twilight Aylmer opened his eyes upon his wife's face and recognized the symbol of imperfection; and when they sat together at the evening hearth his eyes wandered stealthily to her cheek, and beheld, flickering with the blaze of the wood fire, the spectral hand that wrote mortality where he would fain have worshipped. Georgiana soon learned to shudder at his gaze. It needed but a glance with the peculiar expression that his face often wore to change the roses of her cheek into a deathlike paleness, amid which the crimson hand was brought strongly out, like a bas-relief of ruby on the whitest marble.

Late one night when the lights were growing dim, so as hardly to betray the stain on the poor wife's cheek, she herself, for the first time, voluntarily took up the subject.

"Do you remember, my dear Aylmer," said she, with a feeble attempt at a smile, "have you any recollection of a dream last night about this odious hand?"

"None! None whatever!" replied Aylmer, starting; but then he added, in a dry, cold tone, affected for the sake of concealing the real depth of his emotion, "I might well dream of it; for before I fell asleep it had taken a pretty firm hold of my fancy."

"And you did dream of it?" continued Georgiana, hastily;

for she dreaded lest a gush of tears should interrupt what she had to say. "A terrible dream! I wonder that you can forget it. Is it possible to forget this one expression?—'It is in her heart now; we must have it out!' Reflect, my husband; for by all means I would have you recall that dream."

The mind is in a sad state when Sleep, the all-involving, cannot confine her specters within the dim region of her sway, but suffers them to break forth, affrighting this actual life with secrets that perchance belong to a deeper one. Aylmer now remembered his dream. He had fancied himself with his servant Aminadab, attempting an operation for the removal of the birthmark; but the deeper went the knife, the deeper sank the hand, until at length its tiny grasp appeared to have caught hold of Georgiana's heart; whence, however, her husband was inexorably resolved to cut or wrench it away.

When the dream had shaped itself perfectly in his memory, Aylmer sat in his wife's presence with guilty feeling. Truth often finds its way to the mind close muffled in robes of sleep, and then speaks with uncompromising directness of matters in regard to which we practice an unconscious self-deception during our waking moments. Until now he had not been aware of the tyrannizing influence acquired by one idea over his mind, and of the lengths which he might find in his heart to go for the sake of giving himself peace.

"Aylmer," resumed Georgiana, solemnly, "I know not what may be the cost to both of us to rid me of this fatal birthmark. Perhaps its removal may cause cureless deformity; or it may be the stain goes as deep as life itself. Again: do we know that there is a possibility, on any terms, of unclasping the firm gripe of this little hand which was laid upon me before I came into the world?"

"Dearest Georgiana, I have spent much thought upon the subject," hastily interrupted Aylmer. "I am convinced of the perfect practicability of its removal."

"If there be the remotest possibility of it," continued Georgiana, "let the attempt be made at whatever risk. Danger is nothing to me; for life, while this hateful mark makes me the object of your horror and disgust—life is a burden which I would fling down with joy. Either remove this dreadful hand, or take my wretched life! You have deep science. All the world bears witness of it. You have achieved great wonders. Cannot you remove this little, little mark, which I cover with the tips of two small fingers? Is this beyond your power, for the sake of your own peace, and to save your poor wife from madness?"

"Noblest, dearest, tenderest wife," cried Aylmer, rapturously, "doubt not my power. I have already given this matter the deepest thought—thought which might almost have enlightened me to create a being less perfect than yourself. Georgiana, you have led me deeper than ever into the heart of science. I feel myself fully competent to render this dear cheek as faultless as its fellow; and then, most beloved, what will be my triumph when I shall have corrected what Nature left imperfect in her fairest work! Even Pygmalion, when his sculptured woman assumed life, felt not greater ecstasy than mine will be."

"It is resolved, then," said Georgiana, faintly smiling. "And, Aylmer, spare me not, though you should find the birthmark take refuge in my heart at last."

Her husband tenderly kissed her cheek—her right cheek—not that which bore the impress of the crimson hand.

The next day Aylmer apprised his wife of a plan that he had formed whereby he might have opportunity for the intense thought and constant watchfulness which the proposed operation would require; while Georgiana, likewise, would enjoy the perfect repose essential to its success. They were able to seclude themselves in the extensive apartments occupied by Aylmer as a laboratory, and where, during his toilsome youth, he had made discoveries in the elemental powers of Nature that had roused the admiration of all the learned societies in Europe. Seated calmly in this laboratory, the pale philosopher had investigated the secrets of the highest cloud region and of the profoundest mines; he had satisfied himself of the causes that kindled and kept alive the fires of the volcano; and had explained the mystery of fountains, and how it is that they gush forth, some so bright and pure, and others with such rich medicinal virtues, from the dark bosom of the earth. Here, too, at an earlier period, he had studied the wonders of the human frame, and attempted to fathom the very process by which Nature assimilates all her precious influences from earth and air, and from the spiritual world, to create and foster man, her masterpiece. The latter pursuit, however, Aylmer had long laid aside in unwilling recognition of the truth—against which all seekers sooner or later stumble—that our great creative Mother, while she amuses us with apparently working in the broadest sunshine, is yet severely careful to keep her own secrets, and, in spite of her pretended openness, shows us nothing but results. She permits us, indeed, to mar, but seldom to mend, and, like a jealous patentee, on no account to make. Now, however, Aylmer resumed these half-forgotten investigations; not, of course, with such hopes or wishes as first suggested them; but because they involved much physiological truth and lay in the path of his proposed scheme for the treatment of Georgiana.

As he led her over the threshold of the laboratory, Georgiana was cold and tremulous. Aylmer looked cheerfully into her face, with intent to reassure her, but was so startled with the intense glow of the birthmark upon the whiteness of her cheek that he could not restrain a strong convulsive shudder. His wife fainted.

"Aminadab! Aminadab!" shouted Aylmer, stamping violently on the floor.

Forthwith there issued from an inner apartment a man of low stature, but bulky frame, with shaggy hair hanging about his visage, which was grimed with the vapors of the furnace. This personage had been Aylmer's underworker during his whole scientific career, and was admirably fitted for that office by his great mechanical readiness, and the skill with which, while incapable of comprehending a single principle, he executed all the details of his master's experiments. With his vast strength, his shaggy hair, his smoky aspect, and the indescribable earthiness that incrusted him, he seemed to represent man's physical nature; while Aylmer's slender figure, and pale, intellectual face, were no less apt a type of the spiritual element.

"Throw open the door of the boudoir, Aminadab," said Aylmer, "and burn a pastil."

"Yes, master," answered Aminadab, looking intently at the lifeless form of Georgiana; and then he muttered to himself, "If she were my wife, I'd never part with that birthmark."

When Georgiana recovered consciousness she found herself breathing an atmosphere of penetrating fragrance, the gentle potency of which had recalled her from her deathlike faintness. The scene around her looked like enchantment. Aylmer had converted those smoky, dingy, somber rooms, where he had spent his brightest years in recondite pursuits, into a series of beautiful apartments not unfit to be the secluded abode of a lovely woman. The walls were hung with gorgeous curtains, which imparted the combination of grandeur and grace that no other species of adornment can achieve; and as they fell from the ceiling to the floor, their rich and ponderous folds, concealing all angles and straight lines, appeared to shut in the scene from infinite space. For aught Georgiana knew, it might be a pavilion among the clouds. And Aylmer, excluding the sunshine, which would have interfered with his chemical processes, had supplied its place with perfumed lamps, emitting flames of various hue, but all uniting in a soft, impurpled radiance. He now knelt by his wife's side, watching her earnestly, but without alarm; for he was confident in his science, and felt that he could draw a magic circle round her within which no evil might intrude.

"Where am I? Ah, I remember," said Georgiana, faintly; and she placed her hand over her cheek to hide the terrible mark from her husband's eyes.

"Fear not, dearest!" exclaimed he. "Do not shrink from me! Believe me, Georgiana, I even rejoice in this single imperfection, since it will be such a rapture to remove it."

"Oh, spare me!" sadly replied his wife. "Pray do not look at it again. I never can forget that convulsive shudder."

In order to soothe Georgiana, and, as it were, to release her mind from the burden of actual things, Aylmer now put in practice some of the light and playful secrets which science had taught him among its profounder lore. Airy figures, absolutely bodiless ideas, and forms of unsubstantial beauty came and danced before her, imprinting their momentary footsteps on beams of light. Though she had some indistinct idea of the method of these optical phenomena, still the illusion was almost perfect enough to warrant the belief that her husband possessed sway over the spiritual world. Then again, when she felt a wish to look forth from her seclusion, immediately, as if her thoughts were answered, the procession of external existence flitted across a screen. The scenery and the figures of actual life were perfectly represented, but with that bewitching, yet indescribable difference which always makes a picture, an image, or a shadow so much more attractive than the original. When wearied of this, Aylmer bade her cast her eyes upon a vessel containing a quantity of earth. She did so, with little interest at first; but was soon startled to perceive the germ of a plant shooting upward from the soil. Then came the slender stalk; the leaves gradually unfolded themselves; and amid them was a perfect and lovely flower.

"It is magical!" cried Georgiana. "I dare not touch it."

"Nay, pluck it," answered Aylmer—"pluck it, and inhale its brief perfume while you may. The flower will wither in a few moments and leave nothing save its brown seed vessels, but thence may be perpetuated a race as ephemeral as itself."

But Georgiana had no sooner touched the flower than the whole plant suffered a blight, its leaves turning coal-black as if by the agency of fire.

"There was too powerful a stimulus," said Aylmer, thoughtfully.

To make up for this abortive experiment, he proposed to take her portrait by a scientific process of his own invention. It was to be effected by rays of light striking upon a polished plate of metal. Georgiana assented; but, on looking at the result, was afrighted to find the features of the portrait blurred and indefinable; while the minute figure of a hand appeared where the cheek should have been. Aylmer snatched the metallic plate and threw it into a jar of corrosive acid.

Soon, however, he forgot those mortifying failures. In the intervals of study and chemical experiment he came to her flushed and exhausted, but seemed invigorated by her presence, and spoke in glowing language of the resources of his art. He gave a history of the long dynasty of the alchemists, who spent so many ages in quest of the universal solvent by which the golden principle might be elicited from all things vile and base. Aylmer appeared to believe that, by the plainest scientific logic, it was altogether within the limits of possibility to discover this long-sought medium; "but," he added, "a philosopher who should go deep enough to acquire the power would attain too lofty a wisdom to stoop to the exercise of it." Not less singular were his opinions in regard to the elixir vitae. He more than intimated that it was at his option to concoct a liquid that should prolong life for years, perhaps interminably; but that it would produce a discord in Nature which all the world, and chiefly the quaffer of the immortal nostrum, would find cause to curse.

"Aylmer, are you in earnest?" asked Georgiana, looking at him with amazement and fear. "It is terrible to possess such power, or even to dream of possessing it."

"Oh, do not tremble, my love," said her husband. "I would not wrong either you or myself by working such inharmonious effects upon our lives; but I would have you consider how trifling, in comparison, is the skill requisite to remove this little hand."

At the mention of the birthmark, Georgiana, as usual, shrank as if a red-hot iron had touched her cheek.

Again Aylmer applied himself to his labors. She could hear his voice in the distant furnace room giving directions to Aminadab, whose harsh, uncouth, misshapen tones were audible in response, more like the grunt or growl of a brute than human speech. After hours of absence, Aylmer reappeared and proposed that she should now examine his cabinet of chemical products and natural treasures of the earth. Among the former he showed her a small vial, in which, he remarked, was contained a gentle yet most powerful fragrance, capable of impregnating all the breezes that blow across a kingdom. They were of inestimable value, the contents of that little vial; and, as he said so, he threw some of the perfume into the air and filled the room with piercing and invigorating delight.

"And what is this?" asked Georgiana, pointing to a small crystal globe containing a gold-colored liquid. "It is so beautiful to the eye that I could imagine it the elixir of life."

"In one sense it is," replied Aylmer; "or, rather, the elixir of immortality. It is the most precious poison that ever was concocted in this world. By its aid I could apportion the lifetime of any mortal at whom you might point your finger. The strength of the dose would determine whether he were to linger out years, or drop dead in the midst of a breath. No king on his guarded throne could keep his life if I, in my private station, should deem that the welfare of millions justified me in depriving him of it."

"Why do you keep such a terrific drug?" inquired Georgiana in horror.

"Do not mistrust me, dearest," said her husband, smiling; "its virtuous potency is yet greater than its harmful one. But see! Here is a powerful cosmetic. With a few drops of this in a vase of water, freckles may be washed away as easily as the hands are cleansed. A stronger infusion would take the blood out of the cheek, and leave the rosiest beauty a pale ghost."

"Is it with this lotion that you intend to bathe my cheek?" asked Georgiana, anxiously.

"Oh, no," hastily replied her husband; "this is merely superficial. Your case demands a remedy that shall go deeper."

In his interviews with Georgiana, Aylmer generally made minute inquiries as to her sensations and whether the confinement of the rooms and the temperature of the atmosphere agreed with her. These questions had such a particular drift that Georgiana began to conjecture that she was already subjected to certain physical influences, either breathed in with the fragrant air or taken with her food. She fancied likewise, but it might be altogether fancy, that there was a stirring up of her system—a strange, indefinite sensation creeping through her veins, and tingling, half painfully, half pleasurably, at her heart. Still, whenever she dared to look into the mirror, there she beheld herself pale as a white rose and with the crimson birthmark stamped upon her cheek. Not even Aylmer now hated it so much as she.

To dispel the tedium of the hours which her husband found it necessary to devote to the processes of combination and analysis, Georgiana turned over the volumes of his scientific library. In many dark old tomes she met with chapters full of romance and poetry. They were the works of the philosophers of the middle ages, such as Albertus Magnus, Cornelius Agrippa, Paracelsus, and the famous friar who created the prophetic Brazen Head. All these antique naturalists stood in advance of their centuries, yet were imbued with some of their credulity, and therefore were believed, and perhaps imagined themselves to have acquired from the investigation of Nature a power above Nature, and from physics a sway over the spiritual world. Hardly less curious and imaginative were the early volumes of the Transactions of the Royal Society, in which the members, knowing little of the limits of natural possibility, were continually recording wonders or proposing methods whereby wonders might be wrought.

But to Georgiana the most engrossing volume was a large folio from her husband's own hand, in which he had recorded every experiment of his scientific career, its original aim, the methods adopted for its development, and its final success or failure, with the circumstances to which either event was attributable. The book, in truth, was both the history and emblem of his ardent, ambitious, imaginative, yet practical and laborious life. He handled physical details as if there were nothing beyond them; yet spiritualized them all, and redeemed himself from materialism by his strong and eager aspiration towards the infinite. In his grasp the veriest clod of earth assumed a soul. Georgiana, as she read, reverenced Aylmer and loved him more profoundly than ever, but with a less entire dependence on his judgment than heretofore. Much as he had accomplished, she could not but observe that his most splendid successes were almost invariably failures, if compared with the ideal at which he aimed. His brightest diamonds were the merest pebbles, and felt to be so by himself, in comparison with the inestimable gems which lay hidden beyond his reach. The volume, rich with achievements that had won renown for its author, was yet as melancholy a record as ever mortal hand had penned. It was the sad confession and continual exemplification of the shortcomings of the composite man, the spirit burdened with clay and working in matter, and of the despair that assails the higher nature at finding itself so miserably thwarted by the earthly part. Perhaps every man of genius in whatever sphere might recognize the image of his own experience in Aylmer's journal.

So deeply did these reflections affect Georgina that she laid her face upon the open volume and burst into tears. In this situation she was found by her husband.

"It is dangerous to read in a sorcerer's books," said he with a smile, though his countenance was uneasy and displeased. "Georgiana, there are pages in that volume which I can scarcely glance over and keep my senses. Take heed lest it prove as detrimental to you."

"It has made me worship you more than ever," said she.

"Ah, wait for this one success," rejoined he, "then worship me if you will. I shall deem myself hardly unworthy of it. But come, I have sought you for the luxury of your voice. Sing to me, dearest."

So she poured out the liquid music of her voice to quench the thirst of his spirit. He then took his leave with a boyish exuberance of gaiety, assuring her that her seclusion would endure but a little longer, and that the result was already certain. Scarcely had he departed when Georgiana felt irresistibly impelled to follow him. She had forgotten to inform Aylmer of a symptom which for two or three hours past had begun to excite her attention. It was a sensation in the fatal birthmark, not painful, but which induced a restlessness throughout her system. Hastening after her husband, she intruded for the first time into the laboratory.

The first thing that struck her eye was the furnace, that hot and feverish worker, with the intense glow of its fire, which by the quantities of soot clustered above it seemed to have been burning for ages. There was a distilling apparatus in full operation. Around the room were retorts, tubes, cylinders, crucibles, and other apparatus of chemical research. An electrical machine stood ready for immediate use. The atmosphere felt oppressively close, and was tainted with gaseous odors which had been tormented forth by the processes of science. The severe and homely simplicity of the apartment, with its naked walls and brick pavement, looked strange, accustomed as Georgiana had become to the fantastic elegance of her boudoir. But what chiefly, indeed almost solely, drew her attention was the aspect of Aylmer himself.

He was pale as death, anxious and absorbed, and hung over the furnace as if it depended upon his utmost watchfulness whether the liquid which it was distilling should be the draught of immortal happiness or misery. How different from the sanguine and joyous mien that he had assumed for Georgiana's encouragement!

"Carefully now, Aminadab; carefully, thou human machine; carefully, thou man of clay!" muttered Aylmer, more to himself than his assistant. "Now, if there be a thought too much or too little, it is all over."

"Ho! Ho!" mumbled Aminadab. "Look, master! Look!"

Aylmer raised his eyes hastily, and at first reddened, then grew paler than ever, on beholding Georgiana. He rushed towards her and seized her arm with a gripe that left the print of his fingers upon it.

"Why do you come hither? Have you no trust in your husband?" cried he, impetuously. "Would you throw the blight of that fatal birthmark over my labors? It is not well done. Go, prying woman, go!"

"Nay, Aylmer," said Georgiana with the firmness of which

she possessed no stinted endowment, "it is not you that have a right to complain. You mistrust your wife; you have concealed the anxiety with which you watch the development of this experiment. Think not so unworthily of me, my husband. Tell me all the risk we run, and fear not that I shall shrink; for my share in it is far less than your own."

"No, no, Georgiana!" said Aylmer, impatiently. "It must not be."

"I submit," replied she calmly. "And, Aylmer, I shall quaff whatever draught you bring me; but it will be on the same principle that would induce me to take a dose of poison if offered by your hand."

"My noble wife," said Aylmer, deeply moved, "I knew not the height and depth of your nature until now. Nothing shall be concealed. Know, then, that this crimson hand, superficial as it seems, has clutched its grasp into your being with a strength of which I had no previous conception. I have already administered agents powerful enough to do aught except to change your entire physical system. Only one thing remains to be tried. If that fail us we are ruined."

"Why did you hesitate to tell me this?" asked she.

"Because, Georgiana," said Aylmer, in a low voice, "there is danger."

"Danger? There is but one danger—that this horrible stigma shall be left upon my cheek!" cried Georgiana. "Remove it, remove it, whatever be the cost, or we shall both go mad!"

"Heaven knows your words are too true," said Aylmer, sadly. "And now, dearest, return to your boudoir. In a little while all will be tested."

He conducted her back and took leave of her with a solemn tenderness which spoke far more than his words how much was now at stake. After his departure Georgiana became rapt in musings. She considered the character of Aylmer, and did it completer justice than at any previous moment. Her heart exulted, while it trembled, at his honorable love—so pure and lofty that it would accept nothing less than perfection nor miserably make itself contented with an earthlier nature than he had dreamed of. She felt how much more precious was such a sentiment than that meaner kind which would have borne with the imperfection for her sake, and have been guilty of treason to holy love by degrading its perfect idea to the level of the actual; and with her whole spirit she prayed that, for a single moment, she might satisfy his highest and deepest conception. Longer than one moment she well knew it could not be; for his spirit was ever on the march, ever ascending, and each instant required something that was beyond the scope of the instant before.

The sound of her husband's footsteps aroused her. He bore a crystal goblet containing a liquor colorless as water, but bright enough to be the draught of immortality. Aylmer was pale; but it seemed rather the consequence of a highly wrought state of mind and tension of spirit than of fear or doubt.

"The concoction of the draught has been perfect," said he, in answer to Georgiana's look. "Unless all my science have deceived me, it cannot fail."

"Save on your account, my dearest Aylmer," observed his wife, "I might wish to put off this birthmark of mortality by relinquishing mortality itself in preference to any other mode. Life is but a sad possession to those who have attained precisely the degree of moral advancement at which I stand. Were I weaker and blinder, it might be happiness. Were I stronger, it might be endured hopefully. But, being what I find myself, methinks I am of all mortals the most fit to die."

"You are fit for heaven without tasting death!" replied her husband. "But why do we speak of dying? The draught cannot fail. Behold its effect upon this plant."

On the window seat there stood a geranium diseased with yellow blotches, which had overspread all its leaves. Aylmer poured a small quantity of the liquid upon the soil in which it grew. In a little time, when the roots of the plant had taken up the moisture, the unsightly blotches began to be extinguished in a living verdure.

"There needed no proof," said Georgiana, quietly. "Give me the goblet. I joyfully stake all upon your word."

"Drink, then, thou lofty creature!" exclaimed Aylmer, with fervid admiration. "There is no taint of imperfection on thy spirit. Thy sensible frame, too, shall soon be all perfect."

She quaffed the liquid and returned the goblet to his hand.

"It is grateful," said she with a placid smile. "Methinks it is like water from a heavenly fountain; for it contains I know not what of unobtrusive fragrance and deliciousness. It allays a feverish thirst that had parched me for many days. Now, dearest, let me sleep. My earthly senses are closing over my spirit like the leaves around the heart of a rose at sunset."

She spoke the last words with a gentle reluctance, as if it required almost more energy than she could command to pronounce the faint and lingering syllables. Scarcely had they loitered through her lips ere she was lost in slumber. Aylmer sat by her side, watching her aspect with the emotions proper to a man the whole value of whose existence was involved in the process now to be tested. Mingled with this mood, however, was the philosophic investigation characteristic of the man of science. Not the minutest symptom escaped him. A heightened flush of the cheek, a slight irregularity of breath, a quiver of the eyelid, a hardly perceptible tremor through the frame—such were the details which, as the moments passed, he wrote down in his folio volume. Intense thought had set its stamp upon every previous page of that volume, but the thoughts of years were all concentrated upon the last.

While thus employed, he failed not to gaze often at the fatal hand, and not without a shudder. Yet once, by a strange and unaccountable impulse, he pressed it with his lips. His spirit recoiled, however, in the very act; and Georgiana, out of the midst of her deep sleep, moved uneasily and murmured as if in remonstrance. Again Aylmer resumed his watch. Nor was it without avail. The crimson hand, which at first had been strongly visible upon the marble paleness of Georgiana's cheek, now grew more faintly outlined. She remained not less pale than ever; but the birthmark, with every breath that came and went, lost somewhat of its former distinctness. Its presence had been awful; its departure was more awful still. Watch the stain of the rainbow fading out of the sky, and you will know how that mysterious symbol passed away.

"By heaven, it is well-nigh gone!" said Aylmer to himself, in almost irrepressible ecstasy. "I can scarcely trace it now. Success! Success! And now it is like the faintest rose color. The lightest flush of blood across her cheek would overcome it. But she is so pale!"

He drew aside the window curtain and suffered the light of natural day to fall into the room and rest upon her cheek. At the same time he heard a gross, hoarse chuckle, which he had long known as his servant Aminadab's expression of delight.

"Ah, clod! Ah, earthly mass!" cried Aylmer, laughing in a sort of frenzy, "you have served me well! Matter and spirit—earth and heaven—have both done their part in this! Laugh, thing of the senses! You have earned the right to laugh."

These exclamations broke Georgiana's sleep. She slowly unclosed her eyes and gazed into the mirror which her husband had arranged for that purpose. A faint smile flitted over her lips when she recognized how barely perceptible was now that crimson hand which had once blazed forth with such disastrous brilliancy as to scare away all their happiness. But then her eyes sought Aylmer's face with a trouble and anxiety that he could by no means account for.

"My poor Aylmer!" murmured she.

"Poor? Nay, richest, happiest, most favored!" exclaimed he. "My peerless bride, it is successful! You are perfect!"

"My poor Aylmer," she repeated, with a more than human tenderness, "you have aimed loftily; you have done nobly. Do not repent that with so high and pure a feeling, you have rejected the best the earth could offer. Aylmer, dearest Aylmer, I am dying!"

Alas! It was too true! The fatal hand had grappled with the mystery of life, and was the bond by which an angelic spirit kept itself in union with a mortal frame. As the last crimson tint of the birthmark—that sole token of human imperfection—faded from her cheek, the parting breath of the now perfect woman passed into the atmosphere, and her soul, lingering a moment near her husband, took its heavenward flight. Then a hoarse, chuckling laugh was heard again! Thus ever does the gross fatality of earth exult in its invariable triumph over the immortal essence which, in this dim sphere of half development, demands the completeness of a higher state. Yet, had Aylmer reached a profounder wisdom, he need not thus have flung away the happiness which would have woven his mortal life of the selfsame texture with the celestial. The momentary circumstance was too strong for him; he failed to look beyond the shadowy scope of time, and, living once for all in eternity, to find the perfect future in the present.

In addition to such literary masterpieces as David Copperfield, Martin Chuzzlewit, A Tale of Two Cities, *and* The Pickwick Papers, Charles Dickens *(1812–1870) wrote short stories for a variety of British weekly periodicals—"popular fictions" designed to help finance a wide range of extra-literary interests that included charitable organizations, social reform, travels in Europe and America, and the managing of a theatrical company. "A Pair of Gloves" is one such story, and one of several excursions into the realm of mystery and crime. Dickens's most famous criminous work is, of course,* The Mystery of Edwin Drood, *the novel on which he was working at the time of his death. Left unfinished, with no clear notes as to its solution,* Edwin Drood *is itself a baffling mystery that has challenged the intellect and ingenuity of countless scholars and armchair detectives for more than a century.*

A PAIR OF GLOVES
Charles Dickens

"It's a singler story, sir," said Inspector Wield, of the detective police, who, in company with Sergeants Dornton and Mith, paid us another twilight visit, one July evening; "and I've been thinking you might like to know it.

"It's concerning the murder of the young woman, Eliza Grimwood, some years ago, over in the Waterloo Road. She was commonly called the Countess, because of her handsome appearance and her proud way of carrying of herself; and when I saw the poor Countess (I had known her well to speak to), lying dead with her throat cut on the floor of her bedroom, you'll believe me that a variety of reflections calculated to make a man rather low in his spirits came into my head.

"That's neither here nor there. I went to the house the morning after the murder, and examined the body, and made a general observation of the bedroom where it was. Turning down the pillow of the bed with my hand, I found underneath it, a pair of gloves. A pair of gentleman's dress gloves, very dirty; and inside the lining, the letters TR, and a cross.

"Well, sir, I took them gloves away, and I showed 'em to the magistrate, over at Union Hall, before whom the case was. He says, 'Wield,' he says, 'there's no doubt this is a discovery that may lead to something very important; and what you have got to do, Wield, is to find out the owner of these gloves.'

"I was of the same opinion, of course, and I went at it immediately. I looked at the gloves pretty narrowly, and it was my opinion that they had been cleaned. There was a smell of sulphur and rosin about 'em, you know, which cleaned gloves usually have, more or less. I took 'em over to a friend of mine at Kennington, who was in that line, and I put it to him. 'What do you say now? Have these gloves been cleaned?' 'These gloves have been cleaned,' says he. 'Have you any idea who cleaned them?' says I. 'Not at all,' says he; 'I've a very distinct idea who *didn't* clean 'em, and that's myself. But I'll tell you what, Wield, there ain't above eight or nine reg'lar glove cleaners in London—there were not, at that time, it seems—and I think I can give you their addresses, and you may find out, by that means, who did clean 'em.' Accordingly, he gave me the directions, and I went here, and I went there, and I looked up this man, and I looked up that man; but, though they all agreed that the gloves had been cleaned, I couldn't find the man, woman, or child that had cleaned that aforesaid pair of gloves.

"What with this person not being at home, and that person being expected home in the afternoon, and so forth, the inquiry took me three days. On the evening of the third day, coming over Waterloo Bridge from the Surrey side of the river, quite beat, and very much vexed and disappointed, I thought I'd have a shilling's worth of entertainment at the Lyceum Theater to freshen myself up. So I went into the pit, at half-price, and I sat myself down next to a very quiet, modest sort of young man. Seeing I was a stranger (which I thought it just as well to appear to be) he told me the names of the actors on the stage, and we got into conversation. When the play was over, we came out together, and I said, 'We've been very companionable and agreeable, and perhaps you wouldn't object to a drain?' 'Well, you're very good,' says he; 'I *shouldn't* object to a drain.' Accordingly, we went to a public house, near the theater, sat ourselves down in a quiet room upstairs on the first floor, and called for a pint of half-and-half, apiece, and a pipe.

"Well, sir, we put our pipes aboard, and we drank our half-and-half, and sat a talking, very sociably, when the young man says, 'You must excuse me stopping very long,' he says, 'because I'm forced to go home in good time. I must be at work all night.' 'At work all night?' says I. 'You ain't a baker?' 'No,' he says, laughing, 'I ain't a baker.' 'I thought not,' says I, 'you haven't the looks of a baker.' 'No,' says he, 'I'm a glove-cleaner.'

"I never was more astonished in my life than when I heard them words come out of his lips. 'You're a glove-cleaner, are you?' says I. 'Yes,' he says, 'I am.' 'Then, perhaps,' says I, taking the gloves out of my pocket, 'you can tell me who cleaned this pair of gloves? It's a rum story,' I says. 'I was dining over at Lambeth, the other day, at a free-and-easy—quite promiscuous—with a public company—when some gentleman, he left these gloves behind him! Another gentleman and me, you see, we laid a wager of a sovereign that I wouldn't find out who they belonged to. I've spent as much as seven shillings already, in trying to discover; but if you could help me, I'd stand another seven and welcome. You see there's TR and a cross, inside.' '*I* see,' he says. 'Bless you, *I* know these gloves very well! I've seen dozens of pairs belonging to the same party.' 'No?' says I. 'Yes,' says he. 'Then you know who cleaned 'em?' says I. 'Rather so,' says he. 'My father cleaned 'em.'

"'Where does your father live?' says I. 'Just around the corner,' says the young man, 'near Exeter Street, here. He'll tell you who they belong to, directly.' 'Would you come round with me now?' says I. 'Certainly,' says he, 'but you needn't tell my father that you found me at the play, you know, because he mightn't like it.' 'All right!' We went round to the place, and there we found an old man in a white apron, with two or three daughters, all rubbing and cleaning away at lots of gloves, in a front parlor. 'Oh, Father!' says the young man. 'Here's a person been and made a bet about the ownership of a pair of gloves, and I've told him you can settle it.' 'Good evening, sir,' says I to the old gentleman. 'Here's the gloves your son speaks of. Letters TR, you see, and a cross.' 'Oh yes,' he says, 'I know these gloves very well; I've cleaned dozens of pairs of 'em. They belong to Mr. Trinkle, the great upholsterer in Cheapside.' 'Did you get 'em from Mr. Trinkle, direct,' says I, 'if you'll excuse my asking the question?' 'No,' says he; 'Mr. Trinkle always sends 'em to Mr. Phibbs's, the haberdasher's, opposite his shop, and the haberdasher sends 'em to me,' 'Perhaps *you* wouldn't object to a drain?' says I. 'Not in the least!' says he. So I took the old gentleman out, and had a little more talk with him and his son, over a glass, and we parted excellent friends.

"This was late on a Saturday night. First thing on the Monday morning, I went to the haberdasher's shop, opposite Mr. Trinkle's, the great upholsterer's in Cheapside. 'Mr. Phibbs in the way?' 'My name is Phibbs.' 'Oh! I believe you sent this pair of gloves to be cleaned?' 'Yes, I did, for young Mr. Trinkle over the way. There he is in the shop!' 'Oh! That's him in the shop, is it? Him in the green coat?' 'The same individual.' 'Well, Mr. Phibbs, this is an unpleasant affair; but the fact is, I am Inspector Wield of the detective police, and I found these gloves under the pillow of the young woman that was murdered the other day, over in the Waterloo Road.' 'Good heaven!' says he. 'He's a most respectable young man, and if his father was to hear of it, it would be the ruin of him!' 'I'm very sorry for it,' says I, but I must take him into custody.' 'Good heaven!' says Mr. Phibbs, again. 'Can nothing be done?' 'Nothing,' says I. 'Will you allow me to call him over here,' says he, 'that his father may not see it done?' 'I don't object to that,' says I; 'but unfortunately, Mr. Phibbs, I can't allow of any communication between you. If any was attempted, I should have to interfere directly. Perhaps you'll beckon him over here?' Mr. Phibbs went to the door and beckoned, and the young fellow came across the street directly; a smart, brisk young fellow.

" 'Good morning, sir,' says I. 'Good morning, sir,' says he.

'Would you allow me to inquire, sir,' says I, 'if you ever had any acquaintance with a party of the name of Grimwood?' 'Grimwood! Grimwood!' says he. 'No!' 'You know the Waterloo Road?' 'Oh! Of course I know the Waterloo Road!' 'Happen to have heard of a young woman being murdered there?' 'Yes, I read it in the paper, and very sorry I was to read it.' 'Here's a pair of gloves belonging to you that I found under her pillow the morning afterwards!'

"He was in a dreadful state, sir; a dreadful state! 'Mr. Wield,' he says, 'upon my solemn oath I never was there. I never so much as saw her, to my knowledge, in my life!' 'I am very sorry,' says I. 'To tell you the truth, I don't think you *are* the murderer, but I must take you to Union Hall in a cab. However, I think it's a case of that sort that, at present, at all events, the magistrate will hear it in private.'

"A private examination took place, and then it came out that this young man was acquainted with a cousin of the unfortunate Eliza Grimwood, and that, calling to see this cousin a day or two before the murder, he left these gloves upon the table. Who should come in, shortly afterwards, but Eliza Grimwood! 'Whose gloves are these?' she says, taking 'em up. 'Those are Mr. Trinkle's gloves,' says her cousin. 'Oh!' says she. 'They are very dirty, and of no use to him, I am sure. I shall take 'em away for my girl to clean the stoves with.' And she put 'em in her pocket. The girl had used 'em to clean the stoves, and, I have no doubt, had left 'em lying on the bedroom mantlepiece, or on the drawers, or somewhere; and her mistress, looking round to see that the room was tidy, had caught 'em up and put 'em under the pillow where I found 'em.

"That's the story, sir."

Wilkie Collins (1824–1889) is best known to readers of mystery and detective fiction as the author of The Woman in White *and* The Moonstone. *First published in the 1860s in periodicals edited by Collins's close friend, Charles Dickens, these classic novels feature elaborately detailed plots full of red herrings, clever alibis, and cliff-hanging situations—elements that have become the hallmarks of all good detective novels. "The Biter Bit," the first recorded humorous detective story, is one of his many shorter experiments in crime, having first appeared in 1859 in the collection* The Queen of Hearts. *Evidence of the fact that Collins highly valued his tales of mystery and detection is his stated desire that his epitaph should read: "Author of* The Woman in White *and other works of fiction."*

THE BITER BIT
Wilkie Collins

FROM CHIEF INSPECTOR THEAKSTONE, OF THE DETECTIVE
POLICE, TO SERGEANT BULMER OF THE SAME FORCE.

LONDON, *4th July*, 18—

SERGEANT BULMER—This is to inform you that you are wanted
to assist in looking up a case of importance, which will require
all the attention of an experienced member of the force. The
matter of the robbery on which you are now engaged, you will
please shift over to the young man who brings you this letter.
You will tell him all the circumstances of the case, just as they
stand; you will put him up to the progress you have made (if
any) towards detecting the person or persons by whom the
money has been stolen; and you will leave him to make the best
he can of the matter now in your hands. He is to have the whole

47

responsibility of the case, and the whole credit of his success, if he brings it to a proper issue.

So much for the orders that I am desired to communicate to you.

A word in your ear, next, about this new man who is to take your place. His name is Matthew Sharpin; and he is to have the chance given him of dashing into our office at a jump—supposing he turns out strong enough to take it. You will naturally ask me how he comes by this privilege. I can only tell you that he has some uncommonly strong interest to back him in certain high quarters which you and I had better not mention except under our breaths. He has been a lawyer's clerk; and he is wonderfully conceited in his opinion of himself, as well as mean and underhand to look at. According to his own account, he leaves his old trade, and joins ours of his own free will and preference. You will no more believe that than I do. My notion is that he has managed to ferret out some private information in connection with the affairs of one of his master's clients, which makes him rather an awkward customer to keep in the office for the future, and which, at the same time, gives him hold enough over his employer to make it dangerous to drive him into a corner by turning him away. I think the giving him this unheard-of chance among us is, in plain words, pretty much like giving him hush-money to keep him quiet. However that may be, Mr. Matthew Sharpin is to have the case now in your hands; and if he succeeds with it, he pokes his ugly nose into our office, as sure as fate. I put you up to this, Sergeant, so that you may not stand in your own light by giving the new man any cause to complain of you at headquarters, and remain yours,

FRANCIS THEAKSTONE

FROM MR. MATTHEW SHARPIN TO CHIEF INSPECTOR THEAKSTONE

LONDON, *5th July,* 18—

DEAR SIR—Having now been favored with the necessary instructions from Sergeant Bulmer, I beg to remind you of certain directions which I have received, relating to the report of my future proceedings which I am to prepare for examination at headquarters.

The object of my writing, and of your examining what I have written, before you send it in to the higher authorities is, I am informed, to give me, as an untried hand, the benefit of your advice, in case I want it (which I venture to think I shall not) at any stage of my proceedings. As the extraordinary circumstances of the case on which I am now engaged make it impossible for me to absent myself from the place where the robbery was committed, until I have made some progress towards discovering the thief, I am necessarily precluded from consulting you personally. Hence the necessity of my writing down the various details, which might, perhaps, be better communicated by word of mouth. This, if I am not mistaken, is the position in which we are now placed. I state my own impressions on the subject, in writing, in order that we may clearly understand each other at the outset; and have the honor to remain, your obedient servant,

MATTHEW SHARPIN

FROM CHIEF INSPECTOR THEAKSTONE TO MR. MATTHEW SHARPIN

LONDON, *5th July*, 18—

SIR—You have begun by wasting time, ink, and paper. We both of us perfectly well knew the position we stood in towards each other when I sent you with my letter to Sergeant Bulmer. There was not the least need to repeat it in writing. Be so good as to employ your pen, in future, on the business actually in hand.

You have now three separate matters on which to write to me. First, you have to draw up a statement of your instructions received from Sergeant Bulmer, in order to show us that nothing has escaped your memory, and that you are thoroughly acquainted with all the circumstances of the case which has been entrusted to you. Secondly, you are to inform me what it is you propose to do. Thirdly, you are to report every inch of your progress (if you make any) from day to day, and, if need be, from hour to hour as well. This is *your* duty. As to what *my* duty may be, when I want you to remind me of it, I will write and tell you so. In the meantime, I remain, yours,

FRANCIS THEAKSTONE

FROM MR. MATTHEW SHARPIN TO CHIEF INSPECTOR THEAKSTONE

LONDON, *6th July*, 18—

SIR—You are rather an elderly person, and, as such, naturally inclined to be a little jealous of men like me, who are in the prime of their lives and their faculties. Under these circumstances, it is my duty to be considerate towards you, and not to bear too hardly on your small failings. I decline, therefore, altogether, to take offense at the tone of your letter; I give you the full benefit of the natural generosity of my nature; I sponge the very existence of your surly communication out of my memory—in short, Chief Inspector Theakstone, I forgive you, and proceed to business.

My first duty is to draw up a full statement of the instructions I have received from Sergeant Bulmer. Here they are at your service, according to my version of them.

At number 13 Rutherford Street, Soho, there is a stationer's shop. It is kept by one Mr. Yatman. He is a married man, but has no family. Besides Mr. and Mrs. Yatman, the other inmates in the house are a young single man named Jay, who lodges in the front room on the second floor—a shopman, who sleeps in one of the attics—and a servant-of-all-work, whose bed is in the back kitchen. Once a week a charwoman comes for a few hours in the morning only, to help this servant. These are all the persons who, on ordinary occasions, have means of access to the interior of the house, placed, as a matter of course, at their disposal.

Mr. Yatman has been in business for many years, carrying on his affairs prosperously enough to realize a handsome inde-

pendence for a person in his position. Unfortunately for himself
he endeavored to increase the amount of his property by specu-
lating. He ventured boldly in his investments, luck went against
him, and rather less than two years ago he found himself a poor
man again. All that was saved out of the wreck of his property
was the sum of two hundred pounds.

Although Mr. Yatman did his best to meet his altered circumstances by giving up many of the luxuries and comforts to
which he and his wife had been accustomed, he found it impossible to retrench so far as to allow of putting by any money from
the income produced by the shop. The business has been de-
clining of late years—the cheap advertising stationers having
done it injury with the public. Consequently, up to the last
week the only surplus property possessed by Mr. Yatman consisted of the two hundred pounds which had been recovered
from the wreck of his fortune. This sum was placed as a deposit
in a joint-stock bank of the highest possible character.

Eight days ago, Mr. Yatman and his lodger, Mr. Jay, held a
conversation on the subject of the commercial difficulties which
are hampering trade in all directions at the present time. Mr.
Jay (who lives by supplying the newspapers with short paragraphs relating to incidents, offenses, and brief records of remarkable occurrences in general—who is, in short, what they
call a penny-a-liner) told his landlord that he had been in the
city that day, and had heard unfavorable rumors on the subject
of the joint-stock banks. The rumors to which he alluded had already reached the ears of Mr. Yatman from other quarters; and
the confirmation of them by his lodger had such an effect on his
mind—predisposed as it was to alarm by the experience of his
former losses—that he resolved to go at once to the bank and
withdraw his deposit.

It was then getting on towards the end of the afternoon;
and he arrived just in time to receive his money before the bank
closed.

He received the deposit in bank notes of the following
amounts: one fifty-pound note, three twenty-pound notes, six
ten-pound notes, and six five-pound notes. His object in drawing

the money in this form was to have it ready to lay out immediately in trifling loans, on good security, among the small tradespeople of his district, some of whom are sorely pressed for the very means of existence at the present time. Investments of this kind seemed to Mr. Yatman to be the most safe and the most profitable on which he could now venture.

He brought the money back in an envelope placed in his breast pocket; and asked his shopman, on getting home, to look for a small flat tin cash box, which had not been used for years, and which, as Mr. Yatman remembered it, was exactly the right size to hold the bank notes. For some time the cash box was searched for in vain. Mr. Yatman called to his wife to know if she had any idea where it was. The question was overheard by the servant-of-all-work, who was taking up the tea tray at the time, and by Mr. Jay, who was coming downstairs on his way out to the theater. Ultimately the cash box was found by the shopman. Mr. Yatman placed the bank notes in it, secured them by a padlock and put the box in his coat pocket. It stuck out of the coat pocket a very little, but enough to be seen. Mr. Yatman remained at home, upstairs, all the evening. No visitors called. At eleven o'clock he went to bed, and put the cash box, along with his clothes, on a chair by the bedside.

When he and his wife woke the next morning, the box was gone. Payment of the notes was immediately stopped at the Bank of England; but no news of the money has been heard of since that time.

So far, the circumstances of the case are perfectly clear. They point unmistakably to the conclusion that the robbery must have been committed by some person living in the house. Suspicion falls, therefore, upon the servant-of-all-work, upon the shopman, and upon Mr. Jay. The two first knew that the cash box was being inquired for by their master, but did not know what it was he wanted to put into it. They would assume, of course, that it was money. They both had opportunities (the servant, when she took away the tea—and the shopman, when he came, after shutting up, to give the keys of the till to his master) of seeing the cash box in Mr. Yatman's pocket, and of inferring naturally, from its position there, that he intended to take it into his bedroom with him at night.

Mr. Jay, on the other hand, had been told, during the afternoon's conversation on the subject of joint-stock banks, that his landlord had a deposit of two hundred pounds in one of them. He also knew that Mr. Yatman left him with the intention of drawing that money out; and he heard the inquiry for the cash box, afterwards, when he was coming downstairs. He must, therefore, have inferred that the money was in the house, and that the cash box was the receptacle intended to contain it. That he could have had any idea, however, of the place in which Mr. Yatman intended to keep it for the night is impossible, seeing that he went out before the box was found, and did not return till his landlord was in bed. Consequently, if he committed the robbery, he must have gone into the bedroom purely on speculation.

Speaking of the bedroom reminds me of the necessity of noticing the situation of it in the house, and the means that exist of gaining easy access to it at any hour of the night.

The room in question is the back room on the first floor. In consequence of Mrs. Yatman's constitutional nervousness on the subject of fire (which makes her apprehend being burnt alive in her room, in case of accident, by the hampering of the lock if the key is turned in it) her husband has never been accustomed to lock the bedroom door. Both he and his wife are, by their own admission, heavy sleepers. Consequently, the risk to be run by any evil-disposed persons wishing to plunder the bedroom was of the most trifling kind. They could enter the room by merely turning the handle of the door; and if they moved with ordinary caution, there was no fear of their waking the sleepers inside. This fact is of importance. It strengthens our conviction that the money must have been taken by one of the inmates of the house, because it tends to show that the robbery, in this case, might have been committed by persons not possessed of the superior vigilance and cunning of the experienced thief.

Such are the circumstances as they were related to Sergeant Bulmer when he was first called in to discover the guilty parties, and, if possible, to recover the lost bank notes. The strictest inquiry which he could institute failed of producing the smallest fragment of evidence against any of the persons on whom suspicion naturally fell. Their language and behavior, on being informed of the robbery, was perfectly consistent with the language and behavior of innocent people. Sergeant Bulmer felt from the first that this was a case for private inquiry and secret observation. He began by recommending Mr. and Mrs. Yatman to affect a feeling of perfect confidence in the innocence of the persons living under their roof; and he then opened the campaign by employing himself in following the goings and comings, and in discovering the friends, the habits, and the secrets of the maid-of-all-work.

Three days and nights of exertions on his own part, and on that of others who were competent to assist his investigations, were enough to satisfy him that there was no sound cause for suspicion against the girl.

He next practiced the same precaution in relation to the shopman. There was more difficulty and uncertainty in privately clearing up this person's character without his knowledge, but the obstacles were at last smoothed away with tolerable success; and though there is not the same amount of certainty, in this case, which there was in that of the girl, there is still fair reason for supposing that the shopman has had nothing to do with the robbery of the cash box.

As a necessary consequence of these proceedings, the range of suspicion now becomes limited to the lodger, Mr. Jay.

When I presented your letter of introduction to Sergeant Bulmer, he had already made some inquiries on the subject of this young man. The result, so far, has not been at all favorable. Mr. Jay's habits are irregular; he frequents public houses, and seems to be familiarly acquainted with a great many dissolute characters; he is in debt to most of the tradespeople whom he employs; he has not paid his rent to Mr. Yatman for the last month; yesterday evening he came home excited by liquor, and last week he was seen talking to a prizefighter. In short, though

Mr. Jay does call himself a journalist, in virtue of his penny-a-line contributions to the newspapers, he is a young man of low tastes, vulgar manners, and bad habits. Nothing has yet been discovered in relation to him, which redounds to his credit in the smallest degree.

I have now reported, down to the very last details, all the particulars communicated to me by Sergeant Bulmer. I believe you will not find an omission anywhere; and I think you will admit, though you are prejudiced against me, that a clearer statement of facts was never laid before you than the statement I have now made. My next duty is to tell you what I propose to do, now that the case is confided to my hands.

In the first place, it is clearly my business to take up the case at the point where Sergeant Bulmer has left it. On his authority, I am justified in assuming that I have no need to trouble myself about the maid-of-all-work and the shopman. Their characters are now to be considered as cleared up. What remains to be privately investigated is the question of the guilt or innocence of Mr. Jay. Before we give up the notes for lost, we must make sure, if we can, that he knows nothing about them.

This is the plan that I have adopted, with the full approval of Mr. and Mrs. Yatman, for discovering whether Mr. Jay is or is not the person who has stolen the cash box:

I propose, today, to present myself at the house in the character of a young man who is looking for lodgings. The back room on the second floor will be shown to me as the room to let; and I shall establish myself there tonight, as a person from the country who has come to London to look for a situation in a respectable shop or office.

By this means I shall be living next to the room occupied by Mr. Jay. The partition between us is mere lath and plaster. I shall make a small hole in it, near the cornice, through which I can see what Mr. Jay does in his room, and hear every word that is said when any friend happens to call on him. Whenever he is at home, I shall be at my post of observation. Whenever he goes out, I shall be after him. By employing these means of watching him, I believe I may look forward to the discovery of his secret—if he knows anything about the lost bank notes—as to a dead certainty.

What you may think of my plan of observation I cannot undertake to say. It appears to me to unite the invaluable merits of boldness and simplicity. Fortified by this conviction, I close the present communication with feelings of the most sanguine description in regard to the future, and remain your obedient servant,

MATTHEW SHARPIN

FROM THE SAME TO THE SAME

7th July, 18—

SIR—As you have not honored me with any answer to my last communication, I assume that, in spite of your prejudices against me, it has produced the favorable impression on your mind which I ventured to anticipate. Gratified beyond measure by the token of approval which your eloquent silence conveys to me, I proceed to report the progress that has been made in the course of the last twenty-four hours.

I am now comfortably established next door to Mr. Jay; and I am delighted to say that I have two holes in the partition, instead of one. My natural sense of humor has led me into the pardonable extravagance of giving them appropriate names. One I call my peep-hole, and the other my pipe-hole. The name of the first explains itself; the name of the second refers to a small tin pipe, or tube, inserted in the hole, and twisted so that the mouth of it comes close to my ear, while I am standing at my post of observation. Thus, while I am looking at Mr. Jay through my peep-hole, I can hear every word that may be spoken in his room through my pipe-hole.

Perfect candor—a virtue which I have possessed from my childhood—compels me to acknowledge, before I go any further, that the ingenious notion of adding a pipe hole to my proposed peep-hole originated with Mrs. Yatman. This lady—a most intelligent and accomplished person, simple, and yet distinguished, in her manners—has entered into all my little plans with an enthusiasm and intelligence which I cannot too highly praise. Mr. Yatman is so cast down by his loss that he is quite incapable of affording me any assistance. Mrs. Yatman, who is evidently most tenderly attached to him, feels her husband's sad condition of mind even more acutely than she feels the loss of the money; and is mainly stimulated to exertion by her desire to assist in raising him from the miserable state of prostration into which he has now fallen.

"The money, Mr. Sharpin," she said to me yesterday evening, with tears in her eyes, "the money may be regained by rigid economy and strict attention to business. It is my husband's wretched state of mind that makes me so anxious for the discovery of the thief. I may be wrong, but I felt hopeful of success as soon as you entered the house; and I believe, if the wretch who has robbed us is to be found, you are the man to discover him." I accepted this gratifying compliment in the spirit in which it was offered—firmly believing that I shall be found, sooner or later, to have thoroughly deserved it.

Let me now return to business; that is to say, to my peep-hole and my pipe-hole.

I have enjoyed some hours of calm observation of Mr. Jay. Though rarely at home, as I understand from Mrs. Yatman, on ordinary occasions, he has been indoors the whole of this day. That is suspicious, to begin with. I have to report further that he rose at a late hour this morning (always a bad sign in a young man), and that he lost a great deal of time, after he was up, in yawning and complaining to himself of headache. Like other debauched characters, he ate little or nothing for breakfast. His next proceeding was to smoke a pipe—a dirty clay pipe, which a gentleman would have been ashamed to put between his lips. When he had done smoking, he took out pen, ink, and paper, and sat down to write with a groan—whether of remorse for having taken the bank notes, or of disgust at the task before him, I am unable to say. After writing a few lines (too far away from my peep-hole to give me a chance of reading over his shoulder), he leaned back in his chair, and amused himself by humming the tunes of certain popular songs. Whether these do, or do not, represent secret signals by which he communicates with his accomplices remains to be seen. After he had amused himself for some time by humming, he got up and began to walk about the room, occasionally stopping to add a sentence to the paper on his desk. Before long, he went to a locked cupboard and opened it. I strained my eyes eagerly, in expectation of making a discovery. I saw him take something carefully out of the cupboard— he turned round—and it was only a pint bottle of brandy! Having drunk some of the liquor, this extremely indolent reprobate lay down on his bed again, and in five minutes was fast asleep.

After hearing him snoring for at least two hours, I was recalled to my peep-hole by a knock at his door. He jumped up and opened it with suspicious activity.

A very small boy, with a very dirty face, walked in, said, "Please, sir, they're waiting for you," sat down on a chair, with his legs a long way from the ground, and instantly fell asleep! Mr. Jay swore an oath, tied a wet towel round his head, and going back to his paper, began to cover it with writing as fast as his fingers could move the pen. Occasionally getting up to dip the towel in water and tie it on again, he continued at this employment for nearly three hours; then folded up the leaves of writing, woke the boy, and gave them to him, with this remarkable expression: "Now, then, young sleepyhead, quick—march! If you see the governor, tell him to have the money ready when I call for it." The boy grinned, and disappeared. I was sorely tempted to follow "sleepyhead," but, on reflection, considered it safest still to keep my eye on the proceedings of Mr. Jay.

In half an hour's time, he put on his hat and walked out. Of course, I put on my hat and walked out also. As I went downstairs, I passed Mrs. Yatman going up. The lady has been kind enough to undertake, by previous arrangement between us, to search Mr. Jay's room, while he is out of the way, and while I am necessarily engaged in the pleasing duty of following him wherever he goes. On the occasion to which I now refer, he walked straight to the nearest tavern, and ordered a couple of mutton chops for his dinner. I placed myself in the next box to him, and ordered a couple of mutton chops for my dinner. Before I had been in the room a minute, a young man of highly suspicious manners and appearance, sitting at a table opposite, took his glass of porter in his hand and joined Mr. Jay. I pretended to be reading the newspaper, and listened, as in duty bound, with all my might.

"Jack has been here inquiring after you," says the young man.

"Did he leave any message?" asks Mr. Jay.

"Yes," says the other. "He told me, if I met with you, to say that he wished very particularly to see you tonight; and that he would give you a look-in, at Rutherford Street, at seven o'clock."

"All right," says Mr. Jay. "I'll get back in time to see him."

Upon this, the suspicious-looking young man finished his porter, and saying that he was rather in a hurry, took leave of his friend (perhaps I should not be wrong if I said his accomplice) and left the room.

At twenty-five minutes and a half past six—in these serious cases it is important to be particular about time—Mr. Jay finished his chops and paid his bill. At twenty-six minutes and three quarters I finished my chops and paid mine. In ten minutes more I was inside the house in Rutherford Street, and was received by Mrs. Yatman in the passage. That charming woman's face exhibited an expression of melancholy and disappointment which it quite grieved me to see.

"I am afraid, Ma'am," says I, "that you have not hit on any little criminating discovery in the lodger's room?"

She shook her head and sighed. It was a soft, languid, fluttering sigh; and, upon my life, it quite upset me. For the moment I forgot business, and burned with envy of Mr. Yatman.

"Don't despair, Ma'am," I said, with an insinuating mildness which seemed to touch her. "I have heard a mysterious conversation—I know of a guilty appointment—and I expect great things from my peep-hole and my pipe-hole tonight. Pray, don't be alarmed, but I think we are on the brink of a discovery."

Here my enthusiastic devotion to business got the better of my tender feelings. I looked—winked—nodded—left her.

When I got back to my obervatory, I found Mr. Jay digesting his mutton chops in an armchair, with his pipe in his mouth. On his table were two tumblers, a jug of water, and the pint bottle of brandy. It was then close upon seven o'clock. As the hour struck, the person described as "Jack" walked in.

He looked agitated—I am happy to say he looked violently agitated. The cheerful glow of anticipated success diffused itself (to use a strong expression) all over me, from head to foot. With breathless interest I looked through my peep-hole, and saw the visitor—the "Jack" of this delightful case—sit down, facing me, at the opposite side of the table to Mr. Jay. Making allowance for the difference in expression which their countenances just now happened to exhibit, these two abandoned villains were so much alike in other respects as to lead at once to the conclusion that they were brothers. Jack was the cleaner man and the better-dressed of the two. I admit that, at the outset. It is, perhaps, one of my failings to push justice and impartiality to their utmost limits. I am no Pharisee; and where Vice has its redeeming point, I say, let Vice have its due—yes, yes, by all manner of means, let Vice have its due.

"What's the matter now, Jack?" says Mr. Jay.

"Can't you see it in my face?" says Jack. "My dear fellow, delays are dangerous. Let us have done with suspense, and risk it the day after tomorrow."

"So soon as that?" cried Mr. Jay, looking very much astonished. "Well, I'm ready, if you are. But, I say, Jack, is Somebody Else ready too? Are you quite sure of that?"

He smiled as he spoke—a frightful smile—and laid a very strong emphasis on those two words, "Somebody Else." There is evidently a third ruffian, a nameless desperado, concerned in the business.

"Meet us tomorrow," says Jack, "and judge for yourself. Be

in the Regent's Park at eleven in the morning, and look out for us at the turning that leads to the Avenue Road."

"I'll be there," says Mr. Jay. "Have a drop of brandy and water? What are you getting up for? You're not going already?"

"Yes, I am," says Jack. "The fact is, I'm so excited and agitated that I can't sit still anywhere for five minutes together. Ridiculous as it may appear to you, I'm in a perpetual state of nervous flutter. I can't, for the life of me, help fearing that we shall be found out. I fancy that every man who looks twice at me in the street is a spy—"

At those words, I thought my legs would have given way under me. Nothing but strength of mind kept me at my peephole—nothing else, I give you my word of honor.

"Stuff and nonsense!" cried Mr. Jay, with all the effrontery of a veteran in crime. "We have kept the secret up to this time, and we will manage cleverly to the end. Have a drop of brandy and water, and you will feel as certain about it as I do."

Jack steadily refused the brandy and water, and steadily persisted in taking his leave.

"I must try if I can't walk it off," he said. "Remember tomorrow morning—eleven o'clock, Avenue Road side of the Regent's Park."

With those words he went out. His hardened relative laughed desperately, and resumed the dirty clay pipe.

I sat down on the side of my bed, actually quivering with excitement.

It is clear to me that no attempt has yet been made to change the stolen bank notes; and I may add that Sergeant Bulmer was of that opinion also, when he left the case in my hands. What is the natural conclusion to draw from the conversation which I have just set down? Evidently, that the confederates meet tomorrow to take their respective shares in the stolen money, and to decide the safest means of getting the notes changed the day after. Mr. Jay is, beyond a doubt, the leading criminal in this business, and he will probably run the chief risk—that of changing the fifty-pound note. I shall, therefore, still make it my business to follow him—attending at the Regent's Park tomorrow, and doing my best to hear what is said there. If another appointment is made the day after, I shall, of course, go to it. In the meantime, I shall want the immediate assistance of two competent persons (supposing the rascals separate after their meeting) to follow the two minor criminals. It is only fair to add that, if the rogues all retire together, I shall probably keep my subordinates in reserve. Being naturally ambitious, I desire, if possible, to have the whole credit of discovering this robbery to myself.

8th July

I have to acknowledge, with thanks, the speedy arrival of my two subordinates—men of very average abilities, I am afraid; but, fortunately, I shall always be on the spot to direct them.

My first business this morning was, necessarily, to prevent mistakes by accounting to Mr. and Mrs. Yatman for the presence of two strangers on the scene. Mr. Yatman (between ourselves, a poor feeble man) only shook his head and groaned. Mrs. Yatman (that superior woman) favored me with a charming look of intelligence.

"Oh, Mr. Sharpin!" she said. "I am so sorry to see those two men! Your sending for their assistance looks as if you were beginning to be doubtful of success."

I privately winked at her (she is very good in allowing me to do so without taking offense), and told her, in my facetious way, that she labored under a slight mistake.

"It is because I am sure of success, Ma'am, that I send for them. I am determined to recover the money, not for my own sake only, but for Mr. Yatman's sake—and for yours."

I laid a considerable amount of stress on those last three words. She said, "Oh, Mr. Sharpin!" again—and blushed of a heavenly red—and looked down at her work. I could go to the world's end with that woman, if Mr. Yatman would only die.

I sent off the two subordinates to wait, until I wanted them, at the Avenue Road gate of the Regent's Park. Half an hour afterwards I was following in the same direction myself, at the heels of Mr. Jay.

The two confederates were punctual to the appointed time. I blush to record it, but it is nevertheless necessary to state that the third rogue—the nameless desperado of my report, or if you prefer it, the mysterious "Somebody Else" of the conversation between the two brothers—is a Woman! And, what is worse, a young woman! And, what is more lamentable still, a nice-looking woman! I have long resisted a growing conviction that, wherever there is mischief in this world, an individual of the fair sex is inevitably certain to be mixed up in it. After the experience of this morning, I can struggle against that sad conclusion no longer. I give up the sex—excepting Mrs. Yatman, I give up the sex.

The man named "Jack" offered the woman his arm. Mr. Jay placed himself on the other side of her. The three then walked away slowly among the trees. I followed them at a respectful distance. My two subordinates, at a respectful distance also, followed me.

It was, I deeply regret to say, impossible to get near enough to them to overhear their conversation, without running too great a risk of being discovered. I could only infer from their gestures and actions that they were all three talking with extraordinary earnestness on some subject which deeply interested them. After having been engaged in this way a full quarter of an hour, they suddenly turned round to retrace their steps. My presence of mind did not forsake me in this emergency. I signed to the two subordinates to walk on carelessly and pass them, while I myself slipped dexterously behind a tree. As they came by me, I heard "Jack" address these words to Mr. Jay:

"Let us say half-past ten tomorrow morning. And mind you come in a cab. We had better not risk taking one in this neighborhood."

Mr. Jay made some brief reply, which I could not overhear. They walked back to the place at which they had met, shaking hands there with an audacious cordiality which it quite sickened me to see. They then separated. I followed Mr. Jay. My subordinates paid the same delicate attention to the other two.

Instead of taking me back to Rutherford Street, Mr. Jay led me to the Strand. He stopped at a dingy, disreputable-looking house, which, according to the inscription over the door, was a newspaper office, but which, in my judgment, had all the external appearance of a place devoted to the reception of stolen goods.

After remaining inside for a few minutes, he came out, whistling, with his finger and thumb in his waistcoat pocket. A less discreet man than myself would have arrested him on the spot. I remembered the necessity of catching the two confederates, and the importance of not interfering with the appointment that had been made for the next morning. Such coolness as this, under trying circumstances, is rarely to be found, I should imagine, in a young beginner, whose reputation as a detective policeman is still to make.

From the house of suspicious appearance, Mr. Jay betook himself to a cigar divan, and read the magazines over a cheroot. I sat at a table near him, and read the magazines likewise over a cheroot. From the divan he strolled to the tavern and had his chops. I strolled to the tavern and had my chops. When he had done, he went back to his lodging. When I had done, I went back to mine. He was overcome with drowsiness early in the evening, and went to bed. As soon as I heard him snoring, I was overcome with drowsiness, and went to bed also.

Early in the morning my two subordinates came to make their report.

They had seen the man named "Jack" leave the woman near the gate of an apparently respectable villa residence, not far from the Regent's Park. Left to himself, he took a turning to the right, which led to a sort of suburban street, principally inhabited by shopkeepers. He stopped at the private door of one of the houses, and let himself in with his own key—looking about him as he opened the door, and staring suspiciously at my men as they lounged along on the opposite side of the way. These were all the particulars which the subordinates had to communicate. I kept them in my room to attend on me, if needful, and mounted to my peep-hole to have a look at Mr. Jay.

He was occupied in dressing himself, and was taking extraordinary pains to destroy all traces of the natural slovenliness of his appearance. This was precisely what I expected. A vagabond like Mr. Jay knows the importance of giving himself a respectable look when he is going to run the risk of changing a stolen bank note. At five minutes past ten o'clock, he had given the last brush to his shabby hat and the last scouring with bread-crumb to his dirty gloves. At ten minutes past ten he was in the street, on his way to the nearest cab stand, and I and my subordinates were close on his heels.

He took a cab, and we took a cab. I had not overheard them appoint a place of meeting when following them in the park on the previous day; but I soon found that we were proceeding in the old direction of the Avenue Road gate.

The cab in which Mr. Jay was riding turned into the park slowly. We stopped outside, to avoid exciting suspicion. I got out to follow the cab on foot. Just as I did so, I saw it stop, and detected the two confederates approaching it from among the trees. They got in, and the cab was turned about directly. I ran back to my own cab, and told the driver to let them pass him, and then to follow as before.

The man obeyed my directions, but so clumsily as to excite their suspicions. We had been driving after them about three minutes (returning along the road by which we had advanced) when I looked out of the window to see how far they might be ahead of us. As I did this, I saw two hats popped out of the windows of their cab, and two faces looking back at me. I sank into my place in a cold sweat; the expression is coarse, but no other form of words can describe my condition at that trying moment.

"We are found out!" I said faintly to my two subordinates. They stared at me in astonishment. My feelings changed instantly from the depth of despair to the height of indignation.

"It is the cabman's fault. Get out, one of you," I said, with dignity—"get out and punch his head."

Instead of following my directions (I should wish this act of disobedience to be reported at headquarters) they both looked out the window. Before I could pull them back, they both sat down again. Before I could express my just indignation, they both grinned, and said to me, "Please to look out, sir!"

I did look out. The thieves' cab had stopped.

Where?

At a church door!!!

What effect this discovery might have had upon the ordinary run of men, I don't know. Being of a strong religious turn myself, it filled me with horror. I have often read of the unprincipled cunning of criminal persons; but I never before heard of three thieves attempting to double on their pursuers by entering a church! The sacrilegious audacity of that proceeding is, I should think, unparalleled in the annals of crime.

I checked my grinning subordinates by a frown. It was easy to see what was passing in their superficial minds. If I had not been able to look below the surface, I might, on observing two nicely dressed men and one nicely dressed woman enter a church before eleven in the morning on a weekday, have come to the same hasty conclusion at which my inferiors had evidently arrived. As it was, appearances had no power to impose on *me*. I got out, and, followed by one of my men, entered the church. The other man I sent round to watch the vestry door. You may catch a weasel asleep—but not your humble servant, Matthew Sharpin!

We stole up the gallery stairs, diverged to the organ loft, and peered through the curtains in front. There they were all three, sitting in a pew below—yes, incredible as it may appear, sitting in a pew below!

Before I could determine what to do, a clergyman made his appearance in full canonicals, from the vestry door, followed by a clerk. My brain whirled, and my eyesight grew dim. Dark remembrances of robberies committed in vestries floated through my mind. I trembled for the excellent man in full canonicals—even trembled for the clerk.

The clergyman placed himself inside the altar rails. The three desperadoes approached him. He opened his book, and began to read. What?—you will ask.

I answer, without the slightest hesitation: the first lines of the marriage service.

My subordinate had the audacity to look at me, and then to stuff his pocket handkerchief into his mouth. I scorned to pay any attention to him. After I had discovered that the man "Jack" was the bridegroom, and that the man Jay acted the part of father, and gave away the bride, I left the church, followed by my man, and joined the other subordinate outside the vestry door. Some people in my position would now have felt rather crestfallen, and would have begun to think that they had made a very foolish mistake. Not the faintest misgiving of any kind troubled me. I did not feel in the slightest degree depreciated in my own estimation. And even now, after a lapse of three hours, my mind remains, I am happy to say, in the same calm and hopeful condition.

As soon as I and my subordinates were assembled together outside the church, I intimated my intention of still following the other cab, in spite of what had occurred. My reason for deciding on this course will appear presently. The two subordinates were astonished at my resolution. One of them had the impertinence to say to me:

"If you please, sir, who is it that we are after? A man who has stolen money, or a man who has stolen a wife?"

The other low person encouraged him by laughing. Both have deserved an official reprimand; and both, I sincerely trust, will be sure to get it.

When the marriage ceremony was over, the three got into their cab; and once more our vehicle (neatly hidden round the corner of the church, so that they could not suspect it to be near them) started to follow theirs.

We traced them to the terminus of the Southwestern Railway. The newly married couple took tickets for Richmond—

paying their fare with a half-sovereign, and so depriving me of the pleasure of arresting them, which I should certainly have done, if they had offered a bank-note. They parted from Mr. Jay, saying, "Remember the address—Fourteen Babylon Terrace. You dine with us tomorrow week." Mr. Jay accepted the invitation, and added, jocosely, that he was going home at once to get off his clean clothes, and to be comfortable and dirty again for the rest of the day. I have to report that I saw him home safely, and that he is comfortable and dirty again (to use his own disgraceful language) at the present moment.

Here the affair rests, having by this time reached what I may call its first stage.

I know very well what persons of hasty judgment will be inclined to say of my proceedings thus far. They will assert that I have been deceiving myself all through, in the most absurd way; they will declare that the suspicious conversations which I have reported referred solely to the difficulties and dangers of successfully carrying out a runaway match; and they will appeal to the scene in the church, as offering undeniable proof of the correctness of their assertions. So let it be. I dispute nothing up to this point. But I ask a question, out of the depths of my own sagacity as a man of the world, which the bitterest of my enemies will not, I think, find it particularly easy to answer.

Granted the fact of the marriage, what proof does it afford me of the innocence of three persons concerned in that clandestine transaction? It gives me none. On the contrary, it strengthens my suspicions against Mr. Jay and his confederates, because it suggests a distinct motive for their stealing the money. A gentleman who is going to spend his honeymooon at Richmond wants money; and a gentleman who is in debt to all his tradespeople wants money. Is this an unjustifiable imputation of bad motives? In the name of outraged morality, I deny it. These men have combined together, and have stolen a woman. Why should they not combine together, and steal a cash box? I take my stand on the logic of rigid virtue; and I defy all the sophistry of vice to move me an inch out of my position.

Speaking of virtue, I may add that I have put this view of

the case to Mr. and Mrs. Yatman. That accomplished and charming woman found it difficult, at first, to follow the close chain of my reasoning. I am free to confess that she shook her head, and shed tears, and joined her husband in premature lamentation over the loss of the two hundred pounds. But a little careful explanation on my part, and a little attentive listening on hers, ultimately changed her opinion. She now agrees with me, that there is nothing in this unexpected circumstance of the clandestine marriage which absolutely tends to divert suspicion from Mr. Jay, or Mr. "Jack," or the runaway lady. "Audacious hussy" was the term my fair friend used in speaking of her, but let that pass. It is more to the purpose to record that Mrs. Yatman has not lost confidence in me and that Mr. Yatman promises to follow her example, and do his best to look hopefully for future results.

I have now, in the new turn that circumstances have taken, to await advice from your office. I pause for fresh orders with all the composure of a man who has got two strings to his bow. When I traced the three confederates from the church door to the railway terminus, I had two motives for doing so. First, I followed them as a matter of official business, believing them still to have been guilty of the robbery. Secondly, I followed them as a matter of private speculation, with a view of discovering the place of refuge to which the runaway couple intended to retreat, and of making my information a marketable commodity to offer to the young lady's family and friends. Thus, whatever happens, I may congratulate myself beforehand on not having wasted my time. If the office approves of my conduct, I have my plan ready for further proceedings. If the office blames me, I shall take myself off, with my marketable information, to the genteel villa residence in the neighborhood of the Regent's Park. Anyway, the affair puts money into my pocket, and does credit to my penetration as an uncommonly sharp man.

I have only one word more to add, and it is this: If any individual ventures to assert that Mr. Jay and his confederates are innocent of all share in the stealing of the cash box, I, in return, defy that individual—though he may even be Chief Inspector

Theakstone himself—to tell me who has committed the robbery at Rutherford Street, Soho.

> I have the honor to be,
> Your very obedient servant,
>
> MATTHEW SHARPIN

FROM CHIEF INSPECTOR THEAKSTONE TO SERGEANT BULMER

> BIRMINGHAM, *9th July*

SERGEANT BULMER—That empty-headed puppy, Mr. Matthew Sharpin, has made a mess of the case at Rutherford Street, exactly as I expected he would. Business keeps me in this town; so I write to you to set the matter straight. I enclose, with this, the pages of feeble scribble-scrabble which the creature, Sharpin, calls a report. Look them over; and when you have made your way through all the gabble, I think you will agree with me that the conceited booby has looked for the thief in every direction but the right one. You can lay your hand on the guilty person in five minutes, now. Settle the case at once; forward your report to me at this place; and tell Mr. Sharpin that he is suspended till further notice.

> Yours,
>
> FRANCIS THEAKSTONE

FROM SERGEANT BULMER TO CHIEF INSPECTOR THEAKSTONE

> LONDON, *10th July*

INSPECTOR THEAKSTONE—Your letter and enclosure came safe to hand. Wise men, they say, may always learn something, even from a fool. By the time I had got through Sharpin's maundering report of his own folly, I saw my way clear enough to the end of the Rutherford Street case, just as you thought I should. In half an hour's time I was at the house. The first person I saw there was Mr. Sharpin himself.

"Have you come to help me?" says he.

"Not exactly," says I. "I've come to tell you that you are suspended till further notice.'

"Very good," says he, not taken down, by so much as a single peg, in his own estimation. "I thought you would be jealous of me. It's very natural; and I don't blame you. Walk in, pray, and make yourself at home. I'm off to do a little detective business on my own account, in the neighborhood of the Regent's Park. Ta-ta, Sergeant, ta-ta!"

With those words he took himself out of the way—which was exactly what I wanted him to do.

As soon as the maidservant had shut the door, I told her to inform her master that I wanted to say a word to him in private. She showed me into the parlor behind the shop; and there was Mr. Yatman, all alone, reading the newspaper.

"About this matter of the robbery, sir," says I.

He cut me short, peevishly enough—being naturally a poor, weak, womanish sort of man. "Yes, yes, I know," says he. "You have come to tell me that your wonderfully clever man, who has bored holes in my second-floor partition, has made a mistake, and is off the scent of the scoundrel who has stolen my money."

"Yes, sir," says I. "That *is* one of the things I came to tell you. But I have got something else to say, besides that."

"Can you tell me who the thief is?" says he, more pettish than ever.

"Yes, sir," says I, "I think I can."

He put down the newspaper, and began to look rather anxious and frightened.

"Not my shopman?" says he. "I hope, for the man's own sake, it's not my shopman."

"Guess again, sir," says I.

"That idle slut, the maid?" says he.

"She is idle, sir," says I, "and she is also a slut; my first inquiries about her proved as much as that. But she's not the thief."

"Then in the name of heaven, who is?" says he.

"Will you please to prepare yourself for a very disagreeable surprise, sir?" says I. "And in case you lose your temper, will you excuse my remarking that I am the stronger man of the two, and that, if you allow yourself to lay hands on me, I may unintentionally hurt you, in pure self-defense?"

He turned as pale as ashes, and pushed his chair two or three feet away from me.

"You have asked me to tell you, sir, who has taken your money." I went on. "If you insist on my giving you an answer—"

"I do insist," he said, faintly. "Who has taken it?"

"Your wife has taken it," I said very quietly, and very positively at the same time.

He jumped out of the chair as if I had put a knife into him, and struck his fist on the table, so heavily that the wood cracked again.

"Steady, sir," says I. "Flying into a passion won't help you to the truth."

"It's a lie!" says he, with another smack of his fist on the table. "A base, vile, infamous lie! How dare you—"

He stopped, and fell back into the chair again, looked about him in a bewildered way, and ended by bursting out crying.

"When your better sense comes back to you, sir," says I, "I am sure you will be gentleman enough to make an apology for the language you have just used. In the meantime, please to listen, if you can, to a word of explanation. Mr. Sharpin has sent in a report to our inspector, of the most irregular and ridiculous kind; setting down, not only all of his own foolish doings and sayings, but the doings and sayings of Mrs. Yatman as well. In most cases, such a document would have been fit for the waste-paper basket; but, in this particular case, it so happens that Mr. Sharpin's budget of nonsense leads to a certain conclusion, which the simpleton of a writer has been quite innocent of suspecting from the beginning to the end. Of that conclusion I am so sure that I will forfeit my place if it does not turn out that Mrs. Yatman has been practicing upon the folly and conceit of this young man, and that she has tried to shield herself from discovery by purposely encouraging him to suspect the wrong persons. I tell you that confidently; and I will even go further. I will undertake to give a decided opinion as to why Mrs. Yatman took the money, and what she has done with it, or with a part of it. Nobody can look at that lady, sir, without being struck by the great taste and beauty of her dress—"

As I said those last words, the poor man seemed to find his powers of speech again. He cut me short directly, as haughtily as if he had been a duke instead of a stationer.

"Try some other means of justifying your vile calumny against my wife," says he. "Her milliner's bill for the past year is on my file of receipted accounts at this moment."

"Excuse me, sir," says I, "but that proves nothing. Milliners, I must tell you, have a certain rascally custom which comes within the daily experience of our office. A married lady who wishes it can keep two accounts at her dressmaker's: one is the account which her husband sees and pays; the other is the private account, which contains all the extravagant items, and which the wife pays secretly, by installments, whenever she can. According to our usual experience, these installments are mostly squeezed out of the housekeeping money. In your case, I suspect no installments have been paid; proceedings have been threatened; Mrs. Yatman, knowing your altered circumstances, has felt herself driven into a corner; and she has paid her private account out of your cash box."

"I won't believe it," says he. "Every word you speak is an abominable insult to me and to my wife."

"Are you man enough, sir," says I, taking him up short, in order to save time and words, "to get that receipted bill you spoke of just now off the file, and come with me at once to the milliner's shop where Mrs. Yatman deals?"

He turned red in the face at that, got the bill directly, and put on his hat. I took out of my pocketbook the list containing the numbers of the lost notes, and we left the house together immediately.

Arrived at the milliner's (one of the expensive West End houses, as I expected), I asked for a private interview, on important business, with the mistress of the concern. It was not the first time that she and I had met over the same delicate investigation. The moment she set eyes on me, she sent for her husband. I mentioned who Mr. Yatman was, and what we wanted.

"This is strictly private?" inquires her husband. I nodded my head.

"And confidential?" says the wife. I nodded again.

"Do you see any objection, dear, to obliging the sergeant with a sight of the books?" says the husband.

"None in the world, love, if you approve of it," says the wife.

All this while poor Mr. Yatman sat looking the picture of astonishment and distress, quite out of place at our polite conference. The books were brought—and one minute's look at the pages in which Mrs. Yatman's name figured was enough, and more than enough, to prove the truth of every word I had spoken.

There, in one book, was the husband's account, which Mr. Yatman had settled. And there, in the other, was the private account, crossed off also; the date of settlement being the very day after the loss of the cash box. This said private account amounted to the sum of a hundred and seventy-five pounds, odd shillings; and it extended over a period of three years. Not a single installment had been paid on it. Under the last line was an entry to this effect: "Written to for the third time, June 23rd." I pointed to it, and asked the milliner if that meant "last June." Yes, it did mean last June; and she now deeply regretted to say that it had been accompanied by a threat of legal proceedings.

"I thought you gave good customers more than three years' credit?" says I.

The milliner looks at Mr. Yatman, and whispers to me— "Not when a lady's husband gets into difficulties."

She pointed to the account as she spoke. The entries after the time when Mr. Yatman's circumstances became involved were just as extravagant, for a person in his wife's situation, as the entries for the year before that period. If the lady had economized in other things, she had certainly not economized in the matter of dress.

There was nothing left now but to examine the cash book, for form's sake. The money had been paid in notes, the amounts and numbers of which exactly tallied with the figures set down in my list.

After that, I thought it best to get Mr. Yatman out of the house immediately. He was in such a pitiable condition that I called a cab and accompanied him home in it. At first he cried and raved like a child: but I soon quieted him—and I must add, to his credit, that he made me a most handsome apology for his language as the cab drew up at his house door. In return, I tried to give him some advice about how to set matters right, for the future, with his wife. He paid very little attention to me, and went upstairs muttering to himself about a separation. Whether Mrs. Yatman will come cleverly out of the scrape or not seems doubtful. I should say, myself, that she will go into screeching hysterics, and so frighten the poor man into forgiving her. But this is no business of ours. So far as we are concerned, the case is now at an end; and the present report may come to a conclusion along with it.

I remain, accordingly, yours to command,

THOMAS BULMER

P.S. I have to add that, on leaving Rutherford Street, I met Mr. Matthew Sharpin coming to pack up his things.

"Only think!" says he, rubbing his hands in great spirits. "I've been to the genteel villa residence; and the moment I mentioned my business, they kicked me out directly. There were two witnesses of the assault; and it's worth a hundred pounds to me, if it's worth a farthing."

"I wish you joy of your luck," says I.

"Thank you," says he. "When may I pay you the same compliment on finding the thief?"

"Whenever you like," says I, "for the thief is found."

"Just what I expected," says he. "I've done all the work; and now you cut in, and claim all the credit—Mr. Jay, of course?"

"No," says I.

"Who is it then?" says he.

"Ask Mrs. Yatman," says I. "She's waiting to tell you."

"All right! I'd much rather hear it from that charming woman than from you," says he, and goes into the house in a mighty hurry.

What do you think of that, Inspector Theakstone? Would you like to stand in Mr. Sharpin's shoes? I shouldn't, I can promise you!

FROM CHIEF INSPECTOR THEAKSTONE TO MR. MATTHEW SHARPIN

12th July

SIR—Sergeant Bulmer has already told you to consider yourself suspended until further notice. I have now authority to add that your services as a member of the Detective Police are positively declined. You will please to take this letter as notifying officially your dismissal from the force.

I may inform you, privately, that your rejection is not intended to cast any reflection on your character. It merely implies that you are not quite sharp enough for our purpose. If we *are* to have a new recruit among us, we should infinitely prefer Mrs. Yatman.

Your obedient servant,

FRANCIS THEAKSTONE

NOTE ON THE PRECEDING CORRESPONDENCE, ADDED BY MR. THEAKSTONE

The Inspector is not in a position to append any explanations of importance to the last of the letters. It has been discovered that Mr. Matthew Sharpin left the house in Rutherford Street five minutes after his interview outside of it with Sergeant Bulmer—his manner expressing the liveliest emotions of terror and astonishment, and his left cheek displaying a bright patch of red, which might have been the result of a slap on the face from a female hand. He was also heard, by the shopman at Rutherford Street, to use a very shocking expression in reference to Mrs. Yatman; and was seen to clench his fist vindictively as he ran round the corner of the street. Nothing more has been heard of him; and it is conjectured that he has left London with the intention of offering his valuable services to the provincial police.

On the interesting domestic subject of Mr. and Mrs. Yatman still less is known. It has, however, been positively ascertained that the medical attendant of the family was sent for in a great hurry on the day when Mr. Yatman returned from the milliner's shop. The neighboring chemist received, soon afterwards, a prescription of a soothing nature to make up for Mrs. Yatman. The day after, Mr. Yatman purchased some smelling-salts at the shop, and afterwards appeared at the circulating library to ask for a novel, descriptive of high life, that would amuse an invalid lady. It has been inferred from these circumstances, that he has not thought it desirable to carry out his threat of separating himself from his wife—at least in the present (presumed) condition of that lady's sensitive nervous system.

Count Leo Nikolaevich Tolstoy (1828–1910) was a moral philosopher and social reformer as well as a novelist and writer of short stories. During his military service in the Crimean War, he wrote idyllic and semiautobiographical novels—Childhood, Boyhood, Youth—*before turning to more serious works.* Sevastopol Sketches *(1855–56) made a profound impression because of its condemnatory depiction of the ravages of war on soldiers and civilians alike. Tolstoy's most famous and enduring novels are, of course,* War and Peace *(1869) and* Anna Karenina *(1877); the former is particularly remarkable for its panoramic battle scenes of the Napoleonic campaigns in Russia.* "God Sees the Truth But Waits" *is a deceptively simple tale of crime and punishment under Czarist rule.*

GOD SEES THE TRUTH BUT WAITS
Leo N. Tolstoy

In the town of Vladimir lived a young merchant named Ivan Dmitrich Aksionov. He had two shops and a house of his own.

Aksionov was a handsome, fair-haired, curly-headed fellow, full of fun, and very fond of singing. When quite a young man he had been given to drink, and was riotous when he had had too much; but after he married he gave up drinking, except now and then.

One summer Aksionov was going to the Nizhny Fair, and as he bade good-bye to his family, his wife said to him, "Ivan Dmitrich, do not start today; I have had a bad dream about you."

Aksionov laughed, and said, "You are afraid that when I get to the fair I shall go on a spree."

His wife replied: "I do not know what I am afraid of; all I know is that I had a bad dream. I dreamt you returned from the town, and when you took off your cap I saw that your hair was quite gray."

Aksionov laughed. "That's a lucky sign," said he. "See if I don't sell out all my goods, and bring you some presents from the fair."

So he said good-bye to his family, and drove away.

When he had traveled halfway, he met a merchant whom he knew, and they put up at the same inn for the night. They had some tea together, and then went to bed in adjoining rooms.

It was not Aksionov's habit to sleep late, and, wishing to travel while it was still cool, he roused his driver before dawn, and told him to put in the horses.

Then he made his way across to the landlord of the inn (who lived in a cottage at the back), paid his bill, and continued his journey.

When he had gone about twenty-five miles he stopped for the horses to be fed. Aksionov rested awhile in the passage of the inn, then he stepped out into the porch, and ordering a samovar to be heated, got out his guitar and began to play.

Suddenly a troika drove up with tinkling bells and an official alighted, followed by two soldiers. He came to Aksionov and began to question him, asking him who he was and whence he came. Aksionov answered him fully and said, "Won't you have some tea with me?" But the official went on cross-questioning him and asking him, "Where did you spend last night? Were you alone, or with a fellow merchant? Did you see the other merchant this morning? Why did you leave the inn before dawn?"

Aksionov wondered why he was asked all these questions, but he described all that had happened, and then added, "Why do you cross-question me as if I were a thief or robber? I am traveling on business of my own, and there is no need to question me."

Then the official, calling the soldiers, said, "I am the police officer of this district, and I question you because the merchant with whom you spent last night has been found with his throat cut. We must search your things."

They entered the house. The soldiers and the police officer unstrapped Aksionov's luggage and searched it. Suddenly the officer drew a knife out of a bag, crying, "Whose knife is this?"

Aksionov looked, and seeing a bloodstained knife taken from his bag, he was frightened.

"How is it there is blood on this knife?"

Aksionov tried to answer, but could hardly utter a word, and only stammered: "I—don't know—not mine."

Then the police officer said: "This morning the merchant was found in bed with his throat cut. You are the only person who could have done it. The house was locked from inside, and no one else was there. Here is this bloodstained knife in your bag, and your face and manner betray you! Tell me how you killed him, and how much money you stole?"

Aksionov swore he had not done it; that he had not seen the merchant after they had had tea together; that he had no money except eight thousand rubles of his own, and that the knife was not his. But his voice was broken, his face pale, and he trembled with fear as though he were guilty.

The police officer ordered the soldiers to bind Aksionov and to put him in the cart. As they tied his feet together and flung him into the cart, Aksionov crossed himself and wept. His money and goods were taken from him, and he was sent to the nearest town and imprisoned there. Inquiries as to his character were made in Vladimir. The merchants and other inhabitants of that town said that in former days he used to drink and waste his time, but that he was a good man. Then the trial came on: he was charged with murdering a merchant from Ryazan, and robbing him of twenty thousand rubles.

His wife was in despair, and did not know what to believe. Her children were all quite small; one was a baby at her breast. Taking them all with her, she went to the town where her husband was in jail. At first she was not allowed to see him; but after much begging, she obtained permission from the officials, and was taken to him. When she saw her husband in prison dress and in chains shut up with thieves and criminals, she fell down, and did not come to her senses for a long time. Then she drew her children to her, and sat down near him. She told him of things at home, and asked about what had happened to him. He told her all, and she asked, "What can we do now?"

"We must petition the Czar not to let an innocent man perish."

His wife told him that she had sent a petition to the Czar, but it had not been accepted.

Aksionov did not reply, but only looked downcast.

Then his wife said, "It was not for nothing I dreamt your hair had turned gray. You remember? You should not have started that day." And passing her fingers through his hair, she said: "Vanya dearest, tell your wife the truth; was it not you who did it?"

"So you, too, suspect me!" said Aksionov, and, hiding his face in his hands, he began to weep. Then a soldier came to say that the wife and children must go away; and Aksionov said good-bye to his family for the last time.

When they were gone, Aksionov recalled what had been said, and when he remembered that his wife also had suspected him, he said to himself, "It seems that only God can know the truth; it is to Him alone we must appeal, and from Him alone expect mercy."

And Aksionov wrote no more petitions, gave up all hope, and only prayed to God.

Aksionov was condemned to be flogged and sent to the mines. So he was flogged with a knot, and when the wounds made by the knot were healed, he was driven to Siberia with other convicts.

For twenty-six years Aksionov lived as a convict in Siberia. His hair turned white as snow, and his beard grew long, thin, and gray. All his mirth went; he stooped; he walked slowly, spoke little, and never laughed, but he often prayed.

In prison Aksionov learned to make boots, and earned a little money, with which he bought *The Lives of the Saints*. He read this book when there was light enough in the prison; and on Sundays in the prison church he read the lessons and sang in the choir; for his voice was still good.

The prison authorities liked Aksionov for his meekness, and his fellow prisoners respected him: they called him "Grandfather," and "The Saint." When they wanted to petition the prison authorities about anything, they always made Aksionov their spokesman, and when there were quarrels among the prisoners they came to him to put things right, and to judge the matter.

No news reached Aksionov from his home, and he did not even know if his wife and children were still alive.

One day a fresh gang of convicts came to the prison. In the evening the old prisoners collected round the new ones and asked them what towns or villages they came from, and what they were sentenced for. Among the rest Aksionov sat down near the newcomers, and listened with downcast air to what was said.

One of the new convicts, a tall man of sixty with a closely cropped gray beard, was telling the others what he had been arrested for.

"Well, friends," he said, "I only took a horse that was tied to a sledge, and I was arrested and accused of stealing. I said I had only taken it to get home quicker, and had then let it go; besides, the driver was a personal friend of mine. So I said, 'It's all right.' 'No,' said they, 'you stole it.' But how or where I stole it they could not say. I once really did something wrong, and ought by rights to have come here long ago, but that time I was not found out. Now I have been sent here for nothing at all. . . . Eh, but it's lies I'm telling you; I've been to Siberia before, but I did not stay long."

"Where are you from?" asked someone.

"From Vladimir. My family are of that town. My name is Makar, and they also call me Semyonich."

Aksionov raised his head and said: "Tell me, Semyonich, do you know anything of the merchants Aksionov of Vladimir? Are they still alive?"

"Know them? Of course I do. The Aksionovs are rich, though their father is in Siberia: a sinner like ourselves, it seems! As for you, Gran'dad, how did you come here?"

Aksionov did not like to speak of his misfortune. He only sighed and said, "For my sins I have been in prison these twenty-six years."

"What sins?" asked Makar Semyonich.

But Aksionov only said, "Well, well—I must have deserved it!" He would have said no more, but his companions told the newcomers how Aksionov came to be in Siberia; how someone had killed a merchant, and had put the knife among Aksionov's things, and Aksionov had been unjustly condemned.

When Makar Semyonich heard this, he looked at Aksionov, slapped his own knee, and exclaimed, "Well, this is wonderful! Really wonderful! But how old you've grown Gran'dad!"

The others asked him why he was so surprised, and where he had seen Aksionov before; but Makar Semyonich did not reply. He only said: "It's wonderful that we should meet here, lads!"

These words made Aksionov wonder whether this man knew who had killed the merchant, so he said, "Perhaps, Semyonich, you have heard of that affair, or maybe you've seen me before?"

"How could I help hearing? The world's full of rumors. But it's a long time ago, and I've forgotten what I heard."

"Perhaps you heard who killed the merchant?" asked Aksionov.

Makar Semyonich laughed, and replied: "It must have been him in whose bag the knife was found! If someone else hid the knife there, 'He's not a thief till he's caught,' as the saying is. How could anyone put a knife into your bag while it was under your head? It would surely have woke you up."

When Aksionov heard these words, he felt sure this was the man who had killed the merchant. He rose and went away. All that night Aksionov lay awake. He felt terribly unhappy, and all sorts of images rose in his mind. There was the image of his wife as she was when he parted from her to go to the fair. He saw her as if she were present; her face and her eyes rose before him; he heard her speak and laugh. Then he saw his children, quite little, as they were at that time: one with a little cloak on, another at his mother's breast. And then he remembered himself as he used to be—young and merry. He remembered how he sat playing the guitar on the porch of the inn where he was arrested, and how free from care he had been. He saw, in his mind, the place where he was flogged, the executioner, and the people standing around; the chains, the convicts, all the twenty-six years of his prison life, and his premature old age. The thought of it all made him so wretched that he was ready to kill himself.

"And it's all that villain's doing!" thought Aksionov. And his anger was so great against Makar Semyonich that he longed for vengeance, even if he himself should perish for it. He kept repeating prayers all night, but could get no peace. During the day he did not go near Makar Semyonich, nor even look at him.

A fortnight passed in this way. Aksionov could not sleep at night, and was so miserable that he did not know what to do.

One night as he was walking about the prison he noticed some earth that came rolling out from under one of the shelves on which the prisoners slept. He stopped to see what it was. Suddenly Makar Semyonich crept out from under the shelf, and looked up at Aksionov with frightened face. Aksionov tried to pass without looking at him, but Makar seized his hand and told him that he had dug a hole under the wall, getting rid of the earth by putting it into his highboots, and emptying it out every day on the road when the prisoners were driven to their work.

"Just you keep quiet, old man, and you shall get out too. If you blab, they'll flog the life out of me, but I will kill you first."

Aksionov trembled with anger as he looked at his enemy. He drew his hand away, saying, "I have no wish to escape and you have no need to kill me; you killed me long ago. As to telling of you—I may do so or not, as God shall direct."

Next day, when the convicts were led out to work, the convoy of soldiers noticed that one or other of the prisoners emptied some earth out of his boots. The prison was searched and the tunnel found. The Governor came and questioned all the prisoners to find out who had dug the hole. They all denied any knowledge of it. Those who knew would not betray Makar

Semyonich, knowing he would be flogged almost to death. At last the Governor turned to Aksionov whom he knew to be a just man, and said:

"You are a truthful old man; tell me, before God, who dug the hole?"

Makar Semyonich stood as if he were quite unconcerned, looking at the Governor and not so much as glancing at Aksionov. Aksionov's lips and hands trembled, and for a long time he could not utter a word. He thought, "Why should I screen him who ruined my life? Let him pay for what I have suffered. But if I tell, they will probably flog the life out of him, and maybe I suspect him wrongly. And, after all, what good would it be to me?"

"Well, old man," repeated the Governor, "tell me the truth: who has been digging under the wall?"

Aksionov glanced at Makar Semyonich, and said, "I cannot say, your honor. It is not God's will that I should tell! Do what you like with me; I am in your hands."

However much the Governor tried, Aksionov would say no more, and so the matter had to be left.

That night, when Aksionov was lying on his bed and just beginning to doze, someone came quietly and sat down on his bed. He peered through the darkness and recognized Makar.

"What more do you want of me?" asked Aksionov. "Why have you come here?"

Makar Semyonich was silent. So Aksionov sat up and said, "What do you want? Go away, or I will call the guard!"

Makar Semyonich bent close over Aksionov, and whispered, "Ivan Dmitrich, forgive me!"

"What for?" asked Aksionov.

"It was I who killed the merchant and hid the knife among your things. I meant to kill you too, but I heard a noise outside, so I hid the knife in your bag and escaped out of the window."

Aksionov was silent, and did not know what to say. Makar Semyonich slid off the bed shelf and knelt upon the ground. "Ivan Dmitrich," said he, "forgive me! For the love of God, forgive me! I will confess that it was I who killed the merchant, and you will be released and can go to your home."

"It is easy for you to talk," said Aksionov, "but I have suffered for you these twenty-six years. Where could I go to now? ... My wife is dead, and my children have forgotten me. I have nowhere to go. . . ."

Makar Semyonich did not rise, but beat his head on the floor. "Ivan Dmitrich, forgive me!" he cried. "When they flogged me with the knot it was not so hard to bear as it is to see you now ... yet you had pity on me, and did not tell. For Christ's sake forgive me, wretch that I am!" And he began to sob.

When Aksionov heard him sobbing he, too, began to weep. "God will forgive you!" said he. "Maybe I am a hundred times worse than you." And at these words his heart grew light, and the longing for home left him. He no longer had any desire to leave the prison, but only hoped for his last hour to come.

In spite of what Aksionov had said, Makar Semyonich confessed his guilt. But when the order for his release came Aksionov was already dead.

Although he wrote relatively few mystery stories, Ambrose Bierce (1842–1914?) himself became one of the great real-life mysteries when he disappeared in Mexico in 1914, a disappearance that has never been fully explained. (The theory most often espoused is that he fell victim to the rebel soldiers of Pancho Villa.) It is an enigma that Bierce himself would have relished. He was an iconoclast whose sketches, short stories, and political and social-reform newspaper columns made him many enemies and turned the San Francisco literary establishment on its ear in the last quarter of the nineteenth century. His caustic pen and his fascination with death and horror earned him the nickname "Bitter Bierce"; his work has been called, among other things, "paranoid," "malevolent," and "venomous." Such assessments may be applied to "A Watcher by the Dead"—but it is nonetheless a memorable tale, masterfully plotted and masterfully told.

A WATCHER BY THE DEAD
Ambrose BiercE

I

In an upper room of an unoccupied dwelling in the part of San Francisco known as North Beach lay the body of a man, under a sheet. The hour was near nine in the evening; the room was dimly lighted by a single candle. Although the weather was warm, the two windows, contrary to the custom which gives the dead plenty of air, were closed and the blinds drawn down. The furniture of the room consisted of but three pieces—an arm-chair, a small reading stand supporting the candle, and a long kitchen table supporting the body of the man. All these, as also the corpse, seemed to have been recently brought in, for an observer, had there been one, would have seen that all were free from dust, whereas everything else in the room was pretty thickly coated with it, and there were cobwebs in the angles of the walls.

Under the sheet the outlines of the body could be traced,

even the features, these having that unnaturally sharp definition which seems to belong to the faces of the dead, but is really characteristic of those only that have been wasted by disease. From the silence of the room one would rightly have inferred that it was not in the front of the house, facing a street. It really faced nothing but a high breast of rock, the rear of the building being set into a hill.

As a neighboring church clock was striking nine with an indolence which seemed to imply such an indifference to the flight of time that one could hardly help wondering why it took the trouble to strike at all, the single door of the room was opened and a man entered, advancing toward the body. As he did so the door closed, apparently of its own volition; there was a grating, as of a key turned with difficulty, and the snap of the lock bolt as it shot into its socket. A sound of retiring footsteps in the passage outside ensued, and the man was to all appearance a prisoner. Advancing to the table, he stood a moment looking down at the body; then with a slight shrug of the shoulders walked over to one of the windows and hoisted the blind. The darkness outside was absolute, the panes were covered with dust, but by wiping this away he could see that the window was fortified with strong iron bars crossing it within a few inches of the glass and imbedded in the masonry on each side. He examined the other window. It was the same. He manifested no great curiosity in the matter, did not even so much as raise the sash. If he was a prisoner he was apparently a tractable one. Having completed his examination of the room, he seated himself in the armchair, took a book from his pocket, drew the stand with its candle alongside and began to read.

The man was young—not more than thirty—dark in complexion, smooth-shaven, with brown hair. His face was thin and high-nosed, with a broad forehead and a "firmness" of the chin and jaw which is said by those having it to denote resolution. The eyes were gray and steadfast, not moving except with definitive purpose. They were now for the greater part of the time fixed upon his book, but he occasionally withdrew them and turned them to the body on the table, not, apparently, from any dismal fascination which under such circumstances it might be supposed to exercise upon even a courageous person, nor with a conscious rebellion against the contrary influence which might dominate a timid one. He looked at it as if in his reading he had come upon something recalling him to a sense of his surroundings. Clearly this watcher by the dead was discharging his trust with intelligence and composure, as became him.

After reading for perhaps a half-hour he seemed to come to the end of a chapter and quietly laid away the book. He then rose and taking the reading stand from the floor carried it into a corner of the room near one of the windows, lifted the candle from it and returned to the empty fireplace before which he had been sitting.

A moment later he walked over to the body on the table, lifted the sheet and turned it back from the head, exposing a mass of dark hair and a thin face cloth, beneath which the features showed with even sharper definition than before. Shading his eyes by interposing his free hand between them and the candle, he stood looking at his motionless companion with a serious and tranquil regard. Satisfied with his inspection, he pulled the sheet over the face again and returning to the chair, took some matches off the candlestick, put them in the side pocket of his sack coat, and sat down. He then lifted the candle from its socket and looked at it critically, as if calculating how long it would last. It was barely two inches long; in another hour he would be in darkness. He replaced it in the candlestick and blew it out.

II

In a physician's office in Kearny Street three men sat about a table, drinking punch and smoking. It was late in the evening, almost midnight, indeed, and there had been no lack of punch. The gravest of the three, Dr. Helberson, was the host—it was in his rooms they sat. He was about thirty years of age; the others were even younger; all were physicians.

"The superstitious awe with which the living regard the

dead," said Dr. Helberson, "is hereditary and incurable. One needs no more be ashamed of it than of the fact that he inherits, for example, an incapacity for mathematics, or a tendency to lie."

The others laughed. "Oughtn't a man to be ashamed to lie?" asked the youngest of the three, who was in fact a medical student not yet graduated.

"My dear Harper, I said nothing about that. The tendency to lie is one thing; lying is another."

"But do you think," said the third man, "that this superstitious feeling, this fear of the dead, reasonless as we know it to be, is universal? I am myself not conscious of it."

"Oh, but it is 'in your system' for all that," replied Helberson; "it needs only the right conditions—what Shakespeare calls the 'confederate season'—to manifest itself in some very disagreeable way that will open your eyes. Physicians and soldiers are of course more nearly free from it than others."

"Physicians and soldiers! Why don't you add hangmen and headsmen? Let us have in all the assassin classes."

"No, my dear Mancher; the juries will not let the public executioners acquire sufficient familiarity with death to be altogether unmoved by it."

Young Harper, who had been helping himself to a fresh cigar at the sideboard, resumed his seat. "What would you consider conditions under which any man of woman born would become insupportably conscious of his share of our common weakness in this regard?" he asked, rather verbosely.

"Well, I should say that if a man were locked up all night with a corpse—alone—in a dark room—of a vacant house—with no bed covers to pull over his head—and lived through it without going altogether mad, he might justly boast himself not of woman born, nor yet, like Macduff, a product of Caesarean section."

"I thought you never would finish piling up conditions," said Harper, "but I know a man who is neither a physician nor a soldier who will accept them all, for any stake you like to name."

"Who is he?"

"His name is Jarette—a stranger here; comes from my town in New York. I have no money to back him, but he will back himself with loads of it."

"How do you know that?"

"He would rather bet than eat. As for fear—I daresay he thinks it some cutaneous disorder, or possibly a particular kind of religious heresy."

"What does he look like?" Helberson was evidently becoming interested.

"Like Mancher, here—might be his twin brother."

"I accept the challenge," said Helberson, promptly.

"Awfully obliged to you for the compliment, I'm sure," drawled Mancher, who was growing sleepy. "Can't I get into this?"

"Not against me," Helberson said. "I don't want *your* money."

"All right," said Mancher; "I'll be the corpse."

The others laughed.

The outcome of this crazy conversation we have seen.

III

In extinguishing his meager allowance of candle Mr. Jarette's object was to preserve it against some unforeseen need. He may have thought, too, or half thought, that the darkness would be no worse at one time than another, and if the situation became insupportable it would be better to have a means of relief, or even release. At any rate it was wise to have a little reserve of light, even if only to enable him to look at his watch.

No sooner had he blown out the candle and set it on the floor at his side than he settled himself comfortably in the armchair, leaned back and closed his eyes, hoping and expecting to sleep. In this he was disappointed; he had never in his life felt less sleepy, and in a few minutes he gave up the attempt. But what could he do? He could not go groping about in absolute darkness at the risk of bruising himself—at the risk, too, of blundering against the table and rudely disturbing the dead. We all recognize their right to lie at rest, with immunity from all that is harsh and violent. Jarette almost succeeded in making himself believe that considerations of this kind restrained him from risking the collision and fixed him to the chair.

While thinking of this matter he fancied that he heard a faint sound in the direction of the table—what kind of sound he could hardly have explained. He did not turn his head. Why should he—in the darkness? But he listened—why should he not? And listening he grew giddy and grasped the arms of the chair for support. There was a strange ringing in his ears; his head seemed bursting; his chest was oppressed by the constriction of his clothing. He wondered why it was so, and whether these were symptoms of fear. Then, with a long and strong expiration, his chest appeared to collapse, and with the great gasp with which he refilled his exhausted lungs the vertigo left him and he knew that so intently had he listened that he had held his breath almost to suffocation. The revelation was vexatious; he arose, pushed away the chair with his foot, and strode to the center of the room. But one does not stride far in darkness; he began to grope, and finding the wall followed it to an angle, turned, followed it past the two windows and there in another corner came into violent contact with the reading stand, overturning it. It made a clatter that startled him. He was annoyed. "How the devil could I have forgotten where it was?" he muttered, and groped his way along the third wall to the fireplace. "I must put things to rights," said he, feeling the floor for the candle.

Having recovered that, he lighted it and instantly turned his eyes to the table, where, naturally, nothing had undergone any change. The reading stand lay unobserved upon the floor; he had forgotten to "put it to rights." He looked all about the room, dispersing the deeper shadows by movements of the candle in his hand, and crossing over to the door tested it by turning and pulling the knob with all his strength. It did not yield and this seemed to afford him a certain satisfaction; indeed, he secured it more firmly by a bolt which he had not before observed. Returning to his chair, he looked at his watch; it was half-past nine. With a start of surprise he held the watch at his ear. It had not stopped. The candle was now visibly shorter. He again extinguished it, placing it on the floor at his side as before.

Mr. Jarette was not at his ease; he was distinctly dissatisfied with his surroundings, and with himself for being so. "What have I to fear?" he thought. "This is ridiculous and disgraceful; I will not be so great a fool." But courage does not come of saying, "I will be courageous," nor of recognizing its appropriateness to the occasion. The more Jarette condemned himself, the more reason he gave himself for condemnation; the greater the number of variations which he played upon the simple theme of the harmlessness of the dead, the most insupportable grew the discord of his emotions. "What!" he cried aloud in the anguish of his spirit. "What! Shall I, who have not a shade of superstition in my nature—I, who have no belief in immortality—I, who know (and never more clearly than now) that the afterlife is the dream of a desire—shall I lose at once my bet, my honor, and my self-respect, perhaps my reason, because certain savage ancestors dwelling in caves and burrows conceived the monstrous notion that the dead walk by night—that—" Distinctly, unmistakably, Mr. Jarette heard behind him a light, soft sound of footfalls, deliberate, regular, successively nearer!

IV

Just before daybreak the next morning Dr. Helberson and his young friend Harper were driving slowly through the streets of North Beach in the doctor's coupé.

"Have you still the confidence of youth in the courage or stolidity of your friend?" said the elder man. "Do you believe that I have lost this wager?"

"I *know* you have," replied the other, with enfeebling emphasis.

"Well, upon my soul, I hope so."

It was spoken earnestly, almost solemnly. There was a silence for a few moments.

"Harper," the doctor resumed, looking very serious in the shifting half-lights that entered the carriage as they passed the street lamps, "I don't feel altogether comfortable about this business. If your friend had not irritated me by the contemptuous manner in which he treated my doubt of his endurance—purely physical quality—and by the cool incivility of his suggestion that the corpse be that of a physician, I would not have gone on with it. If anything should happen we are ruined, as I fear we deserve to be."

"What can happen? Even if the matter should be taking a serious turn, of which I am not at all afraid, Mancher has only to 'resurrect' himself and explain matters. With a genuine 'subject' from the dissecting room, or one of your late patients, it might be different."

Dr. Mancher, then, had been as good as his promise; he was the "corpse."

Dr. Helberson was silent for a long time, as the carriage, at a snail's pace, crept along the same street it had traveled two or three times already. Presently he spoke: "Well, let us hope that Mancher, if he has had to rise from the dead, has been discreet about it. A mistake in that might make matters worse instead of better."

"Yes," said Harper. "Jarette would kill him. But, Doctor"—looking at his watch as the carriage passed a gas lamp—"it is nearly four o'clock at last."

A moment later the two had quitted the vehicle and were walking briskly toward the long-unoccupied house belonging to the doctor in which they had immured Mr. Jarette in accordance with the terms of the mad wager. As they neared it they met a man running. "Can you tell me," he cried, suddenly checking his speed, "where I can find a doctor?"

"What's the matter?" Helberson asked, noncommittal.

"Go and see for yourself," said the man, resuming his running.

They hastened on. Arrived at the house, they saw several persons entering in haste and excitement. In some of the dwellings nearby and across the way the chamber windows were thrown up, showing a protrusion of heads. All heads were asking questions, none heeding the questions of the others. A few of the windows with closed blinds were illuminated; the inmates of those rooms were dressing to come down. Exactly opposite the door of the house that they sought a street lamp threw a yellow, insufficient light upon the scene, seeming to say that it could disclose a good deal more if it wished. Harper paused at the door and laid a hand upon his companion's arm. "It is all up with us, Doctor," he said in extreme agitation, which contrasted strangely with his free-and-easy words: "the game has gone against us all. Let's not go in there; I'm for lying low."

"I'm a physician," said Dr. Helberson, calmly; "there may be need of one."

They mounted the doorsteps and were about to enter. The door was open; the street lamp opposite lighted the passage into which it opened. It was full of men. Some had ascended the stairs at the farther end, and, denied admittance above, waited for better fortune. All were talking, none listening. Suddenly, on the upper landing there was a great commotion; a man had sprung out of a door and was breaking away from those endeavoring to detain him. Down through the mass of affrighted idlers he came, pushing them aside, flattening them against the wall on one side, or compelling them to cling to the rail on the other, clutching them by the throat, striking them savagely, thrusting them back down the stairs and walking over the fallen. His clothing was in disorder, he was without a hat. His eyes, wild and restless, had in them something more terrifying than his apparently superhuman strength. His face, smooth-shaven, was bloodless, his hair frost-white.

As the crowd at the foot of the stairs, having more freedom, fell away to let him pass Harper sprang forward. "Jarette! Jarette!" he cried.

Dr. Helberson seized Harper by the collar and dragged

him back. The man looked into their faces without seeming to see them and sprang through the door, down the steps, into the street, and away. A stout policeman, who had had inferior success in conquering his way down the stairway, followed a moment later and started in pursuit, all the heads in the windows—those of women and children now—screaming in guidance.

The stairway being now partly cleared, most of the crowd having rushed down to the street to observe the flight and pursuit, Dr. Helberson mounted to the landing, followed by Harper. At a door in the upper passage an officer denied them admittance. "We are physicians," said the doctor, and they passed in. The room was full of men, dimly seen, crowded about a table. The newcomers edged their way forward and looked over the shoulders of those in the front rank. Upon the table, the lower limbs covered with a sheet, lay the body of a man, brilliantly illuminated by the beam of a bull's-eye lantern held by a policeman standing at the feet. The others, excepting those near the head—the officer himself—all were in darkness. The face of the body showed yellow, repulsive, horrible! The eyes were partly open and upturned and the jaw fallen; traces of froth defiled the lips, the chin, the cheeks. A tall man, evidently a doctor, bent over the body with his hand thrust under the shirt front. He withdrew it and placed two fingers in the open mouth. "This man has been about six hours dead," said he. "It is a case for the coroner."

He drew a card from his pocket, handed it to the officer, and made his way toward the door.

"Clear the room—out, all!" said the officer, sharply, and the body disappeared as if it had been snatched away, as shifting the lantern he flashed its beam of light here and there against the faces of the crowd. The effect was amazing! The men, blinded, confused, almost terrified, made a tumultuous rush for the door, pushing, crowding, and tumbling over one another as they fled, like the hosts of Night before the shafts of Apollo. Upon the struggling, trampling mass the officer poured his light without pity and without cessation. Caught in the current, Helberson and Harper were swept out of the room and cascaded down the stairs into the street.

"Good God, Doctor! Did I not tell you that Jarette would kill him?" said Harper, as soon as they were clear of the crowd.

"I believe you did," replied the other, without apparent emotion.

They walked on in silence, block after block. Against the graying east the dwellings of the hill tribes showed in silhouette. The familiar milk wagon was already astir in the streets; the baker's man would soon come upon the scene; the newspaper carrier was abroad in the land.

"It strikes me, youngster," said Helberson, "that you and I have been having too much of the morning air lately. It is unwholesome; we need a change. What do you say to a tour in Europe?"

"When?"

"I'm not particular. I should suppose that four o'clock this afternoon would be early enough."

"I'll meet you at the boat," said Harper.

V

Seven years afterward these two men sat upon a bench in Madison Square, New York, in familiar conversation. Another man, who had been observing them for some time, himself unobserved, approached and, courteously lifting his hat from locks as white as frost, said: "I beg your pardon, gentlemen, but when you have killed a man by coming to life, it is best to change clothes with him, and at the first opportunity make a break for liberty."

Helberson and Harper exchanged significant glances. They were obviously amused. The former then looked the stranger kindly in the eye and replied:

"That has always been my plan. I entirely agree with you as to its advant—"

He stopped suddenly, rose, and went white. He stared at the man, open-mouthed; he trembled visibly.

"Ah!" said the stranger. "I see that you are indisposed, Doctor. If you cannot treat yourself Dr. Harper can do something for you, I am sure."

"Who the devil are you?" said Harper, bluntly.

The stranger came nearer and, bending toward them, said in a whisper: "I call myself Jarette sometimes, but I don't mind telling you, for old friendship, that I am Dr. William Mancher."

The revelation brought Harper to his feet. "Mancher!" he cried; and Helberson added: "It is true, by God!"

"Yes," said the stranger, smiling vaguely, "it is true enough, no doubt."

He hesitated and seemed to be trying to recall something, then began humming a popular air. He had apparently forgotten their presence.

"Look here, Mancher," said the elder of the two, "tell us just what occurred that night—to Jarette, you know."

"Oh, yes, about Jarette," said the other. "It's odd I should have neglected to tell you—I tell it so often. You see I knew, by overhearing him talking to himself, that he was pretty badly frightened. So I couldn't resist the temptation to come to life and have a bit of fun out of him—I couldn't really. That was all right, though certainly I did not think he would take it so seriously; I did not, truly. And afterward—well, it was a tough job changing places with him, and then—damn you! You didn't let me out!"

Nothing could exceed the ferocity with which these last words were delivered. Both men stepped back in alarm.

"We? Why—why," Helberson stammered, losing his self-possession utterly, "we had nothing to do with it."

"Didn't I say you were Drs. Hell-born and Sharper?" inquired the man, laughing.

"My name is Helberson, yes; and this gentleman is Mr. Harper," replied the former, reassured by the laugh. "but we are not physicians now; we are—well, hang it, old man, we are gamblers."

And that was the truth.

"A very good profession—very good, indeed; and, by the way, I hope Sharper here paid over Jarette's money like an honest stakeholder. A very good and honorable profession," he repeated, thoughtfully, moving carelessly away; "but I stick to the old one. I am High Supreme Medical Officer of the Bloomingdale Asylum; it is my duty to cure the superintendent."

H. G. Wells (1866–1946) was a self-made man whose commitment to social justice, world peace, and the dignity of human beings was frustrated by the ills and horrors of the twentieth century. Wells lived through some of the most important technological and social changes in world history—he "saw" both the first airplane flight and the development of nuclear weapons— and as a result he became increasingly pessimistic about the ability of man to achieve the perfection he longed for. He is best known today for his "scientific romances," novels such as The Time Machine *(1895),* The Invisible Man *(1897), and* The War of the Worlds *(1898). Especially noteworthy among his prodigious output of nonfiction is his huge two-volume* Outline of History *(1920), which was very influential in its time. He was a versatile fiction writer, although his non-science fiction works are not widely known today; his* Complete Short Stories *(1927) contains fiction on a wide variety of themes, including the criminous.*

MR. BRISHER'S TREASURE
H. G. Wells

"You can't be *too* careful *whom* you marry," said Mr. Brisher, and pulled thoughtfully with a fat-wristed hand at the lank mustache that hides his want of chin.

"That's why—" I ventured.

"Yes," said Mr. Brisher, with a solemn light in his bleary, blue-gray eyes, moving his head expressively and breathing alcohol intimately at me. "There's lots as 'ave 'ad a try at me—many as I could name in *this* town—but none 'ave done it—none."

I surveyed the flushed countenance, the equatorial expansion, the masterly carelessness of his attire, and heaved a sigh to think that by reason of the unworthiness of woman he must needs be the last of his race.

"I was a smart young chap when I was younger," said Mr.

Brisher. "I 'ad my work cut out. But I was very careful—very. And I got through . . ."

He leaned over the tap-room table and thought visibly on the subject of my trustworthiness. I was relieved at last by his confidence.

"I was engaged once," he said at last, with a reminiscent eye on the shuv-a'penny board.

"So near as that?"

He looked at me. "So near as that. Fact is—" He looked about him, brought his face close to mine, lowered his voice, and fenced off an unsympathetic world with a grimy hand. "If she ain't dead or married to someone else or anything—I'm engaged still. Now." He confirmed this statement with nods and facial contortions. "*Still*," he said, ending the pantomime, and broke into a reckless smile at my surprise. "*Me!*

"Run away," he explained in further confidence, with coruscating eyebrows. "Come 'ome.

"That ain't all.

"You'd hardly believe it," he said, "but I found a treasure. Found a regular treasure."

I fancied this was irony, and did not, perhaps, greet it with proper surprise. "Yes," he said, "I found a treasure. And come 'ome. I tell you I could surprise you with things that has happened to me." And for some time he was content to repeat that he had found a treasure—and left it.

I made no vulgar clamor for a story, but I became attentive to Mr. Brisher's bodily needs, and presently I led him back to the deserted lady.

"She was a nice girl," he said—a little sadly, I thought. "*And* respectable."

He raised his eyebrows and tightened his mouth to express extreme respectability—beyond the likes of us elderly men.

"It was a long way from 'ere. Essex, in fact. Near Colchester. It was when I was up in London—in the buildin' trade. I was a smart young chap then, I can tell you. Slim. 'Ad best clo'es 's good as anybody. 'At—*silk* 'at, mind you." Mr. Brisher's hand shot above his head towards the infinite to indicate a silk hat of the highest. "Umbrella—nice umbrella with a 'orn 'andle. Savin's. Very careful I was. . . ."

He was pensive for a little while, thinking, as we must all come to think sooner or later, of the vanished brightness of youth. But he refrained, as one may do in tap-rooms, from the obvious moral.

"I got to know 'er through a chap what was engaged to 'er sister. She was stopping in London for a bit with an aunt that 'ad a 'am an' beef shop. This aunt was very particular—they was all very particular people, all 'er people was—and wouldn't let 'er sister go out with this feller except 'er other sister, *my* girl that is, went with them. So 'e brought me into it, sort of to ease the crowding. We used to go for walks in Battersea Park of a Sunday afternoon. Me in my topper, and 'im in 'is; and the girls—well—stylish. There wasn't many in Battersea Park 'ad the larf of us. She wasn't what you'd call pretty, but a nicer girl I never met. *I* liked 'er from the start, and, well—though I say it who shouldn't—she liked me. You know 'ow it is, I dessay?"

I pretended I did.

"And when this chap married 'er sister—'im and me was great friends—what must 'e do but arst me down to Colchester, close by where She lived. Naturally I was introduced to 'er people, and, well, very soon, her and me was engaged."

He repeated "engaged."

"She lived at 'ome with 'er father and mother, quite the lady, in a very nice little 'ouse with a garden—and remarkable respectable people they was. Rich, you might call 'em a'most. They owned their own 'ouse—got it out of the Building Society, and cheap because the chap who had it before was a burglar and in prison—and they 'ad a bit of free'old land, and some cottages and money 'nvested—all nice and tight: they was what you'd call snug and warm. I tell you, I was On. Furniture too. Why! They 'ad a pianner, Jane—'er name was Jane—used to play it Sundays, and very nice she played too. There wasn't 'ardly a 'ymn toon in the book she *couldn't* play. . . .

"Many's the evenin' we've met and sung 'ymns there, me and 'er and the 'ole bloomin' rest of 'er family.

"Er father was quite a leadin' man in chapel. You should ha' seen him Sundays, interruptin' the minister and givin' out 'ymns. He had gold spectacles, I remember, and used to look over 'em at you while he sang hearty—he was always great on singing 'earty to the Lord—and when *he* got out o' toon 'arf the people went after 'im—always. 'E was that sort of man. And to walk be'ind 'im in 'is nice black clo'es—'is 'at was a brimmer—made one regular proud to be engaged to such a father-in-law. And when the summer came I went down there and stopped a fortnight.

"Now, you know there was a sort of 'itch," said Mr. Brisher. "We wanted to marry, me and Jane did, and get things settled. But *'e* said I 'ad to get a proper position first. Consequently, there was a 'itch. Consequently, when I went down there, I was anxious to show that I was a good and useful sort of chap. Show I could do pretty nearly everything like. See?"

I made a sympathetic noise.

"And down at the bottom of their garden was a bit of wild part like. So I says to 'im, 'Why don't you 'ave a rockery 'ere?' I says. 'It 'ud look nice.'

" 'Too much expense,' he says.

" 'Not a penny,' says I. 'I'm a dab at rockeries. Lemme make you one.' You see, I'd 'elped my mother make a rockery in the beer garden be'ind 'is tap, so I knew 'ow to do it to rights. 'Lemme make you one,' I says. 'It's 'olidays, but I'm that sort of chap, I 'ate doing nothing,' I says. 'I'll make you one to rights.' And the long and the short of it was, he said I might.

"And that's 'ow I come on the treasure."

"What treasure?" I asked

"Why!" said Mr. Brisher. "The treasure I'm telling you about, what's the reason why I never married."

"What! A treasure—dug up?"

"Yes—buried wealth—treasure trove. Come out of the ground. What I kept on saying—regular treasure." He looked at me with unusual disrespect.

"It wasn't more than a foot deep, not the top of it," he said. "I'd 'ardly got thirsty like, before I come on the corner."

"Go on," I said. "I didn't understand."

"Why! Directly I 'it the box I knew it was treasure. A sort of instinct told me. Something seemed to shout inside of me— 'Now's your chance—lie low.' It's lucky I knew the laws of treasure trove or I'd 'ave been shoutin' there and then. I daresay you know—?"

"Crown bags it," I said, "all but one percent. Go on. It's a shame. What did you do?"

"Uncovered the top of the box. There wasn't anybody in the garden or about like. Jane was 'elping 'er mother do the 'ouse. I *was* excited—I tell you. I tried the lock and then gave a whack at the hinges. Open it came. Silver coins—full! Shining. It made me tremble to see 'em. And jest then—I'm blessed if the dustman didn't come round the back of the 'ouse. It pretty nearly gave me 'eart disease to think what a fool I was to 'ave that money showing. And directly after I 'eard the chap next door—'e was 'olidaying too—I 'eard him watering 'is beans. If only 'e'd looked over the fence!"

"What did you do?"

"Kicked the lid on again and covered it up like a shot, and went on digging about a yard away from it—like mad. And my face, so to speak, was laughing on its own account till I had it hid. I tell you I was regular scared like at my luck. I jest thought that it 'ad to be kep' close and that was all. 'Treasure,' I kep' whisperin' to myself, 'Treasure' and ' 'undreds of pounds, 'undreds, 'undreds of pounds.' Whispering to myself like, and digging like blazes. It seemed to me the box was regular sticking out and showing, like your legs do under the sheets in bed, and I went and put all the earth I'd got out of my 'ole for the rockery slap on top of it. I *was* in a sweat. And in the midst of it all out toddles 'er father. He didn't say anything to me, jest stood behind me and stared, but Jane tol' me afterwards when he went indoors, 'e says, 'That there jackanapes of yours, Jane'—he always called me a jackanapes some'ow—'knows 'ow to put 'is back into it, after all.' Jane said that 'e seemed quite impressed by it, 'e did."

"How long was the box?" I asked suddenly.

" 'Ow long?" said Mr. Brisher.

"Yes—in length?"

"Oh! 'Bout so—by so." Mr. Brisher indicated a moderate-sized trunk.

"*Full?*" said I.

"Full up of silver coins—'arf-crowns, I believe."

"Why!" I cried. "That would mean—hundreds of pounds."

"Thousands," said Mr. Brisher, in a sort of sad calm. "I calc'lated it out."

"But how did they get there?"

"All I know is what I found. What I thought at the time was this. The chap who'd owned the 'ouse before 'er father 'd been a regular slap-up burglar. What you'd call a 'igh-class criminal. Used to drive 'is trap—like Peace did." Mr. Brisher meditated on the difficulties of narration and embarked on a complicated parenthesis. "I don't know if I told you it'd been a burglar's 'ouse before it was my girl's father's, and I knew 'e'd robbed a mail train once, I did know that. It seemed to me—"

"That's very likely," I said. "But what did you do?"

"Sweated," said Mr. Brisher. "Regular run orf me. All that morning I was at it," said Mr. Brisher, "pretending to make that rockery and wondering what I should do. I'd 'ave told 'er father, p'r'aps, only I was doubtful of 'is honesty—I was afraid he might rob me of it like, and give it up to the authorities—and besides, considering I was marrying into the family, I thought it would be nicer like if it came through me. Put me on a better footing, so to speak. Well, I 'ad three days before me left of my 'olidays, so there wasn't no hurry, so I covered it up and went on digging, and tried to puzzle out 'ow I was to make sure of it. Only I couldn't.

"I thought," said Mr. Brisher, "*and* I thought. Once I got regular doubtful whether I'd seen it or not, and went down to it and 'ad it uncovered again, just as her ma came out to 'ang up a bit of washin' she'd done. Jumps again! Afterwards I was just thinking I'd 'ave another go at it, when Jane comes to tell me dinner was ready. 'You'll want it,' she said, 'seeing all the 'ole you've dug.'

"I was in a regular daze all durin' dinner, wondering whether that chap next door wasn't over the fence and filling 'is pockets. But in the afternoon I got easier in my mind—it seemed to me it must 'ave been there so long it was pretty sure to stop a bit longer—and I tried to get up a bit of a discussion to drawr out the old man and see what 'e thought of treasure trove."

Mr. Brisher paused, and affected amusement at the memory.

"The old man was a scorcher," he said; "a regular scorcher."

"What!" said I. "Did he—?"

"It was like this," explained Mr. Brisher, laying a friendly hand on my arm and breathing into my face to calm me. "Just to drawr 'im out, I told a story of a chap I said I knew—pretendin', you know—who'd found a sovring in an overcoat 'e'd borrowed. I said 'e stuck to it, but I said I wasn't sure whether that was right or not. And then the old man began Lor! 'E *did* let me 'ave it!" Mr. Brisher affected an insincere amusement. " 'E was, well—what you might call a rare 'and at snacks. Said that was the sort of friend 'e'd naturally expect me to 'ave. Said 'e'd naturally expect that from the friend of a out-of-work loafer who took up with daughters who didn't belong to 'im. There! I couldn't tell you *arf* 'e said. 'E went on most outrageous. I stood up to 'im about it, just to drawr 'im out. 'Wouldn't you stick to 'arf-sov', not if you found it in the street?' I says. 'Certainly not,' 'e says; 'certainly I wouldn't.' 'What! Not if you found it as a sort of treasure?' 'Young man,' 'e says, 'there's 'igher 'thority than mine'—"Render unto Caesar" '—what is it? Yes. Well, he fetched up that. A rare 'and at 'itting you over the 'ead with the Bible, was the old man. And so he went on. 'E got to such snacks about me at last I couldn't stand it. I'd promised Jane not to answer 'im back, but it got a bit *too* thick. I—I give it 'im. . . ."

Mr. Brisher, by means of enigmatical facework, tried to make me think he had had the best of that argument, but I knew better.

"I went out in a 'uff at last. But not before I was pretty sure I 'ad to lift that treasure by myself. The only thing that kep' me up was thinking 'ow I'd take it out of 'im when I 'ad the cash. . . ."

There was a lengthy pause.

"Now, you'd 'ardly believe it, but all them three days I never 'ad a chance at the blessed treasure, never got out not even a 'arf-crown. There was always a Something—always.

" 'Stonishing thing it isn't thought of more," said Mr. Brisher. "Finding treasure's no great shakes. It's getting it. I don't suppose I slep' a wink any of those nights, thinking where I was to take it, what I was to do with it, 'ow I was to explain it. It made me regular ill. And days I was that dull, it made Jane regular 'uffy. 'You ain't the same chap you was in London,' she says, several times. I tried to lay it on 'er father and 'is snacks, but bless you, she knew better. What must she 'ave but that I'd got another girl on my mind. Said I wasn't true. Well, we had a bit of a row. But I was that set on the treasure, I didn't seem to mind a bit anything she said.

"Well, at last I got a sort of plan. I was always a bit good at planning, though carrying out isn't so much in my line. I thought it all out and settled on a plan. First, I was going to take all my pockets full of these 'ere 'arf-crowns—see?—and afterwards—as I shall tell.

"Well, I got to that state I couldn't think of getting at the treasure again in the daytime, so I waited until the night before I had to go, and then, when everything was still, up I gets and slips down to the back door, meaning to get my pockets full. What must I do in the scullery but fall over a pail? Up gets 'er father with a gun—'e was a light sleeper, was 'er father, and very suspicious—and there was me: 'ad to explain I'd come down to the pump for a drink because my water bottle was bad. 'E didn't let me off a snack or two over that bit, you lay a bob."

"And you mean to say—" I began.

"Wait a bit," said Mr. Brisher. "I say, I'd made my plan. That put the kibosh on one bit, but it didn't 'urt the general scheme not a bit. I went and I finished that rockery next day, as though there wasn't a snack in the world; cemented over the stones, I did, dabbled it green, and everything. I put a dab of green just to show where the box was. They all came and looked at it, and said 'ow nice it was—even 'e was a bit softer like to see it, and all he said was, 'It's a pity you can't always work like that, then you might get something definite to do,' he says.

" 'Yes,' I says—for I couldn't 'elp it—'I put a lot in that rockery,' I says, like that. See? 'I put a lot in that rockery'—meaning—"

"I see," said I—for Mr. Brisher is apt to overelaborate his jokes.

" 'E didn't," said Mr. Brisher. "Not then, anyhow.

" 'Ar'ever—after all that was over, orf I set for London. . . . Orf I set for London. . . ."

Pause.

"On'y I wasn't going to no London," said Mr. Brisher, with sudden animation, and thrusting his face into mine. "No fear! What do *you* think?

"I didn't get no further than Colchester—not a yard.

"I'd left the spade just where I could find it. I'd got everything planned and right. I 'ired a little trap in Colchester, and pretended I wanted to go up to Ipswich and stop the night, and come back next day, and the chap I 'ired it from made me leave two sovrings on it right away, and off I set.

"I didn't go to no Ipswich neither.

"Midnight the 'orse and trap was 'itched by the little road that ran by the cottage where 'e lived—not sixty yards off, it wasn't—and I was at it like a good 'un. It was jest the night for such games—overcast—but a trifle too 'ot, and all round the sky there was summer lightning and presently a thunderstorm. Down it came. First big drops in a sort of fizzle, then 'ail. I kep' on. I whacked at it—I didn't dream the old man would 'ear. I didn't even trouble to go quiet with the spade, and the thunder and lightning and 'ail seemed to excite me like. I shouldn't wonder if I was singing. I got so 'ard at it I clean forgot the thunder and the 'orse and trap. I precious soon got the box showing, and started to lift it. . . ."

"Heavy?" I said.

"I couldn't no more lift it than fly. I *was* sick. I'd never thought of that! I got regular wild—I tell you, I cursed. I got sort of outrageous. I didn't think of dividing it like for the minute, and even then I couldn't 'ave took money about loose in a trap. I hoisted one end sort of wild like, and over the whole show went with a tremenjous noise. Perfeck smash of silver. And then right on the heels of that, flash! Lightning like the day! And there was the back door open and the old man coming down the garden with 'is blooming old gun. He wasn't not a 'undred yards away! I tell you. I was that upset—I didn't think what I was doing. I never stopped—not even to fill my pockets. I went over the fence like a shot, and ran like one o'clock for the trap, cussing and swearing as I went. I *was* in a state. . . .

"And will you believe me, when I got to the place where I'd left the 'orse and trap, they'd gone. Orf! When I saw that I 'adn't a cuss left for it. I jest danced on the grass, and when I'd danced enough I started off to London. . . . I was done."

Mr. Brisher was pensive for an interval. "I was done," he repeated, very bitterly.

"Well?" I said.

"That's all," said Mr. Brisher.

"You didn't go back?"

"No fear. I'd 'ad enough of *that* blooming treasure—any'ow, for a bit. Besides, I didn't know what was done to chaps who tried to collar a treasure trove. I started off for London there and then. . . ."

"And you never went back?"

"Never."

"But about Jane? Did you write?"

"Three times, fishing like. And no answer. We'd parted in a bit of a 'uff on account of 'er being jealous. So that I couldn't make out for certain what it meant.

"I didn't know what to do. I didn't even know whether the old man knew it was me. I sort of kep' an eye open on papers to see when he'd give up that treasure to the Crown, as I hadn't a doubt 'e would, considering 'ow respectable he'd always been."

"And did he?"

Mr. Brisher pursed his mouth and moved his head slowly from side to side. "Not *'im,*" he said.

"Jane was a nice girl," he said, "a thorough nice girl, mind you, *if* jealous, and there's no knowing I mightn't 'ave gone back to 'er after a bit. I thought if he didn't give up the treasure I might 'ave a sort of 'old on 'im.... Well, one day I looks as usual under Colchester—and there I saw 'is name. What for, d'yer think?" I could not guess.

Mr. Brisher's voice sank to a whisper, and once more he spoke behind his hand. His manner was suddenly suffused with a positive joy. "Issuing counterfeit coins," he said. "Counterfeit coins!"

"You don't mean to say—"

"Yes—it. Bad. Quite a long case they made of it. But they got 'im, though he dodged tremenjous. Traced 'is 'aving passed, oh!—nearly a dozen bad 'arf-crowns."

"And you didn't—?"

"No fear. And it didn't do *'im* much good to say it was treasure trove."

Born in Bombay, Rudyard Kipling (1865–1936) was sent by his family to England when he was six; but during his school days he developed an interest in journalism, and later returned to India as a reporter for the Lahore Civil and Military Gazette. *Most of his fiction is set in that teeming country under British rule, beginning with* Plain Tales from the Hills *(1888), a collection of stories that first appeared in the* Gazette. *He followed this with such still-famous works as* Barrack-Room Ballads *(1892),* The Jungle Books *(1894–95),* Captains Courageous *(1897), and* Kim *(1901). Kipling's primary themes of courage, male-bonding, duty, and patriotism have not been held in high regard by some modern critics; but the power of his work is undeniable.* "The Return of Imray" *is one of a small number of his stories that deal with crime and its aftermath on the Indian frontier.*

The Return of Imray
Rudyard KiplinG

Imray achieved the impossible. Without warning, for no conceivable motive, in his youth, at the threshold of his career he chose to disappear from the world—which is to say, the little Indian station where he lived.

Upon a day he was alive, well, happy, and in great evidence among the billiard tables at his club. Upon a morning, he was not, and no manner of search could make sure where he might be. He had stepped out of his place; he had not appeared at his office at the proper time, and his dogcart was not upon the public roads. For these reasons, and because he was hampering, in a microscopical degree, the administration of the Indian Empire, that Empire paused for one microscopical moment to make inquiry into the fate of Imray. Ponds were dragged, wells were plumbed, telegrams were dispatched down the lines of railways and to the nearest seaport town—1,200

miles away; but Imray was not at the end of the drag ropes nor
the telegraph wires. He was gone, and his place knew him no
more. Then the work of the great Indian Empire swept forward,
because it could not be delayed, and Imray from being a man
became a mystery—such a thing as men talk over at their tables
in the club for a month, and then forget utterly. His guns,
horses, and carts were sold to the highest bidder. His superior
officer wrote an altogether absurd letter to his mother, saying
that Imray had unaccountably disappeared, and his bungalow
stood empty.

After three or four months of the scorching hot weather
had gone by, my friend Strickland, of the police, saw fit to rent
the bungalow from the native landlord. This was before he was
engaged to Miss Youghal—an affair which has been described in
another place—and while he was pursuing his investigations
into native life. His own life was sufficiently peculiar, and men
complained of his manners and customs. There was always food
in his house, but there were no regular times for meals. He ate,
standing up and walking about, whatever he might find at the
sideboard, and this is not good for human beings. His domestic
equipment was limited to six rifles, three shotguns, five saddles,
and a collection of stiff-jointed mahseer rods, bigger and
stronger than the largest salmon rods. These occupied one half
of his bungalow, and the other half was given up to Strickland
and his dog Tietjens—an enormous Rampur slut who devoured
daily the rations of two men. She spoke to Strickland in a language of her own; and whenever, walking abroad, she saw
things calculated to destroy the peace of Her Majesty the
Queen-Empress, she returned to her master and laid information. Strickland would take steps at once, and the end of his
labors was trouble and fine and imprisonment for other people.
The natives believed that Tietjens was a familiar spirit, and
treated her with the great reverence that is born of hate and
fear. One room in the bungalow was set apart for her special
use. She owned a bedstead, a blanket, and a drinking trough,
and if anyone came into Strickland's room at night her custom
was to knock down the invader and give tongue till someone

came with a light. Strickland owed his life to her, when he was on the frontier, in search of a local murderer, who came in the gray dawn to send Strickland much farther than the Andaman Islands. Tietjens caught the man as he was crawling into Strickland's tent with a dagger between his teeth; and after his record of iniquity was established in the eyes of the law he was hanged. From that date Tietjens wore a collar of rough silver, and employed a monogram on her night blanket, and the blanket was of double woven Kashmir cloth, for she was a delicate dog.

Under no circumstances would she be separated from Strickland; and once, when he was ill with fever, made great trouble for the doctors, because she did not know how to help her master and would not allow another creature to attempt aid. Macarnaght, of the Indian Medical Service, beat her over her head with a gun butt before she could understand that she must give room for those who could give quinine.

A short time after Strickland had taken Imray's bungalow, my business took me through that station, and naturally, the club quarters being full, I quartered myself upon Strickland. It was a desirable bungalow, eight-roomed and heavily thatched against any chance of leakage from rain. Under the pitch of the roof ran a ceiling cloth which looked just as neat as a white-washed ceiling. Unless you knew how Indian bungalows were built you would never have suspected that above the cloth lay the dark three-cornered cavern of the roof, where the beams and the underside of the thatch harbored all manner of rats, bats, ants, and foul things.

Tietjens met me in the veranda with a bay like the boom of the bell of St. Paul's, putting her paws on my shoulder to show she was glad to see me. Strickland had contrived to claw together a sort of meal which he called lunch, and immediately after it was finished went out about his business. I was left alone with Tietjens and my own affairs. The heat of the summer had broken up and turned to the warm damp of the rains. There was no motion in the heated air, but the rain fell like ramrods on the earth, and flung up a blue mist when it splashed back. The bamboos, and the custard apples, the poinsettias, and the mango trees in the garden stood still while the warm water lashed through them, and the frogs began to sing among the aloe hedges.

A little before the light failed, and when the rain was at its worst, I sat in the back veranda and heard the water roar from the eaves, and scratched myself because I was covered with the thing called prickly heat. Tietjens came out with me and put her head in my lap and was very sorrowful; so I gave her biscuits when tea was ready, and I took tea in the back veranda on account of the little coolness found there. The rooms of the house were dark behind me. I could smell Strickland's saddlery and the oil on his guns, and I had no desire to sit among these things. My own servant came to me in the twilight, the muslin of his clothes clinging tightly to his drenched body, and told me that a gentleman had called and wished to see someone. Very much against my will, but only because of the darkness of the rooms, I went into the naked drawing room, telling my man to bring the lights. There might or might not have been a caller waiting—it seemed to me that I saw a figure by one of the windows—but when the light came there was nothing save the spikes of the rain without, and the smell of the drinking earth in my nostrils. I explained to my servant that he was no wiser than he ought to be, and went back to the veranda to talk to Tietjens. She had gone out into the wet, and I could hardly coax her back to me; even with biscuits with sugar tops. Strickland came home, dripping wet, just before dinner, and the first thing he said was,

"Has anyone called?"

I explained, with apologies, that my servant had summoned me into the drawing room on a false alarm; or that some loafer had tried to call on Strickland, and thinking better of it had fled after giving his name. Strickland ordered dinner, without comment, and since it was a real dinner with a white tablecloth attached, we sat down.

At nine o'clock Strickland wanted to go to bed, and I was tired too. Tietjens, who had been lying underneath the table, rose up, and swung into the least exposed veranda as soon as her master moved to his own room, which was next to the stately chamber set apart for Tietjens. If a mere wife had wished to sleep out of doors in that pelting rain it would not have mattered; but Tietjens was a dog, and therefore the better animal. I looked at Strickland, expecting to see him flay her with a whip. He smiled queerly, as a man would smile after telling some unpleasant domestic tragedy. "She has done this ever since I moved in here," said he. "Let her go."

The dog was Strickland's dog, so I said nothing, but I felt all that Strickland felt in being thus made light of. Tietjens encamped outside my bedroom window, and storm after storm came up, thundered on the thatch, and died away. The lightning spattered the sky as a thrown egg spatters a barn door, but the light was pale blue, not yellow, and looking through my split bamboo blinds, I could see the great dog standing, not sleeping, in the veranda, the hackles alift on her back and her feet anchored as tensely as the drawn wire-rope of a suspension bridge. In the very short pauses of the thunder I tried to sleep, but it seemed that someone wanted me very urgently. He, whoever he was, was trying to call me by name, but his voice was no more than a husky whisper. The thunder ceased, and Tietjens went into the garden and howled at the low moon. Somebody tried to open my door, walked about and about through the house, and stood breathing heavily in the verandas, and just when I was falling asleep I fancied that I heard a wild hammering and clamoring about my head or on the door.

I ran into Strickland's room and asked him whether he was ill and had been calling for me. He was lying on his bed half dressed, a pipe in his mouth. "I thought you'd come," he said. "Have I been walking round the house recently?"

I explained that he had been tramping in the dining room and the smoking room and two or three other places, and he laughed and told me to go back to bed. I went back to bed and slept till the morning, but through all my mixed dreams I was sure I was doing someone an injustice in not attending to his wants. What those wants were I could not tell; but a fluttering, whispering, bolt-fumbling, lurking, loitering Someone was reproaching me for my slackness, and, half awake, I heard the howling of Tietjens in the garden and the threshing of the rain.

I lived in that house for two days. Strickland went to his office daily, leaving me alone for eight or ten hours with Tietjens for my only companion. As long as the full light lasted I was comfortable, and so was Tietjens; but in the twilight she and I moved into the back veranda and cuddled each other for company. We were alone in the house, but nonetheless it was much too fully occupied by a tenant with whom I did not wish to interfere. I never saw him, but I could see the curtains between the rooms quivering where he had just passed through; I could hear the chairs creaking as the bamboos sprung under a weight that had just quitted them; and I could feel when I went to get a book from the dining room that somebody was waiting in the shadows of the front veranda till I should have gone away. Tietjens made the twilight more interesting by glaring into the darkened rooms with every hair erect, and following the motions of something that I could not see. She never entered the rooms, but her eyes moved interestedly: that was quite sufficient. Only when my servant came to trim the lamps and make all light and habitable she would come in with me and spend her time sitting on her haunches, watching an invisible extra man as he moved about behind my shoulder. Dogs are cheerful companions.

I explained to Strickland, gently as might be, that I would go over to the club and find quarters there. I admired his hospitality, was pleased with his guns and rods, but I did not much care for his house and its atmosphere. He heard me out to the end, and then smiled very wearily, but without contempt, for he is a man who understands things. "Stay on," he said, "and see what this thing means. All you have talked about I have known since I took the bungalow. Stay on and wait. Tietjens has left me. Are you going, too?"

I had seen him through one little affair, connected with a heathen idol, that had brought me to the doors of a lunatic asylum, and I had no desire to help him through further experiences. He was a man to whom unpleasantness arrived as do dinners to ordinary people.

Therefore I explained more clearly than ever that I liked him immensely and would be happy to see him in the daytime; but that I did not care to sleep under his roof. This was after dinner, when Tietjens had gone out to lie in the veranda.

" 'Pon my soul, I don't wonder," said Strickland, with his eyes on the ceiling cloth. "Look at that!"

The tails of two brown snakes were hanging between the cloth and the cornice of the wall. They threw long shadows in the lamplight.

"If you are afraid of snakes, of course—" said Strickland.

I hate and fear snakes, because if you look into the eyes of any snake you will see that it knows all and more of the mystery of man's fall, and that it feels all the contempt that the Devil felt when Adam was evicted from Eden. Besides which its bite is generally fatal, and it twists up trouser legs.

"You ought to get your thatch overhauled," I said. "Give me a mahseer rod, and we'll poke 'em down."

"They'll hide among the roof beams," said Strickland. "I can't stand snakes overhead. I'm going up into the roof. If I shake 'em down, stand by with a cleaning rod and break their backs."

I was not anxious to assist Strickland in his work, but I took the cleaning rod and waited in the dining rooom, while Strickland brought a gardener's ladder from the veranda and set it against the side of the room. The snake tails drew themselves up and disappeared. We could hear the dry rushing scuttle of long bodies running over the baggy ceiling cloth. Strickland took a lamp with him, while I tried to make clear to him the danger of hunting snakes between a ceiling cloth and a thatch, apart from the deterioration of property caused by ripping out ceiling cloths.

"Nonsense!" said Strickland. "They're sure to hide near the walls by the cloth. The bricks are too cold for 'em, and the heat of the room is just what they like." He put his hand to the corner of the stuff and ripped it from the cornice. It gave with a great sound of tearing, and Strickland put his head through the opening into the dark of the angle of the roof beams. I set my teeth and lifted the rod, for I had not the least knowledge of what might descend.

"H'm!" said Strickland, and his voice rolled and rumbled in the roof. "There's room for another set of rooms up here, and, by Jove, someone is occupying 'em!"

"Snakes?" I said from below.

"No. It's a buffalo. Hand me up the last two joints of a mahseer rod, and I'll prod it. It's lying on the main roof beam."

I handed up the rod.

"What a nest for owls and serpents! No wonder the snakes live here," said Strickland, climbing farther into the roof. I could see his elbow thrusting with the rod. "Come out of that, whoever you are! Heads below there! It's falling."

I saw the ceiling cloth nearly in the center of the room bag with a shape that was pressing it downwards and downwards towards the lighted lamp on the table. I snatched the lamp out of danger and stood back. Then the cloth ripped out from the walls, tore, split, swayed, and shot down upon the table something that I dared not look at till Strickland had slid down the ladder and was standing by my side.

He did not say much, being a man of few words; but he picked up the loose end of the tablecloth and threw it over the remnants on the table.

"It strikes me," said he, putting down the lamp, "our friend Imray has come back. Oh, you would, would you?"

There was a movement under the cloth, and a little snake wriggled out, to be back-broken by the butt of the mahseer rod. I was sufficiently sick to make no remarks worth recording.

Strickland meditated, and helped himself to drinks. The arrangement under the cloth made no more signs of life.

"Is it Imray?" I said.

Strickland turned back the cloth for a moment and looked. "It is Imray," he said; "and his throat is cut from ear to ear."

Then we spoke, but together and to ourselves: "That's why he whispered about the house."

Tietjens, in the garden, began to bay furiously. A little later her great nose heaved open the dining-room door.

She sniffed and was still. The tattered ceiling cloth hung down almost to the level of the table, and there was hardly room to move away from the discovery.

Tietjens came in and sat down; her teeth bared under her lip and her forepaws planted. She looked at Strickland.

"It's a bad business, old lady," said he. "Men don't climb up into the roofs of their bungalows to die, and they don't fasten up the ceiling cloth behind 'em. Let's think it out."

"Let's think it out somewhere else," I said.

"Excellent idea! Turn the lamps out. We'll get into my room."

I did not turn the lamps out. I went into Strickland's room first, and allowed him to make the darkness. Then he followed me, and we lit tobacco and thought. Strickland thought. I smoked furiously, because I was afraid.

"Imray is back," said Strickland. "The question is—who killed Imray? Don't talk, I've a notion of my own. When I took this bungalow I took over most of Imray's servants. Imray was guileless and inoffensive, wasn't he?"

I agreed; though the heap under the cloth had looked neither one thing nor the other.

"If I call in all the servants they will stand fast in a crowd and lie like Aryans. What do you suggest?"

"Call 'em in one by one," I said.

"They'll run away and give the news to all their fellows," said Strickland. "We must segregate 'em. Do you suppose your servant knows anything about it?"

"He may, for all I know; but I don't think it's likely. He has only been here two or three days," I answered. "What's your notion?"

"I can't quite tell. How the dickens did the man get the wrong side of the ceiling cloth?"

There was a heavy coughing outside Strickland's bedroom door. This showed that Bahadur Khan, his body servant, had wakened from sleep and wished to put Strickland to bed.

"Come in," said Strickland. "It's a very warm night, isn't it?"

Bahadur Khan, a great, green-turbaned, six-foot Mohammedan, said that it was a very warm night; but that there was more rain pending, which, by his Honor's favor, would bring relief to the country.

"It will be so, if God pleases," said Strickland, tugging off his boots. "It is in my mind, Bahadur Khan, that I have worked thee remorselessly for many days—ever since that time when thou first camest into my service. What time was that?"

"Has the Heaven-born forgotten? It was when Imray Sahib went secretly to Europe without warning given; and I—even I—came into the honored service of the protector of the poor."

"And Imray Sahib went to Europe?"

"It is so said among those who were his servants."

"And thou wilt take service with him when he returns?"

"Assuredly, Sahib. He was a good master, and cherished his dependents."

"That is true. I am very tired, but I go buck shooting tomorrow. Give me the little sharp rifle that I use for black buck; it is in the case yonder."

The man stooped over the case, handed barrels, stock, and fore-end to Strickland, who fitted all together, yawning dolefully. Then he reached down to the gun case, took a solid-drawn cartridge, and slipped it into the breech of the .360 Express.

"And Imray Sahib has gone to Europe secretly! That is very strange, Bahadur Khan, is it not?"

"What do I know of the ways of the white man. Heaven-born?"

"Very little, truly. But thou shalt know more anon. It has reached me that Imray Sahib has returned from his so long journeyings, and that even now he lies in the next room."

"Sahib!"

The lamplight slid along the barrels of the rifle as they leveled themselves at Bahadur Khan's broad breast.

"Go and look!" said Strickland. "Take a lamp. Thy master is tired, and he waits thee. Go!"

The man picked up a lamp, and went into the dining room, Strickland following, and almost pushing him with the muzzle of the rifle. He looked for a moment at the black depths behind the ceiling-cloth; at the writhing snake under foot; and last, a gray glaze settling on his face, at the thing under the cloth.

"Hast thou seen?" said Strickland.

"I have seen. I am clay in the white man's hands. What does the Presence do?"

"Hang thee within the month. What else?"

"For killing him? Nay, Sahib, consider. Walking among us, his servants, he cast his eyes upon my child, who was four years old. Him he bewitched, and in ten days he died of the fever—my child!"

"What said Imray Sahib?"

"He said he was a handsome child, and patted him on the head; wherefore my child died. Wherefore I killed Imray Sahib in the twilight, when he had come back from office, and was sleeping. Wherefore I dragged him up into the roof beams and made all fast behind him. The Heaven-born knows all things. I am the servant of the Heaven-born."

Strickland looked at me.

"Thou art witness to this saying? He has killed."

Bahadur Khan stood ashen gray in the light of the one lamp. The need for justification came upon him very swiftly. "I am trapped," he said, "but the offense was that man's. He cast an evil eye upon my child, and I killed and hid him. Only such as are served by devils," he glared at Tietjens, crouched stolidly before him, "only such could know what I did."

"It was clever. But thou shouldst have lashed him to the beam with a rope. Now, thou thyself wilt hang by a rope. Orderly!"

A drowsy policeman answered Strickland's call. He was followed by another. Tietjens sat wondrous still.

"Take him to the police station," said Strickland.

"Do I hang, then?" said Bahadur Khan, making no attempt to escape, and keeping his eyes on the ground.

"If the sun shines or the water runs—yes!" said Strickland.

Bahadur Khan stepped back one long pace, quivered, and stood still.

"Go!" said Strickland.

"Nay; but I go very swiftly," said Bahadur Khan. "Look! I am even now a dead man."

He lifted his foot, and to the little toe there clung the head of the half-killed snake, firm fixed in the agony of death.

"I come of land-holding stock," said Bahadur Khan, rocking where he stood. "It were a disgrace to me to go to the public scaffold: therefore I take this way. Be it remembered that the Sahib's shirts are correctly enumerated, and that there is an extra piece of soap in his washbasin. My child was bewitched, and I slew the wizard. Why should you seek to slay me with the rope? My honor is saved, and—and—I die."

At the end of an hour he died, as they die who are bitten by the little brown *karait*, and the policemen bore him and the thing under the cloth to their appointed places.

"This," said Strickland, very calmly, as he climbed into bed, "is called the nineteenth century. Did you hear what that man said?"

"I heard," I answered. "Imray made a mistake."

"Simply and solely through not knowing the nature of the Oriental, and the coincidence of a little seasonal fever. Bahadur Khan had been with him for four years."

I shuddered. My own servant had been with me for exactly that length of time. When I went over to my own room I found my man waiting, impassive as the copper head on a penny.

"What has befallen Bahadur Khan?" said I.

"He was bitten by a snake and died. The rest the Sahib knows."

"And how much of this matter hast thou known?"

"As much as might be gathered from One coming in the twilight to seek satisfaction. Gently, Sahib. Let me pull off those boots."

I had just settled to the sleep of exhaustion when I heard Strickland shouting from his side of the house—

"Tietjens has come back to her place!"

And so she had. The great deerhound was couched stately on her own bedstead on her own blanket, while, in the next room, the idle, empty ceiling cloth waggled as it trailed on the table.

Anton Chekhov (1860–1904) was one of the very few figures equally renowned as a playwright and fiction writer. (In the United States in this century, Thornton Wilder was almost as successful in the two fields; Arthur Miller and Tennessee Williams each wrote a fair amount of fiction, but were regarded as primarily playwrights.) Chekhov's most famous play, The Sea Gull, *was first produced in 1898; others of note are* Uncle Vanya *(1899),* The Three Sisters *(1901), and* The Cherry Orchard *(1904). The first collection of his humorous writings,* Motley Stories, *was published in 1886; the best of his serious short fictions can be found in the posthumously published* Darling and Other Stories *(1910). The most notable of Chekhov's crime tales is the novella "The Duel," which unfortunately is much too long for this anthology. "The Bet," while it does not deal with a crime per se, is nonetheless a tale of pure suspense and ranks with the best of his prose.*

THE BET
Anton Chekhov

I

It was a dark autumn night. The old banker was pacing from corner to corner of his study, recalling to his mind the party he gave in the autumn fifteen years before. There were many clever people at the party and much interesting conversation. They talked among other things of capital punishment. The guests, among them not a few scholars and journalists, for the most part disapproved of capital punishment. They found it obsolete as a means of punishment, unfitted to a Christian state and immoral. Some of them thought that capital punishment should be replaced universally by life imprisonment.

"I don't agree with you," said the host. "I myself have experienced neither capital punishment nor life imprisonment, but if one may judge a priori, then in my opinion capital punishment is more moral and more humane than imprisonment. Execution kills instantly, life imprisonment kills by degrees.

Who is the more humane executioner, one who kills you in a few seconds or one who draws the life out of you incessantly, for years?"

"They're both equally immoral," remarked one of the guests, "because their purpose is the same, to take away life. The state is not God. It has no right to take away that which it cannot give back, if it should so desire."

Among the company was a lawyer, a young man of about twenty-five. On being asked his opinion, he said:

"Capital punishment and life imprisonment are equally immoral; but if I were offered the choice between them, I would certainly choose the second. It's better to live somehow than not to live at all."

There ensued a lively discussion. The banker, who was then younger and more nervous, suddenly lost his temper, banged his fist on the table, and turning to the young lawyer, cried out:

"It's a lie. I bet you two million you wouldn't stick in a cell even for five years."

"If you mean it seriously," replied the lawyer, "then I bet I'll stay not five but fifteen."

"Fifteen! Done!" cried the banker. "Gentlemen, I stake two million."

"Agreed. You stake two million, I my freedom," said the lawyer.

So this wild, ridiculous bet came to pass. The banker, who at that time had too many millions to count, spoiled and capricious, was beside himself with rapture. During supper he said to the lawyer jokingly:

"Come to your senses, young man, before it's too late. Two million is nothing to me, but you stand to lose three or four of the best years of your life. I say three or four, because you'll never stick it out any longer. Don't forget either, you unhappy man, that voluntary is much heavier than enforced imprisonment. The idea that you have the right to free yourself at any moment will poison the whole of your life in the cell. I pity you."

And now the banker, pacing from corner to corner, recalled all this and asked himself:

"Why did I make this bet? What's the good? The lawyer loses fifteen years of his life and I throw away two million. Will it convince people that capital punishment is worse or better than imprisonment for life? No, no! All stuff and rubbish. On my part, it was the caprice of a well-fed man; on the lawyer's, pure greed of gold."

He recollected further what happened after the evening party. It was decided that the lawyer must undergo his imprisonment under the strictest observation, in a garden wing of the banker's house. It was agreed that during the period he would be deprived of the right to cross the threshold, to see living people, to hear human voices, and to receive letters and newspapers. He was permitted to have a musical instrument, to read books, to write letters, to drink wine and smoke tobacco. By the agreement he could communicate, but only in silence, with the outside world through a little window specially constructed for this purpose. Everything necessary, books, music, wine, he could receive in any quantity by sending a note through the window. The agreement provided for all the minutest details, which made the confinement strictly solitary, and it obliged the lawyer to remain exactly fifteen years from twelve o'clock of November 14, 1870, to twelve o'clock of November 14, 1885. The least attempt on his part to violate the conditions, to escape if only for two minutes before the time, freed the banker from the obligation to pay him the two million.

During the first year of imprisonment, the lawyer, as far as it was possible to judge from his short notes, suffered terribly from loneliness and boredom. From his wing day and night came the sound of the piano. He rejected wine and tobacco. "Wine," he wrote, "excites desires, and desires are the chief foes of a prisoner; besides, nothing is more boring than to drink good wine alone, and tobacco spoils the air in his room." During the first year the lawyer was sent books of a light character; novels with a complicated love interest, stories of crime and fantasy, comedies, and so on.

In the second year the piano was heard no longer and the lawyer asked only for classics. In the fifth year, music was heard again, and the prisoner asked for wine. Those who watched him said that during the whole of that year he was only eating, drinking, and lying on his bed. He yawned often and talked angrily to himself. Books he did not read. Sometimes at nights he would sit down to write. He would write for a long time and tear it all up in the morning. More than once he was heard to weep.

In the second half of the sixth year, the prisoner began zealously to study languages, philosophy, and history. He fell on these subjects so hungrily that the banker hardly had time to get books enough for him. In the space of four years about six hundred volumes were bought at his request. It was while that passion lasted that the banker received the following letter from the prisoner: "My dear jailer, I am writing these lines in six languages. Show them to experts. Let them read them. If they do not find one single mistake, I beg you to give orders to have a gun fired off in the garden. By the noise I shall know that my efforts have not been in vain. The geniuses of all ages and countries speak in different languages; but in them all burns the same flame. Oh, if you knew my heavenly happiness now that I can understand them!" The prisoner's desire was fulfilled. Two shots were fired in the garden by the banker's order.

Later on, after the tenth year, the lawyer sat immovable before his table and read only the New Testament. The banker found it strange that a man who in four years had mastered six hundred erudite volumes should have spent nearly a year in reading one book, easy to understand and by no means thick. The New Testament was then replaced by the history of religions and theology.

During the last two years of his confinement the prisoner read an extraordinary amount, quite haphazard. Now he would apply himself to the natural sciences, then he would read Byron or Shakespeare. Notes used to come from him in which he asked to be sent at the same time a book on chemistry, a textbook of medicine, a novel, and some treatise on philosophy or theology. He read as though he were swimming in the sea among broken pieces of wreckage, and in his desire to save his life was eagerly grasping one piece after another.

II

The banker recalled all this, and thought:

"Tomorrow at twelve o'clock he receives his freedom. Under the agreement, I shall have to pay him two million. If I pay, it's all over with me. I am ruined forever. . . ."

Fifteen years before he had too many millions to count, but now he was afraid to ask himself which he had more of, money or debts. Gambling on the stock exchange, risky speculation, and the recklessness of which he could not rid himself even in old age had gradually brought his business to decay; and the fearless, self-confident, proud man of business had become an ordinary banker, trembling at every rise and fall in the market.

"That cursed bet," murmured the old man clutching his head in despair. . . . "Why didn't the man die? He's only forty years old. He will take away my last farthing, marry, enjoy life, gamble on the exchange, and I will look on like an envious beggar and hear the same words from him every day: 'I'm obliged to you for the happiness of my life. Let me help you.' No, it's too much! The only escape from bankruptcy and disgrace—is that the man should die."

The clock had just struck three. The banker was listening. In the house everyone was asleep, and one could hear only the frozen trees whining outside the windows. Trying to make no sound, he took out of his safe the key of the door which had not been opened for fifteen years, put on his overcoat, and went out of the house. The garden was dark and cold. It was raining. A damp, penetrating wind howled in the garden and gave the trees no rest. Though he strained his eyes, the banker could see neither the ground, nor the white statues, nor the garden wing, nor the trees. Approaching the garden wing, he called the watchman twice. There was no answer. Evidently the watchman had taken shelter from the bad weather and was now asleep somewhere in the kitchen or the greenhouse.

"If I have the courage to fulfill my intention," thought the old man, "the suspicion will fall on the watchman first of all."

In the darkness he groped for the steps and the door and entered the hall of the garden wing, then poked his way into a narrow passage and struck a match. Not a soul was there. Someone's bed, with no bedclothes on it, stood there, and an iron stove loomed dark in the corner. The seals on the door that led into the prisoner's room were unbroken.

When the match went out, the old man, trembling from agitation, peeped into the little window.

In the prisoner's room a candle was burning dimly. The prisoner himself sat by the table. Only his back, the hair on his head, and his hands were visible. Open books were strewn about on the table, the two chairs, and on the carpet near the table.

Five minutes passed and the prisoner never once stirred. Fifteen years' confinement had taught him to sit motionless. The banker tapped on the window with his finger, but the prisoner made no movement in reply. Then the banker cautiously tore the seals from the door and put the key into the lock. The rusty lock gave a hoarse groan and the door creaked. The banker expected instantly to hear a cry of surprise and the sound of steps. Three minutes passed and it was as quiet inside as it had been before. He made up his mind to enter.

Before the table sat a man, unlike an ordinary human being. It was a skeleton, with tight-drawn skin, with long curly hair like a woman's, and a shaggy beard. The color of his face was yellow, of an earthy shade; the cheeks were sunken, the back long and narrow, and the hand upon which he leaned his hairy head was so lean and skinny that it was painful to look upon. His hair was already silvering with gray, and no one who glanced at the senile emaciation of the face would have believed that he was only forty years old. On the table, before his bent head, lay a sheet of paper on which something was written in a tiny hand.

"Poor devil," thought the banker, "he's asleep and probably seeing millions in his dreams. I have only to take and throw this half-dead thing on the bed, smother him a moment with the pillow, and the most careful examination will find no trace of unnatural death. But first let us read what he has written here."

The banker took the sheet from the table and read:

"Tomorrow at twelve o'clock midnight, I shall obtain my freedom and the right to mix with people. But before I leave this room and see the sun I think it necessary to say a few words to you. On my own clear conscience and before God who sees me I declare to you that I despise freedom, life, health, and all that your books call the blessings of the world.

"For fifteen years I have diligently studied earthly life. True, I saw neither the earth nor the people, but in your books I drank fragrant wine, sang songs, hunted deer and wild boar in the forests, loved women. . . . And beautiful women, like clouds ethereal, created by the magic of your poets' genius, visited me by night and whispered to me wonderful tales, which made my head drunken. In your books I climbed the summits of Elburz and Mont Blanc and saw from there how the sun rose in the morning, and in the evening suffused the sky, the ocean, and the mountain ridges with a purple gold. I saw from there how above me lightning glimmered cleaving the clouds; I saw green forests, fields, rivers, lakes, cities; I heard sirens singing, and the playing of the pipes of Pan; I touched the wings of beautiful devils who came flying to me to speak of God. . . . In your books I cast myself into bottomless abysses, worked miracles, burned cities to the ground, preached new religions, conquered whole countries. . . .

"Your books gave me wisdom. All that unwearying human thought created in the centuries is compressed to a little lump in my skull. I know that I am cleverer than you all.

"And I despise your books, despise all worldly blessings and wisdom. Everything is void, frail, visionary, and delusive as a mirage. Though you be proud and wise and beautiful, yet will death wipe you from the face of the earth like the mice underground; and your posterity, your history, and the immortality of your men of genius will be as frozen slag, burnt down together with the terrestrial globe.

"You are mad, and gone the wrong way. You take falsehood for truth and ugliness for beauty. You would marvel if suddenly apple and orange trees should bear frogs and lizards instead of fruit, and if roses should begin to breathe the odor of a sweating horse. So do I marvel at you, who have bartered heaven for earth. I do not want to understand you.

"That I may show you in deed my contempt for that by which you live, I waive the two million of which I once dreamed as of paradise, and which I now despise. That I may deprive myself of my right to them, I shall come out from here five minutes before the stipulated term, and thus shall violate the agreement."

When he had read, the banker put the sheet on the table, kissed the head of the strange man, and began to weep. He went out of the wing. Never at any other time, not even after his terrible losses on the exchange, had he felt such contempt for himself as now. Coming home, he lay down on his bed, but agitation and tears kept him a long time from sleeping. . . .

The next morning the poor watchman came running to him and told him that they had seen the man who lived in the wing climb through the window into the garden. He had gone to the gate and disappeared. The banker instantly went with his servants to the wing and established the escape of his prisoner. To avoid unnecessary rumors he took the paper with the renunciation from the table and, on his return, locked it in his safe.

An important figure in American letters in the early part of this century, Edith Wharton (1862–1937) understood the human condition and wrote of it with considerable sensitivity and intensity. Her best novels were concerned with the subtle interplay of passions in a Victorian society that censured the free expression of passion; among these are the tragic love story Ethan Frome *(1911),* The Age of Innocence *(1920, and the recipient of the 1921 Pulitzer Prize), and four short novels collected in* Old New York *(1924). She also published a wide variety of short fiction, including several tales of mystery and the macabre, as well as poems and travel books in a prolific career that spanned more than forty years. As evidenced by "Bewitched," her themes and her quiet style are all the more mordant for their deceptive simplicity.*

BEWITCHED
Edith WhartoN

I

The snow was still falling thickly when Orrin Bosworth, who farmed the land south of Lonetop, drove up in his cutter to Saul Rutledge's gate. He was surprised to see two other cutters ahead of him. From them descended two muffled figures. Bosworth, with increasing surprise, recognized Deacon Hibben, from North Ashmore, and Sylvester Brand, the widower, from the old Bearcliff Farm.

It was not often that anybody in Hemlock County entered Saul Rutledge's gate; least of all in the dead of winter, and summoned (as Bosworth, at any rate, had been) by Mrs. Rutledge, who passed, even in that unsocial region, for a woman of cold manners and solitary character.

"Hallo, Deacon."

"Well, well, Orrin—" They shook hands.

" 'Day, Bosworth," said Sylvester Brand with a brief nod,

and they walked across to the front door. The Deacon had hardly lifted the knocker when the door opened and Mrs. Rutledge stood before them.

"Walk right in," she said in her usual dead-level tone. She was dressed for the occasion in a black calico with white spots, a collar of crochet lace fastened by a gold brooch, and a gray woolen shawl, crossed under her arms and tied at the back. In her small narrow head the only marked prominence was that of the brow projecting roundly over pale spectacled eyes. Her eyes were of a cold gray, her complexion was an even white. Her age might have been anywhere from thirty-five to sixty.

The room into which she led the three men was at once close and bitterly cold.

"Andy Pond," Mrs. Rutledge cried to someone at the back of the house, "step out and call Mr. Rutledge. You'll likely find him in the woodshed, or round the barn somewheres." She rejoined her visitors. "I presume you folks are wondering what I asked you to come here for," she said, "and I'll allow you didn't expect it was for a party."

No one ventured to respond to this chill pleasantry, and she continued: "We're in trouble here and need advice—Mr. Rutledge and myself do." She cleared her throat and added in a lower tone, her pitilessly clear eyes looking straight before her. "There's a spell been cast over Mr. Rutledge."

The Deacon looked up sharply, an incredulous smile pinching his thin lips. "A spell?"

"That's what I said: he's bewitched."

Bosworth, less tongue-tied than the others, asked with an attempt at humor: "Do you use the word in the strict scripture sense, Mrs. Rutledge?"

"That's how *he* uses it."

The Deacon coughed and cleared his long, rattling throat. "Do you care to give us more particulars before your husband joins us?"

Mrs. Rutledge looked down at her clasped hands, as if considering the question. "No," she said at length, "I'll wait."

A silence fell, during which the four persons present

seemed all to be listening for the sound of a step; but none was heard, and after a minute, Mrs. Rutledge began to speak again.

"It's down by that old shack on Lamer's pond; that's where they meet." Bosworth, whose eyes were on Sylvester Brand's face, fancied he saw a sort of inner flush darken the farmer's heavy leathern skin. Deacon Hibben leaned forward, a glitter of curiosity in his eyes.

"They—*who*, Mrs. Rutledge?"

"My husband, Saul Rutledge . . . and her. . . ."

Sylvester Brand stirred in his seat. "Who do you mean by *her*?" he asked abruptly.

Mrs. Rutledge's body did not move; she simply revolved her head on her long neck and looked at him.

"Your daughter, Sylvester Brand."

The man staggered to his feet with an explosion of inarticulate sound. "My—my daughter? What the hell are you talking about? My daughter? It's a damned lie . . . it's . . . it's . . ."

"Your daughter *Ora*, Mr. Brand," said Mrs. Rutledge slowly.

Bosworth felt an icy chill down his spine. Instinctively he turned his eyes away from Brand, and they rested on the mildewed countenance of Deacon Hibben. Between the blotches it had become white as Mrs. Rutledge's, and the Deacon's eyes burned in the whiteness like live embers among ashes.

Brand gave a laugh: the rusty creaking laugh of one whose springs of mirth are never moved by gaiety. "My daughter *Ora*?" he repeated.

"Yes."

"My *dead* daughter?"

"That's what he says."

"Your husband?"

"That's what Mr. Rutledge says."

Brand rose to his feet. "Is that all?" he queried contemptuously.

"All? Ain't it enough? How long is it since you folks seen Saul Rutledge, any of you?" Mrs. Rutledge flew out at them.

Bosworth, it appeared, had not seen him for nearly a year;

the Deacon had run across him once, for a minute, at the North Ashmore post office, the previous autumn, and acknowledged he wasn't looking any too good then. Brand said nothing but stood irresolute.

"Well, if you wait a minute you'll see with your own eyes; and he'll tell you with his own words. That's what I've got you here for—to see for yourselves what's come over him. Then you'll talk different," she added, twisting her head abruptly towards Sylvester Brand.

The Deacon raised a lean hand of interrogation. "Does your husband know we've been sent for on this business, Mrs. Rutledge?"

Mrs. Rutledge signed assent.

"It was with his consent, then—"

She looked coldly at her questioner. "I guess it had to be," she said. Again Bosworth felt a chill run down his spine. He tried to dissipate the sensation by speaking with an affectation of energy.

"Can you tell us, Mrs. Rutledge, how this trouble you speak of shows itself . . . what makes you think . . . ?"

She looked at him for a moment; then she leaned forward across the rickety bead-work table. A thin smile of disdain narrowed her colorless lips. "I don't think—I know."

"Well—but how?"

She leaned closer, both elbows on the table, her voice dropping. "I seen 'em."

In the ashen light from the veiling of snow beyond the windows the Deacon's little screwed-up eyes seemed to give out red sparks. "Him and the dead?"

"Him and the dead."

"Saul Rutledge and—and Ora Brand?"

"That's so."

Sylvester Brand's chair fell backwards with a crash. He was on his feet again, crimson and cursing. "It's a goddamned fiend-begotten lie. . . ."

"Friend Brand . . . friend Brand . . ." the Deacon protested.

"Here, let me get out of this. I want to see Saul Rutledge himself, and tell him—"

"Well, here he is," said Mrs. Rutledge.

The outer door had opened; they heard the familiar stamping and shaking of a man who rids his garments of their last snowflake before penetrating to the sacred precincts of the best parlor. Then Saul Rutledge entered.

II

As he came in he faced the light from the north window, and Bosworth's first thought was that he looked like a drowned man fished out from under the ice—"self-drowned," he added. But the snow light plays cruel tricks with a man's color, and even with the shape of his features; it must have been partly that, Bosworth reflected, which transformed Saul Rutledge from the straight, muscular fellow he had been a year before into the haggard wretch now before them.

The Deacon sought for a word to ease the horror. "Well, now, Saul—you look's if you'd ought to set right up to the stove. Had a touch of ague, maybe?"

The feeble attempt was unavailing. Rutledge neither moved nor answered. He stood among them silent, incommunicable, like one risen from the dead.

Brand grasped him roughly by the shoulder. "See here, Saul Rutledge, what's this dirty lie your wife tells us you've been putting about?"

Still Rutledge did not move. "It's no lie," he said.

Brand's hand dropped from his shoulder. In spite of the man's rough bullying power he seemed to be indefinably awed by Rutledge's look and tone.

"No lie? You've gone plumb crazy, then, have you?"

Mrs. Rutledge spoke. "My husband's not lying, nor he ain't gone crazy. Don't I tell you I seen 'em?"

Brand laughed. "Him and the dead?"

"Yes."

"Down by the Lamer pond, you say?"

"Yes."

"And when was that, if I might ask?"

"Day before yesterday."

A silence fell on the strangely assembled group. The Deacon at length broke it to say to Mr. Brand: "Brand, in my opinion we've got to see this thing through."

Brand stood for a moment in speechless contemplation, then let himself slowly down into his chair. "I'll see it through."

The two other men and Mrs. Rutledge had remained seated. Saul Rutledge stood before them, like a prisoner at the bar, or rather like a sick man before the physicians who were to heal him. As Bosworth scrutinized that hollow face, so wan under the dark sunburn, so sucked inward and consumed by some hidden fever, there stole over the sound healthy man the thought that perhaps after all, husband and wife spoke the truth, and that they were all at that moment really standing on the edge of some forbidden mystery. Things that the rational mind would reject without a thought seemed no longer so easy to dispose of as one looked at the actual Saul Rutledge and remembered the man he had been a year before. Yes; as the Deacon said, they would have to see it through. . . .

"Sit down then, Saul; draw up to us, won't you?" the Deacon suggested, trying again for a natural tone.

Mrs. Rutledge pushed a chair forward and her husband sat down on it. He stretched out his arms and grasped his knees in his brown bony fingers; in that attitude he remained, turning neither his head nor his eyes.

"Well, Saul," the Deacon continued, "your wife says you thought mebbe we could do something to help you through this trouble, whatever it is."

Rutledge's gray eyes widened a little. "No; I didn't think that. It was her idea to try what could be done."

"I presume, though, since you've agreed to our coming, that you don't object to our putting a few questions?"

Rutledge was silent for a moment; then he said with a visible effort:

"No, I don't object."

"Well—you've heard what your wife says?"

Rutledge made a slight motion of assent.

"And—what have you got to answer? How do you explain ... ?"

Mrs. Rutledge intervened. "How can he explain? I seen 'em."

There was a silence; then Bosworth, trying to speak in an easy reassuring tone, queried: "That so, Saul?"

"That's so."

Brand lifted up his brooding head. "You mean to say you ... you sit here before me and say ..."

The Deacon's hand checked him. "Hold on, friend Brand. We're all of us trying for the facts, ain't we?"

He turned to Rutledge. "We've heard what Mrs. Rutledge says. What's your answer?"

"I don't know as there's any answer. She found us."

"And you mean to tell me the person with you was ... was what you took to be ..." the Deacon's thin voice grew thinner: "Ora Brand?"

Saul Rutledge nodded.

"You knew ... or thought you knew ... you were meeting with the dead?"

Rutledge bent his head again. The snow continued to fall in a steady unwavering sheet against the window, and Bosworth felt as if a winding-sheet were descending from the window to envelop them all in a common grave.

"Think what you're saying! It's against our religion! Ora ... poor child ... died a year ago. I saw you at her funeral, Saul. How can you make such a statement?"

"What else can he do?" thrust in Mrs. Rutledge.

There was another pause. The Deacon laid his quivering fingertips together and moistened his lips.

"Was the day before yesterday the first time?" he asked.

The movement of Rutledge's head was negative.

"Not the first? Then when ..."

"Nigh on a year ago, I reckon."

"God! And you mean to tell us that ever since—?"

"Well... look at him," said his wife. The three men lowered their eyes.

After a moment Bosworth, trying to collect himself, glanced at the Deacon. "Why not ask Saul to make his own statement, if that is what we are here for?"

"That's so," the Deacon assented. He turned to Rutledge. "Will you try to give us your idea of ... of how it began?"

Rutledge tightened his grasp on his gaunt knees. "Well," he said, "I guess it begun way back, afore even I was married to Mrs. Rutledge. ..." He spoke in a low automatic voice, as if some invisible agent were dictating his words, or even uttering them for him. "You know," he added, "Ora and me, we kept company. But she was very young. Mr. Brand here he sent her away. She was gone nigh to three years, I guess. When she come back I was married."

"That's right," Brand said.

"And after she came back did you meet her again?" the Deacon continued.

"Alive?" Rutledge questioned.

"Well—of course," said the Deacon nervously.

Rutledge seemed to consider. "Once I did—only once. There was a lot of other people around. At Cold Corners fair it was."

"Did you talk with her then?"

"Only a minute."

"What did she say?"

His voice dropped. "She said she was sick and knew she was going to die, and when she was dead she'd come back to me."

"And what did you answer?"

"Nothing."

"Did you think anything of it at the time?"

"Well, no. Not till I heard she was dead I didn't. After that I thought of it—and I guess she drew me." He moistened his lips.

"Drew you down to that abandoned house by the pond?"

Rutledge made a faint motion of assent, and the Deacon added: "How . . . did you know it was there she wanted you to come?"

"She . . . just drew me. . . ."

There was a long pause. Mrs. Rutledge opened and closed her narrow lips like some beached shellfish gasping for the tide. Rutledge waited.

"Well, now, Saul, won't you go on with what you was telling us?" the Deacon suggested.

"That's all. There's nothing else."

The Deacon lowered his voice. "She just draws you?"

"Yes."

"Often?"

"That's as it happens. . . ."

"But if it's always there she draws you, man, haven't you the strength to keep away from the place?"

For the first time Rutledge wearily turned his head toward his questioner. A spectral smile narrowed his colorless lips. "Ain't any use. She follers after me. . . ."

Mrs. Rutledge's presence checked the next question. At length the Deacon spoke in a more authoritative tone. "These are forbidden things. You know that, Saul. Have you tried prayer?"

Rutledge shook his head.

"Will you pray with us now?"

Rutledge cast a glance of freezing indifference on his spiritual adviser. "If you folks want to pray, I'm agreeable," he said. But Mrs. Rutledge intervened.

"Prayer ain't any good. In this kind of thing it ain't no manner of use; you know it ain't. I called you here, Deacon, because you remember the last case in this parish. Thirty years ago it was, I guess; but you remember. Lefferts Nash—did praying help *him*? I was a little girl then, but I used to hear my folks talk of it winter nights. Lefferts Nash and Hannah Cory. They drove a stake through her breast. That's what cured him."

Sylvester Brand raised his head. "You're speaking of that old story as if this was the same sort of thing?"

"Ain't it? Ain't my husband pining away the same as Lefferts Nash did? The Deacon here knows—"

The Deacon stirred anxiously in his chair. "These are forbidden things," he repeated. "Supposing your husband is quite sincere in thinking himself haunted, as you might say. Well, even then, what proof have we that the . . . the dead woman . . . is the specter of that poor girl?"

"Proof? Don't he say so? Didn't she tell him? Ain't I seen 'em?" Mrs. Rutledge almost screamed.

The three men sat silent, and suddenly the wife burst out: "A stake through the breast! That's the old way; and it's the only way. The Deacon knows it."

"It's against our religion to disturb the dead."

"Ain't it against your religion to let the living perish as my husband is perishing?" She sprang up with one of her abrupt movements and took the family Bible from the what-not in a corner of the parlor. Putting the book on the table, and moistening a livid fingertip, she turned the pages rapidly, till she came to one on which she laid her hand like a stony paperweight. "See here," she said, and read out in her level chanting voice:

" 'Thou shalt not suffer a witch to live.'

"That's in Exodus, that's where it is," she added, leaving the book open as if to confirm the statement.

The three visitors remained silent, turning about their hats in reluctant hands. Rutledge faced them, still with that empty pellucid gaze which frightened Bosworth. What was he seeing?

"Ain't any of you folks got the grit—" his wife burst out again, half hysterically.

Deacon Hibben held up his hand. "That's no way, Mrs. Rutledge. This ain't a question of having grit. What we want first of all is . . . proof. . . ."

"That's so," said Bosworth, with an explosion of relief, as if the words had lifted something black and crouching from his breast. Involuntarily the eyes of both men had turned to Brand. He stood there, smiling grimly, but did not speak.

"Ain't it so, Brand?" the Deacon prompted him.

"Proof that spooks walk?" the other sneered.

"Well—I presume you want this business settled too?"

The old farmer squared his shoulders. "Yes—I do. But I ain't a sperritualist. How the hell are you going to settle it?"

Deacon Hibben hesitated; then he said, in a low incisive tone: "I don't see but one way—Mrs. Rutledge's."

There was a silence.

"What?" Brand sneered again. "Spying?"

The Deacon's voice sank lower. "If the poor girl *does* walk ... her that's your child ... wouldn't you be the first to want her laid quiet? We all know there've been such cases ... mysterious visitations. . . . Can any one of us here deny it?"

"I've seen 'em," Mrs. Rutledge interjected.

Suddenly Brand fixed his gaze on Rutledge. "See here, Saul Rutledge, you've got to clear up this damned calumny, or I'll know why. You say my dead girl comes to you." He labored with his breath, and then jerked out: "When? You tell me that and I'll be there."

Rutledge's head drooped a little, and his eyes wandered to the window. "Round about sunset mostly."

"You'll know beforehand?"

Rutledge made a sign of assent.

"Well, then—tomorrow, will it be?"

Rutledge made the same sign.

Brand turned to the door. "I'll be there." He strode out between them without another glance or word. Deacon Hibben looked at Mrs. Rutledge. "We'll be there, too," he said, as if she had asked him, but she had not spoken, and Bosworth saw that her thin body was trembling all over. He was glad when he and Hibben were out again in the snow.

III

They thought that Brand wanted to be left to himself, but he turned back to them as they lingered. "You'll meet me down by Lamer's pond tomorrow," he suggested. "I want witnesses. Round about sunset."

They nodded their acquiescence and he drove off under the snow-smothered hemlocks.

"What do you make of this business, Deacon?" Bosworth asked.

The Deacon shook his head. "The man's a sick man—that's sure. Something's sucking the life clean out of him."

But already, in the biting outer air, Bosworth was getting himself under better control. "Looks to me like a bad case of the ague, as you said."

"Well—ague of the mind, then. It's his brain that's sick."

Bosworth shrugged. "He ain't the first in Hemlock County."

"That's so," the Deacon agreed. "It's a worm in the brain, solitude is."

"Well, we'll know this time tomorrow, maybe," said Bosworth. He scrambled into his sleigh and was driving off when he heard his companion calling after him. The Deacon explained that his horse had cast a shoe; would Bosworth drive him down to the forge near North Ashmore, if it wasn't too much out of his way? He didn't want the mare slipping about on the freezing snow, and he could probably get the blacksmith to drive him back and shoe her in Rutledge's shed. Bosworth made room for him under the bearskin, and the two men drove off pursued by a puzzled whinny from the Deacon's old mare.

The shortest way to the forge passed close by Lamer's pond, and Bosworth, since he was in for the business, was not sorry to look the ground over. They jogged along slowly, each thinking his own thoughts.

"That's the house . . . that tumbledown shack over there, I suppose?" the Deacon said, as the road drew near the edge of the frozen pond.

Bosworth reined in his horse and looked through pine trees purpled by the sunset at the crumbling structure. Between two sharply patterned pine boughs he saw the evening star, like a white boat in a sea of green.

His gaze dropped from that fathomless sky and followed the blue-white undulations of the snow. It gave him a curious agitated feeling to think that here, in this icy solitude, in the tumbledown house he had so often passed without heeding it, a dark mystery, too deep for thought, was being enacted. Down that very slope, coming from the graveyard at Cold Corners, the being they called "Ora" must pass toward the pond. His heart began to beat stiflingly. Suddenly he gave an exclamation: "Look!"

He had jumped out of the cutter and was stumbling up the bank toward the slope of snow. On it, turned in the direction of the house by the pond, he had detected a woman's footprints; two; then three; then more. The Deacon scrambled out after him and they stood and stared.

"God—barefoot!" Hibben gasped. "Then it is . . . the dead. . . ."

Bosworth said nothing. But he knew that no live woman would travel with naked feet across that freezing wilderness. Here, then, was the proof the Deacon had asked for—they held it. What should they do with it?

"Supposing we was to drive up nearer—round the turn of the pond, till we get close to the house," the Deacon proposed in a colorless voice. "Mebbe then . . ."

Postponement was a relief. They got into the sleigh and drove on. Two or three hundred yards farther the road turned sharply to the right following the bend of the pond. As they rounded the turn they saw Brand's cutter ahead of them. It was empty, the horse tied to a tree trunk. The two men looked at each other again. This was not Brand's nearest way home.

Evidently he had been actuated by the same impulse which had made them rein in their horse by the pond-side, and then hasten on to the deserted house. Bosworth found himself shivering under his bearskin. "I wish to God the dark wasn't coming on," he muttered. He tethered his horse near Brand's, and he and the Deacon plowed through the snow, in the track of Brand's huge feet.

They had only a few yards to walk to overtake him. He did not hear them following him, and when Bosworth spoke his name he stopped and turned, his heavy face dim and confused, like a darker blot on the dusk. He looked at them dully, but without surprise.

"I wanted to see the place," he said.

The three men came out together in the cleared space before the house. As they emerged from beneath the trees they seemed to have left night behind. The evening star shed a luster on the speckless snow, and Brand, in the lucid circle, stopped with a jerk, and pointed to the same light footprints turned toward the house—the track of a woman in the snow. He stood still, his face working. "Bare feet . . . " he said.

The Deacon piped up in a quavering voice. "The feet of the dead."

Brand remained motionless. "The feet of the dead," he echoed.

Deacon Hibben laid a frightened hand on his arm. "Come away now, Brand; for the love of God come away."

The father hung there, gazing down at those light tracks in the snow—light as fox or squirrel trails they seemed, on the white immensity. Bosworth thought to himself: "The living couldn't walk so light—not even Ora Brand couldn't have, when she lived. . . ."

Brand swung on them abruptly. "*Now!*" he said, moving on as if to an assault, his head bowed forward on his bull neck.

"Now—now? Not in there?" gasped the Deacon. "What's the use? It was tomorrow he said—" He shook like a leaf.

"It's now," said Brand. He went up to the door of the crazy house, pushed it inward, and meeting with an unexpected resistance, thrust his heavy shoulder against the panel. The door collapsed like a playing card, and Brand stumbled after it into the darkness of the hut. The others, after a moment's hesitation, followed.

Bosworth was never quite sure in what order the events that succeeded took place. Coming in out of the snow dazzle, he seemed to be plunging into total darkness. He groped his way across the threshold, caught a sharp splinter of the fallen door in his palm, seemed to see something white and wraithlike surge

up out of the darkest corner of the hut, and then heard a revolver shot at his elbow, and a cry—

Brand had turned back, and was staggering past him
out into the lingering daylight. The sunset, suddenly flushing through the trees, crimsoned his face like blood. He
held a revolver in his hand, and looked about him in his
stupid way.

"They *do* walk then," he said and began to laugh. He bent
his head to examine his weapon. "Better here than in the
churchyard. They shan't dig her up *now*," he shouted out. The
two men caught him by the arms, and Bosworth got the revolver away from him.

IV

The next day Bosworth's sister Loretta, who kept house for him,
asked him, when he came in for his midday dinner, if he had
heard the news.

"What news?"

"Venny Brand's down sick with pneumonia. The Deacon's
been there. I guess she's dying." After a pause she added: "It'll
kill Sylvester Brand, all alone up there."

Venny Brand was buried three days later. The Deacon read
the service; Bosworth was one of the pallbearers. The whole
countryside turned out for Venny Brand was young and handsome, and her dying like that, so suddenly, had the fascination
of tragedy. As pallbearer, Bosworth felt obliged to linger and
say a word to the stricken father. He waited till Brand had
turned from the grave with the Deacon at his side. The three
men stood together for a moment; but not one of them spoke.
Brand's face was the closed door of a vault, barred with wrin-
kles like bands of iron. Finally the Deacon took his hand and
said: "The Lord gave—"

Brand nodded and turned away toward the shed where the
horses were hitched. Bosworth followed him. "Let me drive
along home with you," he suggested.

Brand did not so much as turn his head. "Home? What home?" he said; and the other fell back.

Loretta Bosworth was talking with the other women while the men unblanketed their horses and backed the cutters out into the heavy snow. As Bosworth waited for her, a few feet off, he saw Mrs. Rutledge's tall bonnet lording it above the group.

"Saul ain't here today, Mrs. Rutledge, is he?" one of the village elders piped, turning a benevolent old tortoise-head about on a loose neck, and blinking up into Mrs. Rutledge's marble face.

"No. Mr. Rutledge ain't here. He would'a come for certain, but his aunt Minorca Cummins is being buried down to Stotesbury this very day and he had to go down there. Don't it sometimes seem zif we was all walking right in the Shadow of Death?"

As she moved toward the cutter in which the farmhand was already seated, the Deacon went up to her with visible hesitation. Involuntarily Bosworth also moved nearer. He heard the Deacon say: "I'm glad to hear that Saul is able to be up and around."

She turned her small head on her rigid neck, and lifted the lids of marble.

"Yes, I guess he'll sleep quieter now. And *her* too, maybe, now she don't lay there alone any longer," she added in a low voice, with a sudden twist of her chin toward the fresh black stain in the graveyard snow.

W. Somerset Maugham (1874–1965) was to the British novel, perhaps, what W. S. Gilbert was to British letters and to the stage: the perfect and poised, balanced and graceful exponent of his era. If he lacked some of the harshness of Gilbert's more aphoristic wit, he had somewhat more complexity. His most important novels are Of Human Bondage, The Moon and Sixpence, Cakes and Ale, and The Razor's Edge; his most famous book of stories is Ashenden: The British Agent (1928), the connected adventures of a World War I spy and the first realistic look at a spy's life. Maugham himself served as an intelligence agent in Russia during that war, and depicted the espionage agent as an ordinary person in unusual circumstances—an approach that was later adopted and updated by today's foremost spy novelists, John le Carré, Len Deighton, and Eric Ambler. Maugham was equally adept at the tale of mystery and suspense, as "Before the Party" demonstrates.

BEFORE THE PARTY
W. Somerset Maugham

Mrs. Skinner liked to be in good time. She was already dressed, in black silk as befitted her age and the mourning she wore for her son-in-law, and now she put on her toque. She was a little uncertain about it, since the egrets' feathers which adorned it might very well arouse in some of the friends she would certainly meet at the party acid expostulations; and of course it was shocking to kill those beautiful white birds, in the mating season too, for the sake of their feathers; but there they were, so pretty and stylish, and it would have been silly to refuse them, and it would have hurt her son-in-law's feelings. He had brought them all the way from Borneo and he expected her to be so pleased with them. Kathleen had made herself rather unpleasant about them; she must wish she hadn't now, after what had happened, but Kathleen had never really liked Harold. Mrs. Skinner, standing at her dressing table, placed the toque on her

167

head, it was after all the only nice hat she had, and put in a pin with a large jet knob. If anybody spoke to her about the ospreys she had her answer.

"I know it's dreadful," she would say, "and I wouldn't dream of buying them, but my poor son-in-law brought them back the last time he was home on leave."

That would explain her possession of them and excuse their use. Everyone had been very kind. Mrs. Skinner took a clean handkerchief from a drawer and sprinkled a little eau de cologne on it. She never used scent, and she had always thought it rather fast, but eau de cologne was so refreshing. She was very nearly ready now and her eyes wandered out of the window behind her looking glass. Canon Heywood had a beautiful day for his garden party. It was warm and the sky was blue; the trees had not yet lost the fresh green of the spring. She smiled as she saw her little granddaughter in the strip of garden behind the house busily raking her very own flowerbed. Mrs. Skinner wished Joan were not quite so pale, it was a mistake to have kept her so long in the tropics; and she was so grave for her age, you never saw her run about; she played quiet games of her own invention and watered her garden. Mrs. Skinner gave the front of her dress a little pat, took up her gloves, and went downstairs.

Kathleen was at the writing table in the window busy with lists she was making, for she was honorary secretary of the Ladies' Golf Club and when there were competitions had a good deal to do. But she too was ready for the party.

"I see you've put on your jumper after all," said Mrs. Skinner.

They had discussed at luncheon whether Kathleen should wear her jumper or her black chiffon. The jumper was black and white, and Kathleen thought it was rather smart, but it was hardly mourning. Millicent, however, was in favor of it.

"There's no reason why we should all look as if we'd just come from a funeral," she said. "Harold's been dead eight months."

To Mrs. Skinner it seemed rather unfeeling to talk like that. Millicent was strange since her return from Borneo.

"You're not going to leave off your weeds yet, darling?" she asked.

Millicent did not give a direct answer.

"People don't wear mourning in the way they used," she said. She paused a little and when she went on there was a tone in her voice which Mrs. Skinner thought quite peculiar. It was plain that Kathleen noticed it too, for she gave her sister a curious look. "I'm sure Harold wouldn't wish me to wear mourning for him indefinitely."

"I dressed early because I wanted to say something to Millicent," said Kathleen in reply to her mother's observation.

"Oh?"

Kathleen did not explain. But she put her lists aside and with knitted brows read for the second time a letter from a lady who complained that the committee had most unfairly marked down her handicap from twenty-four to eighteen. It requires a good deal of tact to be honorary secretary to a ladies' golf club. Mrs. Skinner began to put on her new gloves. The sun blinds kept the room cool and dark. She looked at the great wooden hornbill, gaily painted, which Harold had left in her safe-keeping; and it seemed a little odd and barbaric to her, but he had set much store on it. It had some religious significance and Canon Heywood had been greatly struck by it. On the wall, over the sofa, were Malay weapons, she forgot what they were called, and here and there on occasional tables pieces of silver and brass which Harold at various times had sent to them. She had liked Harold and involuntarily her eyes sought his photograph which stood on the piano with photographs of her two daughters, her grandchild, her sister and her sister's son.

"Why, Kathleen, where's Harold's photograph?" she asked.

Kathleen looked round. It no longer stood in its place.

"Someone's taken it away," said Kathleen.

Surprised and puzzled, she got up and went over to the piano. The photographs had been rearranged so that no gap should show.

"Perhaps Millicent wanted to have it in her bedroom," said Mrs. Skinner.

"I should have noticed it. Besides, Millicent has several photographs of Harold. She keeps them locked up."

Mrs. Skinner had thought it very peculiar that her daughter should have no photographs of Harold in her room. Indeed she had spoken of it once, but Millicent had made no reply. Millicent had been strangely silent since she came back from Borneo, and had not encouraged the sympathy Mrs. Skinner would have been so willing to show her. She seemed unwilling to speak of her great loss. Sorrow took people in different ways. Her husband had said the best thing was to leave her alone. The thought of him turned her ideas to the party they were going to.

"Father asked if I thought he ought to wear a top hat," she said. "I said I thought it was just as well to be on the safe side."

It was going to be quite a grand affair. They were having ices, strawberry and vanilla, from Boddy, the confectioner, but the Heywoods were making the iced coffee at home. Everyone would be there. They had been asked to meet the Bishop of Hong Kong, who was staying with the Canon, an old college friend of his, and he was going to speak on the Chinese missions. Mrs. Skinner, whose daughter had lived in the East for eight years and whose son-in-law had been Resident of a district in Borneo, was in a flutter of interest. Naturally it meant more to her than to people who had never had anything to do with the colonies and that sort of thing.

"'What can they know of England who only England know?'" as Mr. Skinner said.

He came into the room at that moment. He was a lawyer, as his father had been before him, and he had offices in Lincoln's Inn Fields. He went up to London every morning and came down every evening. He was only able to accompany his wife and daughters to the Canon's garden party because the Canon had very wisely chosen a Saturday to have it on. Mr. Skinner looked very well in his tailcoat and pepper-and-salt trousers. He was not exactly dressy, but he was neat. He looked like a respectable family solicitor, which indeed he was; his firm never touched work that was not perfectly aboveboard, and if a client went to him with some trouble that was not quite nice, Mr. Skinner would look grave.

"I don't think this is the sort of case that we very much care to undertake," he said. "I think you'd do better to go elsewhere."

He drew towards him his writing block and scribbled a name and address on it. He tore off a sheet of paper and handed it to his client.

"If I were you I think I would go and see these people. If you mention my name I believe they'll do anything they can for you."

Mr. Skinner was clean-shaven and very bald. His pale lips were tight and thin, but his blue eyes were shy. He had no color in his cheeks and his face was much lined.

"I see you've put on your new trousers," said Mrs. Skinner.

"I thought it would be a good opportunity," he answered. "I was wondering if I should wear a buttonhole."

"I wouldn't, Father," said Kathleen. "I don't think it's awfully good form."

"A lot of people will be wearing them," said Mrs. Skinner.

"Only clerks and people like that," said Kathleen. "The Heywoods have had to ask everybody, you know. And besides, we are in mourning."

"I wonder if there'll be a collection after the Bishop's address," said Mr. Skinner.

"I should hardly think so," said Mrs. Skinner.

"I think it would be rather bad form," agreed Kathleen.

"It's as well to be on the safe side," said Mr. Skinner. "I'll give for all of us. I was wondering if ten shillings would be enough or if I must give a pound."

"If you give anything I think you ought to give a pound, Father," said Kathleen.

"I'll see when the time comes. I don't want to give less than any one else, but on the other hand I see no reason to give more than I need."

Kathleen put away her papers in the drawer of the writing table and stood up. She looked at her wrist watch.

"Is Millicent ready?" asked Mrs. Skinner.

"There's plenty of time. We're only asked at four and I don't think we ought to arrive much before half-past. I told Davis to bring the car round at four-fifteen."

Generally, Kathleen drove the car, but on grand occasions like this Davis, who was the gardener, put on his uniform and acted as chauffeur. It looked better when you drove up and naturally Kathleen didn't much want to drive herself when she was wearing her new jumper. The sight of her mother forcing her fingers one by one into her new gloves reminded her that she must put on her own. She smelt them to see if any odor of the cleaning still clung to them. It was very slight. She didn't believe anyone would notice.

At last the door opened and Millicent came in. She wore her widow's weeds. Mrs. Skinner never could get used to them, but of course she knew that Millicent must wear them for a year. It was a pity they didn't suit her; they suited some people. She had tried on Millicent's bonnet once, with its white band and long veil, and thought she looked very well in it. Of course she hoped dear Alfred would survive her, but if he didn't she would never go out of weeds. Queen Victoria never had. It was different for Millicent; Millicent was a much younger woman; she was only thirty-six; it was very sad to be a widow at thirty-six. And there wasn't much chance of her marrying again. Kathleen wasn't very likely to marry now, she was thirty-five; last time Millicent and Harold had come home she had suggested that they should have Kathleen to stay with them; Harold had seemed willing enough, but Millicent said it wouldn't do. Mrs. Skinner didn't know why not. It would give her a chance. Of course they didn't want to get rid of her, but a girl ought to marry, and somehow all the men they knew at home were married already. Millicent said the climate was trying. It was true she was a bad color. No one would think now that Millicent had been the prettier of the two. Kathleen had fined down as she grew older (of course some people said she was too thin), but now that she had cut her hair, with her cheeks red from playing golf in all weathers, Mrs. Skinner thought her quite pretty. No one could say that of poor Millicent; she had lost her figure completely; she had never been tall and now that she had filled out she looked stocky. She was a good deal too fat; Mrs. Skinner supposed it was due to the tropical heat that prevented her from taking exercise. Her skin was sallow and muddy; and her blue eyes, which had been her best feature, had gone quite pale.

"She ought to do something about her neck," Mrs. Skinner reflected. "She's becoming dreadfully jowly."

She had spoken of it once or twice to her husband. He remarked that Millicent wasn't as young as she was: that might be, but she needn't let herself go altogether. Mrs. Skinner made up her mind to talk to her daughter seriously, but of course she must respect her grief and she would wait till the year was up. She was just as glad to have this reason to put off a conversation the thought of which made her slightly nervous. For Millicent was certainly changed. There was something sullen in her face which made her mother not quite at home with her. Mrs. Skinner liked to say aloud all the thoughts that passed through her head, but Millicent when you made a remark (just to say something you know) had an awkward habit of not answering so that you wondered whether she had heard. Sometimes Mrs. Skinner found it so irritating that not to be quite sharp with Millicent she had to remind herself that poor Harold had only been dead eight months.

The light from the window fell on the window's heavy face as she advanced silently, but Kathleen stood with her back to it. She watched her sister for a moment.

"Millicent, there's something I want to say to you," she said. "I was playing golf with Gladys Heywood this morning."

"Did you beat her?" asked Millicent.

Gladys Heywood was the Canon's only unmarried daughter.

"She told me something about you which I think you ought to know."

Millicent's eyes passed beyond her sister to the little girl watering flowers in the garden.

"Have you told Annie to give Joan her tea in the kitchen, Mother?" she said.

"Yes, she'll have it when the servants have theirs."

Kathleen looked at her sister coolly.

"The Bishop spent two or three days at Singapore on his way home," she went on. "He's very fond of traveling. He's been to Borneo and he knows a good many of the people that you know."

"He'll be interested to see you, dear," said Mrs. Skinner. "Did he know poor Harold?"

"Yes, he met him at Kuala Solor. He remembers him very well. He says he was shocked to hear of his death."

Millicent sat down and began to put on her black gloves. It seemed strange to Mrs. Skinner that she received these remarks with complete silence.

"Oh, Millicent," she said, "Harold's photo has disappeared. Have you taken it?"

"Yes, I put it away."

"I should have thought you'd like to have it out."

Once more Millicent said nothing. It really was an exasperating habit.

Kathleen turned slightly in order to face her sister.

"Millicent, why did you tell us that Harold died of fever?"

The widow made no gesture; she looked at Kathleen with steady eyes, but her sallow skin darkened with a flush. She did not reply.

"What *do* you mean, Kathleen?" asked Mr. Skinner, with surprise.

"The Bishop says that Harold committed suicide."

Mrs. Skinner gave a startled cry, but her husband put out a deprecating hand.

"Is it true, Millicent?"

"It is."

"But why didn't you tell us?"

Millicent paused for an instant. She fingered idly a piece of Brunei brass which stood on the table by her side. That too had been a present from Harold.

"I thought it better for Joan that her father should be thought to have died of fever. I didn't want her to know anything about it."

"You've put us in an awfully awkward position," said Kathleen, frowning a little. "Gladys Heywood said she thought it rather nasty of me not to have told her the truth. I had the greatest difficulty in getting her to believe that I knew absolutely nothing about it. She said her father was rather put out. He says, after all the years we've known one another, and considering that he married you, and the terms we've been on, and all that, he does think we might have had confidence in him. And at all events if we didn't want to tell him the truth we needn't have told him a lie."

"I must say I sympathize with him there," said Mr. Skinner acidly.

"Of course I told Gladys that we weren't to blame. We only told them what you told us."

"I hope it didn't put off your game," said Millicent.

"Really, my dear, I think that is a most improper observation," exclaimed her father.

He rose from his chair, walked over to the empty fireplace, and from force of habit stood in front of it with parted coattails.

"It was my business," said Millicent, "and if I chose to keep it to myself I didn't see why I shouldn't."

"It doesn't look as if you had any affection for your mother if you didn't even tell her," said Mrs. Skinner.

Millicent shrugged her shoulders.

"You might have known it was bound to come out," said Kathleen.

"Why? I didn't expect that two gossiping old parsons would have nothing else to talk about than me."

"When the Bishop said he'd been to Borneo it's only natural that the Heywoods should ask him if he knew you and Harold."

"All that's neither here nor there," said Mr. Skinner. "I think you should certainly have told us the truth and we could have decided what was the best thing to do. As a solicitor I can tell you that in the long run it only makes things worse if you attempt to hide them."

"Poor Harold," said Mrs. Skinner, and the tears began to trickle down her raddled cheeks. "It seems dreadful. He was always a good son-in-law to me. Whatever induced him to do such a dreadful thing?"

"The climate."

"I think you'd better give us all the facts, Millicent," said her father.

"Kathleen will tell you."

Kathleen hesitated. What she had to say really was rather dreadful. It seemed terrible that such things should happen to a family like theirs.

"The Bishop says he cut his throat."

Mrs. Skinner gasped and she went impulsively up to her bereaved daughter. She wanted to fold her in her arms.

"My poor child," she sobbed.

But Millicent withdrew herself.

"Please don't fuss me, Mother. I really can't stand being mauled about."

"Really, Millicent," said Mr. Skinner, with a frown.

He did not think she was behaving very nicely.

Mrs. Skinner dabbed her eyes carefully with her handkerchief and with a sigh and a little shake of the head returned to her chair. Kathleen fidgeted with the long chain she wore round her neck.

"It does seem rather absurd that I should have to be told the details of my brother-in-law's death by a friend. It makes us all look such fools. The Bishop wants very much to see you, Millicent; he wants to tell you how much he feels for you." She paused, but Millicent did not speak. "He says that Millicent had been away with Joan and when she came back she found poor Harold lying dead on his bed."

"It must have been a great shock," said Mr. Skinner.

Mrs. Skinner began to cry again, but Kathleen put her hand gently on her shoulder.

"Don't cry, Mother," she said. "It'll make your eyes red and people will think it so funny."

They were all silent while Mrs. Skinner, drying her eyes, made a successful effort to control herself. It seemed very strange to her that at this very moment she should be wearing in her toque the ospreys that poor Harold had given her.

"There's something else I ought to tell you," said Kathleen.

Millicent looked at her sister again, without haste, and her eyes were steady, but watchful. She had the look of a person who is waiting for a sound which he is afraid of missing.

"I don't want to say anything to wound you, dear," Kathleen went on, "but there's something else and I think you ought to know it. The Bishop says that Harold drank."

"Oh, my dear, how dreadful!" cried Mrs. Skinner. "What a shocking thing to say. Did Gladys Heywood tell you? What did you say?"

"I said it was entirely untrue."

"This is what comes of making secrets of things," said Mr. Skinner irritably. "It's always the same. If you try and hush a thing up all sorts of rumors get about which are ten times worse than the truth."

"They told the Bishop in Singapore that Harold had killed himself while he was suffering from delirium tremens. I think for all our sakes you ought to deny that, Millicent."

"It's such a dreadful thing to have said about anyone who's dead," said Mrs. Skinner. "And it'll be so bad for Joan when she grows up."

"But what is the foundation of this story, Millicent?" asked her father. "Harold was always very abstemious."

"Here," said the widow.

"Did he drink?"

"Like a fish."

The answer was so unexpected, and the tone so sardonic, that all three of them were startled.

"Millicent, how can you talk like that of your husband when he's dead?" cried her mother, clasping her neatly gloved hands. "I can't understand you. You've been so strange since you came back. I could never have believed that a girl of mine could take her husband's death like that."

"Never mind about that, Mother," said Mr. Skinner. "We can go into all that later."

He walked to the window and looked out at the sunny little garden, and then walked back into the room. He took his pince-nez out of his pocket and, though he had no intention of putting them on, wiped them with his handkerchief. Millicent looked at him and in her eyes, unmistakably, was a look of irony which was quite cynical. Mr. Skinner was vexed. He had finished his week's work and he was a free man till Monday morning. Though he had told his wife that this garden party was a great nuisance and he would much sooner have tea quietly in his own garden, he had been looking forward to it. He did not care very much about Chinese missions, but it would be interesting to meet the Bishop. And now this! It was not the kind of thing he cared to be mixed up in; it was most unpleasant to be told on a sudden that his son-in-law was a drunkard and a suicide. Millicent was thoughtfully smoothing her white cuffs. Her coolness irritated him; but instead of addressing her he spoke to his younger daughter.

"Why don't you sit down, Kathleen? Surely there are plenty of chairs in the room."

Kathleen drew forward a chair and without a word seated herself. Mr. Skinner stopped in front of Millicent and faced her.

"Of course I see why you told us Harold had died of fever. I think it was a mistake, because that sort of thing is bound to come out sooner or later. I don't know how far what the Bishop has told the Heywoods coincides with the facts, but if you will take my advice you will tell us everything as circumstantially as you can; then we can see. We can't hope that it will go no further now that Canon Heywood and Gladys know. In a place like this people are bound to talk. It will make it easier for all of us if we at all events know the exact truth."

Mrs. Skinner and Kathleen thought he put the matter very well. They waited for Millicent's reply. She had listened with an impassive face; that sudden flush had disappeared and it was once more, as usual, pasty and sallow.

"I don't think you'll much like the truth if I tell it you," she said.

"You must know that you can count on our sympathy and understanding," said Kathleen gravely.

Millicent gave her a glance and the shadow of a smile flickered across her set mouth. She looked slowly at the three of them. Mrs. Skinner had an uneasy impression that she looked at them as though they were mannequins at a dressmaker's. She seemed to live in a different world from theirs and to have no connection with them.

"You know, I wasn't in love with Harold when I married him," she said reflectively.

Mrs. Skinner was on the point of making an exclamation when a rapid gesture of her husband, barely indicated, but after so many years of married life perfectly significant, stopped her. Millicent went on. She spoke with a level voice, slowly, and there was little change of expression in her tone.

"I was twenty-seven, and no one else seemed to want to marry me. It's true he was forty-four, and it seemed rather old, but he had a very good position, hadn't he? I wasn't likely to get a better chance."

Mrs. Skinner felt inclined to cry again, but she remembered the party.

"Of course I see now why you took his photograph away," she said dolefully.

"Don't, Mother," exclaimed Kathleen.

It had been taken when he was engaged to Millicent and was a very good photograph of Harold. Mrs. Skinner had always thought him quite a fine man. He was heavily built, tall and perhaps a little too fat, but he held himself well, and his presence was imposing. He was inclined to be bald, even then, but men did go bald very early nowadays, and he said that topees, sun helmets, you know, were very bad for the hair. He had a small dark mustache and his face was deeply burned by the sun. Of course his best feature was his eyes; they were brown and large, like Joan's. His conversation was interesting. Kathleen said he was pompous, but Mrs. Skinner didn't think him so, she didn't mind it if a man laid down the law; and when she saw, as she very soon did, that he was attracted by Millicent she began to like him very much. He was always very attentive to Mrs. Skinner and she listened as though she were really interested when he spoke of his district and told her of the big game he had killed. Kathleen said he had a pretty good opinion of himself, but Mrs. Skinner came of a generation which accepted without question the good opinion that men had of themselves. Millicent saw very soon which way the wind blew and, though she said nothing to her mother, her mother knew if Harold asked her she was going to accept him.

Harold was staying with some people who had been thirty years in Borneo and they spoke well of the country. There was no reason why a woman shouldn't live there comfortably; of course the children had to come home when they were seven; but Mrs. Skinner thought it unnecessary to trouble about that yet. She asked Harold to dine and she told him they were always in to tea. He seemed to be at a loose end and when his visit to his old friends was drawing to a close she told him they would be very much pleased if he would come and spend a fortnight with them. It was towards the end of this that Harold and Millicent became engaged. They had a very pretty wedding, they went to Venice for their honeymoon, and then they started for the East. Millicent wrote from the various ports at which the ship touched. She seemed happy.

"People were very nice to me at Kuala Solor," she said. Kuala Solor was the chief town of the state of Sembulu. "We stayed with the Resident and everyone asked us to dinner. Once or twice I heard men ask Harold to have a drink but he refused; he said he had turned over a new leaf now he was a married man. I didn't know why they laughed. Mrs. Gray, the Resident's wife, told me they were all so glad Harold was married. She said it was dreadfully lonely for a bachelor on one of the outstations. When we left Kuala Solor Mrs. Gray said good-bye to me so funnily that I was quite surprised. It was as if she was solemnly putting Harold in my charge."

They listened to her in silence. Kathleen never took her eyes off her sister's impassive face, but Mr. Skinner stared straight in front of him at the Malay arms, *krises* and *parangs*, which hung on the wall above the sofa on which his wife sat.

"It wasn't till I went back to Kuala Solor a year and a half later that I found out why their manner had seemed so odd," Millicent gave a queer little sound like the echo of a scornful laugh. "I knew then a good deal that I hadn't known before. Harold came to England that time in order to marry. He didn't much mind who it was. Do you remember how we spread ourselves out to catch him, Mother? We needn't have taken so much trouble."

"I don't know what you mean, Millicent," said Mrs. Skinner, not without acerbity, for the insinuation of scheming did not please her. "I saw he was attracted by you."

Millicent shrugged her heavy shoulders.

"He was a confirmed drunkard. He used to go to bed every night with a bottle of whisky and empty it before morning. The Chief Secretary told him he'd have to resign unless he stopped drinking. He said he'd give him one more chance. He could take his leave then and go to England. He advised him to marry so that when he got back he'd have someone to look after him. Harold married me because he wanted a keeper. They took bets in Kuala Solor on how long I'd make him stay sober."

"But he was in love with you," Mrs. Skinner interrupted. "You don't know how he used to speak to me about you, and at that time you're speaking of, when you went to Kuala Solor to have Joan, he wrote me such a charming letter about you."

Millicent looked at her mother again and a deep color dyed her sallow skin. Her hands, lying on her lap, began to tremble a little. She thought of those first months of her married life. The Government launch took them to the mouth of the river and they spent the night at the bungalow which Harold said jokingly was their seaside residence. Next day they went upstream in a *prahu*. From the novels she had read she expected the rivers of Borneo to be dark and strangely sinister, but the sky was blue, dappled with little white clouds, and the green of the mangroves and the nipas, washed by the flowing water, glistened in the sun. On each side stretched the pathless jungle, and in the distance, silhouetted against the sky, was the rugged outline of a mountain. The air in the early morning was fresh and buoyant. She seemed to enter upon a friendly, fertile land, and she had a sense of spacious freedom. They watched the banks for monkeys sitting on the branches of the tangled trees and once Harold pointed out something that looked like a log and said it was a crocodile. The Assistant Resident, in ducks and a topee, was at the landing stage to meet them, and a dozen trim little soldiers were lined up to do them honor. The Assistant Resident was introduced to her. His name was Simpson.

"By Jove, sir," he said to Harold, "I'm glad to see you back. It's been deuced lonely without you."

The Resident's bungalow, surrounded by a garden in which grew wildly all manner of gay flowers, stood on the top of a low hill. It was a trifle shabby and the furniture was sparse, but the rooms were cool and of generous size.

"The *kampong* is down there," said Harold, pointing.

Her eyes followed his gesture, and from among the coconut trees rose the beating of a gong. It gave her a queer little sensation in the heart.

Though she had nothing much to do the days passed easily enough. At dawn a boy brought them their tea and they lounged about the veranda, enjoying the fragrance of the morning (Harold in a singlet and a sarong, she in a dressing gown), till it was time to dress for breakfast. Then Harold went to his office and she spent an hour or two learning Malay. After tiffin he went back to his office while she slept. A cup of tea revived them both and they went for a walk or played golf on the nine-hole links which Harold had made on a level piece of cleared jungle below the bungalow. Night fell at six and Mr. Simpson came along to have a drink. They chatted till their late dinner hour, and sometimes Harold and Mr. Simpson played chess. The balmy evenings were enchanting. The fireflies turned the bushes just below the veranda into coldly sparkling, tremulous beacons, and flowering trees scented the air with sweet odors. After dinner they read the papers which had left London six weeks before and presently went to bed. Millicent enjoyed being a married woman, with a house of her own, and she was pleased with the native servants, in their gay sarongs, who went about the bungalow, with bare feet, silent but friendly. It gave her a pleasant sense of importance to be the wife of the Resident. Harold impressed her by the fluency with which he spoke the language, by his air of command, and by his dignity. She went into the courthouse now and then to hear him try cases. The multifariousness of his duties and the competent way in which he performed them aroused her respect. Mr. Simpson told her that Harold understood the natives as well as any man in the country. He had the combination of firmness, tact, and good humor which was essential in dealing with that timid, revengeful, and suspicious race. Millicent began to feel a certain admiration for her husband.

They had been married nearly a year when two English naturalists came to stay with them for a few days on their way to the interior. They brought a pressing recommendation from the Governor and Harold said he wanted to do them proud. Their arrival was an agreeable change. Millicent asked Mr. Simpson to dinner (he lived at the Fort and only dined with them on Sunday nights), and after dinner the men sat down to play bridge. Millicent left them presently and went to bed, but they were so noisy that for some time she could not get to sleep. She did not know at what hour she was awakened by Harold staggering into the room. She kept silent. He made up his mind to have a bath before getting into bed; the bathhouse was just below their room and he went down the steps that led to it. Apparently he slipped, for there was a great clatter, and he began to swear. Then he was violently sick. She heard him sluice the buckets of water over himself and in a little while, walking very cautiously this time, he crawled up the stairs and slipped into bed. Millicent pretended to be asleep. She was disgusted.

Harold was drunk. She made up her mind to speak about it in the morning. What would the naturalists think of him? But in the morning Harold was so dignified that she hadn't quite the determination to refer to the matter. At eight Harold and she, with their two guests, sat down to breakfast. Harold looked round the table.

"Porridge," he said. "Millicent, your guests might manage a little Worcester Sauce for breakfast, but I don't think they'll much fancy anything else. Personally I shall content myself with a whisky and soda."

The naturalists laughed, but shamefacedly.

"Your husband's a terror," said one of them.

"I should not think I had properly performed the duties of hospitality if I sent you sober to bed on the first night of your visit," said Harold, with his round, stately way of putting things.

Millicent, smiling acidly, was relieved to think that her guests had been as drunk as her husband. The next evening she sat up with them and the party broke up at a reasonable hour. But she was glad when the strangers went on with their journey. Their life resumed its placid course. Some months later Harold went on a tour of inspection of his district and came back with a bad attack of malaria. This was the first time she had seen the disease of which she had heard so much, and when he recovered it did not seem strange to her that Harold was very shaky. She found his manner peculiar. He would come back from the office and stare at her with glazed eyes; he would stand on the veranda, swaying slightly, but still dignified, and make long harangues about the political situation in England; losing the thread of his discourse, he would look at her with an archness which his natural stateliness made somewhat disconcerting and say:

"Pulls you down dreadfully, this confounded malaria. Ah, little woman, you little know the strain it puts upon a man to be an empire builder."

She thought that Mr. Simpson began to look worried, and once or twice, when they were alone, he seemed on the point of saying something to her which his shyness at the last moment prevented. The feeling grew so strong that it made her nervous, and one evening when Harold, she knew not why, had remained later than usual at the office she tackled him.

"What have you got to say to me, Mr. Simpson?" she broke out suddenly.

He blushed and hesitated.

"Nothing. What makes you think I have anything in particular to say to you?"

Mr. Simpson was a thin, weedy youth of four and twenty, with a fine head of waving hair which he took great pains to plaster down very flat. His wrists were swollen and scarred with mosquito bites. Millicent looked at him steadily.

"If it's something to do with Harold, don't you think it would be kinder to tell me frankly?"

He grew scarlet now. He shuffled uneasily on his rattan chair. She insisted.

"I'm afraid you'll think it awful cheek," he said at last. "It's rotten of me to say anything about my chief behind his back. Malaria's a rotten thing, and after one's had a bout of it one feels awfully down and out."

He hesitated again. The corners of his mouth sagged as if he were going to cry. To Millicent he seemed like a little boy.

"I'll be as silent as the grave," she said with a smile, trying to conceal her apprehension. "Do tell me."

"I think it's a pity your husband keeps a bottle of whisky at the office. He's apt to take a nip more often than he otherwise would."

Mr. Simpson's voice was hoarse with agitation. Millicent felt a sudden coldness shiver through her. She controlled herself, for she knew that she must not frighten the boy if she were to get out of him all there was to tell. He was unwilling to speak. She pressed him, wheedling, appealing to his sense of duty, and at last she began to cry. Then he told her that Harold had been drunk more or less for the last fortnight; the natives were talking about it, and they said that soon he would be as bad as he had been before his marriage. He had been in the habit of drinking a good deal too much then, but details of that time, notwithstanding all her attempts, Mr. Simpson resolutely declined to give her.

"Do you think he's drinking now?" she asked.

"I don't know."

Millicent felt herself on a sudden hot with shame and anger. The Fort, as it was called because the rifles and the ammunition were kept there, was also the courthouse. It stood opposite the Resident's bunaglow in a garden of its own. The sun was just about to set and she did not need a hat. She got up and walked across. She found Harold in the office behind the large hall in which he administered justice. There was a bottle of whisky in front of him. He was smoking cigarettes and talking to three or four Malays who stood in front of him listening with obsequious and at the same time scornful smiles. His face was red.

The natives vanished.

"I came to see what you were doing," she said.

He rose, for he always treated her with elaborate politeness, and lurched. Feeling himself unsteady he assumed an elaborate stateliness of demeanor.

"Take a seat, my dear, take a seat. I was detained by press of work."

She looked at him with angry eyes.

"You're drunk," she said.

He stared at her, his eyes bulging a little, and a haughty look gradually traversed his large and fleshy face.

"I haven't the remotest idea what you mean," he said.

She had been ready with a flow of wrathful expostulation, but suddenly she burst into tears. She sank into a chair and hid her face. Harold looked at her for an instant, then the tears began to trickle down his cheeks; he came towards her with outstretched arms and fell heavily on his knees. Sobbing, he clasped her to him.

"Forgive me, forgive me," he said. "I promise you it shall not happen again. It was that damned malaria."

"It's so humiliating," she moaned.

He wept like a child. There was something very touching

in the self-abasement of that big dignified man. Presently Millicent looked up. His eyes, appealing and contrite, sought hers.

"Will you give me your word of honor that you'll never touch liquor again?"

"Yes, yes. I hate it."

It was then she told him that she was with child. He was overjoyed.

"That is the one thing I wanted. That'll keep me straight."

They went back to the bungalow. Harold bathed himself and had a nap. After dinner they talked long and quietly. He admitted that before he married her he had occasionally drunk more than was good for him: in outstations it was easy to fall into bad habits. He agreed to everything that Millicent asked. And during the months before it was necessary for her to go to Kuala Solor for her confinement Harold was an excellent husband, tender, thoughtful, proud, and affectionate: he was irreproachable. A launch came to fetch her; she was to leave him for six weeks, and he promised faithfully to drink nothing during her absence. He put his hands on her shoulders.

"I never break a promise," he said in his dignified way. "But even without it, can you imagine that while you are going through so much, I should do anything to increase your troubles?"

Joan was born. Millicent stayed at the Resident's and Mrs. Gray, his wife, a kindly creature of middle age, was very good to her. The two women had little to do during the long hours they were alone but to talk, and in course of time Millicent learned everything there was to know of her husband's alcoholic past. The fact which she found most difficult to reconcile herself to was that Harold had been told that the only condition upon which he would be allowed to keep his post was that he should bring back a wife. It caused in her a dull feeling of resentment. And when she discovered what a persistent drunkard he had been she felt vaguely uneasy. She had a horrid fear that during her absence he would not have been able to resist the craving. She went home with her baby and a nurse. She spent a night at the mouth of the river and sent a messenger in a canoe to announce her arrival. She scanned the landing stage anxiously as the launch approached it. Harold and Mr. Simpson were standing there. The trim little soldiers were lined up. Her heart sank, for Harold was swaying slightly, like a man who seeks to keep his balance on a rolling ship, and she knew he was drunk.

It wasn't a very pleasant homecoming. She had almost forgotten her mother and father and her sister who sat there silently listening to her. Now she roused herself and became once more aware of their presence. All that she spoke of seemed very far away.

"I knew that I hated him then," she said. "I could have killed him."

"Oh, Millicent, don't say that," cried her mother. "Don't forget that he's dead, poor man."

Millicent looked at her mother, and for a moment a scowl darkened her impassive face. Mr. Skinner moved uneasily.

"Go on," said Kathleen.

"When he found out that I knew all about him he didn't bother very much more. In three months he had another attack of d.t.'s."

"Why didn't you leave him?" said Kathleen.

"What would have been the good of that? He would have been dismissed from the service in a fortnight. Who was to keep me and Joan? I had to stay. And when he was sober I had nothing to complain of. He wasn't in the least in love with me, but he was fond of me: I hadn't married him because I was in love with him but because I wanted to be married. I did everything I could to keep liquor from him; I managed to get Mr. Gray to prevent whisky being sent from Kuala Solor, but he got it from the Chinese. I watched him as a cat watches a mouse. He was too cunning for me. In a little while he had another outbreak. He neglected his duties. I was afraid complaints would be made. We were two days from Kuala Solor and that was our safeguard, but I suppose something was said, for Mr. Gray wrote a private letter of warning to me. I showed it to Harold. He stormed and blustered, but I saw he was frightened, and for two or three months he was quite sober. Then he began again. And so it went on till our leave became due.

"Before we came to stay here I begged and prayed him to be careful. I didn't want any of you to know what sort of a man I had married. All the time he was in England he was all right, and before we sailed I warned him. He'd grown to be very fond of Joan, and very proud of her, and she was devoted to him. She always liked him better than she liked me. I asked him if he wanted to have his child grow up knowing that he was a drunkard, and I found out that at last I'd got a hold on him. The thought terrified him. I told him that *I* wouldn't allow it, and if he ever let Joan see him drunk I'd take her away from him at once. Do you know, he grew quite pale when I said it. I fell on my knees that night and thanked God because I'd found a way of saving my husband.

"He told me that if I would stand by him he would have another try. We made up our minds to fight the thing together. And he tried so hard. When he felt as though he *must* drink he came to me. You know he was inclined to be rather pompous: with me he was humble, he was like a child; he depended on me. Perhaps he didn't love me when he married me, but he loved me then, me and Joan. I'd hated him, because of the humiliation, because when he was drunk and tried to be dignified and impressive he was loathsome; but now I got a strange feeling in my heart. It wasn't love, but it was a queer, shy tenderness. He was something more than my husband; he was like a child that I'd carried under my heart for long and weary months. He was so proud of me and, you know, I was proud too. His long speeches didn't irritate me anymore, and I only thought his stately ways rather funny and charming. At last we won. For two years he never touched a drop. He lost his craving entirely. He was even able to joke about it.

"Mr. Simpson had left us then and we had another young man called Francis.

" 'I'm a reformed drunkard, you know, Francis,' Harold said to him once. 'If it hadn't been for my wife I'd have been sacked long ago. I've got the best wife in the world, Francis.'

"You don't know what it meant to me to hear him say that. I felt that all I'd gone through was worthwhile. I was so happy."

She was silent. She thought of the broad, yellow, and turbid river on whose banks she had lived so long. The egrets, white and gleaming in the tremulous sunset, flew down the stream in a flock, flew low and swift, and scattered. They were like a ripple of snowy notes, sweet and pure and springlike, which an unseen hand drew forth, a divine arpeggio, from an unseen harp. They fluttered along between the green banks, wrapped in the shadows of evening, like the happy thoughts of a contented mind.

"Then Joan fell ill. For three weeks we were very anxious. There was no doctor nearer than Kuala Solor and we had to put up with the treatment of a native dispenser. When she grew well again I took her down to the mouth of the river in order to give her a breath of sea air. We stayed there a week. It was the first time I had been separated from Harold since I went away to have Joan. There was a fishing village, on piles, not far from us, but really we were quite alone. I thought a great deal about Harold, so tenderly, and all at once I knew that I loved him. I was so glad when the *prahu* came to fetch us back, because I wanted to tell him. I thought it would mean a good deal to him. I can't tell you how happy I was. As we rowed upstream the headman told me that Mr. Francis had had to go upcountry to arrest a woman who had murdered her husband. He had been gone a couple of days.

"I was surprised that Harold was not on the landing stage to meet me; he was always very punctilious about that sort of thing; he used to say that husband and wife should treat one another as politely as they treated acquaintances; and I could not imagine what business had prevented him. I walked up the little hill on which the bungalow stood. The *ayah* brought Joan behind me. The bungalow was strangely silent. There seemed to be no servants about and I could not make it out; I wondered if Harold hadn't expected me so soon and was out. I went up the steps. Joan was thirsty and the *ayah* took her to the servants' quarters to give her something to drink. Harold was not in the sitting room. I called him, but there was no answer. I was disappointed, because I should have liked him to be there. I went into our bedroom. Harold wasn't out after all; he was lying on the bed asleep. I was really very much amused because he always pretended he never slept in the afternoon. He said it was an unnecessary habit that we white people got into. I went up to the bed softly. I thought I would have a joke with him. I opened the mosquito curtains. He was lying on his back, with nothing on but a sarong, and there was an empty whisky bottle by his side. He was drunk.

"It had begun again. All my struggles for so many years were wasted. My dream was shattered. It was all hopeless. I was seized with rage."

Millicent's face grew once again darkly red and she clenched the arms of the chair she sat in.

"I took him by the shoulders and shook him with all my might. 'You beast,' I cried, 'you beast.' I was so angry I don't know what I did, I don't know what I said. I kept on shaking him. You don't know how loathsome he looked, that large fat man, half naked; he hadn't shaved for days, and his face was bloated and purple. He was breathing heavily. I shouted at him, but he took no notice. I tried to drag him out of bed, but he was too heavy. He lay there like a log. 'Open your eyes,' I screamed. I shook him again. I hated him. I hated him all the more because for a week I'd loved him with all my heart. He'd let me down. He'd let me down. I wanted to tell him what a filthy beast he was. I could make no impression on him. 'You shall open your eyes,' I cried. I was determined to make him look at me."

The widow licked her dry lips. Her breath seemed hurried. She was silent.

"If he was in that state I should have thought it best to have let him go on sleeping," said Kathleen.

"There was a *parang* on the wall by the side of the bed. You know how fond Harold was of curios."

"What's a *parang*?" said Mrs. Skinner.

"Don't be silly, Mother," her husband replied irritably. "There's one on the wall immediately behind you."

He pointed to the Malay sword on which for some reason his eyes had been unconsciously resting. Mrs. Skinner drew quickly into the corner of the sofa, with a little frightened gesture, as though she had been told that a snake lay curled up beside her.

"Suddenly the blood spurted out from Harold's throat. There was a great red gash right across it."

"Millicent," cried Kathleen, springing up and almost leaping towards her, "what in God's name do you mean?"

Mrs. Skinner stood staring at her with wide startled eyes, her mouth open.

"The *parang* wasn't on the wall anymore. It was on the bed. Then Harold opened his eyes. They were just like Joan's."

"I don't understand," said Mr. Skinner. "How could he have committed suicide if he was in the state you describe?"

Kathleen took her sister's arm and shook her angrily.

"Millicent, for God's sake, explain."

Millicent released herself.

"The *parang* was on the wall, I told you. I don't know what happened. There was all the blood and Harold opened his eyes. He died almost at once. He never spoke, but he gave a sort of gasp."

At last Mr. Skinner found his voice.

"But, you wretched woman, it was murder."

Millicent, her face mottled with red, gave him such a look of scornful hatred that he shrank back. Mrs. Skinner cried out.

"Millicent, you didn't do it, did you?"

Then Millicent did something that made them all feel as though their blood were turned to ice in their veins. She chuckled.

"I don't know who else did," she said.

"My God," muttered Mr. Skinner.

Kathleen had been standing bolt upright, with her hands to her heart, as though its beating were intolerable.

"And what happened then?" she said.

"I screamed. I went to the window and flung it open. I called for the *ayah*. She came across the compound with Joan. 'Not Joan,' I cried. 'Don't let her come.' She called the cook and told him to take the child. I cried to her to hurry. And when she came I showed her Harold. 'The *Tuan's* killed himself!' I cried. She gave a scream and ran out of the house.

"No one would come near. They were all frightened out of their wits. I wrote a letter to Mr. Francis, telling him what had happened, and asking him to come at once."

"How do you mean you told him what had happened."

"I said, on my return from the mouth of the river, I'd found Harold with his throat cut. You know, in the tropics you have to bury people quickly. I got a Chinese coffin, and the soldiers dug a grave behind the Fort. When Mr. Francis came Harold had been buried for nearly two days. He was only a boy. I could do anything I wanted with him. I told him I'd found the *parang* in Harold's hand and there was no doubt he'd killed himself in an attack of delirium tremens. I showed him the empty bottle. The servants said he'd been drinking hard ever since I left to go to the sea. I told the same story at Kuala Solor. Everyone was very kind to me, and the Government granted me a pension."

For a little while nobody spoke. At last Mr. Skinner gathered himself together.

"I am a member of the legal profession. I'm a solicitor. I have certain duties. We've always had a most respectable practice. You've put me in a monstrous position."

He fumbled, searching for the phrases that played at hide and seek in his scattered wits. Millicent looked at him with scorn.

"What are you going to do about it?"

"It was murder, that's what it was; do you think I can possibly connive at it?"

"Don't talk nonsense, Father," said Kathleen sharply. "You can't give your own daughter up."

"You've put me in a monstrous position," he repeated.

Millicent shrugged her shoulders again.

"You made me tell you. And I've borne it long enough by myself. It was time that all of you bore it too."

At that moment the door was opened by the maid.

"Davis has brought the car round, sir," she said.

Kathleen had the presence of mind to say something, and the maid withdrew.

"We'd better be starting," said Millicent.

"I can't go to the party now," cried Mrs. Skinner, with horror. "I'm far too upset. How can we face the Heywoods? And the Bishop will want to be introduced to you."

Millicent made a gesture of indifference. Her eyes held their ironical expression.

"We must go, Mother," said Kathleen. "It would look so funny if we stayed away." She turned on Millicent furiously. "Oh, I think the whole thing is such frightfully bad form."

Mrs. Skinner looked helplessly at her husband. He went to her and gave her his hand to help her up from the sofa.

"I'm afraid we must go, Mother," he said.

"And me with the ospreys in my toque that Harold gave me with his own hands," she moaned.

He led her out of the room. Kathleen followed close on their heels, and a step or two behind came Millicent.

"You'll get used to it, you know," she said quietly. "At first I thought of it all the time, but now I forget it for two or three days together. It's not as if there was any danger."

They did not answer. They walked through the hall and out of the front door. The three ladies got into the back of the car and Mr. Skinner seated himself beside the driver. They had no self-starter; it was an old car, and Davis went to the bonnet to crank it up. Mr. Skinner turned round and looked petulantly at Millicent.

"I ought never to have been told," he said. "I think it was most selfish of you."

Davis took his seat and they drove off to the Canon's garden party.

Winner of the Nobel Prize for Literature in 1932, John Galsworthy (1867–1933) was a graduate of Oxford who became a barrister in 1890. His career before the bench was short-lived, however, as he soon followed an inner desire to write novels and plays. His most significant work, and that which most strongly influenced the Nobel committee, is his multivolume study of the Forsyte family, which includes The Man of Property *(1906),* Indian Summer of a Forsyte *(1918),* In Chancery *(1920),* Awakening *(1920), and* To Let *(1921). As* The Forsyte Saga, *the collected books (and the long-running television series based on them) constitute an entertaining look at the lives of an upper-middle-class British family, the Yuppies of their day. Modern critics have not been kind to Galsworthy, but he was nonetheless a gifted writer, as "The Neighbors" clearly shows.*

THE NEIGHBORS
John Galsworthy

In the remote country, nature at first sight so serene, so simple, will soon intrude on her observer a strange discomfort; a feeling that some familiar spirit haunts the old lanes, rocks, wasteland, and trees, and has the power to twist all living things around into some special shape befitting its genius.

When moonlight floods the patch of moorland about the center of the triangle between the little towns of Hartland, Torrington, and Holsworthy, a pagan spirit steals forth through the wan gorse; gliding round the stems of the lonely, gibbetlike fir trees, peeping out among the reeds of the white marsh. That spirit has the eyes of a borderer, who perceives in every man a possible foe. And, in fact, this high corner of the land has remained border to this day, where the masterful, acquisitive invader from the North dwells side by side with the unstable, proud, quick-blooded Celt-Iberian.

In two cottages crowning some fallow land two families used to live side by side. That long white dwelling seemed all one, till the eye, peering through the sweetbrier which smothered the right-hand half, perceived the rude, weather-beaten presentment of a Running Horse, denoting the presence of intoxicating liquors; and in a window of the left-hand half, that strange conglomeration of edibles and shoe-leather which proclaims the one shop of a primitive hamlet.

These married couples were by name Sandford at the eastern, and Leman at the western end; and he who saw them for the first time thought: "What splendid-looking people!"

They were all four above the average height, and all four as straight as darts. The innkeeper, Sandford, was a massive man, stolid, grave, light-eyed, with big fair mustaches, who might have stepped straight out of some Norseman's galley. Leman was lean and lathy, a regular Celt, with an amiable, shadowy, humorous face. The two women were as different as the men. Mrs. Sandford's fair, almost transparent cheeks colored easily, her eyes were gray, her hair pale brown; Mrs. Leman's hair was of a lusterless jet-black, her eyes the color of a peaty stream, and her cheeks had the close creamy texture of old ivory.

Those accustomed to their appearance soon noted the qualifications of their splendor. In Sandford, whom neither sun nor wind ever tanned, there was a look as if nothing would ever turn him from acquisition of what he had set his heart on; his eyes had the idealism of the worshipper of property, ever marching towards a heaven of great possessions. Followed by his cowering spaniel, he walked to his fields (for he farmed as well as kept the inn) with a tread that seemed to shake the lanes, disengaging an air of such heavy and complete insulation that even the birds were still. He rarely spoke. He was not popular. He was feared, no one quite knew why.

On Mrs. Sandford, for all her pink and white, sometimes girlish look, he had set the mark of his slow, heavy domination. Her voice was seldom heard. Once in a while, however, her reserve would yield to garrulity, as of water flowing through a broken dam. In these outbursts she usually spoke of her neighbors, the Lemans, deploring the state of their marital relations. "A woman," she would say, "must give way to a man sometimes; I've had to give way to Sandford myself, I have." Her lips, from long compression, had become thin as the edge of a teacup; all her character seemed to have been driven down below the surface of her long, china-white face. She had not broken, but she had chipped; her edges had become jagged, sharp. The consciousness, that she herself had been beaten to the earth, seemed to inspire in her that waspish feeling towards Mrs. Leman—"a woman with a proud temper," as she would say in her almost ladylike voice; "a woman who's never bowed down to a man—that's what she'll tell you herself. 'Tisn't the drink that makes Leman behave so mad, 'tis because she won't give way to him. We're glad to sell drink to anyone we can, of course; but 'tisn't that what's making Leman so queer. 'Tis her."

Leman, whose long figure was often to be seen seated on the wooden bench of his neighbor's stone-flagged little inn, had, indeed, begun to have the soaked look and scent of a man never quite drunk, and hardly ever sober. He spoke slowly, his tongue seemed thickening; he no longer worked; his humorous, amiable face had grown hangdog and clouded. All the village knew of his passionate outbreaks and bursts of desperate weeping; and of two occasions when Sandford had been compelled to wrest a razor from him. People took a morbid interest in this rapid deterioration, speaking of it with misgiving and relish, unanimous in their opinion that—"summat'd 'appen about that; the drink wer duin' for George Leman, *that* it wer, praaperly!"

But Sandford—that blond, ashy-looking Teuton—was not easy of approach, and no one cared to remonstrate with him; his taciturnity was too impressive, too impenetrable. Mrs. Leman, too, never complained. To see this black-haired woman, with her stoical, alluring face, come out for a breath of air and stand in the sunlight, her baby in her arms, was to have looked on a very woman of the Britons. In conquering races the men, they say, are superior to the women; in conquered races, the women to the men. She was certainly superior to Leman. That woman might be bent and mangled, she could not be broken; her pride was too simple, too much a physical part of her. No one ever saw a word pass between her and Sandford. It was almost as if the old racial feelings of this borderland were pursuing in these two their unending conflict. For there they lived, side by side under the long, thatched roof, this great primitive, invading male, and that black-haired, lithe-limbed woman of an older race, avoiding each other, never speaking—as much too much for their own mates as they were, perhaps, worthy of each other.

In this lonely parish, houses stood far apart, yet news traveled down the May-scented lanes and over the whin-covered moor with a strange speed; blown perhaps by the west wind, whispered by the pagan genius of the place in his wanderings, or conveyed by small boys on large farm horses.

On Whit-Monday it was known that Leman had been drinking all Sunday; for he had been heard on Sunday night shouting out that his wife had robbed him, and that her children were not his. All next day he was sitting in the bar of the inn soaking steadily. Yet on Tuesday morning Mrs. Leman was serving in her shop as usual—a really noble figure, with that lusterless black hair of hers—very silent, and ever sweetening her eyes to her customers. Mrs. Sandford, in one of her bursts of garrulity, complained bitterly of the way her neighbors had "gone on" the night before. But unmoved, ashy, stolid as ever, Sandford worked in the most stony of his fields.

That hot, magnificent day wore to its end; a night of extraordinary beauty fell. In the gold moonlight the shadows of the lime-tree leaves lay, blacker than any velvet, piled one on the other at the foot of the little green. It was very warm. A cuckoo called on till nearly midnight. A great number of little moths were out; and the two broad meadows which fell away from the hamlet down to the stream were clothed in a glamorous haze of their own moonlit buttercups. Where that marvelous moonlight spread out across the moor it was all pale witchery; only the three pine trees had strength to resist the wan gold of their fair visitor, and brooded over the scene like the ghosts of three great gallows. The long white dwelling of "the neighbors," bathed in that vibrating glow, seemed to be exuding a refulgence of its own. Beyond the stream a nightjar hunted, whose fluttering harsh call tore the garment of the scent-laden still air. It was long before sleep folded her wings.

A little past twelve o'clock there was the sound of a double shot. By five o'clock next morning the news had already traveled far; and before seven, quite a concourse had gathered to watch two mounted constables take Leman on Sandford's pony to Bideford jail. The dead bodies of Sandford and Mrs. Leman lay—so report ran—in the locked bedroom at Leman's end of the neighbors' house. Mrs. Sandford, in a state of collapse, was being nursed at a neighboring cottage. The Leman children had been taken to the Rectory. Alone of the dwellers in those two cottages, Sandford's spaniel sat in a gleam of early sunlight under the eastern porch, with her nose fixed to the crack beneath the door.

It was vaguely known that Leman had "done for 'em"; of the how, the why, the when, all was conjecture. Nor was it till the assizes that the story of that night was made plain, from Leman's own evidence, read from a dirty piece of paper:

"I, George Leman, make this confession—so help me God! When I came up to bed that evening, I was far gone in liquor and so had been for two days off and on, which Sandford knows. My wife was in bed. I went up, and I said to her: 'Get up!' I said; 'do what I tell you for once!' 'I will not!' she said. So I pulled the bedclothes off her. When I saw her all white like that, with her black hair, it turned me queer, and I ran downstairs and got my gun, and loaded it. When I came upstairs again, she was against the door. I pushed, and she pushed back. She didn't call out, or say one word—but pushed; she was never one to be afraid. I was the stronger, and I pushed in the door. She stood up against the bed, defying me with her mouth tight shut, the way she had; and I put up my gun to shoot her. It was then that Sandford came running up the stairs and knocked the gun out of my hand with his stick. He hit me a blow over the heart with his fist, and I fell down against the wall and couldn't move. And he said: 'Keep quiet,' he said, 'you dog!' Then he looked at her. 'And as for you,' he said, 'you bring it on yourself! You can't bow down, can't you? *I'll* bow you down for once!' And he took and raised his stick. But he didn't strike her, he just looked at her in her nightdress, which was torn at the shoulders, and her black hair ragged. She never said a word, but smiled at him. Then he caught hold of her by the arms, and they stood there. I saw her eyes; they were as black as two sloes. He seemed to go all weak of a sudden, and white as the wall. It was like as they were struggling which was the better of them, meaning to come to one another at the end. I saw what was in them as clear as I see this paper. I got up and crept round, and I took the gun and pointed it, and pulled the triggers one after the other, and they fell dead, first him, then her; they fell quietly, neither of them made a noise. I went out and lay down on the grass. They found me there when they came to take me. This is all I have to write, but it is true that I was far gone in liquor, which I had of him. . . ."

P(elham) G(renville) Wodehouse (1881–1975) was the most cele-brated fiction humorist since Mark Twain. His amazing career spanned the first seventy-five years of this century: He was still chronicling the adventures of Jeeves, Bertie Wooster, Mr. Mul-liner, Stanley Featherstonehaugh Ukridge, and the many other characters who populated his very special world at the time of his death at age ninety-four. Wodehouse was a lifelong devotee of the mystery story, and much of his fiction contains criminous elements—the novels Leave It to Psmith *and* Laughing Gas, *for instance, and such short stories as "Without the Option" (which features that inimitable duo, Jeeves and Bertie Wooster). The best of his comic capers can be found in the posthumously pub-lished collection,* Wodehouse on Crime *(1981).*

WITHOUT THE OPTION

P. G. Wodehouse

The evidence was all in. The machinery of the law had worked without a hitch. And the beak, having adjusted a pair of pince-nez which looked as though they were going to do a nose dive any moment, coughed like a pained sheep and slipped us the bad news.

"The prisoner, Wooster," he said—and who can paint the shame and agony of Bertram at hearing himself so described?—"will pay a fine of five pounds."

"Oh, rather!" I said. "Absolutely! Like a shot!"

I was dashed glad to get the thing settled at such a reasonable figure. I gazed across what they call the sea of faces till I picked up Jeeves, sitting at the back. Stout fellow, he had come to see the young master through his hour of trial.

"I say, Jeeves," I sang out, "have you got a fiver? I'm a bit short."

"Silence!" bellowed some officious blighter.

"It's all right," I said; "just arranging the financial details. Got the stuff, Jeeves?"

"Yes, sir."

"Good egg!"

"Are you a friend of the prisoner?" asked the beak.

"I am in Mr. Wooster's employment, Your Worship, in the capacity of gentleman's personal gentleman."

"Then pay the fine to the clerk."

"Very good, Your Worship."

The beak gave a coldish nod in my direction, as much as to say that they might now strike the fetters from my wrists; and having hitched up the pince-nez once more, proceeded to hand poor old Sippy one of the nastiest looks ever seen in Bosher Street police court.

"The case of the prisoner Leon Trotsky—which," he said, giving Sippy the eye again, "I am strongly inclined to think an assumed and fictitious name—is more serious. He has been convicted of a wanton and violent assault upon the police. The evidence of the officer has proved that the prisoner struck him in the abdomen, causing severe internal pain, and in other ways interfered with him in the execution of his duties. I am aware that on the night following the annual aquatic contest between the universities of Oxford and Cambridge a certain license is traditionally granted by the authorities, but aggravated acts of ruffianly hooliganism like that of the prisoner Trotsky cannot be overlooked or palliated. He will serve a sentence of thirty days in the Second Division without the option of a fine."

"No, I say—here—hi—dash it all!" protested poor old Sippy.

"Silence!" bellowed the officious blighter.

"Next case," said the beak. And that was that.

The whole affair was most unfortunate. Memory is a trifle blurred; but as far as I can piece together the facts, what happened was more or less this:

Abstemious cove though I am as a general thing, there is one night in the year when, putting all other engagements aside, I am rather apt to let myself go a bit and renew my lost youth, as it were. The night to which I allude is the one following the annual aquatic contest between the universities of Oxford and Cambridge; or, putting it another way, Boat-Race Night. Then, if ever, you will see Bertram under the influence. And on this occasion, I freely admit, I had been doing myself rather juicily, with the result that when I ran into old Sippy opposite the Empire I was in quite fairly bonhomous mood. This being so, it cut me to the quick to perceive that Sippy, generally the brightest of revelers, was far from being his usual sunny self. He had the air of a man with a secret sorrow.

"Bertie," he said as we strolled along toward Piccadilly Circus, "the heart bowed down by weight of woe to weakest hope will cling." Sippy is by way of being an author, though mainly dependent for the necessaries of life on subsidies from an old aunt who lives in the country, and his conversation often takes a literary turn. "But the trouble is that I have no hope to cling to, weak or otherwise. I am up against it, Bertie."

"In what way, laddie?"

"I've got to go tomorrow and spend three weeks with some absolutely dud—I will go further—some positively scaly friends of my Aunt Vera. She has fixed the thing up, and may a nephew's curse blister every bulb in her garden."

"Who are these hounds of hell?" I asked.

"Some people named Pringle. I haven't seen them since I was ten, but I remember them at that time striking me as England's premier warts."

"Tough luck. No wonder you've lost your morale."

"The world," said Sippy, "is very gray. How can I shake off this awful depression?"

It was then that I got one of those bright ideas one does get round about eleven-thirty on Boat-Race Night.

"What you want, old man," I said, "is a policeman's helmet."

"Do I, Bertie?"

"If I were you, I'd just step straight across the street and get that one over there."

"But there's a policeman inside it. You can see him distinctly."

"What does that matter?" I said. I simply couldn't follow his reasoning.

Sippy stood for a moment in thought.

"I believe you're absolutely right," he said at last. "Funny I never thought of it before. You really recommend me to get that helmet?"

"I do, indeed."

"Then I will," said Sippy, brightening up in the most remarkable manner.

So there you have the posish, and you can see why, as I left the dock a free man, remorse gnawed at my vitals. In his twenty-fifth year, with life opening out before him and all that sort of thing, Oliver Randolph Sipperley had become a jailbird, and it was all my fault. It was I who had dragged that fine spirit down into the mire, so to speak, and the question now arose: What could I do to atone?

Obviously the first move must be to get in touch with Sippy and see if he had any last messages and what not. I pushed about a bit, making inquiries, and presently found myself in a little dark room with whitewashed walls and a wooden bench. Sippy was sitting on the bench with his head in his hands.

"How are you, old lad?" I asked in a hushed, bedside voice.

"I'm a ruined man," said Sippy, looking like a poached egg.

"Oh, come," I said. "it's not so bad as all that. I mean to say, you had the swift intelligence to give a false name. There won't be anything about you in the papers."

"I'm not worrying about the papers. What's bothering me is, how can I go and spend three weeks with the Pringles, starting today, when I've got to sit in a prison cell with a ball and chain on my ankle?"

"But you said you didn't want to go."

"It isn't a question of wanting, fathead. I've got to go. If I don't my aunt will find out where I am. And if she finds out that I am doing thirty days, without the option, in the lowest dungeon beneath the castle moat—well, where shall I get off?"

I saw his point.

"This is not a thing we can settle for ourselves," I said gravely. "We must put our trust in a higher power. Jeeves is the man we must consult."

And having collected a few of the necessary data, I shook his hand, patted him on the back, and tooled off home to Jeeves.

"Jeeves," I said, when I had climbed outside the pick-me-up which he had thoughtfully prepared against my coming, "I've got something to tell you; something important; something that vitally affects one whom you have always regarded with—one whom you have always looked upon—one whom you have—well, to cut a long story short, as I'm not feeling quite myself—Mr. Sipperley."

"Yes, sir?"

"Jeeves, Mr. Souperley is in the sip."

"Sir?"

"I mean, Mr. Sipperley is in the soup."

"Indeed, sir?"

"And all owing to me. It was I who, in a moment of mistaken kindness, wishing only to cheer him up and give him something to occupy his mind, recommended him to pinch that policeman's helmet."

"Is that so, sir?"

"Do you mind not intoning the responses, Jeeves?" I said. "This is a most complicated story for a man with a headache to have to tell, and if you interrupt you'll make me lose the thread. As a favor to me, therefore, don't do it. Just nod every now and then to show that you're following me."

I closed my eyes and marshaled the facts.

"To start with then, Jeeves, you may or may not know that Mr. Sipperley is practically dependent on his Aunt Vera."

"Would that be Miss Sipperley of the Paddock, Beckley-on-the-Moor, in Yorkshire, sir?"

"Yes. Don't tell me you know her!"

"Not personally, sir. But I have a cousin residing in the village who has some slight acquaintance with Miss Sipperley. He has described her to me as an imperious and quick-tempered old lady.... But I beg your pardon, sir, I should have nodded."

"Quite right, you should have nodded. Yes, Jeeves, you should have nodded. But it's too late now."

I nodded myself. I hadn't had my eight hours the night before, and what you might call a lethargy was showing a tendency to steal over me from time to time.

"Yes, sir?" said Jeeves.

"Oh—ah—yes," I said, giving myself a bit of a hitch up. "Where had I got to?"

"You were saying that Mr. Sipperley is practically dependent upon Miss Sipperley, sir."

"Was I?"

"You were, sir."

"You're perfectly right; so I was. Well, then, you can readily understand, Jeeves, that he has got to take jolly good care to keep in with her. You get that?"

Jeeves nodded.

"Now mark this closely: The other day she wrote to old Sippy, telling him to come down and sing at her village concert. It was equivalent to a royal command, if you see what I mean, so Sippy couldn't refuse in so many words. But he had sung at her village concert once before and had got the bird in no uncertain manner, so he wasn't playing any return dates. You follow so far, Jeeves?"

Jeeves nodded.

"So what did he do, Jeeves? He did what seemed to him at the moment a rather brainy thing. He told her that, though he would have been delighted to sing at her village concert, by a most unfortunate chance an editor had commissioned him to write a series of articles on the colleges of Cambridge and he was obliged to pop down there at once and would be away for quite three weeks. All clear up to now?"

Jeeves inclined the coconut.

"Whereupon, Jeeves, Miss Sipperley wrote back, saying

that she quite realized that work must come before pleasure—pleasure being her loose way of describing the act of singing songs at the Beckley-on-the-Moor concert and getting the laugh from the local toughs; but that, if he was going to Cambridge, he must certainly stay with her friends, the Pringles, at their house just outside the town. And she dropped them a line telling them to expect him on the twenty-eighth, and they dropped another line saying right-ho, and the thing was settled. And now Mr. Sipperley is in the jug, and what will be the ultimate outcome or upshot? Jeeves, it is a problem worthy of your great intellect. I rely on you."

"I will do my best to justify your confidence, sir."

"Carry on, then. And meanwhile pull down the blinds and bring a couple more cushions and heave that small chair this way so that I can put my feet up, and then go away and brood and let me hear from you in—say, a couple of hours, or maybe three. And if anybody calls and wants to see me, inform them that I am dead."

"Dead, sir?"

"Dead. You won't be so far wrong."

It must have been well toward evening when I woke up with a crick in my neck but otherwise somewhat refreshed. I pressed the bell.

"I looked in twice, sir," said Jeeves, "but on each occasion you were asleep and I did not like to disturb you."

"The right spirit, Jeeves. . . . Well?"

"I have been giving close thought to the little problem which you indicated, sir, and I can see only one solution."

"One is enough. What do you suggest?"

"That you go to Cambridge in Mr. Sipperley's place, sir."

I stared at the man. Certainly I was feeling a good deal better than I had been a few hours before; but I was far from being in a fit condition to have rot like this talked to me.

"Jeeves," I said sternly, "pull yourself together. This is mere babble from the sickbed."

"I fear I can suggest no other plan of action, sir, which will extricate Mr. Sipperley from his dilemma."

"But think! Reflect! Why, even I, in spite of having had a disturbed night and a most painful morning with the minions of the law, can see that the scheme is a loony one. To put the finger on only one leak in the thing, it isn't me these people want to see; it's Mr. Sipperley. They don't know me from Adam."

"So much the better, sir. For what I am suggesting is that you go to Cambridge, affecting actually to be Mr. Sipperley."

This was too much.

"Jeeves," I said, and I'm not half sure there weren't tears in my eyes, "surely you can see for yourself that this is pure banana oil. It is not like you to come into the presence of a sick man and gibber."

"I think the plan I have suggested would be practicable, sir. While you were sleeping, I was able to have a few words with Mr. Sipperley, and he informed me that Professor and Mrs. Pringle have not set eyes upon him since he was a lad of ten."

"No, that's true. He told me that. But even so, they would be sure to ask him questions about my aunt—or rather his aunt. Where would I be then?"

"Mr. Sipperley was kind enough to give me a few facts respecting Miss Sipperley, sir, which I jotted down. With these, added to what my cousin has told me of the lady's habits, I think you would be in a position to answer any ordinary question."

There is something dashed insidious about Jeeves. Time and again since we first came together he has stunned me with some apparently driveling suggestion or scheme or ruse or plan of campaign, and after about five minutes has convinced me that it is not only sound but fruity. It took nearly a quarter of an hour to reason me into this particular one, it being considerably the weirdest to date; but he did it. I was holding out pretty firmly, when he suddenly clinched the thing.

"I would certainly suggest, sir," he said, "that you left London as soon as possible and remained hid for some little time in some retreat where you would not be likely to be found."

"Eh? Why?"

"During the last hour Mrs. Spenser Gregson has been on the telephone three times, sir, endeavoring to get into communication with you."

"Aunt Agatha!" I cried, paling beneath my tan.

"Yes, sir. I gathered from her remarks that she had been reading in the evening paper a report of this morning's proceedings in the police court."

I hopped from the chair like a jack rabbit of the prairie. If Aunt Agatha was out with her hatchet, a move was most certainly indicated.

"Jeeves," I said, "this is a time for deeds, not words. Pack—and that right speedily."

"I have packed, sir."

"Find out when there is a train for Cambridge."

"There is one in forty minutes, sir."

"Call a taxi."

"A taxi is at the door, sir."

"Good!" I said. "Then lead me to it."

The Maison Pringle was quite a bit of a way out of Cambridge, a mile or two down the Trumpington Road; and when I arrived everybody was dressing for dinner. So it wasn't till I had shoved on the evening raiment and got down to the drawing room that I met the gang.

"Hullo-ullo!" I said, taking a deep breath and floating in.

I tried to speak in a clear and ringing voice, but I wasn't feeling my chirpiest. It is always a nervous job for a diffident and unassuming bloke to visit a strange house for the first time; and it doesn't make the thing any better when he goes there pretending to be another fellow. I was conscious of a rather pronounced sinking feeling, which the appearance of the Pringles did nothing to allay.

Sippy had described them as England's premier warts, and it looked to me as if he might be about right. Professor Pringle was a thinnish, baldish, dyspeptic-lookingish cove with an eye like a haddock, while Mrs. Pringle's aspect was that of one who had had bad news round about the year 1900 and never really got over it. And I was just staggering under the impact of these two when I was introduced to a couple of ancient females with shawls all over them.

"No doubt you remember my mother?" said Professor Pringle mournfully, indicating Exhibit A.

"Oh—ah!" I said, achieving a bit of a beam.

"And my aunt," sighed the prof, as if things were getting worse and worse.

"Well, well, well!" I said, shooting another beam in the direction of Exhibit B.

"They were saying only this morning that they remembered you," groaned the prof, abandoning all hope.

There was a pause. The whole strength of the company gazed at me like a family group out of one of Edgar Allan Poe's less cheery yarns, and I felt my *joie de vivre* dying at the roots.

"I remember Oliver," said Exhibit A. She heaved a sigh. "He was such a pretty child. What a pity! What a pity!"

Tactful, of course, and calculated to put the guest completely at his ease.

"I remember Oliver," said Exhibit B, looking at me in much the same way as the Bosher Street beak had looked at Sippy before putting on the black cap. "Nasty little boy! He teased my cat."

"Aunt Jane's memory is wonderful, considering that she will be eighty-seven next birthday," whispered Mrs. Pringle with mournful pride.

"What did you say?" asked the Exhibit suspiciously.

"I said your memory was wonderful."

"Ah!" The dear old creature gave me another glare. I could see that no beautiful friendship was to be looked for by Bertram in this quarter. "He chased my Tibby all over the garden, shooting arrows at her from a bow."

At this moment a cat strolled out from under the sofa and made for me with its tail up. Cats always do take to me, which made it all the sadder that I should be saddled with Sippy's criminal record. I stopped to tickle it under the ear, such being my invariable policy, and the Exhibit uttered a piercing cry.

"Stop him! Stop him!"

She leaped forward, moving uncommonly well for one of her years and, having scooped up the cat, stood eyeing me with bitter defiance, as if daring me to start anything. Most unpleasant.

"I like cats," I said feebly.

It didn't go. The sympathy of the audience was not with me. And conversation was at what you might call a low ebb when the door opened and a girl came in.

"My daughter Heloise," said the prof moodily, as if he hated to admit it.

I turned to mitt the female, and stood there with my hand out, gaping. I can't remember when I've had such a nasty shock.

I suppose everybody has had the experience of suddenly meeting somebody who reminded them frightfully of some fearful person. I mean to say, by way of an example, once when I was golfing in Scotland I saw a woman come into the hotel who was the living image of my Aunt Agatha. Probably a very decent sort, if I had only waited to see, but I didn't wait. I legged it that evening, utterly unable to stand the spectacle. And on another occasion I was driven out of a thoroughly festive nightclub because the headwaiter reminded me of my Uncle Percy.

Well, Heloise Pringle, in the most ghastly way, resembled Honoria Glossop.

I think I may have told you before about this Glossop scourge. She was the daughter of Sir Roderick Glossop, the loony doctor, and I had been engaged to her for about three weeks, much against my wishes, when the old boy most fortunately got the idea that I was off my rocker and put the bee on the proceedings. Since then the mere thought of her had been enough to make me start out of my sleep with a loud cry. And this girl was exactly like her.

"Er—how are you?" I said.

"How do you do?"

Her voice put the lid on it. It might have been Honoria
herself talking. Honoria Glossop has a voice like a lion tamer
making some authoritative announcement to one of the troupe,
and so had this girl. I backed away convulsively and sprang into
the air as my foot stubbed itself against something squashy. A
sharp yowl rent the air, followed by an indignant cry, and I
turned to see Aunt Jane on all fours, trying to put things right
with the cat, which had gone to earth under the sofa. She gave
me a look, and I could see that her worst fears had been realized.

At this juncture dinner was announced—not before I was
ready for it.

"Jeeves," I said, when I got him alone that night, "I am no
faintheart, but I am inclined to think that this binge is going to
prove a shade above the odds."

"You are not enjoying your visit, sir?"

"I am not, Jeeves. Have you seen Miss Pringle?"

"Yes, sir, from a distance."

"The best way to see her. Did you observe her keenly?"

"Yes, sir."

"Did she remind you of anybody?"

"She appeared to me to bear a remarkable likeness to her
cousin, Miss Glossop, sir."

"Her cousin! You don't mean to say she's Honoria Glossop's
cousin!"

"Yes, sir. Mrs. Pringle was a Miss Blatherwick—the younger of two sisters, the elder of whom married Sir Roderick Glossop."

"Great Scott! That accounts for the resemblance."

"Yes, sir."

"And what a resemblance, Jeeves! She even talks like Miss
Glossop."

"Indeed, sir? I have not yet heard Miss Pringle speak."

"You have missed little. And what it amounts to, Jeeves, is
that, though nothing will induce me to let old Sippy down, I
can see that this visit is going to try me high. At a pinch, I could
stand the prof and wife. I could even make the effort of a life-

time and bear up against Aunt Jane. But to expect a man to mix daily with the girl Heloise—and to do it, what is more, on lemonade, which is all there was to drink at dinner—is to ask too much of him. What shall I do, Jeeves?"

"I think that you should avoid Miss Pringle's society as much as possible."

"The same great thought had occurred to me," I said.

It is all very well, though, to talk airily about avoiding a female's society; but when you are living in the same house with her, and she doesn't want to avoid you, it takes a bit of doing. It is a peculiar thing in life that the people you most particularly want to edge away from always seem to cluster round like a poultice. I hadn't been twenty-four hours in the place before I perceived that I was going to see a lot of this pestilence.

She was one of those girls you're always meeting on the stairs and in passages. I couldn't go into a room without seeing her drift in a minute later. And if I walked in the garden she was sure to leap out at me from a laurel bush or the onion bed or something. By about the tenth day I had begun to feel absolutely haunted.

"Jeeves," I said, "I have begun to feel absolutely haunted."

"Sir?"

"This woman dogs me. I never seem to get a moment to myself. Old Sippy was supposed to come here to make a study of the Cambridge colleges, and she took me round about fifty-seven this morning. This afternoon I went to sit in the garden, and she popped up through a trap and was in my midst. This evening she cornered me in the morning room. It's getting so that, when I have a bath, I wouldn't be a bit surprised to find her nestling in the soap dish."

"Extremely trying, sir."

"Dashed so. Have you any remedy to suggest?"

"Not at the moment, sir. Miss Pringle does appear to be distinctly interested in you, sir. She was asking me questions this morning respecting your mode of life in London."

"What?"

"Yes, sir."

I stared at the man in horror. A ghastly thought had struck me. I quivered like an aspen.

At lunch that day a curious thing had happened. We had just finished mangling the cutlets and I was sitting back in my chair, taking a bit of an easy before being allotted my slab of boiled pudding, when, happening to look up, I caught the girl Heloise's eye fixed on me in what seemed to me a rather rummy manner. I didn't think much about it at the time, because boiled pudding is a thing you have to give your undivided attention to if you want to do yourself justice; but now, recalling the episode in the light of Jeeves's words, the full sinister meaning of the thing seemed to come home to me.

Even at the moment, something about that look had struck me as oddly familiar, and now I suddenly saw why. It had been the identical look which I observed in the eye of Honoria Glossop in the days immediately preceding our engagement—the look of a tigress that has marked down its prey.

"Jeeves, do you know what I think?"

"Sir?"

I gulped slightly.

"Jeeves," I said, "listen attentively. I don't want to give the impression that I consider myself one of those deadly coves who exercise an irresistible fascination over one and all and can't meet a girl without wrecking her peace of mind in the first half-minute. As a matter of fact, it's rather the other way with me, for girls on entering my presence are mostly inclined to give me the raised eyebrow and the twitching upper lip. Nobody, therefore, can say that I am a man who's likely to take alarm unnecessarily. You admit that, don't you?"

"Yes, sir."

"Nevertheless, Jeeves, it is a known scientific fact that there is a particular style of female that does seem strangely attracted to the sort of fellow I am."

"Very true, sir."

"I mean to say, I know perfectly well that I've got, roughly speaking, half the amount of brain a normal bloke ought to possess. And when a girl comes along who has about twice the regular allowance, she too often makes a beeline for me with the love light in her eyes. I don't know how to account for it, but it is so."

"It may be Nature's provision for maintaining the balance of the species, sir."

"Very possibly. Anyway, it has happened to me over and over again. It was what happened in the case of Honoria Glossop. She was notoriously one of the brainiest women of her year at Girton, and she just gathered me in like a bull pup swallowing a piece of steak."

"Miss Pringle, I am informed, sir, was an even more brilliant scholar than Miss Glossop."

"Well, there you are! Jeeves, she looks at me."

"Yes, sir?"

"I keep meeting her on the stairs and in passages."

"Indeed, sir?"

"She recommends me books to read, to improve my mind."

"Highly suggestive, sir."

"And at breakfast this morning, when I was eating a sausage, she told me I shouldn't, as modern medical science held that a four-inch sausage contained as many germs as a dead rat. The maternal touch, you understand; fussing over my health."

"I think we may regard that, sir, as practically conclusive."

I sank into a chair, thoroughly pipped.

"What's to be done, Jeeves?"

"We must think, sir."

"You think. I haven't the machinery."

"I will most certainly devote my very best attention to the matter, sir, and will endeavor to give satisfaction."

Well, that was something. But I was ill at ease. Yes, there is no getting away from it, Bertram was ill at ease.

Next morning we visited sixty-three more Cambridge colleges, and after lunch I said I was going to my room to lie down. After staying there for half an hour to give the coast time to clear, I shoved a book and smoking materials in my pocket, and climbing out of a window, shinned down a convenient water pipe into the garden. My objective was the summerhouse, where it seemed to me that a man might put in a quiet hour or so without interruption.

It was extremely jolly in the garden. The sun was shining, the crocuses were all to the mustard, and there wasn't a sign of Heloise Pringle anywhere. The cat was fooling about on the lawn, so I chirruped to it and it gave a low gargle and came trotting up. I had just got it in my arms and was scratching it under the ear when there was a loud shriek from above, and there was Aunt Jane half out the window. Dashed disturbing.

"Oh, right-ho," I said.

I dropped the cat, which galloped off into the bushes, and dismissing the idea of bunging a brick at the aged relative, went on my way, heading for the shrubbery. Once safely hidden there, I worked round till I got to the summerhouse. And, believe me, I had hardly got my first cigarette nicely under way when a shadow fell on my book and there was young Sticketh-Closer-Than-a-Brother in person.

"So there you are," she said.

She seated herself by my side, and with a sort of gruesome playfulness jerked the gasper out of the holder and heaved it through the door.

"You're always smoking," she said, a lot too much like a lovingly chiding young bride for my comfort. "I wish you wouldn't. It's so bad for you. And you ought not to be sitting out here without your light overcoat. You want someone to look after you."

"I've got Jeeves."

She frowned a bit.

"I don't like him," she said.

"Eh? Why not?"

"I don't know. I wish you would get rid of him."

My flesh absolutely crept. And I'll tell you why. One of the first things Honoria Glossop had done after we had become engaged was to tell me she didn't like Jeeves and wanted him shot out. The realization that this girl resembled Honoria not only in body but in blackness of soul made me go all faint.

"What are you reading?"

She picked up my book and frowned again. The thing was one I had brought down from the old flat in London, to glance at in the train—a fairly zippy effort in the detective line called *The Trail of Blood*. She turned the pages with a nasty sneer.

"I can't understand you liking nonsense of this—" She stopped suddenly: "Good gracious!"

"What's the matter?"

"Do you know Bertie Wooster?"

And then I saw that my name was scrawled right across the title page, and my heart did three back somersaults.

"Oh—er—well—that is to say—well, slightly."

"He must be a perfect horror. I'm surprised that you can make a friend of him. Apart from anything else, the man is practically an imbecile. He was engaged to my Cousin Honoria at one time, and it was broken off because he was next door to insane. You should hear my Uncle Roderick talk about him!"

I wasn't keen.

"Do you see much of him?"

"A goodish bit."

"I saw in the paper the other day that he was fined for making a disgraceful disturbance in the street."

"Yes, I saw that."

She gazed at me in a foul, motherly way.

"He can't be a good influence for you," she said. "I do wish you would drop him. Will you?"

"Well—" I began. And at this point old Cuthbert, the cat, having presumably found it a bit slow by himself in the bushes, wandered in with a matey expression on his face and jumped on my lap. I welcomed him with a good deal of cordiality. Though but a cat, he did make a sort of third at this party; and he afforded a good excuse for changing the conversation.

"Jolly birds, cats," I said.

She wasn't having any.

"Will you drop Bertie Wooster?" she said, absolutely ignoring the cat motif.

"It would be so difficult."

"Nonsense! It only needs a little willpower. The man surely can't be so interesting a companion as all that. Uncle Roderick says he is an invertebrate waster."

I could have mentioned a few things that I thought Uncle Roderick was, but my lips were sealed, so to speak.

"You have changed a great deal since we last met," said the Pringle disease reproachfully. She bent forward and began to scratch the cat under the ear. "Do you remember, when we were children together, you used to say that you would do anything for me?"

"Did I?"

"I remember once you cried because I was cross and wouldn't let you kiss me."

I didn't believe it at the time, and I don't believe it now. Sippy is in many ways a good deal of a chump, but surely even at the age of ten he cannot have been such a priceless ass as that. I think the girl was lying, but that didn't make the position of affairs any better. I edged away a couple of inches and sat staring before me, the old brow beginning to get slightly bedewed.

And then suddenly—well, you know how it is, I mean. I suppose everyone has had that ghastly feeling at one time or another of being urged by some overwhelming force to do some absolutely blithering act. You get it every now and then when you're in a crowded theater and something seems to be egging you on to shout "Fire!" and see what happens. Or you're talking to someone and all at once you feel, "Now, suppose I suddenly biffed this bird in the eye!"

Well, what I'm driving at is this, at this juncture, with her shoulder squashing against mine and her back hair tickling my nose, a perfectly loony impulse came sweeping over me to kiss her.

"No, really?" I croaked.

"Have you forgotten?"

She lifted the old onion and her eyes looked straight into mine. I could feel myself skidding. I shut my eyes. And then from the doorway there spoke the most beautiful voice I had ever heard in my life:

"Give me that cat!"

I opened my eyes. There was good old Aunt Jane, that queen of her sex, standing before me, glaring at me as if I were a vivisectionist and she had surprised me in the middle of an experiment. How this pearl among women had tracked me down I don't know, but there she stood, bless her dear, intelligent old soul, like the rescue party in the last reel of a motion picture.

I didn't wait. The spell was broken and I legged it. As I went, I heard that lovely voice again.

"He shot arrows at my Tibby from a bow," said this most deserving and excellent octogenarian.

For the next few days all was peace. I saw comparatively little of Heloise. I found the strategic value of that water pipe outside my window beyond praise. I seldom left the house now by any other route. It seemed to me that, if only the luck held like this, I might after all be able to stick this visit out for the full term of the sentence.

But meanwhile, as they used to say in the movies—

The whole family appeared to be present and correct as I came down to the drawing room a couple of nights later. The Prof, Mrs. Prof, the two Exhibits, and the girl Heloise were scattered about at intervals. The cat slept on the rug, the canary in its cage. There was nothing, in short, to indicate that this was not just one of our ordinary evenings.

"Well, well, well!" I said cheerily. "Hullo-ullo-ullo!"

I always like to make something in the nature of an entrance speech, it seeming to me to lend a chummy tone to the proceedings.

The girl Heloise looked at me reproachfully.

"Where have you been all day?" she asked.

"I went to my room after lunch."

"You weren't there at five."

"No. After putting in a spell of work on the good old colleges I went for a stroll. Fellow must have exercise if he means to keep fit."

"*Mens sana in corpore sano,*" observed the prof.

"I shouldn't wonder," I said cordially.

At this point, when everything was going as sweet as a nut and I was feeling on top of my form, Mrs. Pringle suddenly soaked me on the base of the skull with a sandbag. Not actually, I don't mean. No, no. I speak figuratively, as it were.

"Roderick is very late," she said.

You may think it strange that the sound of that name should have sloshed into my nerve centers like a half-brick. But, take it from me, to a man who has had any dealings with Sir Roderick Glossop there is only one Roderick in the world—and that is one too many.

"Roderick?" I gurgled.

"My brother-in-law, Sir Roderick Glossop, comes to Cambridge tonight," said the prof. "He lectures at St. Luke's tomorrow. He is coming here to dinner."

And while I stood there, feeling like the hero when he discovers that he is trapped in the den of the Secret Nine, the door opened.

"Sir Roderick Glossop," announced the maid or some such person, and in he came.

One of the things that get this old crumb so generally disliked among the better element of the community is the fact that he has a head like the dome of St. Paul's and eyebrows that want bobbing or shingling to reduce them to anything like reasonable size. It is a nasty experience to see this bald and bushy bloke advancing on you when you haven't prepared the strategic railways in your rear.

As he came into the room I backed behind a sofa and commended my soul to God. I didn't need to have my hand read to know that trouble was coming to me through a dark man.

He didn't spot me at first. He shook hands with the prof and wife, kissed Heloise, and waggled his head at the Exhibits.

"I fear I am somewhat late," he said. "A slight accident on the road, affecting what my chauffeur termed the —"

And then he saw me lurking on the outskirts and gave a startled grunt, as if I hurt him a good deal internally.

"This—" began the prof, waving in my direction.

"I am already acquainted with Mr. Wooster."

"This," went on the prof, "is Miss Sipperley's nephew, Oliver. You remember Miss Sipperley?"

"What do you mean?" barked Sir Roderick. Having had so much to do with loonies has given him a rather sharp and authoritative manner on occasion. "This is that wretched young man, Bertram Wooster. What is all this nonsense about Olivers and Sipperleys?"

The prof was eyeing me with some natural surprise. So were the others. I beamed a bit weakly.

"Well, as a matter of fact—" I said.

The prof was wrestling with the situation. You could hear his brain buzzing.

"He said he was Oliver Sipperley," he moaned.

"Come here!" bellowed Sir Roderick. "Am I to understand that you have inflicted yourself on this household under the pretense of being the nephew of an old friend?"

It seemed a pretty accurate description of the facts.

"Well—er—yes," I said.

Sir Roderick shot an eye at me. It entered the body somewhere about the top stud, roamed around inside for a bit, and went out at the back.

"Insane! Quite insane, as I knew from the first moment I saw him."

"What did he say?" asked Aunt Jane.

"Roderick says this young man is insane," roared the prof.

"Ah!" said Aunt Jane, nodding. "I thought so. He climbs down waterpipes."

"Does what?"

"I've seen him—ah, many a time!"

Sir Roderick snorted violently.

"He ought to be under proper restraint. It is abominable that a person in his mental condition should be permitted to roam the world at large. The next stage may quite easily be homicidal."

It seemed to me that, even at the expense of giving old Sippy away, I must be cleared of this frightful charge. After all, Sippy's number was up anyway.

"Let me explain," I said. "Sippy asked me to come here."

"What do you mean?"

"He couldn't come himself, because he was jugged for biffing a cop on Boat-Race Night."

Well, it wasn't easy to make them get the hang of the story, and even when I'd done it it didn't seem to make them any chummier towards me. A certain coldness about expresses it, and when dinner was announced I counted myself out and pushed off rapidly to my room. I could have done with a bit of dinner, but the atmosphere didn't seem just right.

"Jeeves," I said, having shot in and pressed the bell, "we're sunk."

"Sir?"

"Hell's foundations are quivering and the game is up."

He listened attentively.

"The contingency was one always to have been anticipated as a possibility, sir. It only remains to take the obvious step."

"What's that?"

"Go and see Miss Sipperley, sir."

"What on earth for?"

"I think it would be judicious to apprise her of the facts yourself, sir, instead of allowing her to hear of them through the medium of a letter from Professor Pringle. That is to say, if you are still anxious to do all in your power to assist Mr. Sipperley."

"I can't let Sippy down. If you think it's any good—"

"We can but try, sir. I have an idea, sir, that we may find Miss Sipperley disposed to look leniently upon Mr. Sipperley's misdemeanor."

"What makes you think that?"

"It's just a feeling that I have, sir."

"Well, if you think it would be worth trying—How do we get there?"

"The distance is about a hundred and fifty miles, sir. Our best plan would be to hire a car."

"Get it at once," I said.

The idea of being a hundred and fifty miles away from Heloise Pringle, not to mention Aunt Jane and Sir Roderick Glossop, sounded about as good to me as anything I had ever heard.

The Paddock, Beckley-on-the-Moor, was about a couple of parasangs from the village, and I set out for it next morning, after partaking of a hearty breakfast at the local inn, practically without a tremor. I suppose when a fellow has been through it as I had in the last two weeks his system becomes hardened. After all, I felt, whatever this aunt of Sippy's might be like, she wasn't Sir Roderick Glossop, so I was that much on velvet from the start.

The Paddock was one of those medium-sized houses with a goodish bit of very tidy garden and a carefully rolled gravel drive curving past a shrubbery that looked as if it had just come back from the dry cleaner—the sort of house you take one look at and say to yourself, "Somebody's aunt lives there." I pushed on up the drive, and as I turned the bend I observed in the middle distance a woman messing about by a flower bed with a trowel in her hand. If this wasn't the female I was after, I was very much mistaken, so I halted, cleared the throat, and gave tongue.

"Miss Sipperley?"

She had had her back to me, and at the sound of my voice she executed a sort of leap, or bound, not unlike a barefoot dancer who steps on a tin tack halfway through the Vision of Salome. She came to earth and goggled at me in a rather goofy manner. A large, stout female with a reddish face.

"Hope I didn't startle you," I said.

"Who are you?"

"My name's Wooster. I'm a pal of your nephew Oliver."

Her breathing had become more regular.

"Oh?" she said. "When I heard your voice I thought you were someone else."

"No, that's who I am. I came up here to tell you about Oliver."

"What about him?"

I hesitated. Now that we were approaching what you might call the nub, or crux, of the situation, a good deal of my breezy confidence seemed to have slipped from me.

"Well, it's rather a painful tale, I must warn you."

"Oliver isn't ill? He hasn't had an accident?"

She spoke anxiously, and I was pleased at this evidence of human feeling. I decided to shoot the works with no more delay.

"Oh, no, he isn't ill," I said; "and as regards having accidents, it depends on what you call an accident. He's in chokey."

"In what?"

"In prison."

"In prison!"

"It was entirely my fault. We were strolling along on Boat-Race Night and I advised him to pinch a policeman's helmet."

"I don't understand."

"Well, he seemed depressed, don't you know; and rightly or wrongly, I thought it might cheer him up if he stepped across the street and collared a policeman's helmet. He thought it a good idea, too, so he started doing it, and the man made a fuss and Oliver sloshed him."

"Sloshed him?"

"Biffed him—smote him a blow—in the stomach."

"My nephew Oliver hit a policeman in the stomach?"

"Absolutely in the stomach. And the next morning the beak sent him to the bastille for thirty days without the option."

I was looking at her a bit anxiously all this while to see how she was taking the thing, and at this moment her face seemed suddenly to split in half. For an instant she appeared to be all mouth, and then she was staggering about the grass, shouting with laughter and waving the trowel madly.

It seemed to me a bit of luck for her that Sir Roderick

Glossop wasn't on the spot. He would have been calling for the strait-waistcoat in the first half-minute.

"You aren't annoyed?" I said.

"Annoyed?" She chuckled happily. "I've never heard such a splendid thing in my life."

I was pleased and relieved. I had hoped the news wouldn't upset her too much, but I had never expected it to go with such a roar as this.

"I'm proud of him," she said.

"That's fine."

"If every young man in England went about hitting policemen in the stomach, it would be a better country to live in."

I couldn't follow her reasoning, but everything seemed to be all right; so after a few more cheery words I said good-bye and legged it.

"Jeeves," I said when I got back to the inn, "everything's fine. But I am far from understanding why."

"What actually occurred when you met Miss Sipperley, sir?"

"I told her Sippy was in the jug for assaulting the police. Upon which she burst into hearty laughter, waved her trowel in a pleased manner, and said she was proud of him."

"I think I can explain her apparently eccentric behavior, sir. I am informed that Miss Sipperley has had a good deal of annoyance at the hands of the local constable during the past two weeks. This has doubtless resulted in a prejudice on her part against the force as a whole."

"Really? How was that?"

"The constable has been somewhat overzealous in the performance of his duties, sir. On no fewer than three occasions in the last ten days he has served summonses upon Miss Sipperley—for exceeding the speed limit in her car; for allowing her dog to appear in public without a collar; and for failing to abate a smoky chimney. Being in the nature of an autocrat, if I may use the term, in the village, Miss Sipperley has been accustomed to do these things in the past with impunity, and the constable's unexpected zeal has made her somewhat ill disposed to policemen as a class and consequently disposed to look upon such assaults as Mr. Sipperley's in a kindly and broadminded spirit."

I saw his point.

"What an amazing bit of luck, Jeeves!"

"Yes, sir."

"Where did you hear all this?"

"My informant was the constable himself, sir. He is my cousin."

I gaped at the man. I saw, so to speak, all.

"Good Lord, Jeeves! You didn't bribe him?"

"Oh, no, sir. But it was his birthday last week, and I gave him a little present. I have always been fond of Egbert, sir."

"How much?"

"A matter of five pounds, sir."

I felt in my pocket.

"Here you are," I said. "And another fiver for luck."

"Thank you very much, sir."

"Jeeves," I said, "you move in a mysterious way your wonders to perform. You don't mind if I sing a bit, do you?"

"Not at all, sir," said Jeeves.

Aldous Huxley (1894–1963) wrote on a wide variety of topics in a variety of forms—plays, essays, poetry, novels, and short stories. His 1932 dystopian novel Brave New World *is considered one of the landmark works of its type, a reputation enhanced by its appearance just as fascism was coming to power in Germany. Despite his background (he was one of a distinguished English family of scholars and scientists) Huxley was infatuated with mysticism and openly experimented with hallucinatory drugs toward the end of his life, engaging in practices he seemed to be warning against in* Brave New World. *Among his other novels, three stand out:* Chrome Yellow *(1921),* Those Barren Leaves *(1925), and* Point Counter Point *(1928). His short fiction can be found in his* Collected Short Stories *(1957). "The Gioconda Smile" is the only one of these to deal directly with a criminous theme.*

The Gioconda Smile
Aldous Huxley

"Miss Spence will be down directly, sir."

"Thank you," said Mr. Hutton, without turning round. Janet Spence's parlormaid was so ugly—ugly on purpose, it always seemed to him, malignantly, criminally ugly—that he could not bear to look at her more than was necessary. The door closed. Left to himself, Mr. Hutton got up and began to wander round the room, looking with meditative eyes at the familiar objects it contained.

Photographs of Greek statuary, photographs of the Roman Forum, colored prints of Italian masterpieces, all very safe and well known. Poor, dear Janet, what a prig—what an intellectual snob! Her real taste was illustrated in that watercolor by the pavement artist, the one she had paid half a crown for (and thirty-five shillings for the frame). How often he had heard her tell the story, how often expatiate on the beauties of that skillful imitation of an oleograph! "A real Artist in the streets," and you could hear the capital A in Artist as she spoke the words. She made you feel that part of his glory had entered into Janet Spence when she tendered him that half-crown for the copy of the oleograph. She was implying a compliment to her own taste and penetration. A genuine Old Master for half a crown. Poor, dear Janet!

Mr. Hutton came to a pause in front of a small oblong mirror. Stooping a little to get a full view of his face, he passed a white, well-manicured finger over his mustache. It was as curly, as freshly auburn as it had been twenty years ago. His hair still retained its color, and there was no sign of baldness yet—only a certain elevation of the brow. "Shakespearean," thought Mr. Hutton, with a smile, as he surveyed the smooth and polished expanse of his forehead.

Others abide our question, thou art free. . . . Footsteps in the sea . . . Majesty . . . Shakespeare, thou shouldst be living at this hour. No, that was Milton, wasn't it? Milton, the Lady of Christ's. There was no lady about him. He was what the women would call a manly man. That was why they liked him—for the curly auburn mustache and the discreet redolence of tobacco. Mr. Hutton smiled again; he enjoyed making fun of himself. Lady of Christ's? No, no. He was the Christ of Ladies. Very pretty, very pretty. The Christ of Ladies. Mr. Hutton wished there were somebody he could tell the joke to. Poor, dear Janet wouldn't appreciate it, alas!

He straightened himself up, patted his hair, and resumed his peregrination. Damn the Roman Forum; he hated those dreary photographs.

Suddenly he became aware that Janet Spence was in the room, standing near the door. Mr. Hutton started, as though he had been taken in some felonious act. To make these silent and spectral appearances was one of Janet Spence's peculiar talents. Perhaps she had been there all the time, had seen him looking at himself in the mirror. Impossible! But, still, it was disquieting.

"Oh, you gave me such a surprise," said Mr. Hutton, recovering his smile and advancing with outstretched hand to meet her.

Miss Spence was smiling too: her Gioconda smile, he had once called it in a moment of half ironical flattery. Miss Spence had taken the compliment seriously, and had always tried to live up to the Leonardo standard. She smiled on his silence while Mr. Hutton shook hands; that was part of the Gioconda business.

"I hope you're well," said Mr. Hutton. "You look it."

What a queer face she had! That small mouth pursed forward by the Gioconda expression into a little snout with a round hole in the middle as though for whistling—it was like a penholder seen from the front. Above the mouth a well-shaped nose, finely aquiline. Eyes large, lustrous, and dark, with the largeness, luster, and darkness that seems to invite sties and an occasional bloodshot suffusion. They were fine eyes, but unchangingly grave. The penholder might do its Gioconda trick, but the eyes never altered in their earnestness. Above them, a pair of boldly arched, heavily penciled black eyebrows lent a surprising air of power, as of a Roman matron, to the upper portion of the face. Her hair was dark and equally Roman; Agrippina from the brows upward.

"I thought I'd just look in on my way home," Mr. Hutton went on. "Ah, it's good to be back here"—he indicated with a wave of his hand the flowers in the vases, the sunshine and greenery beyond the windows—"it's good to be back in the country after a stuffy day of business in town."

Miss Spence who had sat down, pointed to a chair at her side.

"No, really, I can't sit down," Mr. Hutton protested. "I must get back to see how poor Emily is. She was rather seedy this morning." He sat down, nevertheless. "It's these wretched liver chills. She's always getting them. Women—" He broke off and coughed, so as to hide the fact that he had uttered. He was about to say that women with weak digestions ought not to marry; but the remark was too cruel, and he didn't really believe it. Janet Spence, moreover, was a believer in eternal flames and spiritual attachments. "She hopes to be well enough," he added, "to see you at luncheon tomorrow. Can you come? Do!" He smiled persuasively. "It's my invitation too, you know."

She dropped her eyes, and Mr. Hutton almost thought that he detected a certain reddening of the cheek. It was a tribute; he stroked his mustache.

"I should like to come if you think Emily's really well enough to have a visitor."

"Of course. You'll do her good. You'll do us both good. In married life three is often better company than two."

"Oh, you're cynical."

Mr. Hutton always had a desire to say "Bow-wow-wow" whenever the last word was spoken. It irritated him more than any other word in the language. But instead of barking he made haste to protest.

"No, no. I'm only speaking a melancholy truth. Reality doesn't always come up to the ideal, you know. But that doesn't make me believe any the less in the ideal. Indeed, I believe in it passionately—the ideal of a matrimony between two people in perfect accord. I think it's realizable. I'm sure it is."

He paused significantly and looked at her with an arch expression. A virgin of thirty-six, but still unwithered; she had her charms. And there was something really rather enigmatic about her. Miss Spence made no reply but continued to smile. There were times when Mr. Hutton got rather bored with the Gioconda. He stood up.

"I must really be going now. Farewell, mysterious Gioconda." The smile grew intenser, focused itself, as it were, in a narrower snout. Mr. Hutton made a cinquecento gesture, and kissed her extended hand. It was the first time he had done such a thing; the action seemed not to be resented. "I look forward to tomorrow."

"Do you?"

For answer Mr. Hutton once more kissed her hand, then turned to go. Miss Spence accompanied him to the porch.

"Where's your car?" she asked.

"I left it at the gate of the drive."

"I'll come and see you off."

"No, no." Mr. Hutton was playful, but determined. "You must do no such thing. I simply forbid you."

"But I should like to come," Miss Spence protested, throwing a rapid Gioconda at him.

Mr. Hutton held up his hand. "No," he repeated, and then, with a gesture that was almost the blowing of a kiss, he started to run down the drive, lightly on his toes, with long, bounding strides like a boy's. He was proud of that run; it was quite marvelously youthful. Still, he was glad the drive was no longer. At the last bend, before passing out of sight of the house, he halted and turned round. Miss Spence was still standing on the steps, smiling her smile. He waved his hand, and this time quite definitely and overtly wafted a kiss in her direction. Then, breaking once more into his magnificent canter, he rounded the last dark promontory of trees. Once out of sight of the house he let his high paces decline to a trot, and finally to a walk. He took out his handkerchief and began wiping his neck inside his collar. What fools, what fools! Had there ever been such an ass as poor, dear Janet Spence? Never, unless it was himself. Decidedly he was the more malignant fool, since he, at least, was aware of his folly and still persisted in it. Why did he persist? Ah, the problem that was himself, the problem that was other people.

He had reached the gate. A large, prosperous-looking motor was standing at the side of the road.

"Home, M'Nab." The chauffeur touched his cap. "And stop at the crossroads on the way, as usual," Mr. Hutton added, as he opened the door of the car. "Well?" he said, speaking into the obscurity that lurked within.

"Oh, Teddy Bear, what an age you've been!" It was a fresh and childish voice that spoke the words. There was the faintest hint of Cockney impurity about the vowel sounds.

Mr. Hutton bent his large form and darted into the car with the agility of an animal regaining its burrow.

"Have I?" he said, as he shut the door. The machine began to move. "You must have missed me a lot if you found the time so long." He sat back in the low seat; a cherishing warmth enveloped him.

"Teddy Bear . . ." and with a sigh of contentment a charming little head declined onto Mr. Hutton's shoulder. Ravished, he looked down sideways at the round, babyish face.

"Do you know, Doris, you look like the pictures of Louise de Kerouaille." He passed his fingers through a mass of curly hair.

"Who's Louise de Kera-whatever-it-is?" Doris spoke from remote distances.

"She was, alas! *Fuit.* We shall all be 'was' one of these days. Meanwhile . . ."

Mr. Hutton covered the babyish face with kisses. The car rushed smoothly along. M'Nab's back through the front window was stonily impassive, the back of a statue.

"Your hands," Doris whispered. "Oh, you mustn't touch me. They give me electric shocks."

Mr. Hutton adored her for the virgin imbecility of the words. How late in one's existence one makes the discovery of one's body!

"The electricity isn't in me, it's in you." He kissed her again, whispering her name several times: Doris, Doris, Doris. The scientific appellation of the sea mouse, he was thinking as he kissed the throat she offered him, white and extended like the throat of a victim awaiting the sacrificial knife. The sea mouse was a sausage with iridescent fur: very peculiar. Or was Doris the sea cucumber, which turns itself inside out in moments of alarm? He would really have to go to Naples again, just to see the aquarium. These sea creatures were fabulous, unbelievably fantastic.

"Oh, Teddy Bear!" (More zoology; but he was only a land animal. His poor little jokes!) "Teddy Bear, I'm so happy."

"So am I," said Mr. Hutton. Was it true?

"But I wish I knew if it were right. Tell me, Teddy Bear, is it right or wrong?"

"Ah, my dear, that's just what I've been wondering for the last thirty years."

"Be serious, Teddy Bear. I want to know if this is right; if it's right that I should be here with you and that we should love one another, and that it should give me electric shocks when you touch me."

"Right? Well, it's certainly good that you should have electric shocks rather than sexual repressions. Read Freud; repressions are the devil."

"Oh, you don't help me. Why aren't you ever serious? If only you knew how miserable I am sometimes, thinking it's not right. Perhaps, you know, there is a hell, and all that. I don't know what to do. Sometimes I think I ought to stop loving you."

"But could you?" asked Mr. Hutton, confident in the powers of his seduction and his mustache.

"No, Teddy Bear, you know I couldn't. But I could run away, I could hide from you, I could lock myself up and force myself not to come to you."

"Silly little thing!" He tightened his embrace.

"Oh, dear, I hope it isn't wrong. And there are times when I don't care if it is."

Mr. Hutton was touched. He had a certain protective affection for this little creature. He laid his cheek against her hair and so, interlaced, they sat in silence, while the car, swaying and pitching a little as it hastened along, seemed to draw in the white road and the dusty hedges towards it devouringly.

"Good-bye, good-bye."

The car moved on, gathered speed, vanished round a curve, and Doris was left standing by the signpost at the crossroads, still dizzy and weak with the languor born of those kisses and the electrical touch of those gentle hands. She had to take a deep breath, to draw herself up deliberately, before she was strong enough to start her homeward walk. She had half a mile in which to invent the necessary lies.

Alone, Mr. Hutton suddenly found himself the prey of an appalling boredom.

* * *

Mrs. Hutton was lying on the sofa in her boudoir, playing patience. In spite of the warmth of the July evening a wood fire was burning on the hearth. A black Pomeranian, extenuated by the heat and the fatigues of digestion, slept before the blaze.

"Phew! Isn't it rather hot in here?" Mr. Hutton asked as he entered the room.

"You know I have to keep warm, dear." The voice seemed breaking on the verge of tears. "I get so shivery."

"I hope you're better this evening."

"Not much, I'm afraid."

The conversation stagnated. Mr. Hutton stood leaning his back against the mantelpiece. He looked down at the Pomeranian lying at his feet, and with the toe of his right boot he rolled the little dog over and rubbed its white-flecked chest and belly. The creature lay in an inert ecstasy. Mrs. Hutton continued to play patience. Arrived at an impasse, she altered the position of one card, took back another, and went on playing. Her patiences always came out.

"Dr. Libbard thinks I ought to go to Llandrindod Wells this summer."

"Well—go, my dear—go, most certainly."

Mr. Hutton was thinking of the events of the afternoon: how they had driven, Doris and he, up to the hanging wood, had left the car to wait for them under the shade of the trees, and walked together out into the windless sunshine of the chalk down.

"I'm to drink the waters for my liver, and he thinks I ought to have massage and electric treatment, too."

Hat in hand, Doris had stalked four blue butterflies that were dancing together round a scabious flower with a motion that was like the flickering of blue fire. The blue fire burst and scattered into whirling sparks; she had given chase, laughing and shouting like a child.

"I'm sure it will do you good, my dear."

"I was wondering if you'd come with me, dear."

"But you know I'm going to Scotland at the end of the month."

Mrs. Hutton looked up at him entreatingly. "It's the journey," she said. "The thought of it is such a nightmare. I don't know if I can manage it. And you know I can't sleep in hotels. And then there's the luggage and all the worries. I can't go alone."

"But you won't be alone. You'll have your maid with you." He spoke impatiently. The sick woman was usurping the place of the healthy one. He was being dragged back from the memory of the sunlit down and the quick, laughing girl, back to this unhealthy, overheated room and its complaining occupant.

"I don't think I shall be able to go."

"But you must, my dear, if the doctor tells you to. And, besides, a change will do you good."

"I don't think so."

"But Libbard thinks so, and he knows what he's talking about."

"No, I can't face it. I'm too weak. I can't go alone." Mrs. Hutton pulled a handkerchief out of her black silk bag, and put it to her eyes.

"Nonsense, my dear, you must make the effort."

"I had rather be left in peace to die here." She was crying in earnest now.

"O Lord! Now do be reasonable. Listen now, please." Mrs. Hutton only sobbed more violently. "Oh, what is one to do?" He shrugged his shoulders and walked out of the room.

Mr. Hutton was aware that he had not behaved with proper patience; but he could not help it. Very early in his manhood he had discovered that not only did he not feel sympathy for the poor, the weak, the diseased, and deformed; he actually hated them. Once, as an undergraduate, he spent three days at a mission in the East End. He had returned, filled with a profound and ineradicable disgust. Instead of pitying, he loathed the unfortunate. It was not, he knew, a very comely emotion; and he had been ashamed of it at first. In the end he had decided that it was temperamental, inevitable, and had felt no further qualms. Emily had been healthy and beautiful when he married her. He had loved her then. But now—was it his fault that she was like this?

Mr. Hutton dined alone. Food and drink left him more benevolent than he had been before dinner. To make amends for his show of exasperation he went up to his wife's room and offered to read to her. She was touched, gratefully accepted the offer, and Mr. Hutton, who was particularly proud of his accent, suggested a little light reading in French.

"French? I am so fond of French." Mrs. Hutton spoke of the language of Racine as though it were a dish of green peas.

Mr. Hutton ran down to the library and returned with a yellow volume. He began reading. The effort of pronouncing perfectly absorbed his whole attention. But how good his accent was! The fact of its goodness seemed to improve the quality of the novel he was reading.

At the end of fifteen pages an unmistakable sound aroused him. He looked up; Mrs. Hutton had gone to sleep. He sat still for a little while, looking with a dispassionate curiosity at the sleeping face. Once it had been beautiful; once, long ago, the sight of it, the recollection of it, had moved him with an emotion profounder, perhaps, than any he had felt before or since. Now it was lined and cadaverous. The skin was stretched tightly over the cheekbones, across the bridge of the sharp, birdlike nose. The closed eyes were set in profound bone-rimmed sockets. The lamplight striking on the face from the side emphasized with light and shade its cavities and projections. It was the face of a dead Christ by Morales.

Le squelette était invisible
Au temps heureux de l'art païen.

He shivered a little, and tiptoed out of the room.

On the following day Mrs. Hutton came down to luncheon. She had had some unpleasant palpitations during the night, but she was feeling better now. Besides, she wanted to do honor to her guest. Miss Spence listened to her complaints about

Llandrindod Wells, and was loud in sympathy, lavish with advice. Whatever she said was always said with intensity. She leaned forward, aimed, so to speak, like a gun, and fired her words. Bang! The charge in her soul was ignited, the words whizzed forth at the narrow barrel of her mouth. She was a machine gun riddling her hostess with sympathy. Mr. Hutton had undergone similar bombardments, mostly of a literary or philosophic character—bombardments of Maeterlinck, of Mrs. Besant, of Bergson, of William James. Today the missiles were medical. She talked about insomnia, she expatiated on the virtues of harmless drugs and beneficent specialists. Under the bombardment Mrs. Hutton opened out, like a flower in the sun.

Mr. Hutton looked on in silence. The spectacle of Janet Spence evoked in him an unfailing curiosity. He was not romantic enough to imagine that every face masked an interior physiognomy of beauty or strangeness, that every woman's small talk was like a vapor hanging over mysterious gulfs. His wife, for example, and Doris; they were nothing more than what they seemed to be. But with Janet Spence it was somehow different. Here one could be sure that there was some kind of queer face behind the Gioconda smile and the Roman eyebrows. The only question was: What exactly was there? Mr. Hutton could never quite make out.

"But perhaps you won't have to go to Llandrindod after all," Miss Spence was saying. "If you get well quickly Dr. Libbard will let you off."

"I only hope so. Indeed, I do really feel rather better today."

Mr. Hutton felt ashamed. How much was it his own lack of sympathy that prevented her from feeling well every day? But he comforted himself by reflecting that it was only a case of feeling, not of being better. Sympathy does not mend a diseased liver or a weak heart.

"My dear, I wouldn't eat those red currants if I were you," he said, suddenly solicitous. "You know that Libbard has banned everything with skins and pips."

"But I am so fond of them," Mrs. Hutton protested, "and I feel so well today."

"Don't be a tyrant," said Miss Spence, looking first at him and then at his wife. "Let the poor invalid have what she fancies; it will do her good." She laid her hand on Mrs. Hutton's arm and patted it affectionately two or three times.

"Thank you, my dear." Mrs. Hutton helped herself to the stewed currants.

"Well, don't blame me if they make you ill again."

"Do I ever blame you, dear?"

"You have nothing to blame me for," Mr. Hutton answered playfully. "I am the perfect husband."

They sat in the garden after luncheon. From the island of shade under the old cypress tree they looked out across a flat expanse of lawn, in which the parterres of flowers shone with a metallic brilliance.

Mr. Hutton took a deep breath of the warm and fragrant air. "It's good to be alive," he said.

"Just to be alive," his wife echoed, stretching one pale, knot-jointed hand into the sunlight.

A maid brought the coffee; the silver pots and the little blue cups were set on a folding table near the group of chairs.

"Oh, my medicine!" exclaimed Mrs. Hutton. "Run in and fetch it, Clara, will you? The white bottle on the sideboard."

"I'll go," said Mr. Hutton. "I've got to go and fetch a cigar in any case."

He ran in towards the house. On the threshold he turned round for an instant. The maid was walking back across the lawn. His wife was sitting up in her deck chair, engaged in opening her white parasol. Miss Spence was bending over the table, pouring out the coffee. He passed into the cool obscurity of the house.

"Do you like sugar in your coffee?" Miss Spence inquired.

"Yes, please. Give me rather a lot. I'll drink it after my medicine to take the taste away."

Mrs. Hutton leaned back in her chair, lowering the sunshade over her eyes, so as to shut out from her vision the burning sky.

Behind her, Miss Spence was making a delicate clinking among the coffee cups.

"I've given you three large spoonfuls. That ought to take the taste away. And here comes the medicine."

Mr. Hutton had reappeared, carrying a wineglass, half full of a pale liquid.

"It smells delicious," he said, as he handed it to his wife.

"That's only the flavoring." She drank it off at a gulp, shuddered, and made a grimace. "Ugh, it's so nasty. Give me my coffee."

Miss Spence gave her the cup; she sipped at it. "You've made it like syrup. But it's very nice, after that atrocious medicine."

At half-past three Mrs. Hutton complained that she did not feel as well as she had done, and went indoors to lie down. Her husband would have said something about the red currants, but checked himself; the triumph of an "I told you so" was too cheaply won. Instead, he was sympathetic, and gave her his arm to the house.

"A rest will do you good," he said. "By the way, I shan't be back till after dinner."

"But why? Where are you going?"

"I promised to go to Johnson's this evening. We have to discuss the war memorial, you know."

"Oh, I wish you weren't going." Mrs. Hutton was almost in tears. "Can't you stay? I don't like being alone in the house."

"But, my dear, I promised—weeks ago." It was a bother having to lie like this. "And now I must get back and look after Miss Spence."

He kissed her on the forehead and went out again into the garden. Miss Spence received him aimed and intense.

"Your wife is dreadfully ill," she fired off at him.

"I thought she cheered up so much when you came."

"That was purely nervous, purely nervous. I was watching

her closely. With a heart in that condition and her digestion wrecked—yes, wrecked—anything might happen."

"Libbard doesn't take so gloomy a view of poor Emily's health." Mr. Hutton held open the gate that led from the garden into the drive; Miss Spence's car was standing by the front door.

"Libbard is only a country doctor. You ought to see a specialist."

He could not refrain from laughing. "You have a macabre passion for specialists."

Miss Spence held up her hand in protest. "I am serious. I think poor Emily is in a very bad state. Anything might happen—at any moment."

He handed her into the car and shut the door. The chauffeur started the engine and climbed into his place, ready to drive off.

"Shall I tell him to start?" He had no desire to continue the conversation.

Miss Spence leaned forward and shot a Gioconda in his direction, "Remember, I expect you to come and see me again soon."

Mechanically he grinned, made a polite noise, and, as the car moved forward, waved his hand. He was happy to be alone.

A few minutes afterwards Mr. Hutton himself drove away. Doris was waiting at the crossroads. They dined together twenty miles from home, at a roadside hotel. It was one of those bad, expensive meals which are only cooked in country hotels frequented by motorists. It revolted Mr. Hutton, but Doris enjoyed it. She always enjoyed things. Mr. Hutton ordered a not very good brand of champagne. He was wishing he had spent the evening in his library.

When they started homewards Doris was a little tipsy and extremely affectionate. It was very dark inside the car, but looking forward, past the motionless form of M'Nab, they could see a bright and narrow universe of forms and colors scooped out of the night by the electric headlamps.

It was after eleven when Mr. Hutton reached home. Dr.

Libbard met him in the hall. He was a small man with delicate hands and well-formed features that were almost feminine. His brown eyes were large and melancholy. He used to waste a great deal of time sitting at the bedside of his patients, looking sadness through those eyes and talking in a sad, low voice about nothing in particular. His person exhaled a pleasing odor, decidedly antiseptic but at the same time suave and discreetly delicious.

"Libbard?" said Mr. Hutton in surprise. "You here? Is my wife ill?"

"We tried to fetch you earlier," the soft, melancholy voice replied. "It was thought you were at Mr. Johnson's, but they had no news of you there."

"No, I was detained. I had a breakdown," Mr. Hutton answered irritably. It was tiresome to be caught out in a lie.

"Your wife wanted to see you urgently."

"Well, I can go now." Mr. Hutton moved towards the stairs.

Dr. Libbard laid a hand on his arm. "I am afraid it's too late."

"Too late?" He began fumbling with his watch; it wouldn't come out of the pocket.

"Mrs. Hutton passed away half an hour ago."

The voice remained even in its softness, the melancholy of the eyes did not deepen. Dr. Libbard spoke of death as he would speak of a local cricket match. All things were equally vain and equally deplorable.

Mr. Hutton found himself thinking of Janet Spence's words. At any moment—at any moment. She had been extraordinarily right.

"What happened?" he asked. "What was the cause?"

Dr. Libbard explained. It was heart failure brought on by a violent attack of nausea, caused in its turn by the eating of something of an irritant nature. Red currants? Mr. Hutton suggested. Very likely. It had been too much for the heart. There was chronic valvular disease: something had collapsed under the strain. It was all over; she could not have suffered much.

* * *

"It's a pity they should have chosen the day of the Eton and Harrow match for the funeral," old General Grego was saying as he stood, his top hat in his hand, under the shadow of the lych-gate, wiping his face with his handkerchief.

Mr. Hutton overheard the remark and with difficulty restrained a desire to inflict grievous bodily pain on the General. He would have liked to hit the old brute in the middle of his big red face. Monstrous great mulberry, spotted with meal! Was there no respect for the dead? Did nobody care? In theory he didn't much care; let the dead bury their dead. But here, at the graveside, he had found himself actually sobbing. Poor Emily, they had been pretty happy once. Now she was lying at the bottom of a seven-foot hole. And here was Grego complaining that he couldn't go to the Eton and Harrow match.

Mr. Hutton looked round at the groups of black figures that were drifting slowly out of the churchyard towards the fleet of cabs and motors assembled in the road outside. Against the brilliant background of the July grass and flowers and foliage, they had a horribly alien and unnatural appearance. It pleased him to think that all these people would soon be dead, too.

That evening Mr. Hutton sat up late in his library reading the life of Milton. There was no particular reason why he should have chosen Milton; it was the book that first came to hand, that was all. It was after midnight when he had finished. He got up from his armchair, unbolted the French windows, and stepped out onto the little paved terrace. The night was quiet and clear. Mr. Hutton looked at the stars and at the holes between them, dropped his eyes to the dim lawns and hueless flowers of the garden, and let them wander over the farther landscape, black and gray under the moon.

He began to think with a kind of confused violence. There were the stars, there was Milton. A man can be somehow the peer of stars and night. Greatness, nobility. But is there seriously a difference between the noble and the ignoble? Milton, the stars, death, and himself—himself. The soul, the body; the higher and the lower nature, Perhaps there was something in it, after all. Milton had a god on his side and righteousness. What had he? Nothing, nothing whatever. There were only Doris's little breasts. What was the point of it all? Milton, the stars, death, and Emily in her grave, Doris and himself—always himself . . .

Oh, he was a futile and disgusting being. Everything convinced him of it. It was a solemn moment. He spoke aloud: "I will, I will." The sound of his own voice in the darkness was appalling; it seemed to him that he had sworn that infernal oath which binds even the gods: "I will, I will." There had been New Year's Days and solemn anniversaries in the past, when he had felt the same contritions and recorded similar resolutions. They had all thinned away, these resolutions, like smoke, into nothingness. But this was a greater moment and he had pronounced a more fearful oath. In the future it was to be different. Yes, he would live by reason; he would be industrious; he would curb his appetites; he would devote his life to some good purpose. It was resolved and it would be so.

In practice he saw himself spending his mornings in agricultural pursuits, riding round with the bailiff, seeing that his land was farmed in the best modern way—silos and artificial manures and continuous cropping and all that. The remainder of the day should be devoted to serious study. There was that book he had been intending to write for so long—*The Effect of Diseases on Civilization.*

Mr. Hutton went to bed humble and contrite, but with a sense that grace had entered into him. He slept for seven and a half hours, and woke to find the sun brilliantly shining. The emotions of the evening had been transformed by a good night's rest into his customary cheerfulness. It was not until a good many seconds after his return to conscious life that he remembered his resolution, his Stygian oath. Milton and death seemed somehow different in the sunlight. As for the stars, they were not there. But the resolutions were good; even in the daytime he could see that. He had his horse saddled after breakfast, and rode round the farm with the bailiff. After luncheon he read Thucydides on the plague at Athens. In the evening he made a few notes on malaria in southern Italy. While he was undressing he remembered that there was a good anecdote in Skelton's jest-book about the sweating sickness. He would have made a note of it if only he could have found a pencil.

On the sixth morning of his new life Mr. Hutton found among his correspondence an envelope addressed in that peculiarly vulgar handwriting which he knew to be Doris's. He opened it, and began to read. She didn't know what to say; words were so inadequate. His wife dying like that, and so suddenly—it was too terrible. Mr. Hutton sighed, but his interest revived somewhat as he read on:

"Death is so frightening, I never think of it when I can help it. But when something like this happens, or when I am feeling ill or depressed, then I can't help remembering it is there so close, and I think about all the wicked things I have done and about you and me, and I wonder what will happen. And I am so frightened. I am so lonely, Teddy Bear, and so unhappy, and I don't know what to do. I can't get rid of the idea of dying, I am so wretched and helpless without you. I didn't mean to write you; I meant to wait till you were out of mourning and could come and see me again, but I was so lonely and miserable, Teddy Bear, I had to write. I couldn't help it. Forgive me, I want you so much; I have nobody in the world but you. You are so good and gentle and understanding; there is nobody like you. I shall never forget how good and kind you have been to me, and you are so clever and know so much, I can't understand how you ever came to pay any attention to me, I am so dull and stupid, much less like me and love me, because you do love me a little, don't you, Teddy Bear?"

Mr. Hutton was touched with shame and remorse. To be thanked like this, worshipped for having seduced the girl—it was too much. It had just been a piece of imbecile wantonness. Imbecile, idiotic: there was no other way to describe it. For, when all was said, he had derived very little pleasure from it. Taking all things together, he had probably been more bored than amused. Once upon a time he had believed himself to be a hedonist. But to be a hedonist implies a certain process of reasoning, a deliberate choice of known pleasures, a rejection of known pains. This had been done without reason, against it. For he knew beforehand—so well, so well—that there was no interest or pleasure to be derived from these wretched affairs. And yet each time the vague itch came upon him he succumbed, involving himself once more in the old stupidity. There had been Maggie, his wife's maid, and Edith, the girl on the farm, and Mrs. Pringle, and the waitress in London, and others—there seemed to be dozens of them. It had all been so stale and boring. He knew it would be; he always knew. And yet, and yet . . . Experience doesn't teach.

Poor little Doris! He would write to her kindly, comfortingly, but he wouldn't see her again. A servant came to tell him that his horse was saddled and waiting. He mounted and rode off. That morning the old bailiff was more irritating than usual.

Five days later Doris and Mr. Hutton were sitting together on the pier at Southend. Doris, in white muslin with pink garnishings, radiated happiness; Mr. Hutton, legs outstretched and chair tilted, had pushed the panama back from his forehead, and was trying to feel like a tripper. That night, when Doris was asleep, breathing and warm by his side, he recaptured, in this moment of darkness and physical fatigue, the rather cosmic emotion which had possessed him that evening, not a fortnight ago, when he had made his great resolution. And so his solemn oath had already gone the way of so many other resolutions. Unreason had triumphed; at the first itch of desire he had given way. He was hopeless, hopeless.

For a long time he lay with closed eyes, ruminating his humiliation. The girl stirred in her sleep. Mr. Hutton turned over and looked in her direction. Enough faint light crept in between the half-drawn curtains to show her bare arm and shoulder, her neck, and the dark tangle of hair on the pillow. She was beautiful, desirable. Why did he lie there moaning over his sins? What did it matter? If he were hopeless, then so be it; he would make the best of his hopelessness. A glorious sense of irresponsibility suddenly filled him. He was free, magnificently free. In a kind of exaltation he drew the girl towards him. She woke, bewildered, almost frightened under his rough kisses.

The storm of his desire subsided into a kind of serene merriment. The whole atmosphere seemed to be quivering with enormous silent laughter.

"Could anyone love you as much as I do, Teddy Bear?" The question came faintly from distant worlds of love.

"I think I know somebody who does," Mr. Hutton replied. The submarine laughter was swelling, rising, ready to break the surface of silence and resound.

"Who? Tell me. What do you mean?" The voice had come very close; charged with suspicion, anguish, indignation, it belonged to this immediate world.

"A—ah!"

"Who?"

"You'll never guess." Mr. Hutton kept up the joke until it began to grow tedious, and then pronounced the name "Janet Spence."

Doris was incredulous. "Miss Spence of the Manor? That old woman?" It was too ridiculous. Mr. Hutton laughed too.

"But it's quite true," he said. "She adores me." Oh, the vast joke. He would go and see her as soon as he returned—see and conquer, "I believe she wants to marry me," he added.

"But you wouldn't . . . you don't intend . . ."

The air was fairly crepitating with humor. Mr. Hutton laughed aloud. "I intend to marry you," he said. It seemed to him the best joke he had ever made in his life.

When Mr. Hutton left Southend he was once more a married man. It was agreed that, for the time being, the fact should be kept secret. In the autumn they would go abroad together, and the world should be informed. Meanwhile he was to go back to his own house and Doris to hers.

The day after his return he walked over in the afternoon to see Miss Spence. She received him with the old Gioconda.

"I was expecting you to come."

"I couldn't keep away," Mr. Hutton gallantly replied.

They sat in the summerhouse. It was a pleasant place—a little old stucco temple bowered among dense bushes of evergreen. Miss Spence had left her mark on it by hanging up over the seat a blue-and-white Della Robbia plaque.

"I am thinking of going to Italy this autumn," said Mr. Hutton. He felt like a ginger-beer bottle, ready to pop with bubbling humorous excitement.

"Italy . . ." Miss Spence closed her eyes ecstatically. "I feel drawn there too."

"Why not let yourself be drawn?"

"I don't know. One somehow hasn't the energy and initiative to set out alone."

"Alone . . ." Ah, sound of guitars and throaty singing! "Yes, traveling alone isn't much fun."

Miss Spence lay back in her chair without speaking. Her eyes were still closed. Mr. Hutton stroked his mustache. The silence prolonged itself for what seemed a very long time.

Pressed to stay to dinner, Mr. Hutton did not refuse. The fun had hardly started. The table was laid in the loggia. Through its arches they looked out onto the sloping garden, to the valley below and the farther hills. Light ebbed away; the heat and silence were oppressive. A huge cloud was mounting up the sky, and there were distant breathings of thunder. The thunder drew nearer, a wind began to blow, and the first drops of rain fell. The table was cleared. Miss Spence and Mr. Hutton sat on in the growing darkness.

Miss Spence broke a long silence by saying meditatively:

"I think everyone has a right to a certain amount of happiness, don't you?"

"Most certainly." But what was she leading up to? Nobody makes generalizations about life unless they mean to talk about themselves. Happiness: he looked back on his own life, and saw a cheerful, placid existence disturbed by no great griefs or discomforts or alarms. He had always had money and freedom; he had been able to do very much as he wanted. Yes, he supposed he had been happy—happier than most men. And now he was

not merely happy; he had discovered in irresponsibility the secret of gaiety. He was about to say something about his happiness when Miss Spence went on speaking.

"People like you and me have a right to be happy sometime in our lives."

"Me?" said Mr. Hutton surprised.

"Poor Henry! Fate hasn't treated either of us very well."

"Oh, well, it might have treated me worse."

"You're being cheerful. That's brave of you. But don't
think I can't see behind the mask."

Miss Spence spoke louder and louder as the rain came
down more and more heavily. Periodically the thunder cut
across her utterances. She talked on, shouting against the noise.

"I have understood you so well and for so long."

A flash revealed her, aimed and intent, leaning towards
him. Her eyes were two profound and menacing gun barrels.
The darkness re-engulfed her.

"You were a lonely soul seeking a companion soul. I could
sympathize with you in your solitude. Your marriage . . ."

The thunder cut short the sentence. Miss Spence's voice
became audible once more with the words:

" . . . could offer no companionship to a man of your stamp.
You needed a soul mate."

A soul mate—he! A soul mate. It was incredibly fantastic.
"Georgette Leblanc, the ex-soul mate of Maurice Maeterlinck."
He had seen that in the paper a few days ago. So it was thus that
Janet Spence had painted him in her imagination—a soul-
mater. And for Doris he was a picture of goodness and the clev-
erest man in the world. And actually, really, he was what? Who
knows?

"My heart went out to you. I could understand; I was
lonely, too." Miss Spence laid her hand on his knee. "You were
so patient." Another flash. She was still aimed, dangerously.
"You never complained. But I could guess—I could guess."

"How wonderful of you!" So he was an *âme incomprise.*
"Only a woman's intuition . . ."

The thunder crashed and rumbled, died away, and only the

sound of the rain was left. The thunder was his laughter, magnified, externalized. Flash and crash, there it was again, right on top of them.

"Don't you feel that you have within you something that is akin to this storm?" He could imagine her leaning forward as she uttered the words. "Passion makes one the equal of the elements."

What was his gambit now? Why, obviously, he should have said "Yes," and ventured on some unequivocal gesture. But Mr. Hutton suddenly took fright. The ginger beer in him had gone flat. The woman was serious—terribly serious. He was appalled.

Passion? "No," he desperately answered. "I am without passion."

But his remark was either unheard or unheeded, for Miss Spence went on with a growing exaltation, speaking so rapidly, however, and in such a burningly intimate whisper that Mr. Hutton found it very difficult to distinguish what she was saying. She was telling him, as far as he could make out, the story of her life. The lightning was less frequent now, and there were long intervals of darkness. But at each flash he saw her still aiming towards him, still yearning forward with a terrifying intensity. Darkness, the rain, and then flash! Her face was there, close at hand. A pale mask, greenish white; the large eyes, the narrow barrel of the mouth, the heavy eyebrows. Agrippina, or wasn't it rather—yes, wasn't it rather George Robey?

He began devising absurd plans for escaping. He might suddenly jump up, pretending he had seen a burglar—Stop thief! Stop thief!—and dash off into the night in pursuit. Or should he say that he felt faint, a heart attack? Or that he had seen a ghost—Emily's ghost—in the garden? Absorbed in his childish plotting, he had ceased to pay any attention to Miss Spence's words. The spasmodic clutching of her hand, recalled his thoughts.

"I honored you for that, Henry," she was saying.

Honored him for what?

"Marriage is a sacred tie, and your respect for it, even when the marriage was, as it was in your case, an unhappy one, made me respect you and admire you and—shall I dare say the word?"

Oh, the burglar, the ghost in the garden? But it was too late.

" . . . yes, love you, Henry, all the more. But we're free now, Henry."

Free? There was a movement in the dark, and she was kneeling on the floor by his chair.

"Oh, Henry, Henry, I have been unhappy, too."

Her arms embraced him, and by the shaking of her body he could feel that she was sobbing. She might have been a suppliant crying for mercy.

"You mustn't, Janet," he protested. Those tears were terrible, terrible. "Not now, now now! You must be calm; you must go to bed." He patted her shoulder, then got up, disengaging himself from her embrace. He left her still crouching on the floor beside the chair on which he had been sitting.

Groping his way into the hall, and without waiting to look for his hat, he went out of the house, taking infinite pains to close the front door noiselessly behind him. The clouds had blown over, and the moon was shining from a clear sky. There were puddles all along the road, and a noise of running water rose from the gutters and ditches. Mr. Hutton splashed along, not caring if he got wet.

How heartrendingly she had sobbed! With the emotions of pity and remorse that the recollection evoked in him there was a certain resentment: Why couldn't she have played the game that he was playing—the heartless, amusing game? Yes, but he had known all the time that she wouldn't, she couldn't play that game; he had known and persisted.

What had she said about passion and the elements? Something absurdly stale, but true, true. There she was, a cloud black-bosomed and charged with thunder, and he, like some absurd little Benjamin Franklin, had sent up a kite into the heart of the menace. Now he was complaining that his toy had drawn the lightning.

She was probably still kneeling by that chair in the loggia, crying.

But why hadn't he been able to keep up the game? Why had his irresponsibility deserted him, leaving him suddenly sober in a cold world? There were no answers to any of his questions. One idea burned steady and luminous in his mind— the idea of flight. He must get away at once.

"What are you thinking about, Teddy Bear?"

"Nothing."

There was a silence. Mr. Hutton remained motionless, his elbows on the parapet of the terrace, his chin in his hands, looking down over Florence. He had taken a villa on one of the hilltops to the south of the city. From a little raised terrace at the end of the garden one looked down a long fertile valley onto the town and beyond it to the bleak mass of Monte Morello and, eastward of it, to the peopled hill of Fiesole, dotted with white houses. Everything was clear and luminous in the September sunshine.

"Are you worried about anything?"

"No, thank you."

"Tell me, Teddy Bear."

"But, my dear, there's nothing to tell." Mr. Hutton turned round, smile, and patted the girl's hand. "I think you'd better go in and have your siesta. It's too hot for you here."

"Very well, Teddy Bear. Are you coming too?"

"When I've finished my cigar."

"All right. But do hurry up and finish it, Teddy Bear." Slowly, reluctantly, she descended the steps of the terrace and walked towards the house.

Mr. Hutton continued his contemplation of Florence. He had need to be alone. It was good sometimes to escape from Doris and the restless solicitude of her passion. He had never known the pains of loving hopelessly, but he was experiencing now the pains of being loved. These last weeks had been a period of growing discomfort. Doris was always with him, like an obsession, like a guilty conscience. Yes, it was good to be alone.

He pulled an envelope out of his pocket and opened it; not without reluctance. He hated letters; they always contained something unpleasant—nowadays, since his second marriage. This was from his sister. He began skimming through the insulting home truths of which it was composed. The words "indecent haste," "social suicide," "scarcely cold in her grave," "person of the lower classes," all occurred. They were inevitable now in any communication from a well-meaning and right-thinking relative. Impatient, he was about to tear the stupid letter to pieces when his eye fell on a sentence at the bottom of the third page. His heart beat with uncomfortable violence as he read it. It was too monstrous! Janet Spence was going about telling everyone that he had poisoned his wife in order to marry Doris. What damnable malice! Ordinarily a man of the suavest temper, Mr. Hutton found himself trembling with rage. He took the childish satisfaction of calling names—he cursed the woman.

Then suddenly he saw the ridiculous side of the situation. The notion that he should have murdered anyone in order to marry Doris! If they only knew how miserably bored he was. Poor, dear Janet! She had tried to be malicious; she had only succeeded in being stupid.

A sound of footsteps aroused him; he looked round. In the garden below the little terrace the servant girl of the house was picking fruit. A Neapolitan, strayed somehow as far north as Florence, she was a specimen of the classical type—a little debased. Her profile might have been taken from a Sicilian coin of a bad period. Her features, carved floridly in the grand tradition, expressed an almost perfect stupidity. Her mouth was the most beautiful thing about her; the calligraphic hand of nature had richly curved it into an expression of mulish bad temper. . . . Under her hideous black clothes, Mr. Hutton divined a powerful body, firm and massive. He had looked at her before with a vague interest and curiosity. Today the curiosity defined and focused itself into a desire. An idyll of Theocritus. Here was the woman; he, alas, was not precisely like a goatherd on the volcanic hills. He called to her.

"Armida!"

The smile with which she answered him was so provocative, attested so easy a virtue, that Mr. Hutton took fright. He was on the brink once more—on the brink. He must draw back, oh! Quickly, quickly, before it was too late. The girl continued to look up at him.

"*Ha chiamato?*" she asked at last.

Stupidity or reason? Oh, there was no choice now. It was imbecility every time.

"*Scendo,*" he called back to her. Twelve steps led from the garden to the terrace. Mr. Hutton counted them. Down, down, down, down. . . . He saw a vision of himself descending from one circle of the inferno to the next—from a darkness full of wind and hail to an abyss of stinking mud.

For a good many days the Hutton case had a place on the front page of every newspaper. There had been no more popular murder trial since George Smith had temporarily eclipsed the European War by drowning in a warm bath his seventh bride. The public imagination was stirred by this tale of a murder brought to light months after the date of the crime. Here, it was felt, was one of those incidents in human life, so notable because they are so rare, which do definitely justify the ways of God to man. A wicked man had been moved by an illicit passion to kill his wife. For months he had lived in sin and fancied security—only to be dashed at last more horribly into the pit he had prepared for himself. Murder will out, and here was a case of it. The readers of the newspapers were in a position to follow every movement of the hand of God. There had been vague, but persistent, rumors in the neighborhood; the police had taken action at last. Then came the exhumation order, the postmortem examination, the inquest, the evidence of the experts, the verdict of the coroner's jury, the trial, the condemnation. For once Providence had done its duty, obviously, grossly, didactically, as in a melodrama. The newspapers were right in making of the case the staple intellectual food of a whole season.

Mr. Hutton's first emotion when he was summoned from Italy to give evidence at the inquest was one of indignation. It was a monstrous, a scandalous thing that the police should take such idle, malicious gossip seriously. When the inquest was over he would bring an action for malicious prosecution against the Chief Constable; he would sue the Spence woman for slander.

The inquest was opened; the astonishing evidence unrolled itself. The experts had examined the body, and had found traces of arsenic; they were of the opinion that the late Mrs. Hutton had died of arsenic poisoning.

Arsenic poisoning . . . Emily had died of arsenic poisoning? After that, Mr. Hutton learned with surprise that there was enough arsenicated insecticide in his greenhouses to poison an army.

It was now, quite suddenly, that he saw it: There was a case against him. Fascinated, he watched it growing, growing, like some monstrous tropical plant. It was enveloping him, surrounding him; he was lost in a tangled forest.

When was the poison administered? The experts agreed that it must have been swallowed eight or nine hours before death. About lunchtime? Yes, about lunchtime. Clara, the parlormaid, was called. Mrs. Hutton, she remembered, had asked her to go and fetch her medicine. Mr. Hutton had volunteered to go instead; he had gone alone. Miss Spence—ah, the memory of the storm, the white, aimed face! The horror of it all!—Miss Spence confirmed Clara's statement, and added that Mr. Hutton had come back with the medicine already poured out in a wineglass, not in the bottle.

Mr. Hutton's indignation evaporated. He was dismayed, frightened. It was all too fantastic to be taken seriously, and yet this nightmare was a fact—it was actually happening.

M'Nab had seen them kissing, often. He had taken them for a drive on the day of Mrs. Hutton's death. He could see them reflected in the windscreen, sometimes out of the tail of his eye.

The inquest was adjourned. That evening Doris went to

bed with a headache. When he went to her room after dinner, Mr. Hutton found her crying.

"What's the matter?" He sat down on the edge of her bed and began to stroke her hair. For a long time she did not answer, and he went on stroking her hair mechanically, almost unconsciously; sometimes, even, he bent down and kissed her bare shoulder. He had his own affairs, however, to think about. What had happened? How was it that the stupid gossip had actually come true? Emily had died of arsenic poisoning. It was absurd, impossible. The order of things had been broken, and he was at the mercy of an irresponsibility. What had happened, what was going to happen? He was interrupted in the midst of his thoughts.

"It's my fault—it's my fault!" Doris suddenly sobbed out. "I shouldn't have loved you; I oughtn't to have let you love me. Why was I ever born?"

Mr. Hutton didn't say anything, but looked down in silence at the abject figure of misery lying on the bed.

"If they do anything to you I shall kill myself."

She sat up, held him for a moment at arm's length, and looked at him with a kind of violence, as though she were never to see him again.

"I love you, I love you, I love you." She drew him, inert and passive, towards her, clasped him, pressed herself against him. "I didn't know you loved me as much as that, Teddy Bear. But why did you do it—why did you do it?"

Mr. Hutton undid her clasping arms and got up. His face became very red. "You seem to take it for granted that I murdered my wife," he said. "It's really too grotesque. What do you all take me for? A cinema hero?" He had begun to lose his temper. All the exasperation, all the fear and bewilderment of the day, was transformed into a violent anger against her. "It's all such damned stupidity. Haven't you any conception of a civilized man's mentality? Do I look the sort of man who'd go about slaughtering people? I suppose you imagined I was so insanely in love with you that I could commit any folly. When will you women understand that one isn't insanely in love? All one asks for is a quiet life, which you won't allow one to have. I don't know what the devil ever induced me to marry you. It was all a damned stupid, practical joke. And now you go about saying I'm a murderer. I won't stand it."

Mr. Hutton stamped towards the door. He had said horrible things, he knew—odious things that he ought speedily to unsay. But he wouldn't. He closed the door behind him.

"Teddy Bear!" He turned the handle; the latch clicked into place. "Teddy Bear!" The voice that came to him through the closed door was agonized. Should he go back? He ought to go back. He touched the handle, then withdrew his fingers and quickly walked away. When he was halfway down the stairs he halted. She might try to do something silly—throw herself out of the window or God knows what! He listened attentively; there was no sound. But he pictured her very clearly, tiptoeing across the room, lifting the sash as high as it would go, leaning out into the cold night air. It was raining a little. Under the window lay the paved terrace. How far below? Twenty-five or thirty feet? Once, when he was walking along Piccadilly, a dog had jumped out of a third-story window of the Ritz. He had seen it fall; he had heard it strike the pavement. Should he go back? He was damned if he would; he hated her.

He sat for a long time in the library. What had happened? What was happening? He turned the question over and over in his mind and could find no answer. Suppose the nightmare dreamed itself out to its horrible conclusion. Death was waiting for him. His eyes filled with tears; he wanted so passionately to live. "Just to be alive." Poor Emily had wished it too, he remembered: "Just to be alive." There were still so many places in this astonishing world unvisited, so many queer delightful people still unknown, so many lovely women never so much as seen. The huge white oxen would still be dragging their wains along the Tuscan roads, the cypresses would still go up, straight as pillars, to the blue heaven; but he would not be there to see them. And the sweet southern wines—Tear of Christ and Blood of Judas—others would drink them, not he. Others would walk down the obscure and narrow lanes between the bookshelves in

the London Library, sniffing the dusty perfume of good literature, peering at strange titles, discovering unknown names, ex-
ploring the fringes of vast domains of knowledge. He would be
lying in a hole in the ground. And why, why? Confusedly he felt
that some extraordinary kind of justice was being done. In the
past he had been wanton and imbecile and irresponsible. Now
Fate was playing as wantonly, as irresponsibly, with him. It was
tit for tat, and God existed after all.

He felt that he would like to pray. Forty years ago he used
to kneel by his bed every evening. The nightly formula of
his childhood came to him almost unsought from some long
unopened chamber of the memory. "God bless Father and
Mother, Tom and Cissie and the baby, Mademoiselle and Nurse,
and everyone that I love, and make me a good boy. Amen."
They were all dead now—all except Cissie.

His mind seemed to soften and dissolve; a great calm descended upon his spirit. He went upstairs to ask Doris's forgive-
ness. He found her lying on the couch at the foot of the bed. On
the floor beside her stood a blue bottle of liniment, marked
"Not to be taken"; she seemed to have drunk about half of it.

"You didn't love me," was all she said when she opened her
eyes to find him bending over her.

Dr. Libbard arrived in time to prevent any very serious
consequences. "You mustn't do this again," he said while Mr.
Hutton was out of the room.

"What's to prevent me?" she asked defiantly.

Dr. Libbard looked at her with his large, sad eyes. "There's
nothing to prevent you," he said. "Only yourself and your baby.
Isn't it rather bad luck on your baby, not allowing it to come
into the world because you want to go out of it?"

Doris was silent for a time. "All right," she whispered. "I
won't."

Mr. Hutton sat by her bedside for the rest of the night. He
felt himself now to be indeed a murderer. For a time he persuaded himself that he loved this pitiable child. Dozing in his
chair, he woke up, stiff and cold, to find himself drained dry, as
it were, of every emotion. He had become nothing but a tired

and suffering carcass. At six o'clock he undressed and went to bed for a couple of hours' sleep. In the course of the same afternoon the coroner's jury brought in a verdict of "Willful Murder," and Mr. Hutton was committed for trial.

Miss Spence was not at all well. She had found her public appearances in the witness box very trying, and when it was all over she had something that was very nearly a breakdown. She slept badly, and suffered from nervous indigestion. Dr. Libbard used to call every other day. She talked to him a great deal—mostly about the Hutton case. . . . Her moral indignation was always on the boil. Wasn't it appalling to think that one had had a murderer in one's house. Wasn't it extraordinary that one could have been for so long mistaken about the man's character. (But she had had an inkling from the first.) And then the girl he had gone off with—so low-class, so little better than a prostitute. The news that the second Mrs. Hutton was expecting a baby—the posthumous child of a condemned and executed criminal—revolted her; the thing was shocking—an obscenity. Dr. Libbard answered her gently and vaguely, and prescribed bromides.

One morning he interrupted her in the midst of her customary tirade. "By the way," he said in his soft, melancholy voice, "I suppose it was really you who poisoned Mrs. Hutton."

Miss Spence stared at him for two or three seconds with enormous eyes, and then quietly said, "Yes." After that she started to cry.

"In the coffee, I suppose."

She seemed to nod assent. Dr. Libbard took out his fountain pen, and in his neat, meticulous calligraphy wrote out a prescription for a sleeping draught.

The early novels and novellas of James M. Cain (1892–1977)—
The Postman Always Rings Twice, Serenade, Love's Lovely
Counterfeit, Double Indemnity—*earned him a worldwide reputation as a master of hard-boiled realism. Although he was not a
crime writer per se, much of his work deals with murder; he employed a spare, elemental style reminiscent of Hemingway's, a
style that, as one critic has written, "possesses the sleeve-hold-
ing, hypnotic power of an Ancient Mariner's tale." Cain wrote
relatively few short stories, and most of his small output has
either been widely reprinted ("Dead Man," "Brush Fire") or
collected in the posthumously published* The Baby in the Icebox
*(1981). A few of his stories have escaped reprinting, however;
"Cigarette Girl," which first appeared in the mystery magazine*
Manhunt *in 1953, is one of these—a surprising oversight, considering its distinctive Cain style and content.*

CIGARETTE GIRL
James M. CaiN

I'd never so much as laid eyes on her before going in this place, the Here's How, a nightclub on Route 1, a few miles north of Washington, on business that was 99 percent silly, but that I had to keep to myself. It was around eight at night, with hardly anyone there, and I'd just taken a table, ordered a drink, and started to unwrap a cigar when a whiff of perfume hit me, and she swept by with cigarettes. As to what she looked like, I had only a rear view, but the taffeta skirt, crepe blouse, and silver earrings were quiet, and the chassis was choice, call it fancy, a little smaller than medium. So far, a cigarette girl, nothing to rate any cheers, but not bad either, for a guy unattached who'd like an excuse to linger.

But then she made a pitch, or what I took for a pitch. Her middle-aged customer was trying to tell her some joke, and taking so long about it the proprietor got in the act. He was a big, bland, blocky guy, with kind of a decent face, but he went and whispered to her as though to hustle her up, for some reason apparently, I couldn't quite figure it out. She didn't much seem to like it, until her eye caught mine. She gave a little pout, a little shrug, a little wink, and then just stood there, smiling.

Now I know this pitch and it's nice, because of course I smiled back, and with that I was on the hook. A smile is nature's freeway: it has lanes, and you can go any speed you like, except you can't go back. Not that I wanted to, as I suddenly changed my mind about the cigar I had in my hand, stuck it back in my pocket, and wigwagged for cigarettes. She nodded, and when she came over said: "You stop laughing at me."

"Who's laughing? Looking."

"Oh, of course. That's different."

I picked out a pack, put down my buck, and got the surprise of my life: She gave me change. As she started to leave, I said: "You forgot something, maybe?"

"That's not necessary."

"For all this I get, I should pay."

"All what, sir, for instance?"

"I told you: the beauty that fills my eye."

"The best things in life are free."

"On that basis, fair lady, some of them, here, are tops. Would you care to sit down?"

"Can't."

"Why not?"

"Not allowed. We got rules."

With that she went out toward the rear somewhere, and I noticed the proprietor again, just a short distance away, and realized he'd been edging in. I called him over and said: "What's the big idea? I was talking to her."

"Mister, she's paid to work."

"Yeah, she mentioned about rules, but now they got other things too. Four Freedoms, all kinds of stuff. Didn't anyone ever tell you?"

"I heard of it, yes."

"You're Mr. Here's How?"

"Jack Conner, to my friends."

I took a V from my wallet, folded it, creased it, pushed it toward him. I said: "Jack, little note of introduction I generally carry around. I'd like you to ease these rules. She's cute, and I crave to buy her a drink."

He didn't see any money, and stood for a minute thinking. Then: "Mister, you're off on the wrong foot. In the first place, she's not a cigarette girl. Tonight, yes, when the other girl is off. But not regular, no. In the second place, she's not any chiselly-wink that orders rye, drinks tea, takes the four bits you slip her, the four I charge for the drink—and is open to propositions. She's class. She's used to class—out west, with people that have it, and that brought her east when they came. In the third place she's a friend, and before I eased any rules I'd have to know more about you, a whole lot more, than this note tells me."

"My name's Cameron."

"Pleased to meet you and all that, but as to who you are, Mr. Cameron, and what you are, I still don't know—"

"I'm a musician."

"Yeah? What instrument?"

"Any of them. Guitar, mainly."

Which brings me to what I was doing there. I do play the guitar, play it all day long, for the help I get from it, as it gives me certain chords, the big ones that people go for, and heads me off from some others, the fancy ones on the piano, that other musicians go for. I'm an arranger, based in Baltimore, and had driven down on a little tune detecting. The guy who takes most of my work, Art Lomak, the band leader, writes a few tunes himself, and had gone clean off his rocker about one he said had been stolen, or thefted as they call it. It was one he'd been playing a little, to try it and work out bugs, with lyric and title to come, soon as the idea hit him. And then he rang me, with screams. It had already gone on the air, as twenty people had told him, from this same little honky-tonk, as part of a ten o'clock spot on the Washington FM pickup. He begged me to be here tonight, when the trio started their broadcast, pick up such dope as I could, and tomorrow give him the lowdown.

That much was right on the beam, stuff that goes on every day, a routine I knew by heart. But his tune had angles, all of them slightly peculiar. One was, it had already been written, though it was never a hit and was almost forgotten, in the days when states were hot, under the title "Nevada." Another was, it had been written even before that, by a gent named Giuseppe Verdi, as part of the *Sicilian Vespers,* under the title "O Tu Palermo." Still another was, Art was really burned and seemed to have no idea where the thing had come from. They just can't get it, those big schmalzburgers like him, that what leaks out of their head might, just once, have leaked in. But the twist, the reason I had to come and couldn't just play it for laughs, was: Art could have been right. Maybe the lift *was* from him, not from the original opera, or from the first theft, "Nevada." It's a natural for a three quarters beat, and that's how Art had been playing it. So if that's how they were doing it here, instead of with "Nevada" 's four fourths, which followed the Verdi signature, there might still be plenty of work for the lawyers Art had put on it, with screams, same like to me.

Silly, almost.

Spooky.

But maybe, just possibly, moola.

So Jack, this boss character, by now had smelled something fishy and suddenly took a powder, to the stand where the fiddles were parked, as of course the boys weren't there yet, and came back with a Spanish guitar. I took it, thanked him, and tuned. To kind of work it around in the direction of Art's little problem, and at the same time make like there was nothing at all to conceal, I said I'd come on account of his band, to catch it during the broadcast, as I'd heard it was pretty good. He didn't react, which left me nowhere, but I thought it well to get going.

I played him "Night and Day," no Segovia job, but plenty good, for free. On "day and night," where it really opens up, I knew things to do, and talk suddenly stopped among the scattering of people that were in there. When I finished there was some little clapping, but still he didn't react, and I gave thought to mayhem. But then a buzzer sounded, and he took another powder, out toward the rear this time, where she had disappeared. I began a little beguine, but he was back. He bowed, picked up his V, bowed again, said: "Mr. Cameron, the guitar did it. She heard you, and you're in."

"Will you set me up for two?"

"Hold on, there's a catch."

He said until midnight, when one of his men would take over, she was checking his orders. "That means she handles the money, and if she's not there, I could just as well close down. You're invited back with her, but she can't come out with you."

"Oh. Fine."

"Sir, you asked for it."

It wasn't quite the way I'd have picked to do it, but the main thing was the girl, and I followed him through the OUT door, the one his waiters were using, still with my Spanish guitar. But then, all of a sudden, I loved it and felt even nearer to her.

This was the works of the joint, with a little office at one side, service bar on the other, range rear and center, the crew in white all around, getting the late stuff ready. But high on a stool, off by herself, on a little railed-in platform where waiters would have to pass, she was waving at me, treating it all as a joke. She called down: "Isn't this a balcony scene for you? You have to play me some music!"

I whapped into it quick, and when I told her it was *Romeo and Juliet*, she said it was just what she'd wanted. By then Jack had a stool he put next to hers, so I could sit beside her, back of her little desk. He introduced us, and it turned out her name was Stark. I climbed up and there we were, out in the middle of the air and yet in a way private, as the crew played it funny, to the extent they played it at all but mostly were too busy even to look. I put the guitar on the desk and kept on with the music. By the time I'd done some *Showboat* she was calling me Bill and to me she was Lydia. I remarked on her eyes, which were green and showed up bright against her creamy skin and ashy blond hair. She remarked on mine, which are light, watery blue, and I wished I was something besides tall, thin, and red-haired. But it was kind of cute when she gave a little pinch and nipped one of my freckles, on my hand back of the thumb.

Then Jack was back, with Champagne iced in a bucket, which I hadn't ordered. When I remembered my drink, the one I *had* ordered, he said scotch was no good, and this would be on him. I thanked him, but after he'd opened and poured, and I'd leaned the guitar in a corner and raised my glass to her, I said: "What's made him so friendly?"

"Oh, Jack's always friendly."

"Not to me. Oh, no."

"He may have thought I had it coming. Some little thing to cheer me. My last night in the place."

"You going away?"

"M'm-h'm."

"When?"

"Tonight."

"That why you're off at twelve?"

"Jack tell you that?"

"He told me quite a lot."

"Plane leaves at one. Bag's gone already. It's at the airport, all checked and ready to be weighed."

She clinked her glass to mine, took a little sip, and drew a deep, trembly breath. As for me, I felt downright sick, just why I couldn't say, as it had to all be strictly allegro, with nobody taking it serious. It stuck in my throat a little when I said: "Well—happy landings. Is it permitted to ask which way the plane is taking you?"

"Home."

"And where's that?"

"It's—not important."

"The West, I know that much?"

"What else did Jack tell you?"

I took it, improvised, and made up a little stuff, about her high-toned friends, her being a society brat, spoiled as all get-out, and the heavy dough she was used to—a light rib, as I thought. But it hadn't gone very far when I saw it was missing bad. When I cut it off, she took it. She said: "Some of that's true, in a way. I was—fortunate, we'll call it. But—you still have no idea have you, Bill, what I really am?"

"I've been playing by ear."

"I wonder if you want to know?"

"If you don't want to, I'd rather you didn't say."

None of it was turning out quite as I wanted, and I guess maybe I showed it. She studied me a little and asked: "The silver I wear, that didn't tell you anything? Or my giving you change for your dollar? It didn't mean anything to you that a girl would run a straight game?"

"She's not human."

"It means she's a gambler."

And then: "Bill, does that shock you?"

"No, not at all."

"I'm not ashamed of it. Out home, it's legal. You know where that is now?"

"Oh! *Oh!*"

"Why oh? And *oh?*"

"Nothing. It's—Nevada, isn't it?"

"Something wrong with Nevada?"

"No! I just woke up, that's all."

I guess that's what I said, but whatever it was, she could hardly miss the upbeat in my voice. Because, of course, that wrapped it all up pretty, not only the tune, which the band would naturally play for her, but her too, and who she was. Society dame, to tell the truth, hadn't pleased me much, and maybe that was one reason my rib was slightly off key. But gambler I could go for, a little cold, a little dangerous, a little brave. When she was sure I had really bought it, we were close again, and after a nip on the freckle her fingers slid over my hand. She said play her "Smoke"—the smoke she had in her eyes. But I didn't, and we just sat there some little time.

And then, a little bit at a time, she began to spill it: "Bill, it was just plain cockeyed. I worked in a club, the Paddock, in Reno, a regular institution. Tony Rocco—Rock—owned it, and was the squarest bookie ever—why he was a senator, a civic, and everything. And I worked for him, running his wires, practically being his manager, with a beautiful salary, a bonus at Christmas, and everything. And then wham, it struck. This federal thing. This ten percent tax on gross. And we were out of business. It just didn't make sense. Everything else was exempted. Wheels and boards and slots, whatever you could think of, but us. Us and the numbers racket, in Harlem and Florida and Washington."

"Take it easy."

"That's right, Bill. Thanks."

"Have some wine."

". . . Rock, of course, was fixed. He had property, and for the building, where the Paddock was, he got two hundred fifty thousand—or so I heard. But then came the tip on Maryland."

That crossed me up, and instead of switching her off, I asked her what she meant. She said: "That Maryland would legalize wheels."

"What do you smoke in Nevada?"

"Oh, I didn't believe it. And Rock didn't. But Mrs. Rock went nuts about it. Oh well, she had a reason."

"Dark, handsome reason?"

"I don't want to talk about it, but that reason took the Rocks for a ride, for every cent they got for the place, and tried to take me too, for other things besides money. When they went off to Italy, they thought they had it fixed; he was to keep me at my salary, in case Maryland *would* legalize, and if not, to send me home, with severance pay, as it's called. And instead of that—"

"I'm listening."

"I've said too much."

"What's this guy to you?"

"Nothing! I never even saw him until the three of us stepped off the plane—with our hopes. In a way it seemed reasonable. Maryland has tracks, and they help with the taxes. Why not wheels?"

"And *who* is this guy?"

"I'd be ashamed to say, but I'll say this much: I won't be a kept floozy. I don't care who he thinks he is, or—"

She bit her lip, started to cry, and really shut up then. To switch off, I asked why she was working for Jack, and she said: "Why not? You can't go home in a barrel. But he's been swell to me."

Saying people were swell seemed to be what she liked, and she calmed down, letting her hand stay when I pressed it in both of mine. Then we were really close, and I meditated if we were close enough that I'd be warranted in laying it on the line, she should let that plane fly away and not go to Nevada at all. But while I was working on that, business was picking up, with waiters stopping by to let her look at their trays, and I hadn't much chance to say it, whatever I wanted to say. Then, through the IN door, a waiter came through with a tray that had a wine bottle on it. A guy followed him in, a little noisy guy, who said the bottle was full and grabbed it off the tray. He had hardly gone out again when Jack was in the door, watching him as he staggered back to the table. The waiter swore the bottle was empty, but all Jack did was nod.

Then Jack came over to her, took another little peep through the window in the OUT door, which was just under her balcony, and said: "Lydia, what did you make of him?"

"Why—he's drunk, that's all."

"You notice him, Mr. Cameron?"

"No—except it crossed my mind he wasn't as tight as the act he was putting on."

"Just what crossed *my* mind! How could he get that drunk on a split of Napa red? What did he want back here?"

By now the waiter had gone out on the floor and come back, saying the guy wanted his check. But as he started to shuffle it out of the bunch he had tucked in his vest, Jack stopped him and said: "He don't get any check—not till I give the word. Tell Joe I said stand by and see he don't get out. *Move!*"

The waiter had looked kind of blank but hustled out as told, and then Jack looked at her. He said: "Lady, I'll be back. I'm taking a look around."

He went, and she drew another of her long, trembly

breaths. I cut my eye around, but no one had noticed a thing, and yet it seemed kind of funny they'd all be slicing bread, wiping glass, or fixing cocktail setups, with Jack mumbling it low out of the side of his mouth. I had a creepy feeling of things going on, and my mind took it a little, fitting it together, what she had said about the bag checked at the airport, the guy trying to make her, and most of all the way Jack had acted the second she showed with her cigarettes, shooing her off the floor, getting her out of sight. She kept staring through the window, at the drunk where he sat with his bottle, and seemed to ease when a captain I took to be Joe planted himself pretty solid in a spot that would block off a run-out.

Then Jack was back, marching around, snapping his fingers, giving orders for the night. But as he passed the back door, I noticed his hand touched the lock, as though putting the catch on. He started back to the floor but stopped as he passed her desk, and shot it quick in a whisper: "He's out there, Lydia, parked in back. This drunk, like I thought, is a finger he sent in to spot you, but he won't be getting out till you're gone. You're leaving for the airport right now."

"Will you call me a cab, Jack?"

"Cab? I'm taking you."

He stepped near me and whispered: "Mr. Cameron, I'm sorry, this little lady has to leave for—"

"I know about that."

"She's in danger—"

"I've also caught on to that."

"From a no-good imitation goon that's been trying to get to her here, which is why I'm shipping her out. I hate to break this up, but if you'll ride with us, Mr. Cameron—"

"I'll follow you down."

"That's right, you have your car. It's Friendship Airport, just down the road."

He told her to get ready while he was having his car brought up and the boy who would take her place on the desk was changing his clothes. Step on it, he said, but wait until he came back. He went out on the floor and marched past the drunk without even turning his head. But she sat watching me. She said: "You're not coming, are you?"

"Friendship's a little cold."

"But not mine, Bill, no."

She got off her stool, stood near me and touched my hair. She said: "Ships that pass in the night pass so close, so close." And then: "I'm ashamed, Bill, I'd have to go for this reason. I wonder, for the first time, if gamblings's really much good." She pulled the chain of the light, so we were half in the dark. Then she kissed me. She said: "God bless and keep you, Bill."

"And you, Lydia."

I felt her tears on my cheek, and then she pulled away and stepped to the little office, where she began putting a coat on and tying a scarf on her head. She looked so pretty it came to me I still hadn't given her the one little bouquet I'd been saving for the last. I picked up the guitar and started "Nevada."

She wheeled, but what stared at me were eyes as hard as glass. I was so startled I stopped, but she kept right on staring. Outside a car door slammed, and she listened at the window beside her. Then at last she looked away, to peep through the venetian blind. Jack popped in, wearing his coat and hat, and motioned her to hurry. But he caught something and said, low yet so I could hear him: "Lydia! What's the matter?"

She stalked over to me, with him following along, pointed her finger, and then didn't say it but spat it: "He's the finger— that's what's the matter, that's all. He played "Nevada," as though we hadn't had enough trouble with it already. And Vanny heard it. He hopped out of his car and he's under the window right now."

"Then OK, let's go."

I was a little too burned to make with the explanations and took my time, parking the guitar, sliding off, and climbing down, to give them a chance to blow. But she still had something to say, and to me, not to him. She pushed her face up to mine, and mocking how I had spoken, yipped: "Oh! . . . *Oh!*

OH!" Then she went, with Jack. Then I went, clumping after.

Then it broke wide open.

The drunk, who was supposed to sit there, conveniently boxed in while she went slipping out, turned out more of a hog-calling type, and instead of playing his part jumped up and yelled: "Vanny! *Vanny!* Here she comes! She's leaving! VANNY!"

He kept it up while women screamed all over, then pulled a gun from his pocket and let go at the ceiling, so it sounded like the field artillery, as shots always do when fired inside a room. Jack jumped for him and hit the deck as his feet shot from under him on the slippery wood of the dance floor. Joe swung, missed, swung again, and landed, so Mr. Drunk went down. But when Joe scrambled for the gun, there came this voice through the smoke: "Hold it! As you were—and leave that gun alone."

Then hulking in came this short-necked, thick-shouldered thing, in homburg hat, double-breasted coat, and white muffler, one hand in his pocket, the other giving an imitation of a movie gangster. He said keep still and nobody would get hurt, but "I won't stand for tricks." He helped Jack up, asked how he'd been. Jack said: "Young man, let me tell you something—"

"How you been, I asked."

"Fine, Mr. Rocco."

"Any telling, Jack—I'll do it."

Then to her: "Lydia, how've *you* been?"

"That doesn't concern you."

The she burst out about what he had done to his mother, the gyp he'd handed his father, and his propositions to her, and I got it at last who this idiot was. He listened, but right in the middle of it he waved his hand toward me and asked: "Who's this guy?"

"Vanny, I think you know."

"Guy, are you the boyfriend?"

"If so I don't tell you."

I sounded tough, but my belly didn't feel that way. They had it some more, and he connected me with the tune and seemed to enjoy it a lot that it had told him where to find her, on the broadcast and here now tonight. But he kept creeping closer to where we were all lined up with the drunk stretched on the floor, the gun under his hand, and I suddenly felt the prickle that Vanny was really nuts and in a minute meant to kill her. It also crossed my mind that a guy who plays the guitar has a left hand made of steel, from squeezing down on the strings, and is a dead sure judge of distance to the last eighth of an inch. I prayed I could forget it, told myself I owed her nothing at all, that she'd turned on me cold with no good reason. I concentrated, to dismiss the thought entirely.

No soap.

I grabbed for my chord and got it.

I choked down on his hand, the one he held in his pocket, while hell broke loose in the place with women screaming, men running, and fists trying to help. I had the gun hand all right, but when I reached for the other he twisted, butted, and bit, and for that long I thought he'd get loose and that I was a gone pigeon. The gun barked, and a piledriver hit my leg. I went down. Another gun spoke and he went down beside me. Then there was Jack, the drunk's gun in his hand, stepping in close and firing again to make sure.

I blacked out.

I came to, and then she was there, a knife in her hand, ripping the cloth away from the outside of my leg, grabbing napkins, stanching blood, while somewhere ten miles off I could hear Jack's voice as he yelled into a phone. On the floor right beside me was something under a tablecloth.

That went on for some time, with Joe calming things down and some people sliding out. The band came in, and I heard a boy ask for his guitar. Somebody brought it to him. And then, at last, came the screech of sirens, and she whispered some thanks to God.

Then, while the cops were catching up, with me, with Jack, and what was under the cloth, we both went kind of haywire, me laughing, she crying, and both in each other's arms. I said: "Lydia, Lydia, you're not taking that plane. They legalize things in Maryland, one thing specially, except that instead of wheels they generally use a ring."

Still holding my leg with one hand she pulled me close with the other, kissed me and kept on kissing me, and couldn't speak at all. All legalized now, is what I started to tell about—with Jack as best man, naturally.

One of the most famous and honored of American playwrights, Arthur Miller is especially noted for his probing analyses of family relations, as in his autobiographical All My Sons *and* Death of a Salesman. *The production of the latter in 1947 made his reputation, and its brilliance has somewhat overshadowed such other fine and important plays as* The Crucible (1955), *an attack on the methods of Senator Joseph McCarthy;* A View from the Bridge, *which won the New York Drama Critics Circle Award and the Pulitzer Prize in 1953; and* Incident at Vichy (1964), *which deals with anti-Semitism. Once married to actress Marilyn Monroe, Miller wrote the screenplay for her last film,* The Misfits, *basing it on his 1957* Esquire *story of the same title. Others of his too-little-known short stories can be found in the collection* I Don't Need You Any More (1968).

IT TAKES A THIEF
Arthur MilleR

Some people are laughing in our neighborhood these nights, but most of us are just waiting, like the Sheltons. It is simply unbelievable, it came out so right.

Here is this man, Mr. Shelton, a middle-aged man with what they call a nice family and a nice home. Ordinary kind of businessman, tired every night, sits around on Sundays, pinochle and so on. The point is, he's been doing all right the past few years. Automobiles. His used cars were shipped to California, Florida—wherever the war plants were springing up. Did fine. Then the war ended. The new cars started coming through and then the strikes made them scarce. But people wanted them very badly. Very, very badly. He did fine. Very, very fine.

One night not long ago he and his wife decided to take in a nightclub, and she put on her two diamond rings, the bracelet, and some of her other frozen cash, and they locked up the house—the children are all married and don't live home any-more—and they were off for a trip to the city.

Nobody knows what they did in the city, but they stayed out till three in the morning. Late enough for Shelton to get a headful. The drive home was slow and careful because the car was one of his brand-new ones and he couldn't see well in his condition. Nevertheless, when he put the key in the front-door lock he was able to notice that the door swung open at a touch, whereas it usually took some jiggling of the latch. They went in and turned on the living-room lights, and then they saw it.

The drawer of the desk was lying on the floor, and the rug was littered with check stubs and stationery. The Sheltons rushed into the dining room and saw at once that the sterling-silver service was gone from the massive serving table. Shelton clutched at his heart as though he were going to suffocate, and Mrs. Shelton thrust her fingers into her hair and screamed. At this stage, of course, there was only the sensation that an alien presence had passed through their home. Perhaps they even imagined that the thief was still there. In wild fright they ran to the stairs and up to their bedroom, and Shelton tripped and fell over a bureau drawer that the thief had left on the threshold. Mrs. Shelton helped him up and made him lie down on the colonial bed and she massaged his heart while they both looked anxiously toward the closet door, which stood open.

When he had caught his breath, he pushed her aside and went into the closet and turned on the light. She crowded in beside him as soon as she saw the terrible expression on his face. The safe. The little steel safe that had always stood in the corner of the closet covered with dress boxes and old clothes, the safe was looking up at them from the corner with its door open. Shelton simply stood there panting. It was Mrs. Shelton who got to her knees and felt inside.

Nothing. Nothing was left. The safe was empty. Mrs. Shelton, on her knees in the closet, screamed again. Perhaps they felt once more the presence, the terrifying presence of the thief, for they rushed one behind the other down the stairs, and Shelton picked up the telephone.

The instrument shook in his hand as he bent over close to the dial and spun it around. Mrs. Shelton moved up and down beside him, clasping and unclasping her hands and weeping. "Oh, my God!"

"Police!" Shelton roared into the telephone as soon as he heard the operator's calm voice. "My house has been robbed. We just got home and—"

His voice caught Mrs. Shelton just as she was about to dig her fingers into her hair again. For an instant she stood perfectly still, then she turned suddenly and swung her arm out and clapped her hand over Shelton's mouth. Infuriated, he attempted to knock her hand away. Then his eyes met hers. They stood that way, looking into each other's eyes; and then Shelton's hand began to shake violently and he dropped the telephone with a loud bang onto the marble tabletop and collapsed into a high-backed, Italian-type chair. Mrs. Shelton replaced the telephone on its cradle as the operator's anxious voice flowed out of it.

They were both too frightened to speak for a few minutes. The same thing was rushing through their heads and there was no need to say what it was. Only a solution was needed, and neither of them could find it. At last Mrs. Shelton said, "You didn't give the operator the name or address. Maybe—"

"We'll see," he said, and went into the living room and stretched out on the couch.

Mrs. Shelton went to the front windows and drew the shades. Then she came back to the couch and proceeded to walk up and down beside it, her breasts rising and falling with the heavy rhythm of her breathing.

Nothing happened for nearly an hour. They even made a pass at undressing, just as though he had not shouted frantically into the telephone that his house had been robbed. But they were hardly out of their clothes when the doorbell rang. In dressing gown and slippers Shelton went down the stairs with his wife behind him. In the presence of strangers he always knew how to look calm, so much so that when he opened the door and let the two policemen in, he appeared almost sleepy.

The question of his having hung up without giving his name was cleared away first: He had been too excited to give the detail to the operator. The officers then went about inspecting the premises. That completed, Shelton and his wife sat in the living room with them and gave a detailed description of the seven pieces of jewelry that had been taken from the safe, and the silver service, and the old Persian lamb coat, and the other items, all of which were noted in a black-covered pad that one policeman wrote in. When Shelton had closed the door behind the two officers, he stood thinking for a while, and his wife waited for his word. Finally he said, "We'll report the jewelry to the insurance company tomorrow."

"What about the money?"

"How can I mention the money?"

She knew there was no answer to that one, but it was hard, nevertheless, to give up $91,000 without a complaint.

In bed they lay without moving. Thinking. "What'll we do," she asked, "if they find the crook and he's still got the money?"

A long time later, Shelton said, "They never catch thieves."

Eight days passed, in fact, before Shelton's opinion was proved wrong. The telephone rang at dinnertime. He covered the mouthpiece with his palm and turned to his wife. "They want me to come down and identify the stuff." There was a quavering note in his voice.

"What about the money?" she whispered.

"They didn't mention the money," he said, questioning her with his eyes.

"Maybe tell them you're too sick to go now."

"I'll have to go sometime."

"Try to find out first if they found the money."

"I can't *ask* them, can I?" he said angrily, and turned again to the telephone and said he would be right over.

He drove slowly. The new, purring engine, the $1,900 car for which he could easily get $4,000 cash carried him effortlessly toward the police station. He drove slumped in the seat. As though to rehearse, he kept repeating the same sentence in his mind: I am simply a dealer, I am simply a dealer; I keep that much cash on hand to buy cars with. It sounded all right, businesslike. But was it possible they were that dumb? Maybe. They were just plain cops. Plain cops might not realize that $91,000 was too much to have in a safe for that purpose. And still, it was possible they would not stumble on the truth at all, not know that cash in a home safe was probably not entered on any ledger or income-tax form. Cops did not know much about big money, he felt. And yet—$91,000. Oh, $91,000! His insides grew cool at the thought of it. Not $20,000 or $40,000, not even $75,000, but $91,000. His retirement, his whole future ease, his very sureness of gait lay entirely in that money. It had become a tingling sensation for him, a smell, a feeling, a taste—$91,000 cash money in his safe at home. He had even stopped bothering to read the papers in the past year. Nothing that happened in the world could touch him while he had $91,000 in his closet.

There were three policemen sitting in the room when he entered. He identified himself, and they asked him to sit down. One of them went out. The remaining two were in shirt-sleeves and seemed to be merely waiting around. In a little while a gray-haired man entered, followed by a detective who carried a cheap canvas zipper bag which he set on a desk near the door. The detective introduced himself to Shelton, and asked him to repeat his description of the jewelry. Shelton did so in some detail, answering more specific questions as they occurred to the detective.

The gray-haired man had slumped into a chair. Now he sat staring at the floor. Shelton slowly realized, as he described the jewelry, that this was the thief; for the man seemed resigned, very tired, and completely at home in the situation.

The detective went at last to the desk and opened the zipper bag and laid out the jewelry for Shelton to inspect. Shelton glanced at it and said it was his, picking up a wedding ring which had his name and his wife's engraved on the inside.

"We'll have the coat for you by tomorrow and maybe the

silver, too," the detective said, idly arranging the jewelry in a pattern on the desk as he spoke. Shelton felt that the detective was getting at something from the way he played with the jewelry. The detective completed the pattern on the desk and then turned his broad, dark face toward Shelton and said, "Is there anything else you lost?"

Shelton's hand, of its own accord, moved toward his heart as he said, "That's all I can remember."

The detective turned his whole body now and sat easily on the edge of the desk. "You didn't lose any money?"

The gray-haired thief raised his head, a mystified look clouding his face.

"Money?" asked Shelton. And yet he could not help adding, "What money?" Just curiously.

"We found this on him," the detective said, reaching into the bag and taking out five rolled-up wads of money wrapped in red rubber bands. Shelton's heart hurt him when he saw the rubber bands, because they, more than any of the other items, were peculiarly his. They were the rubber bands he always used in his office.

"There's ninety-one thousand dollars here," the detective said.

The thief was looking up at Shelton from his chair, an expression of wounded bewilderment drawing his brows together. The detective merely sat on the desk, an observer; the moment suddenly belonged only to Shelton and the thief.

Shelton stared at the money without any expression on his face. It was too late to think fast; he had no idea what sort of mind this stolid detective had, and he dared not hesitate long enough to sound the man out. A detective, Shelton knew, is higher than a cop; is more like a businessman, knows more. This one looks smart, and yet maybe . . .

Shelton broke into a smile and touched one of the wads of bills that lay on the desk. (Oh, the $91,000; oh, the touch of it!) Sweat was running down his back; his heart pained like a wound. He smiled and stalled for time. "That's a lot of money," he said softly, frantically studying the detective's eyes for a sign.

But the detective was impassive and said, "Is it yours?"

"Mine?" Shelton said, with a weak laugh. Longingly he looked at the solid wads. "I wish it were, but it isn't. I don't keep ninety-one thou—"

The thief, a tall man, stood up quickly and pointed to the money. "What the hell is *this?*" he shouted, amazed.

The detective moved toward him, and he sat down again. "It's his. I took it out of the safe with the other stuff."

"Take it easy," the detective said.

"Where did I get it, then?" the thief demanded in a more frightened tone. "What're you trying to do, pin another job on me? I only pulled one, that's all! You asked me and I told you." And, pointing directly up at Shelton's face, he said, "He's pullin' something!"

The detective, as he turned to Shelton, was an agonizingly expressionless man who seemed to have neither pulse nor point of view. He simply stood there, the law with two little black eyes. "You're sure," he said, "that this is not your money?"

"I ought to know," Shelton said, laughing calmly.

The detective seemed to catch the absurdity of it, and very nearly smiled. Then he turned to the thief and, with a nod of his head, motioned him outside. The two policemen walked out behind him.

They were alone. The detective, without a word, returned to the desk and put the jewelry back into the zipper bag. Without turning his head, he said that they would return the stuff to Shelton in the morning. And then he picked up one of the heavy wads, but instead of dropping it into the bag he hefted it thoughtfully in his palm and turned his head to Shelton. "Lot of dough," he said.

"I'll say," Shelton agreed.

The detective continued placing the wads in the bag. Shelton stood a little behind him and to one side, watching as best he could for the slightest change in the man's expression. But there was none; the detective might have been asleep but for his open eyes. Shelton wanted to leave—immediately. It was impossible to know what was happening in the detective's head.

And yet Shelton dared not indicate his desperation. He smiled again, and shifted his weight easily to one foot and started to button his coat, and said—as if the question were quite academic—"What do you fellas do with money like that?"

The detective zipped the bag shut. "Money like what?" he asked evenly.

A twinge of pain shot through Shelton's chest at the suspicious reserve in the detective's question. "I mean, money that's not claimed," he amended.

The detective walked past him toward the door. "We wait," he said, and opened the door.

"I mean, supposing it's never claimed?" Shelton asked, following him, still smiling as though with idle curiosity.

"Hot money is never claimed," the detective said. "We'll just wait. Then we'll start looking around."

"I see."

Shelton walked with the detective to the door of the precinct station, and he even talked amiably, and then they said a pleasant good night.

Staring at the pavement rolling under the wheels of his car, he could summon neither feeling nor thought. It was only when he opened the door of his house, the house that had once contained the fortune of his life, that his numbness flowed away, and he felt weak and ill.

"There must be a way to get it back," she began.

"How?"

"You mean to tell me—?"

"I mean to tell you!" he shouted, and got to his feet. "What'll I do, break into the station house?"

But they've got laws against robbery!"

In reply, Shelton pulled his collar open and climbed the stairs and went to bed.

These days, Shelton rides to business very slowly. The few friends he has on the block have grown accustomed to the gray and haunted stare in his eyes. The children seem to quiet down as he guides his car through their street games.

Sometimes he goes by the police station, and passing it he slows down and peers through the car window at it, but he always continues on.

And when a police car rolls into the block on its ordinary tour, people can be seen stopping to watch until it passes his house. Nobody has said anything, of course, but we are waiting with Shelton for that awful moment when the white coupé pulls up at his door. And it must, of course.

Thirty days, maybe two months from now, it will turn the corner and slow down, and gradually, ominously, come to a stop.

The house is very quiet these nights—almost silent. The shades are drawn, and it is seldom that you see anyone going in or out. The Sheltons are waiting.

"Murder on the Waterfront" has the same background—"the violent, vivid, restless, corrupted" New York waterfront of the early fifties—as On the Waterfront, *the classic 1954 film starring Marlon Brando and Rod Steiger for which Budd Schulberg wrote the Academy Award-winning screenplay. As both the film and this story attest, Schulberg is a writer with a strong social sensibility. (Among his other achievements, he was a founder of the Watts Writers Workshop, an institution dedicated to helping young black writers.) His career began with a screenplay coauthored with F. Scott Fitzgerald for the 1939 film* Winter Carnival; *but it was his 1941 novel,* What Makes Sammy Run, *that brought him his first major recognition. Among his other works is* The Harder They Fall *(1947), a devastating indictment of corruption in boxing that was filmed in 1955 with Humphrey Bogart in one of his last roles.*

MURDER ON THE WATERFRONT
Budd SchulberG

The alarm was about to ring when Matt Gillis reached out his bearlike, heavy-muscled arm and shut it off. Habit. Half-past six. Summer with the light streaming in around the patched window shades, and winter when half-past six was black as midnight. Matt stretched his heavyweight, muscular body and groaned. Habit woke you up at half-past six every morning, but habit didn't make you like it—not on these raw winter mornings when the wind blew in from the sea, whipping along the waterfront with an intensity it seemed to reserve for longshoremen. He shivered in anticipation.

Matt listened to the wind howling through the narrow canyon of Eleventh Street and thought to himself: another day, another icy-fingered, stinking day. He pushed one foot from under the covers to test the temperature, and then quickly withdrew it into the warmth of the double bed again. Cold.

295

Damn that janitor, Lacey—the one they all called Rudolph because of his perpetually red nose. Never enough heat in the place. Well, the landlord was probably saying, what do they expect for twenty-five a month?

Matt rolled over heavily, ready for the move into his work clothes.

"Matt?" his wife Franny murmured, feeling for him drowsily in the dark. "I'll get up; fix you some coffee."

"It's all right." His buxom Fran. Matt patted her. Her plump-pretty Irish face was still swollen with sleep. For a moment he remembered her as she had been fifteen years ago: the prettiest kid in the neighborhood—bright, flirty, sky-blue eyes and a pug nose, a little bit of a girl smothered in Matt's big arms, a child in the arms of a grizzly. Now she was plump all over, something like him on a smaller, softer scale, as if she had had to grow along his lines to keep him company.

"Matt, you don't mind me gettin' fat?" she had whispered to him one night in the wide, metal-frame bed after the kids finally had fallen asleep.

"Naw, you're still the best-lookin' woman in the neighborhood," Matt had said gallantly.

"At least you can always find me in the dark," Fran had giggled. They had got to laughing then, until Fran had to stop him because everything Matt did, he did big—laugh, fight, eat, drink, tell off the mob in the union. Even when he thought he was talking normally, he shouted, he bellowed, so when he had chuckled there in the bed, the children—Tom and Mickey and Kate and Johnny and Peggy, the five they had had so far—had stirred in their beds and Fran had said, "Shhh, if the baby wakes up you'll be walkin' the floor with her."

Matt swung his long legs out of the bed and felt the cold touch of the linoleum. He sat there a moment in his long underwear, thinking—he wasn't sure of what; the day ahead, the days of his youth, the time his old man came home from the pier with three fingers off his right hand (copper sheeting—cut off at the knuckle nice and clean), and all those years the old man battled for his compensation. It was all the old man could talk about, finally, and got to be a joke—never to Pop, but to Matt and his brothers when they were big enough to support him.

Big Matt sat there on the edge of the bed rubbing sleep out of his eyes, thinking, thinking, while his wife, warm and sweet and full in her nightgown, half rose behind him and whispered, "Coffee? Let me get up and make you a cup of coffee." She wanted to say more; she wanted to say, "Look, Matt honey, I know what it is to go down there to the shape-up when the sun is still climbing up the backs of the buildings. I know what it is for you to stand there with three-four hundred other men and have the hiring boss, Fisheye Moran, look you over like you was so much meat in a butcher shop. I know what it is for you to go to work every morning like you had a job—only you haven't got a job unless Fisheye, the three-time loser put there by the Village mob, hands you a brass check." She wanted to say, "Yes, and I know what it is for you to be left standing in the street; I know what you feel when the hiring boss looks through you with those pale blue fisheyes that give him his name." *That's all today, come back tomorra.*

Matt was on his feet now, a burly bear in his long underwear, stretching and groaning to push himself awake. Fran started to get up, but he put his big hand on her shoulder and pushed her back into the warm bed. Well, all right. She was glad to give in. When could a body rest except these precious few minutes in the early morning? "You be careful now, Matt. You be careful. Don't get in no trouble."

Fran knew her Matt, the Irish-thick rebel of Local 474, one of the lionhearted—or foolhardy—handful who dared speak up against the Lippy Keegan mob, which had the longshore local in their pocket, and the loading racket, the lunch-hour gambling, and all the other sidelines that bring in a quick dollar on the docks. Lippy and his goons ran the neighborhood like storm troopers, and longshoremen who knew what was good for them went along with Keegan's boys and took what they could get. Matt was always trying to get others to back him up, but the fear was too deep. "Matt, I got me wife and kids to think about; leave me alone," they'd say, and push their thirty cents across the bar for another whiskey.

Matt tried to make as little noise as possible as he went down the creaky stairway. He closed the tenement door behind him and stood a moment in the clammy morning, feeling the weather. He zipped up his windbreaker and pulled his old cap down on his forehead. Then he drew his head down into the heavy collar, threw out his chest, and turned his face into the wind. It was a big, strong-boned, beefy face, with a heavy jaw and a broken nose, a face that had taken plenty. Over the years the Keegan boys had developed a begrudging respect for Matt. They had hit him with everything and he still kept coming on. The gift of getting up—that's what they called it on the waterfront.

Matt ducked into the Longdock Bar & Grill on the corner across the street from the pier. It was full of longshoremen grabbing a cup of coffee and maybe some ham and eggs before drifting over to the shape-up. There were men of all sizes and ages, with weatherbeaten faces like Matt's, many of them with flattened noses, trophies of battles on the docks and in the barrooms; here and there were ex-pugs with big-time memories: the cheers of friends and five hundred dollars for an eight-rounder. Threading through the dock workers was a busy little man whose name was Billy Morgan, though everybody called him "J.P." because he was the moneylender for the mob. If you didn't work, J.P. was happy to lend you a deuce or half a bill, at 10 percent a week. If you fell too far behind, J.P. whispered to Fisheye, and Fisheye threw you a couple of days' work until the loan was paid off. They had you coming and going, the mob. Matt looked at J.P. and turned away.

Over in the corner were a couple of Lippy's pistols, Specs Sinclair, a mild-looking, pasty-skinned man who didn't look like an enforcer but had maybe a dozen stiffs to his credit, and Feets McKenna, a squat muscle man who could rough-and-tumble with the best. Feets was sergeant-at-arms for the local. Specs, for whom signing his name was a lot of writing, was recording secretary. Matt looked straight at them to show he wasn't backing away, ever. Union officials. Only three-time losers need apply.

Matt pushed his way into the group at the short-order counter. They were men dressed like himself, in old trousers and flannel shirts, with old caps worn slightly askew in the old-country way. They all knew Matt and respected the way he stood up; but a stand-up guy, as they called him, was nobody you wanted to get close to. Not if you wanted to work and stay in one piece in Lippy Keegan's sector of the harbor.

Matt was waiting for his coffee when he felt a fist smash painfully into his side. He winced and started an automatic counter at whoever it was, and then he looked down and grinned. He should have known. It was Runt Nolan, whose hundred ring battles and twenty-five years of brawling on the docks were stamped into his flattened face. But a life of beatings had failed to deaden the twinkle in his eyes. Runt Nolan was always seeing the funny side, even when he was looking down the business end of a triggerboy's .38. Where other longshoremen turned away in fear from Lippy's pistoleros, Runt always seemed to take a perverse delight in baiting them. Sometimes they laughed him off and sometimes, if he went on provoking them—and longshoremen were watching to see if Runt could get away with it—they would oblige him with a blackjack or a piece of pipe. Runt had a head like a rock and more lives than a pair of cats, and the stories of his miraculous recoveries from these beatings had become a riverfront legend.

Once they had left him around the corner in the alley lying facedown in his own blood, after enough blows on the noggin to crack the skull of a horse; and an hour later, when everyone figured he was on his way to the morgue, damned if he didn't stagger back into the Longdock and pound the bar for whiskey. "I should worry what they do to me, I'm on borried time," Runt Nolan liked to say.

Runt grinned when he saw Matt rub his side with mock resentment. "Mornin', Matt me lad, just wanted t' see if you was in condition."

"Don't be worryin' about my condition. One more like that and I'll stand you right on your head."

"Come on, you big blowhard, I'm ready for you." Runt fell into a fierce boxing stance and jabbed his small knuckle-broken left fist into Matt's face.

Matt got his coffee and a sinker and sat down at one of the small tables with Runt. Runt was rarely caught eating. He seemed to consider the need for solid food something of a disgrace, a sign of weakness. Whiskey and beer and maybe once a day a corned-beef sandwich—that was Runt's diet, and in the face of medical science it had kept him wiry and resilient at fifty-five.

"What kind of a boat we got today?" Matt asked. Runt lived in a two-dollar hotel above the Longdock Bar and he was usually up on his shipping news.

"Bananas," Runt said, drawing out the middle vowel in disgust.

"Bananas!" Matt groaned. Bananas meant plenty of shoulder work, toting the heavy stalks out of the hold. A banana carrier was nothing less than a human pack mule. There was only one good thing about bananas: the men who worked steady could afford to lay off bananas, and so there was always a need for extra hands. The docker who had no *in* with the hiring boss, and even the fellow who was on the outs with the Keegan mob, stood a chance of picking up a day on bananas.

By the time Matt and Runt reached the pier, ten minutes before the seven-thirty whistle, there were already a couple of hundred men on hand, warming themselves around fires in metal barrels and shifting their feet to keep the numbness away. Some of them were hardworking men with families, professional longshoremen whose Ireland-born fathers had moved cargo before them. And some of them were only a peg above the bum, casuals who drifted in for a day now and then to keep themselves in drinking money. Some of them were big men with powerful chests, large, raw-faced men who looked like throwbacks to the days of bare-knuckle fights-to-a-finish. Some of them were surprisingly slight, wizen-faced men in castoff clothing, the human flotsam of the waterfront.

Fisheye came out of the pier, flanked by a couple of the boys, "Flash" Gordon and "Blackie" McCook. There were about three hundred longshoremen waiting for jobs now. Obediently they formed themselves into a large horseshoe so Fisheye could look them over. Meat in a butcher shop. The men Fisheye wanted were the ones who worked. You kicked back part of your day's pay to Fisheye or did favors for Lippy if you wanted to work regular. You didn't have to have a record, but a couple of years in a respectable pen didn't do you any harm.

"I need two hundred banana carriers." Fisheye's hoarse voice seemed to take its pitch from the foghorns that barked along the Hudson. Jobs for two hundred men at a coveted $2.27 an hour. The three, maybe four hundred men eyed one another in listless rivalry. "You—and you—Pete—OK, Slim . . ." Fisheye was screening the men with a cold, hard look. Nearly twenty years ago a broken-down dockworker had gone across the street from the shape-up. "No work?" the bartender had said, perfunctorily, and the old man had answered, "Nah, he just looked right through me with those blasted fisheyes of his." Fisheye—it had made the bartender laugh, and the name had stuck.

Anger felt cold and uncomfortable in Matt's stomach as he watched Fisheye pass out those precious tabs. He didn't mind seeing the older men go in, the ones he had shaped with for years, especially family men like himself. What gave him that hateful, icy feeling in his belly was seeing the young kids go ahead of him, new-generation hoodlums like the fresh-faced Skelly kid who boasted of the little muscle jobs he did for Lippy and the boys as his way of paying off for steady work. Young Skelly had big ideas, they said around the bar. One of these days he might be crowding Lippy himself. That's how it went down here. "Peaches" Maloney had been number one—Until Lippy dumped him into the gutter outside the Longdock. Matt had seen them come and go. And all the time he had stood up proud and hard while lesser men got the work tabs and the gravy.

Fisheye almost had his two hundred men now. He put his hand on Runt Nolan's shoulder. "All right, you little sawed-off rat, go on in. But remember I'm doin' ya a favor. One word out of line and I'll bounce ya off the ship."

Runt tightened his hands into fists, wanting to stand up and speak his mind. But a day was a day and he hadn't worked steady enough lately to keep himself in beers. He looked over at Matt with a helpless defiance and went on into the pier.

Matt waited, thinking about Fran and the kids. And he waited, thinking at Fisheye: It ain't right, it ain't right, a bum like you havin' all this power. He couldn't keep it out of his face. Fisheye flushed and glared back at him and picked men all around Matt to round out his two hundred. He shoved Matt's face in it by coming toward him as if he were going to pick him and then reaching over his shoulder for Will Murphy, a toothless old sauce hound whom Matt could outwork five for one. There never had been enough caution in Matt, and now he felt himself trembling with anger. He was grabbing Fisheye before he had time to think it out, holding the startled boss by the thick lapels of his windbreaker.

"Listen to me, you fatheaded bum. If you don't put me on today I'll break you in two. I got kids to feed. You hear me, Fisheye?"

Fisheye pulled himself away and looked around for help. Blackie and young Skelly moved in.

"OK, boys," Fisheye said, when he saw they were there. "I c'n handle this myself. This bigmouth is dumb, but he's not so dumb he wants to wind up in the river. Am I right, Matt me lad?"

In the river. A senseless body kicked off the stringpiece into the black and secretive river, while the city looked the other way. Cause of death: accidental drowning. Dozens and dozens of good men had been splashed into the dark river like so much garbage. Matt knew some of the widows who had stories to tell, if only someone would listen. In the river. Matt drew away from Fisheye. What was the use? Outnumbered and outgunned. But one of these days—went the dream—he and Runt would get some action in the local, some following; they'd call a real election and—

Behind Matt a big truck blasted its horn, ready to drive into the pier. Fisheye thumbed Matt to one side. "All right, get moving, you're blocking traffic, we got a ship to turn around." Matt spat into the gutter and walked away.

Back across the street in the Longdock, Matt sat with a beer in front of him, automatically watching the morning television: some good-looking, fast-talking dame selling something—yatta-ta yatta-ta yatta-ta. In the old days, at least you had peace and quiet in the Longdock until the boys with the work tabs came in for lunch. Matt walked up the riverfront to another gin mill and sat with another beer. Now and then a fellow like himself would drift in, on the outs with Lippy and open to Matt's arguments about getting up a petition to call an honest union election: about time we got the mob's foot off'n our necks; sure, they're tough, but if there's enough of us . . . it was the old dream of standing up like honest-to-God Americans instead of like oxen with rings in their noses.

Matt thought he was talking quiet but even his whisper had volume, and farther down the bar Feets and Specs were taking it in. They weren't frowning or threatening, but just looking, quietly drinking and taking it all in.

When Matt finished his beer and said see-ya-later, Specs and Feets rose dutifully and followed him out. A liner going downriver let out a blast that swallowed up all the other sounds in the harbor. Matt didn't hear them approach until Feets had a hand on his shoulder. Feets was built something like Matt, round and hard. Specs was slight and not much to look at. He wore very thick glasses. He had shot the wrong fellow once. Lippy had told him to go out and buy a new pair of glasses and warned him not to slip up that way again.

"What d'ya say, Matt?" Feets asked, and from his tone no one could have thought them anything but friends.

"Hello, Feets, Specs," Matt said.

"Listen, Matt, we'd like to talk to you a minute," Feets said.

"Then talk," Matt said. "As long as it's only talk, go ahead."

"Why do you want to give us so much trouble?" Specs said—any defiance of power mystified him. "You should straighten yourself out, Matt. You'd be working three-four days a week if you just learned to keep that big yap of yours shut."

"I didn't know you were so worried about whether I worked or not."

"Matt, don't be such a thickheaded mick," Feets argued. "Why be agitatin' alla time? You ain't gonna get anywheres, that's for sure. All ya do is louse yourself up with Lippy."

Matt said something short and harsh about Lippy. Feets and Specs looked pained, as if Matt were acting in bad taste.

"I wish you wouldn't say stuff like that," Specs said. His face got very white when he was ready for action. On the waterfront he had a reputation for enjoying the trigger squeezing. "You keep saying that stuff and we'll have to do something about it. You know how Lippy is."

Matt thought a moment about the danger of saying what he wanted to say: Fran and the kids home waiting for money he'd have to borrow from the moneylender. Why look for trouble? Why buck for the bottom of the river? Was it fair to Fran? Why couldn't he be like so many other longshoremen—like Flanagan, who had no love for Lippy Keegan but went along to keep food on the table? Lippy ran the piers just like he owned them. You didn't have to like Lippy, but it sure made life simpler if he liked you.

Matt thought about all this, but he couldn't help himself. He was a self-respecting man, and it galled him that a pushy racketeer—a graduate of the old Arsenal Mob—and a couple of punks could call themselves a union. I shouldn't say this, Matt was thinking, and he was already saying it:

"Yeah, I know how Lippy is. Lippy is gonna get the surprise of his stinkin' life one of these days. Lippy is gonna find
himself—"

"You dumb harp," Feets said. "You must like to get hit in
the head."

"There's lots I like better," Matt admitted. "But I sure as
hell won't back away from it."

Feets and Specs looked at each other and the glance said
clearly: What are you going to do with a thickhead like this?
They shrugged and walked away from Matt, back to their
places at the bar. Later in the day they would give Lippy a full
account and find out the next move. This Matt Gillis was giving
their boss a hard time. Everything would be lovely down here if
it wasn't for this handful of talk-back guys. They leaned on the
bar with a reassuring sense that they were on the side of peace
and stability, that Matt Gillis was asking for trouble.

Matt met Runt in the Longdock around five-thirty. Runt
was buying because he had the potatoes in his pocket. They
talked about this petition they were getting up to call a regular
meeting. Runt had been talking to a couple of old-timers in his
hatch gang who were half scared to death and half ready to go
along. And there were maybe half a dozen young fellows who
had young ideas and no use for the old ways of buying jobs from
Fisheye and coming on the double whenever Lippy whistled.
Another round or two and it was suppertime.

"Have another ball, Matt. The money's burnin' a hole in
me pocket."

"Thank, Runt, but I gotta get home. The wife'll be hittin'
me with a mop." This was a familiar, joking threat in the Gillis
domain.

Matt wiped his mouth with his sleeve and rubbed his
knuckles on Runt's head. "Now don't get in no arguments. You
watch yourself now." It was bad business, Matt knew, bucking
the mob and hitting the bottle at the same time. They could
push you into the drink some night and who was to say you
weren't dead drunk, just another "death by accidental drowning."

Matt was worried about Runt as he walked up the dark side street to his tenement. Runt took too many chances. Runt liked to say, "I had me fun and I drunk me fill. What've I got to lose?"

I better keep my eye on the little fella now that we're pushin' so hard for this up-and-up election, Matt was thinking, when he felt something solid whop him just behind the ear. The blow had force enough to drop a horse, but Matt half turned, made a club of his right hand and was ready to wield it when the something solid whopped him again at the back of his head. He thought it was the kid, the Skelly punk, there with Feets, but he wasn't sure. It was dark and his head was coming apart. In a bad dream something was swinging at him on the ground—hobnailed shoes, the finishing touch. Feets, they called him. The darkness closed in over him like a black tarpaulin. . . .

Everybody was talking at once and—was it time for him to get up and shape?—he was sprawled on the bed in his room. Go 'way, lemme sleep.

"Matt, listen, this is Doc Wolff." The small, lean-faced physician was being pushed and breathed on. "The rest of you go on, get out of here."

Half the tenement population was crowded into the Gillises' narrow flat. Mrs. Geraghty, who was always like that, took the kids up to eat at her place. Doc Wolff washed out the ugly wounds in Matt's scalp. Half the people in the neighborhood owed him money he would never see—or ask for. Some of the old-timers still owed his father, who insisted on practicing at seventy-five. Father and son had patched up plenty of wounds like these. They were specialists on blackjack, steel-pipe, and gun-butt contusions. Jews in an Irish district, they never took sides, verbally, in the endless guerrilla war between the dock mob and the "insoigents." All they could do, when a longshoreman got himself in a fix like this, was to overlook the bill. The Wolffs were still poor from too much overlooking.

"Is it serious, Doctor?"

"We'd better X-ray, to make sure it isn't a skull fracture. I'd like to keep him in St. Vincent's a couple of days."

It was no fracture, just a couple of six-inch gashes and a concussion—a neat professional job performed according to instructions. "Don't knock him out of the box for good. Just leave him so he'll have something to think about for a week or two."

On the second day Runt came up with a quart and the good news that the men on the dock were signing the petition. The topping of Matt had steamed them up, where Lippy had figured it would scare them off. Runt said he thought they had enough men, maybe a couple of dozen, to call a rank-and-file meeting.

Father Conley, a waterfront priest with savvy and guts, had offered the rectory library as a haven.

But that night Fran sat at the side of Matt's bed in the ward for a long talk-to. She had a plan. It had been on her mind for a long time. This was her moment to push it through. Her sister's husband worked for a storage company. The pay was good, the work was regular, and best of all there weren't any Lippy Keegans muscling you if you didn't play it their way. This brother-in-law said there was an opening for Matt. He could come in on a temporary basis and maybe work his way into regular union membership if he liked it. The brother-in-law had a little pull in that direction.

"Please, Matt, Please." It was Fran's domestic logic against his bulldog gift of fighting back. If he was a loner like Runt Nolan he could stand up to Lippy and Specs and Feets and young Skelly and the rest of that trash all he wanted. But was it fair to Fran and the kids to pass up a sure seventy-five dollars a week in order to go hungry and bloody on the piers?

"Why does it always have to be you that sticks his neck out? Next time it'll be worse. They'll . . ."

Yes, Matt knew. The river: Lippy Keegen's silent partner, the old North River, waiting for him in the dark.

"OK, Franny," Matt was saying under his bandages. "OK. Tell Denny"—that was the brother-in-law—"I'll take the job."

In the storage vaults it was nice and quiet. The men came right to work from their homes. There was none of that stopping in at the corner and shooting the breeze about ships coming in and where the jobs might be—no hit or miss. The men were different too: good steady workers who had been there for years, not looking for any excitement. It seemed funny to Matt not to be looking behind him to see if any of Lippy's boys were on his tail, funny to have money in his pockets without having to worry how he was going to pay it back to the loan sharks.

When Matt had been there three weeks, Fran went out and bought herself a new dress—the first new one in almost two years. And the following Sunday they went up to the park and had lunch at the cafeteria near the zoo—their first visit to a restaurant in Lord knows when. Fran put her hand in Matt's and said, "Oh, Matt, isn't this better? Isn't this how people are supposed to live?"

Matt said yeah, he guessed so. It was good to see Fran happy and relaxed, no longer worried about food on the table for the kids, or whether he'd get home in one piece. Only—he couldn't put it into words, but when he got back to work on the fifth floor of the huge storage building, he knew what was going to come over him.

And next day it did, stronger than at any time since he started. He wondered what Runt was doing, and Jocko and Bagles and Timmy and the rest of the gang in the Longdock. He hadn't been in since the first week he started at the storage. The fellows had all asked him how he was feeling and how he liked the new job, but he felt something funny about them, as if they were saying, "Well, you finally let Lippy run you off the docks, huh, Matt?" "All that big talk about cleaning up the union and then you fold like an accordion, huh, Matt?" It was in their eyes—even Runt's.

"Well, I'm glad to see you got smart and put your hook away," Runt actually said. "Me, I'd do the same if I was a family man. But I always run too fast for the goils to catch me." Runt laughed and poked Matt lightly, but there was something about it wasn't the same.

Matt ran into Runt on the street a week or so later and asked him how everything was going. He had heard the neighborhood scuttlebutt about a new meeting coming up in the parish house. A government labor man was going to talk to them on how to get their rights. Father Conley had pulled in a trade-union lawyer for them and everything seemed to be moving ahead.

But Runt was secretive with Matt. Matt felt the brush; he was an outsider now. Runt had never said a word in criticism of Matt's withdrawal from the waterfront—just occasional cracks about fellows like himself who were too dumb to do anything else but stand their ground and fight it out. But it got under Matt's skin. He had the face of a bruiser, and inlanders would think of him as "tough-looking." But actually Matt was thin-skinned, emotional, hypersensitive. Runt wouldn't even tell him the date of the secret meeting, just asked him how he liked the storage job.

"It's a real good deal," Matt said. No seven-thirty shape-up. No muscle men masquerading as shop stewards. The same check every week. What more could he want?

What more than stacking cardboard containers in a long tunnel-like room illuminated by neon tubing? Matt wondered what there was about the waterfront. Why did men humiliate themselves by standing like cattle in the shape-up? What was so good about swinging a cargo hook—hoisting cement, copper ore, coffee, noxious cargoes that tickled your throat and maybe were slowly poisoning you?

But that didn't tell the whole story, Matt was thinking as he handled the storage containers automatically. There was the salt air; there were the ships coming in from Spain, from South America, Greece, all over the world. There was the way the river sparkled on a bright day. And there was the busy movement of the harbor: the sound of the ferries, the tugs, the barges, the freighters, and the great luxury ladies with their autocratic noses in the air. There were the different kinds of cargoes to handle—furs, perfume, sardines, cognac—and who was to blame them if they got away with a bottle or two; it wasn't pil-

ferage on the waterfront until you trucked it away. There was
the teamwork of a good gang working the cargo from the hatch
and over the deck to the pier: the winch men, the deck men, the
hatch boss, the high-low drivers, everybody moving together to
an unstated but strongly felt rhythm that could be thrown off if
just one man in a twenty-three-man gang didn't know his job.
And then there were the breaks for lunch—not cold sandwiches
in a metal container, but a cut of hot roast beef in the bar across
the street, with a cold beer to wash it down. And there was the
talk of last night's fight or today's ball game or the latest cute
trick pulled off by the longshore racketeers.

The waterfront: the violent, vivid, restless, corrupted,
"we're-doin'-lovely" waterfront.

Matt felt that way for days and said nothing about it. He'd
sit in the front room with his shoes off, drinking beer, reading
the tabloids, and wondering until it ached him what Runt and
the boys were up to.

One evening when he came home, Flanagan and Bennett
and some of the other neighbors were busy talking on the steps.
Matt heard. "Maybe he's just on one of his periodicals and he's
sleeping it off somewheres." And, "He coulda shipped out
somewhere. He used to be an A.B. and he's just ornery enough
to do it." And Matt heard, "When he gets his load on, anything
c'n happen. He could walk off the end of the pier into the river
and think he was home in bed."

Runt Nolan! No hide nor hair of him in three days, Flanagan said. Matt ran upstairs to tell Fran. She saw the look in his
eyes when he talked about Runt, who always said he was "on
borried time." "Now, Matt, no use getting yourself excited.
Wait and see. Now, Matt." She saw the look in his eyes was the
old look, before he settled for the cozy inland job with the storage company.

He paced up and down, but the children got on his nerves
and he went over to talk to Father Conley. The father was just
as worried as Matt. Specs had been warning Runt not to hold
any more meetings in the rectory. Specs had told Runt to take it
easy for his own good.

Matt went home after a while, but he couldn't sleep. At one-thirty in the morning he put his clothes back on and went down to the Longdock. What's the story, and news of Runt?

Nine days later there was news of Runt. The police department had made contact with Runt, by means of a grappling hook probing the soft, rotten bottom of the river. Runt wasn't "on borried time" anymore. He had paid back every minute of it. Cause of death: accidental drowning. On the night of his disappearance, Runt had been seen wandering the gin mills in a state of inebriation. In other words, bagged. There were no marks of violence on Runt. How could anyone prove he hadn't slipped? The good old North River, Lippy's silent partner, had done it again.

It was a good funeral. Everybody in the neighborhood was there—even Lippy Keegan, and Specs and Skelly with the rest of the boys. After the mass, Father Conley came out on the sidewalk, and Matt and some of the others who were closest to Runt gathered around to hear what the father had to say.

They had seen the father steamed before but never like this. "Accident my eye," he said. "If they think we're going to take this lying down, they're dumber than I think they are."

"What can we do, Father?"

Everybody looked around. It was Flanagan, who had come up behind Matt; Flanagan, who always played it very cozy with the Keegans. But like most of the others, he had liked having Runt around—that cocky little bantam. The Longdock wouldn't be the same without him. It looked like Runt, at the bottom of the river, had done more damage to Lippy than when he was around the docks shooting off his mouth.

Father Conley said, "We're going to keep this case alive. We'll question every single person who talked to Runt the day they hit him in the head. We'll keep needling the police for action. Keegan hasn't heard the end of Runt Nolan."

"Now's the time to put somebody up to run for president against Lippy," the Bennett kid said.

Everybody looked at Matt. Matt looked down at his uncomfortable black shoes. He would have given anything to have been with Runt the night Keegan's cowboys caught up with the little guy.

"That's right, keep pressing them," Father Conley said. "Maybe they don't know it yet, but times are changing. One of these days you're going to knock them out of the box for good." He looked at Matt and said, "I can help you. But I can't do it for you. It takes leadership."

Matt looked down at the sidewalk. He always felt strange in his dark blue suit. He looked over at Fran, talking with some of the other wives. In his mind, Fran and the storage company and the welfare of the kids were all churning around with Runt and what Father Conley was saying and the faces of these dockworkers looking at him and waiting for him. . . .

The morning after the funeral Matt's alarm clock split the silence at six-thirty. Matt swung his legs over the side of the bed. Fran stirred behind him. "I'll get up make you some coffee." She sat up and they looked at each other.

"I'm sorry, Fran, I—"

"Don't be," she said.

Even before what happened to Runt, she had felt it coming. And on the way home from church he had said, "All the fellers liked Runt. There'll be hell to pay. Now's the time to get 'em movin' in the right direction."

Fran, sitting up in bed behind him, said, "Don't get in no more trouble than you can help, Matt."

Matt stood up and stretched, groaned, and reached for his pants. "Don't worry, I'm gonna watch myself, I ain't gonna take no crazy chances like Runt, Lord-'ve-mercy-on-'im."

She wasn't even disappointed about the storage job. A storage man is a storage man, a longshoreman is a longshoreman. In the deepest part of her mind she had known that all along.

"I'll get up make you some coffee," she said again, as she had a thousand times before, as she would—if he was lucky—a thousand times again.

For a moment he roughed her up affectionately. "You're

gettin' fat, honey." Then he was pulling his wool checkerboard shirt on over his long underwear. If there was enough work, Fisheye was liable to pick him, just to make it look good in case there was an investigation.

The cargo hook felt good in his belt. He zipped up his windbreaker, told Fran not to worry, set his cap at the old-country angle, and tried not to make too much noise on the creaky stairway as he made his way down through the sleeping tenement.

Flanagan was coming out of his door as Matt reached the bottom landing. The old docker was yawning and rubbing sleep out of his eyes, but he grinned when he saw who it was.

"Matt me lad, we'll be needin' ya, that's for sure."

We. It had taken Flanagan a long time to get his mouth around that *we*. There wasn't any *we* over at the storage company. Matt nodded to Flanagan, a little embarrassed, and fussed with his cap like a pitcher.

"Once a stand-up guy, always a stand-up guy, huh, Matt?"

Matt grunted. He didn't want them to make too much of a deal out of it. Matt felt better when he got outside and the wind came blowing into his face. It felt good—like the cargo hook on his hip, familiar and good.

As they reached the corner, facing the elevated railroad tracks that ran along the river, two figures came up from a basement—Specs Sinclair and young Skelly. Specs had a bad cold. He was a sinus sufferer in the wintertime. He wished he was down in Miami scoring on the horses.

"So you want more?" he said to Matt, daubing his nose with a damp handkerchief. "We run you out of here once, but you ain't satisfied. What's a matter, you lookin' to wear cement shoes?"

Matt gazed at him and felt pleased and excited that he was back with this old hoodlum Sinclair and this punk Skelly. They were like old friends in reverse.

"Quit racing your motor," Matt said. "It ain't gonna be so easy this time. None of us is gonna go wanderin' around alone half gassed like Runt Nolan. We're stickin' together now. And

Father Conley's got the newspapers watchin'. You hit me in the head and next thing you know they'll hit you with ten thousand volts."

Specs looked at Skelly. Everything was getting a little out of hand, there was no doubt about it. In the old days you could knock off an old bum like Nolan and that was the end of it. This Matt Gillis, why didn't he stay in cold storage? For the first time in his life Specs worried whether Lippy Keegan would know the next move.

Matt crossed the street and pushed open the door of the Longdock. Everybody knew he was back. Everybody was going to be watching him. He wished Runt would come over and stick him in the side with a left hand. He knew it wasn't very likely, but it made him feel better to wonder if that scrappy little son-of-a-biscuit-eater was going to be watching too.

Although some critics have attempted to minimize his contributions to American letters, John Steinbeck (1902–1968) was one of the most important writers of this century. Such novels as Of Mice and Men *(1937),* The Grapes of Wrath *(1939, and the recipient of a Pulitzer Prize the following year),* Cannery Row *(1944), and* East of Eden *(1952) are major accomplishments in their depiction of the unremitting struggle of people who depend on the soil to sustain themselves, who maintain dignity though poor and oppressed and thus emerge as heroic (if often defeated) figures. Steinbeck, who was awarded the 1962 Nobel Prize for Literature and the Presidential Medal of Freedom in 1964, wrote many different types of fiction, not a little of it spiced with humor both subtle and ribald. The novel* Sweet Thursday *(1954) is one example of his comic abilities; "How Mr. Hogan Robbed a Bank," a story written late in his career and first published in* The New Yorker, *is another.*

HOW MR. HOGAN ROBBED A BANK
John Steinbeck

On the Saturday before Labor Day, 1955, at 9:04½ A.M., Mr. Hogan robbed a bank. He was forty-two years old, married, and the father of a boy and a girl, named John and Joan, twelve and thirteen respectively. Mrs. Hogan's name was Joan and Mr. Hogan's name was John, but since they called themselves Papa and Mama that left their names free for the children, who were considered smart for their ages, each having jumped a grade in school. The Hogans lived at 215 East Maple Street, in a brown-shingle house with white trim—there are two; 215 is the one across from the street light and it is the one with the big tree in the yard, either oak or elm—the biggest tree in the whole street, maybe in the whole town.

John and Joan were in bed at the time of the robbery, for it was Saturday. At 9:10 A.M., Mrs. Hogan was making the cup of tea she always had. Mr. Hogan went to work early. Mrs. Hogan drank her tea slowly, scalding hot, and read her fortune in the tea leaves. There was a cloud and a five-pointed star with two short points in the bottom of the cup, but that was at 9:12 and the robbery was all over by then.

The way Mr. Hogan went about robbing the bank was very interesting. He gave it a great deal of thought and had for a long time, but he did not discuss it with anyone. He just read his newspaper and kept his own counsel. But he worked it out to his own satisfaction that people went to too much trouble robbing banks and that got them in a mess. The simpler the better, he always thought. People went in for too much hullabaloo and hanky-panky. If you didn't do that, if you left hanky-panky out, robbing a bank would be a relatively sound venture—barring accidents, of course, of an improbable kind, but then they could happen to a man crossing the street or anything. Since Mr. Hogan's method worked fine, it proved that his thinking was sound. He often considered writing a little booklet on his technique when the how-to rage was running so high. He figured out the first sentence, which went: "To successfully rob a bank, forget all about hanky-panky."

Mr. Hogan was not just a clerk at Fettucci's grocery store. He was more like the manager. Mr. Hogan was in charge, even hired and fired the boy who delivered groceries after school. He even put in orders with the salesmen, sometimes when Mr. Fettucci was right in the store too, maybe talking to a customer. "You do it, John," he would say and he would nod at the customer, "John knows the ropes. Been with me—how long you been with me, John?"

"Sixteen years."

"Sixteen years. Knows the business as good as me. John, why he even banks the money."

And so he did. Whenever he had a moment, Mr. Hogan went into the storeroom on the alley, took off his apron, put on his necktie and coat, and went back through the store to the cash register. The checks and bills would be ready for him inside the bankbook with a rubber band around it. Then he went next door and stood at the teller's window and handed the checks and bankbook through to Mr. Cup and passed the time of day with him too. Then, when the bankbook was handed back, he checked the entry, put the rubber band around it, and walked next door to Fettucci's grocery and put the bankbook in the cash register, continued on to the storeroom, removed his coat and tie, put on his apron, and went back into the store ready for business. If there was no line at the teller's window, the whole thing didn't take more than five minutes, even passing the time of day.

Mr. Hogan was a man who noticed things, and when it came to robbing the bank, this trait stood him in good stead. He had noticed, for instance, where the big bills were kept right in the drawer under the counter and he had noticed also what days there were likely to be more than other days. Thursday was payday at the American Can Company's local plant, for instance, so there would be more then. Some Fridays people drew more money to tide them over the weekend. But it was even-steven, maybe not a thousand dollars' difference, between Thursdays and Fridays and Saturday mornings. Saturdays were not terribly good because people didn't come to get money that early in the morning, and the bank closed at noon. But he thought it over and came to the conclusion that the Saturday before a long weekend in the summer would be the best of all. People going on trips, vacations, people with relatives visiting, and the bank closed Monday. He thought it out and looked, and sure enough the Saturday morning before Labor Day the cash drawer had twice as much money in it—he saw it when Mr. Cup pulled out the drawer.

Mr. Hogan thought about it during all that year, not all the time, of course, but when he had some moments. It was a busy year too. That was the year John and Joan had the mumps and Mrs. Hogan got her teeth pulled and was fitted for a denture. That was the year when Mr. Hogan was Master of the Lodge, with all the time that takes. Larry Shield died that year—he was Mrs. Hogan's brother and was buried from the Hogan house at 215 East Maple. Larry was a bachelor and had a room in the Pine Tree House and he played pool nearly every night. He

worked at the Silver Diner, but that closed at nine and so Larry
would go to Louie's and play pool for an hour. Therefore, it was
a surprise when he left enough so that after funeral expenses
there were twelve hundred dollars left. And even more surprising that he left a will in Mrs. Hogan's favor, but his double-
barreled twelve-gauge shotgun he left to John Hogan, Jr. Mr.
Hogan was pleased, although he never hunted. He put the shotgun away in the back of the closet in the bathroom, where he
kept his things, to keep it for young John. He didn't want children handling guns and he never bought any shells. It was some
of that twelve hundred that got Mrs. Hogan her dentures. Also,
she bought a bicycle for John and a doll buggy and walking-
talking doll for Joan—a doll with three changes of dresses and a
little suitcase, complete with play makeup. Mr. Hogan thought
it might spoil the children, but it didn't seem to. They made just
as good marks in school and John even got a job delivering
papers. It was a very busy year. Both John and Joan wanted to
enter the W. R. Hearst National "I Love America" Contest and
Mr. Hogan thought it was almost too much, but they promised
to do the work during their summer vacation, so he finally
agreed.

II

During that year, no one noticed any difference in Mr. Hogan.
It was true, he was thinking about robbing the bank, but he only
thought about it in the evening when there was neither a lodge
meeting nor a movie they wanted to go to, so it did not become
an obsession and people noticed no change in him.

He studied everything so carefully that the approach of
Labor Day did not catch him unprepared or nervous. It was hot
that summer and the hot spells were longer than usual. Saturday
was the end of two weeks' heat without a break and people
were irritated with it and anxious to get out of town, although
the country was just as hot. They didn't think of that. The children were excited because the "I Love America" essay contest

was due to be concluded and the winners announced, and the first prize was an all-expense-paid two days' trip to Washington, D.C., with every fixing—hotel room, three meals a day, and side trips in a limousine—not only for the winner, but for an accompanying chaperone; visit to the White House—shake hands with the President—everything. Mr. Hogan thought they were getting their hopes too high and he said so.

"You've got to be prepared to lose," he told his children. "There're probably thousands and thousands entered. You get your hopes up and it might spoil the whole autumn. Now I don't want any long faces in this house after the contest is over."

"I was against it from the start," he told Mrs. Hogan. That was the morning she saw the Washington Monument in her teacup, but she didn't tell anybody about that except Ruth Tyler, Bob Tyler's wife. Ruthie brought over her cards and read them in the Hogan kitchen, but she didn't find a journey. She did tell Mrs. Hogan that the cards were often wrong. The cards had said Mrs. Winkle was going on a trip to Europe and the next week Mrs. Winkle got a fishbone in her throat and choked to death. Ruthie, just thinking out loud, wondered if there was any connection between the fishbone and the ocean voyage to Europe. "You've got to interpret them right." Ruthie did say she saw money coming to the Hogans.

"Oh, I got that already from poor Larry," Mrs. Hogan explained.

"I must have got the past and future cards mixed," said Ruthie. "You've got to interpret them right."

Saturday dawned a blaster. The early morning weather report on the radio said, "Continued hot and humid, light scattered rain Sunday night and Monday." Mrs. Hogan said, "Wouldn't you know? Labor Day." And Mr. Hogan said, "I'm sure glad we didn't plan anything." He finished his egg and mopped the plate with his toast. Mrs. Hogan said, "Did I put coffee on the list?" He took the paper from his handkerchief pocket and consulted it. "Yes, coffee, it's here."

"I had a crazy idea I forgot to write it down," said Mrs.

Hogan. "Ruth and I are going to Altar Guild this afternoon. It's at Mrs. Alfred Drake's. You know, they just came to town. I can't wait to see their furniture."

"They trade with us," said Mr. Hogan. "Opened an account last week. Are the milk bottles ready?"

"On the porch."

Mr. Hogan looked at his watch just before he picked up the bottles and it was five minutes to eight. He was about to go down the stairs, when he turned and looked back through the opened door at Mrs. Hogan. She said, "Want something, Papa?"

"No," he said. "No," and he walked down the steps.

He went down to the corner and turned right on Spooner, and Spooner runs into Main Street in two blocks, and right across from where it runs in, there is Fettucci's and the bank around the corner and the alley beside the bank. Mr. Hogan picked up a handbill in front of Fettucci's and unlocked the door. He went through the storeroom, opened the door to the alley, and looked out. A cat tried to force its way in, but Mr. Hogan blocked it with his foot and leg and closed the door. He took off his coat and put on his long apron, tied the strings in a bowknot behind his back. Then he got the broom from behind the counter and swept out behind the counters and scooped the sweepings into a dustpan; and, going through the storeroom, he opened the door to the alley. The cat had gone away. He emptied the dustpan into the garbage can and tapped it smartly to dislodge a piece of lettuce leaf. Then he went back to the store and worked for a while on the order sheet. Mrs. Clooney came in for a half a pound of bacon. She said it was hot and Mr. Hogan agreed. "Summers are getting hotter," he said.

"I think so myself," said Mrs. Clooney. "How's Mrs. standing up?"

"Just fine," said Mr. Hogan. "She's going to Altar Guild."

"So am I. I just can't wait to see their furniture," said Mrs. Clooney, and she went out.

III

Mr. Hogan put a five-pound hunk of bacon on the slicer and stripped off the pieces and laid them on wax paper and then he put the wax-paper-covered squares in the cooler cabinet. At ten minutes to nine, Mr. Hogan went to a shelf. He pushed a spaghetti box aside and took down a cereal box, which he emptied in the little closet toilet. Then, with a banana knife, he cut out the Mickey Mouse mask that was on the back. The rest of the box he took to the toilet and tore up the cardboard and flushed it down. He went into the store then and yanked a piece of string loose and tied the ends through the side holes of the mask and then he looked at his watch—a large silver Hamilton with black hands. It was two minutes to nine.

Perhaps the next four minutes were his only time of nervousness at all. At one minute to nine, he took the broom and went out to sweep the sidewalk and he swept it very rapidly—was sweeping it, in fact, when Mr. Warner unlocked the bank door. He said good morning to Mr. Warner and a few seconds later the bank staff of four emerged from the coffee shop. Mr. Hogan saw them across the street and he waved at them and they waved back. He finished the sidewalk and went back in the store. He laid his watch on the little step of the cash register. He sighed very deeply, more like a deep breath than a sigh. He knew that Mr. Warner would have the safe open now and he would be carrying the cash trays to the teller's window. Mr. Hogan looked at the watch on the cash register step. Mr. Kenworthy paused in the store entrance, then shook his head vaguely and walked on and Mr. Hogan let out his breath gradually. His left hand went behind his back and pulled the bowknot on his apron, and then the black hand on his watch crept up on the four minute mark and covered it.

Mr. Hogan opened the charge account drawer and took out the store pistol, a silver-colored Iver Johnson .38. He moved quickly to the storeroom, slipped off his apron, put on his coat, and stuck the revolver in his side pocket. The Mickey Mouse mask he shoved up under his coat where it didn't show. He opened the alley door and looked up and down and stepped quickly out, leaving the door slightly ajar. It is sixty feet to where the alley enters Main Street, and there he paused and looked up and down and then he turned his head toward the center of the street as he passed the bank window. At the bank's swinging door, he took out the mask from under his coat and put it on. Mr. Warner was just entering his office and his back was to the door. The top of Will Cup's head was visible through the teller's grill.

Mr. Hogan moved quickly and quietly around the end of the counter and into the teller's cage. He had the revolver in his right hand now. When Will Cup turned his head and saw the revolver, he froze. Mr. Hogan slipped his toe under the trigger of the floor alarm and he motioned Will Cup to the floor with the revolver and Will went down quick. Then Mr. Hogan opened the cash drawer and with two quick movements he piled the large bills from the tray together. He made a whipping motion to Will on the floor, to indicate that he should turn over and face the wall, and Will did. Then Mr. Hogan stepped back around the counter. At the door of the bank he took off the mask, and as he passed the window he turned his head toward the middle of the street. He moved into the alley, walked quickly to the storeroom, and entered. The cat had got in. It watched him from a pile of canned goods cartons. Mr. Hogan went to the toilet closet and tore up the mask and flushed it. He took off his coat and put on his apron. He looked out into the store and then moved to the cash register. The revolver went back into the charge account drawer. He punched No Sale and, lifting the top drawer, distributed the stolen money underneath the top tray and then pulled the tray forward and closed the register, and only then did he look at his watch and it was 9:07½.

He was trying to get the cat out of the storeroom when the commotion boiled out of the bank. He took his broom and went out on the sidewalk. He heard all about it and offered his opinion when it was asked for. He said he didn't think the fellow could get away—where could he get to? Still, with the holiday coming up—

It was an exciting day. Mr. Fettucci was as proud as though it were his bank. The sirens sounded around town for hours. Hundreds of holiday travelers had to stop at the road blocks set up all around the edge of town and several sneaky-looking men had their cars searched.

Mrs. Hogan heard about it over the phone and she dressed earlier than she would have ordinarily and came to the store on her way to Altar Guild. She hoped Mr. Hogan would have seen or heard something new, but he hadn't. "I don't see how the fellow can get away," he said.

Mrs. Hogan was so excited, she forgot her own news. She only remembered when she got to Mrs. Drake's house, but she asked permission and phoned the store the first moment she could. "I forgot to tell you. John's won honorable mention."

"What?"

"In the 'I Love America' contest."

"What did he win?"

"Honorable mention."

"Fine. Fine—anything come with it?"

"Why, he'll get his picture and his name all over the country. Radio too. Maybe even television. They've already asked for a photograph of him."

"Fine," said Mr. Hogan. "I hope it don't spoil him." He put up the receiver and said to Mr. Fettucci, "I guess we've got a celebrity in the family."

Fettucci stayed open until nine on Saturdays. Mr. Hogan ate a few snacks from cold cuts, but not much, because Mrs. Hogan always kept his supper warming.

It was 9:05, or :06, or :07, when he got back to the brown-shingle house at 215 East Maple. He went in through the front door and out to the kitchen where the family was waiting for him.

"Got to wash up," he said, and went up to the bathroom. He turned the key in the bathroom door and then he flushed the toilet and turned on the water in the basin and tub while he counted the money. Eight thousand three hundred and twenty dollars. From the top shelf of the storage closet in the bathroom, he took down the big leather case that held his Knight Templar's uniform. The plumed hat lay there on its form. The white ostrich feather was a little yellow and needed changing. Mr. Hogan lifted out the hat and pried the form up from the bottom of the case. He put the money in the form and then he thought again and removed two bills and shoved them in his side pocket. Then he put the form back over the money and laid the hat on top and closed the case and shoved it back on the top shelf. Finally he washed his hands and turned off the water in the tub and the basin.

In the kitchen, Mrs. Hogan and the children faced him, beaming. "Guess what some young man's going on?"

"What?" asked Mr. Hogan.

"Radio," said John. "Monday night. Eight o'clock."

"I guess we got a celebrity in the family," said Mr. Hogan.

Mrs. Hogan said, "I just hope some young lady hasn't got her nose out of joint."

Mr. Hogan pulled up to the table and stretched his legs. "Mama, I guess I got a fine family," he said. He reached in his pocket and took out two five-dollar bills. He handed one to John. "That's for winning," he said. He poked the other bill at Joan. "And that's for being a good sport. One celebrity and one good sport. What a fine family!" He rubbed his hands together and lifted the lid of the covered dish. "Kidneys," he said. "Fine."

And that's how Mr. Hogan did it.

One of a large number of Jewish-American writers who achieved prominence in the 1950s, Bernard Malamud (1914–1986) is perhaps best known to general readers as the author of The Natural *(1952), that brilliant novel about baseball and the American dream which was the basis for the recent Robert Redford film of the same title. Malamud was among this country's most honored writers; his awards include the National Book Award in 1959 and 1967, the Pulitzer Prize in 1967 (for his novel* The Fixer), *and the O. Henry Award for short fiction in 1969 and 1973. Further evidence of his mastery of the modern short story are the entries in his 1973 collection,* Rembrandt's Hat, *and the mordant tale that follows.*

My Son the Murderer
Bernard Malamud

He wakes feeling his father is in the hallway, listening. He listens to him sleep and dream. Listening to him get up and fumble for his pants. He won't put on his shoes. To him not going to the kitchen to eat. Staring with shut eyes in the mirror. Sitting an hour on the toilet. Flipping the pages of a book he can't read. To his anguish, loneliness. The father stands in the hall. The son hears him listen.

My son the stranger, he won't tell me anything.

I open the door and see my father in the hall. Why are you standing there, why don't you go to work?

On account of I took my vacation in the winter instead of the summer like I usually do.

What the hell for if you spend it in this dark smelly hallway, watching my every move? Guessing what you can't see. Why are you always spying on me?

My father goes to the bedroom and after a while sneaks out in the hallway again, listening.

I hear him sometimes in his room but he don't talk to me and I don't know what's what. It's a terrible feeling for a father. Maybe someday he will write me a letter. My dear father . . .

My dear son Harry, open up your door. My son the prisoner.

My wife leaves in the morning to stay with my married daughter, who is expecting her fourth child. The mother cooks and cleans for her and takes care of the three children. My daughter is having a bad pregnancy, with high blood pressure, and lays in bed most of the time. This is what the doctor advised her. My wife is gone all day. She worries something is wrong with Harry. Since he graduated college last summer he is alone, nervous, in his own thoughts. If you talk to him, half the time he yells if he answers you. He reads the papers, smokes, he stays in his room. Or once in a while he goes for a walk in the street.

How was the walk, Harry?

A walk.

My wife advised him to go look for work, and a couple of times he went, but when he got some kind of an offer he didn't take the job.

It's not that I don't want to work. It's that I feel bad.

So why do you feel bad?

I feel what I feel. I feel what is.

Is it your health, sonny? Maybe you ought to go to a doctor?

I asked you not to call me by that name anymore. It's not my health. Whatever it is I don't want to talk about it. The work wasn't the kind I want.

So take something temporary in the meantime, my wife said to him.

He starts to yell. Everything's temporary. Why should I add more to what's temporary? My gut feels temporary. The goddamn world is temporary. On top of that I don't want temporary work. I want the opposite of temporary, but where is it? Where do you find it?

My father listens in the kitchen.

My temporary son.

She says I'll feel better if I work, I say I won't. I'm twenty-two since December, a college graduate, and you know where you can stick that. At night I watch the news programs. I watch the war from day to day. It's a big burning war on a small screen. It rains bombs and the flames go higher. Sometimes I lean over and touch the war with the flat of my hand. I wait for my hand to die.

My son with the dead hand.

I expect to be drafted any day but it doesn't bother me the way it used to. I won't go. I'll go to Canada or somewhere I can go.

The way he is frightens my wife and she is glad to go to my daughter's house early in the morning to take care of the three children. I stay with him in the house but he don't talk to me.

You ought to call up Harry and talk to him, my wife says to my daughter.

I will sometime but don't forget there's nine years' difference between our ages. I think he thinks of me as another mother around and one is enough. I used to like him when he was a little boy but now it's hard to deal with a person who won't reciprocate to you.

She's got high blood pressure. I think she's afraid to call.

I took two weeks off from my work. I'm a clerk at the stamps window in the post office. I told the superintendent I wasn't feeling so good, which is no lie, and he said I should take sick leave. I said I wasn't that sick, I only needed a little vacation. But I told my friend Moe Berkman I was staying out because Harry has me worried.

I understand what you mean, Leo. I got my own worries and anxieties about my kids. If you got two girls growing up you got hostages to fortune. Still in all we got to live. Why don't you come to poker on this Friday night? We got a nice game going. Don't deprive yourself of a good form of relaxation.

I'll see how I feel by Friday, how everything is coming along. I can't promise you.

Try to come. These things, if you give them time, all pass away. If it looks better to you, come on over. Even if it don't look so good, come on over anyway because it might relieve your tension and worry that you're under. It's not so good for your heart at your age if you carry that much worry around.

It's the worst kind of worry. If I worry about myself I know what the worry is. What I mean, there's no mystery. I can say to myself, Leo you're a big fool, stop worry about nothing—over what, a few bucks? Over my health that has always stood up pretty good although I have my ups and downs? Over that I'm now close to sixty and not getting any younger? Everybody that don't die by age fifty-nine gets to be sixty. You can't beat time when it runs along with you. But if the worry is about somebody else, that's the worst kind. That's the real worry because if he won't tell you, you can't get inside the other person and find out why. You don't know where's the switch to turn off. All you do is worry more.

So I wait out in the hall.

Harry, don't worry so much about the war.

Please don't tell me what to worry about or what not to worry about.

Harry, your father loves you. When you were a little boy, every night when I came home you used to run to me. I picked you up and lifted you up to the ceiling. You liked to touch it with your small hand.

I don't want to hear about that anymore. It's the very thing I don't want to hear. I don't want to hear about when I was a child.

Harry, we live like strangers. All I'm saying is I remember better days. I remember when we weren't afraid to show we loved each other.

He says nothing.

Let me cook you an egg.

An egg is the last thing in the world I want.

So what do you want?

He put his coat on. He pulled his hat off the clothes tree and went down into the street.

Harry walked along Ocean Parkway in his long overcoat and creased brown hat. His father was following him and it filled him with rage.

He walked at a fast pace up the broad avenue. In the old days there was a bridle path at the side of the walk where the concrete bicycle path was now. And there were fewer trees, their black branches cutting the sunless sky. At the corner of Avenue X, just about where you can smell Coney Island, he crossed the street and began to walk home. He pretended not to see his father cross over, though he was infuriated. The father crossed over and followed his son home. When he got to the house he figured Harry was upstairs already. He was in his room with the door shut. Whatever he did in his room he was already doing.

Leo took out his small key and opened the mailbox. There were three letters. He looked to see if one of them was, by any chance, from his son to him. My dear father, let me explain myself. The reason I act as I do . . . There was no such letter. One of the letters was from the Post Office Clerks Benevolent Society, which he slipped into his coat pocket. The other two letters were for Harry. One was from the draft board. He brought it up to his son's room, knocked on the door and waited.

He waited for a while.

To the boy's grunt he said, There is a draft-board letter here for you. He turned the knob and entered the room. His son was lying on his bed with his eyes shut.

Leave it on the table.

Do you want me to open it for you, Harry?

No, I don't want you to open it. Leave it on the table. I know what's in it.

Did you write them another letter?

That's my goddamn business.

The father left it on the table.

The other letter to his son he took into the kitchen, shut the door, and boiled up some water in a pot. He thought he would read it quickly and seal it carefully with a little paste, then go downstairs and put it back in the mailbox. His wife would take it out with her key when she returned from their daughter's house and bring it up to Harry.

The father read the letter. It was a short letter from a girl. The girl said Harry had borrowed two of her books more than six months ago and since she valued them highly she would like him to send them back to her. Could he do that as soon as possible so that she wouldn't have to write again?

As Leo was reading the girl's letter Harry came into the kitchen and when he saw the surprised and guilty look on his father's face, he tore the letter out of his hands.

I ought to murder you the way you spy on me.

Leo turned away, looking out of the small kitchen window into the dark apartment-house courtyard. His face burned, he felt sick.

Harry read the letter at a glance and tore it up. He then tore up the envelope marked personal.

If you do this again don't be surprised if I kill you. I'm sick of you spying on me.

Harry, you are talking to your father.

He left the house.

Leo went into his room and looked around. He looked in the dresser drawers and found nothing unusual. On the desk by the window was a paper Harry had written on. It said: Dear Edith, why don't you go fuck yourself? If you write me another letter I'll murder you.

The father got his hat and coat and left the house. He ran slowly for a while, running then walking, until he saw Harry on the other side of the street. He followed him, half a block behind.

He followed Harry to Coney Island Avenue and was in time to see him board a trolley bus going to the island. Leo had to wait for the next one. He thought of taking a taxi and following the trolley bus, but no taxi came by. The next bus came by fifteen minutes later and he took it all the way to the island. It was February and Coney Island was wet, cold, and deserted. There were few cars on Surf Avenue and few people on the streets. It felt like snow. Leo walked on the boardwalk amid snow flurries, looking for his son. The gray sunless beaches were empty. The hot-dog stands, shooting galleries, and bathhouses were shuttered up. The gunmetal ocean, moving like melted lead, looked freezing. A wind blew in off the water and worked its way into his clothes so that he shivered as he walked. The wind whitecapped the leaden waves and the slow surf broke on the empty beaches with a quiet roar.

He walked in the blow almost to Sea Gate, searching for his son, and then walked back again. On his way toward Brighton Beach he saw a man on the shore standing in the foaming surf. Leo hurried down the boardwalk stairs and onto the ribbed-sand beach. The man on the roaring shore was Harry, standing in water to the tops of his shoes.

Leo ran to his son. Harry, it was a mistake, excuse me, I'm sorry I opened your letter.

Harry did not move. He stood in the water, his eyes on the swelling leaden waves.

Harry, I'm frightened. Tell me what's the matter. My son, have mercy on me.

I'm frightened of the world, Harry thought. It fills me with fright.

He said nothing.

A blast of wind lifted his father's hat and carried it away over the beach. It looked as though it were going to be blown into the surf, but then the wind blew it toward the boardwalk, rolling like a wheel along the wet sand. Leo chased after his hat. He chased it one way, then another, then toward the water. The wind blew the hat against his legs and he caught it. By now he was crying. Breathless, he wiped his eyes with icy fingers and returned to his son at the edge of the water.

He is a lonely man. This is the type he is. He will always be lonely.

My son who made himself into a lonely man.

Harry, what can I say to you? All I can say to you is who says life is easy? Since when? It wasn't for me and it isn't for you. It's life, that's the way it is—what more can I say? But if a person don't want to live what can he do if he's dead? Nothing. Nothing is nothing, it's better to live.

Come home, Harry, he said. It's cold here. You'll catch a cold with your feet in the water.

Harry stood motionless in the water and after a while his father left. As he was leaving, the wind plucked his hat off his head and sent it rolling along the shore.

My father listens in the hallway. He follows me in the street. We meet at the edge of the water.

He runs after his hat.

My son stands with his feet in the ocean.

Joyce Carol Oates is challenged only by Robert Stone or Thomas Pynchon for the position of the most successful and influential writer of her generation. Her novel Them *won the National Book Award in 1969; she has appeared in more than a dozen O. Henry anthologies (winning first prize twice, second prize twice, and earning a special citation for her contribution to the American short story) and in almost twenty volumes of* Best American Short Stories; *she is a member of the National Institute of Arts and Letters and a recipient of the Guggenheim Fellowship. The aspects of violence and/or the criminous in Oates's work have been in evidence from her earliest short stories. They can be found most vividly in* Expensive People (1968), *a Nabokovian novel narrated in deadpan style by a murderer; in the stories in her 1977 collection* Night-Side; *and in "Sentimental Journey," perhaps her most terrifying short story.*

SENTIMENTAL JOURNEY
Joyce Carol Oates

Dear Warren, wrote Annie Quirt on the eve of her thirty-first birthday, *I wonder if you remember me . . . ? I don't really care, I think I am writing to you because I can't sleep tonight, because I have been thinking of you, almost obsessed with memories of you. . . .* Obsessed? Annie wondered if that did not sound too extreme; even pathological. But it was true. She crushed out her cigarette and wrote: *I remember you so vividly . . . the khaki jacket from Army Surplus, worn at the elbows . . . those tennis shoes of yours that came to your ankles and were sometimes unlaced, or was it that the laces had broken and you'd knotted them . . . ? I remember you hunched over your desk, taking notes in a big loose-leaf notebook like the kind high school students use. . . . You were so earnest, so serious, so hardworking, unlike the others, unlike certain friends of yours who didn't deserve your friendship and who took advantage of you.* Annie was writing on plain sheets of paper, hurriedly, almost feverishly, not stopping to read what she had written. She felt rather sick but such feelings did not count: she had vowed, in this new phase of her life, to transcend and to obliterate the merely physical. *You were so good, Warren. I think that was it. So good. Innocent... loyal... sweet... funny.... You had a temper, I remember that, I remember how angry you got with Tony, once, when he was drunk and arguing stupidly about... about what?... how the great philosophers were only expressing the prejudices of their eras?... and you rejected what he said, you were truly angry, and passionate, and I realized for the first time the depth of your character....* How crude, how pathetic! Annie lit another cigarette and turned over the page and continued the letter. She knew her words were absurd, grotesquely sentimental; she knew that Warren, even sweet little Warren Breck, would probably laugh at them; she knew, even as she wrote, her hand aching, that she would not dare mail the letter. Nevertheless she wrote, as quickly as possible, not allowing herself time to think. The emotion that was coursing through her was too powerful to contain. It was like grief, somehow concentrated in her eyes and throat and upper chest. She felt like crying. She had been crying, earlier. Ugly wracking sobs, dry sobs, that were incomprehensible. *I knew so little about life then, about the value of a genuine friendship... I didn't have time for such things... I was always in a hurry, in a rush, it took me a long time to see how shallow a person Tony was, and how I had wasted...* Ten years ago! A decade! Could it be possible, a decade had passed and Annie Quirt, who had always imagined herself so tough and sly and independent, who had been enormously self-confident because of her looks, and the great good luck of her girlhood, was writing to a boy she hardly remembered, a friend of the boy she had loved in college, or had deluded herself into believing she loved...? Annie laughed aloud. She was bent over the kitchen table, a cigarette burning in her left hand, her hair falling into her eyes. The light was poor; she hadn't wanted to put the overhead light on, for fear of attracting her sister's attention; as she wrote a fluid, dancing blur followed her words. *It's two* A.M. *and I've given up trying to sleep. Earlier tonight I was leafing through some of my college books, paperbacks I hadn't looked at for a decade, and I came across something you had written . . . at the back of* The Republic . . . *you couldn't remember, couldn't possibly remember . . . we must have been joking around. . . . That eight* A.M. *class on the top floor of Brennan Hall, us in the back row, Dr. Hotchkiss with his yellow-white hair like a wig and his stammer when he got excited . . . remember, you and he argued, you were the only person in the class he respected, I think. I know. I was too ignorant to appreciate . . .* She looked up, startled. A footstep? A soft thudding sound of some kind? She made a gesture to crush out the cigarette; it would put her at a disadvantage, if Jean saw her smoking when she had stated her intention to quit. But the kitchen was smoky anyway. . . . *I remember a day in early spring, at that ugly Victorian mansion you and the others rented rooms in, remember? . . . it was four stories high, painted a ghastly red-orange, the brick was crumbling, most of the windows in the basement were broken. . . . Tony and Dave and that girl with the braids, the nursing student, and I, do you remember? . . . knocked on your door and disturbed you studying . . . you had an exam in organic chemistry the next morning, you sitting at your desk barechested . . . so pale! . . . I remember how pale you were! It was hot in the room, the radiators couldn't be turned off. We wanted you to come with us out to, what was that place, Erlich's, for a beer. . . . You seemed so lonely then, so alone. I knew you wanted to come with us but at the same time you had to study, I could see how torn you were, I told Tony to leave you alone, to stop bullying you. . . . And then it was the end of the semester: then it was graduation: everything was over and we never saw each other again.* What if Warren were married? It was entirely possible. It was even rather likely. He had been shy, almost to the point of pain; but he had been quite normal. At one of the rare parties he'd attended, once, he had danced with Annie and had engaged her in a long earnest confused conversation, and his feeling for her had been plain, almost embarrassingly obvious. She had liked him well enough, as a minor personage in the exciting drama of her life; but she had not felt, really, any affection for him at the time. All her energies had gone into love: into that relationship with Tony. She had not even valued her friendships with girls she had known for years, during that time. How she disliked herself, that earlier self!—how richly she deserved the various disappointments that had followed! *I think I am writing, Warren, just to reach out to you, to say hello, I don't expect you to reply, I want only . . . I would like . . . what do I want? . . . just to know if you're alive, and happy, and if your plans for medical school worked out. . . . I assume they did. Of course they did. You are probably established now and practicing medicine and probably you are married also, and your wife will resent this letter; I advise you just to scan it and think of me, of Annie Quirt, the redhead, remember? . . . Tony Engel's girl? . . . and then rip the letter up, throw it away. . . .*

"Annie?"

She looked around, startled, It was Jean in her nightgown, barefooted; her older sister Jean blinking at her. Annie saw, but chose not to interpret, her sister's look of apprehension.

"What are you—? Are you writing something? I saw the light on, I noticed your bed was empty—"

"I'm writing a letter," Annie said quietly.

"A letter?"

"Yes, a letter. To a friend. I have friends, I write letters to them occasionally; do you mind? I didn't think I was disturbing you."

Jean relaxed visibly. She tried to smile.

"Of course you weren't disturbing me, Annie, I just woke up and wondered and for a moment . . . for a moment I was, you know, a little worried."

"You were worried," Annie repeated. She and Jean stared at each other for a long moment. At such times Annie kept her expression stiff and neutral: she was Jean's baby sister, she and Jean had always liked each other, it was not Jean she disliked. In fact, in a way, she rather liked Jean's sisterliness—she liked being fussed over, worried over, grieved over, to a certain extent. She did appreciate Jean's generosity, leaving her husband and three children for more than a week, just to stay with Annie in Annie's small, crowded, depressing apartment. But if she thought of Jean and of Jean's love, if she thought of Jean's undisguised sorrow that first day, she might break down; she might succumb to those dry wracking sobs. And this would distress her sister all the more. "But why should you be worried?" she said calmly. "We've been over this already. I am perfectly well now . . . I've regained my old sense of, what was it? . . . not humor but skepticism, cynicism . . . or sin? My sense of sin," she said, smiling broadly. "Yes. I've regained it. So you can stop worrying. You can go back home to your loving husband and your beautiful children, you can dismiss the baby-sitter, you can move back into your enviable life . . . right? Because Annie has regained her sense of sin and knows right from wrong now and has learned her lesson well."

"Who are you writing to, Annie?" Jean asked. She stepped forward though she must have known Annie would cover the sheets of paper with her arms, to hide them; Annie did this without really thinking, as a reflex. It was an insulting gesture but Jean did not appear to mind. ". . . To *him?*"

"No," Annie said quickly, curtly.

"Well, I . . . As long as . . . I'm glad, I mean, that . . ."

"Of course I'm not writing to *him,*" Annie said angrily. Her voice was trembling. "He's gone, he's forgotten. He's dead. To me he's dead. *Dead.* . . . No, I'm writing to a friend, an old friend. I'm writing to someone you don't know. A friend. From college. One of the few worthwhile . . . one of the . . . He doesn't know about my life now but if he did he wouldn't judge, he liked me for myself, for . . . for myself . . . he wouldn't judge. . . . Just a friend, Jean, nobody you know or have to concern yourself with. All right?"

"Yes. All right," Jean said softly.

Priscilla Ann Quirt, she was: in her innermost heart did she love herself too dearly, or despise herself? An urbane, courteous young doctor at the mental health clinic of the university where

Annie had done graduate work, some years ago, had spoken of her poor *self-image*. She did not value herself enough, he believed. Wasn't it a pity, he said, covertly eyeing her, or pretending to covertly eye her in order to flatter her, when she was obviously very intelligent?—and very attractive as well. Wasn't it a pity, he said, that she could not adjust her inner vision of herself, to bring it more in line with reality?

". . . bring it more in line with reality," Annie repeated. She frowned. She was not playing the role of a near-mute, disingenuous girl; she was consciously playing at playing a role, in order to show this wise bastard what she thought of him. "Yes. I will try. *Bring my inner vision more in line with reality.*"

"You don't approve of yourself," he said, reddening. "There's nothing wrong with you—with your mind. The drugs scared you and that's quite natural, in fact that's a good thing—you're too sensitive for anything so crude. Your system can't take it. But there's nothing wrong with your mind, with your sanity; with what we call sanity. Do you understand? It's almost as if you have a problem of vision, of measurement . . . from the inside you see one image of yourself, but no one else sees that image. You have to work hard, don't you?—to make other people see that image."

"Yes," Annie said. "All right."

"All right what?"

"I agree, I see your point, I'm impressed with your insight and kindliness and wisdom. I'm very grateful," Annie said.

He stared at her. For a while he said nothing.

"I'm very grateful but I have to leave now," Annie said. "I have a class. I'm teaching a class. If you won't give me another prescription for those pills—"

"No. I won't."

"—then I have nothing more to say, or to ask of you."

As she opened the door she heard him say something. But when she turned, smiling anxiously, for an instant almost vulnerable—when she turned, he was merely staring at her, blank-faced, assessing. His eye dropped to her hips, to the long stretch of thigh outlined by the tight jeans she wore, then to her legs, her leather boots, to the floor. And that was that.

Yet others told her she was egotistical: she valued herself too much, could never love anyone as she loved herself. Her image of herself was exaggerated, magnified. Jean would never have accused her of such self-love, nor would her mother—who loved Annie best, in that desperate, hopeless, rather exotic way in which mothers love certain children, knowing their love is misplaced; but her father had told her, several times. Her father was an unusual man—the owner of a small but fairly profitable dairy farm who was also a lay minister and also a part-time music instructor in the county public schools. He was abrupt, outspoken, with a temper as bad as Annie's; she supposed she had inherited it from him, along with his tall athletic frame and his too-bright red hair and pale, creamy-pale complexion. "You love yourself too much," he had said. Twelve years old at the time, Annie had been weeping because she was so tall. Five feet eight and a half. And growing, always growing. Growing! She wept because she was the tallest student in her class and because she was the smartest student, because she had no friends, because she felt superior to the friends she had, and could not resist making wise remarks about them; she wept because her skin had broken out and her fantasies of cold, hard, careless beauty were being mocked. She locked herself in the bathroom and stared at her image, weeping angrily, hopelessly. She hated her body, her small hard breasts!—hated them. She hated her red hair, which drew all eyes to it. Even on the street, even on the Greyhound bus, she felt people look at her—adults, not her classmates, grown men and women who should have ignored her, since she was still a child. Men stared, especially. Men stared. And she hated them, hated their watchfulness—though at times she courted it—at times she hated them for watching her and then, as she drew closer, losing interest in her. *Too young*, they might have thought. *Not pretty enough*, they might have thought. She ran home filled with an inexplicable, senseless rage—locked herself in the bathroom and wept. Her father shouted at her to unlock the door. "You love yourself too much, it's a kind of sickness," he said in distaste. "What does it matter how tall you are?—or if you have pimples? What does it matter to anyone except you? The world exists, you know, apart from you." For several years they had battled—she had hated him, had really hated him; now, an adult, she recalled her hatred with amazement and almost with a kind of pride, that she had been capable of such passion. She had not understood her father, really. She had thought it unjust that he should accuse her of lovir g herself when she despised herself, wished to be anyone except Annie Quirt, anyone, any other girl; wasn't that proof of her innocence? She had thought that contentment was an indication of self-esteem, not knowing that discontent, of the kind that raged in her, was far more egotistical.

"Who should I love, then?" she said, sneering. "You?—Mother? Jean? Bill?—*God*?"

"You might begin with any of us," he said, mildly, "and work your way up to God."

She had not understood him then when he spoke like that, nor did she understand him now. Her father's faith embarrassed her. It was so calm, so effortless, it so lacked the kind of combative spirit she had witnessed in others—in other "believers"—that she could not relate to it at all. So she never referred to it, and she tried not to think of it. About the self-love, though, she believed he might be right. Someday she must write a letter home, a spare ascetic letter, and tell him he was right after all—that should please him.

"What does it matter, whether we love or hate ourselves," she said, talking to herself as she sometimes did, making dinner one evening a few days after her sister had left. ". . . if the results are identical. . . ."

Her thirty-first birthday had come and gone. Now she was into her thirty-second year. She would have liked to feel something—a sense of panic, of loss. Instead she felt only that queer suspension, which she had begun to feel some years earlier, past the highest point of her adolescent spirit, her rather ruthless idealism—a queer numb suspension, as if she were waiting for something to happen without any faith that it would happen. Still, she must wait.

The doorbell rang. When she went to open it, rather timidly, she saw that it was no one she knew—it was Warren Breck.

"Of course I didn't forget you. Never. How could I forget you . . . ?" he said, smiling. He shook his head as if with the absurdity of the idea. "And your letter, your lovely marvelous letter . . . your letter came at a crucial time in my life, how did you know? . . . how could you have known what it would mean to me?

They had been holding hands, almost gripping each other's hands. Annie knew she had gone white, deathly pale. In this man's presence she no longer felt familiar to herself, she felt estranged, unpleasantly excited, she could not help staring and staring at him. She loved him. She *loved* him. He was the Warren Breck of ten years ago, his brown hair cut, still, in the same styleless fashion; the lenses of his glasses thick, so that his pale brown eyes were enlarged, and looked appealing, like a child's eyes; his clothes not quite the same clothes but just as ill-fitting—a dark brown plaid sports coat and dark brown trousers, a white cotton shirt of the kind boys wore, for play, the neck stretched from having been pulled over his head many times. He had a wristwatch that was rather fashionable, however—a thick leather band with more than one buckle, like something a motorcyclist might wear. It gave his long, slender, rather bony hands a look of dramatic strength.

They held hands and talked. They talked for hours. She offered him dinner—he tried to eat but was too excited—she was too excited—so she offered him wine and he drank several glasses, distractedly, all the while staring at her. His voice was high, childlike, absolutely the voice of a decade ago, when he had raised it to question Dr. Hotchkiss or Tony or one of the others, frail in texture and yet quite fearless, in a way superbly confident. She remembered him, she remembered him so clearly! She kept interrupting him to laugh, to kiss him on the cheek, to squeeze his hand and his arm gaily, with an almost frantic triumph. He had come to her—he had actually come to her. To *her*. He must have half loved her, as she had sensed. But he had been too timid to approach her. Too shy, beside his friend Tony. Still, he must have sensed how she had liked him ... how very fond she'd been of him ... perhaps in a way she had loved him, had loved him all along. ... Hadn't she kissed him once, at a party? Drunk, all of them, and noisy, and completely happy—hadn't she kissed poor Warren Breck good night, despite his obvious embarrassment and the alarm and resentment of the poor plain girl he was with? She had loved him all along, she believed. All those years.

"Maybe you really did sense that I'd come to a crisis in my life," Warren said. "I know it's ridiculous, but ... but why not? There are mystical connections between people sometimes ... between people who are, you know, sympathetic with each other. There are these connections, I'm sure. As a scientist and a rationalist I'm opposed to such things, even to entertaining them," he said, grinning, "but as a human being ... as one who has experienced certain coincidences, certain small miracles. ... Do you think it might be possible, Annie?"

"Yes? What? That I sensed—?"

"That I communicated with you somehow—"

"Yes, I think it's true," Annie said passionately. "I know it's true."

They kissed. Both were trembling. Annie caught her breath, suddenly frightened, awkward as a young girl; for an instant she seemed not to know how to kiss, where to place her lips. She was so intensely aware of him. He was warm, nervous, giddy from the wine, as she was, tense, extremely self-conscious. *She loved him. And she was kissing him.*

"I know it's true," Annie whispered.

"Nothing much has happened to me," Annie said slowly, as if she were telling the truth; as if the truth rather astonished her. "I'm the same person I was at the age of twenty-one. Really, I'm the same as I was at the age of ... of fifteen or twelve. Aren't you? Yes? I thought so. Nothing much has happened, it's as if I've been running in place for years," she said dreamily.

"You look exactly the same," Warren said. His voice was not so shrill now; he sounded loving. "You're even more beautiful, maybe. I used to stare at your hair, watch the sunlight in it, it was hypnotic, so many angles of light . . . hypnotic. *He* didn't appreciate you enough, didn't value you enough."

Annie chose not to pursue that subject.

They lay together in Annie's narrow bed. Without his glasses Warren looked even younger. There was something ethereal about his face: the large solemn eyes, the thin lips which did not quite close over his front teeth, the slightly receding chin. Strange, that she should have thought him homely, once—he was sweet-faced, appealing, utterly delightful. She took his face in her hands and kissed him. She could not resist kissing him, like that; could not resist touching him. He was grateful for affection, like a puppy. As a lover he was rather nervous, at times frantic—but Annie did not care, she understood his anxiety and his excitement—they must become better acquainted with each other, with each other's bodies—and hadn't he been almost monastic for years?—so she did not care, it really did not matter to her. Love forgave such things. Love did not even notice such things. They lay together, in each other's arms, delighted as children, giggling, whispering, sharing secrets, reminiscing. Was it a dream?—it was so lovely! It was so perfect. Annie slept, and woke, and moved into his arms; and slept again; and, waking, they tried to make love, self-consciously; and then they lay together like conspirators, in a kind of dream, contained within the dream, not wishing to wake. Again and again one of them would exclaim: "It's incredible—seeing you again. I can hardly believe it. A miracle, isn't it? A miracle?"

He had brought a single large suitcase that contained all his "meaningful" belongings. Books and notebooks, mainly, but some clothes as well. He left Lake City, Florida, on the very day that Annie's letter had arrived: she had looked up his parents' address in the Rochester, New York, telephone book at the main library, had sent it there, asking them to forward it. Though the letter had been written in a feverish haste she had, the next morning, calmly put it into an envelope without rereading it, drove to the library, calmly and deliberately addressed the envelope, and mailed it within the hour. And Warren's parents had forwarded it to him in Lake City . . . and so he had come to her, making the long trip in two days. "I didn't even want to take time to write back," he said. "I just had to get here. To you."

"I love you," Annie whispered, starting to cry.

Like newlyweds, they were, those first several days. There was no question of Warren staying elsewhere—she had insisted he move in with her. And he had seemed to expect that. Annie's apartment was on the sixth floor of an undistinguished stucco building on the very border of an excellent residential neighborhood, and not far from one of the city's larger parks. Advertised as a "luxury" apartment, it was really quite ordinary, even shabby; and it was very small. A narrow bedroom looking out upon a wall some fifteen feet away, a living room with a tiny "dining area," a kitchen so small that Annie could make meals standing in one place, merely bending and stretching; a windowless, depressing bathroom that was also used for the cats' litter. When Jean had stayed with her it had been claustrophobic, but with Warren it seemed rather cozy. If they bumped into each other, if they got in each other's way, they merely hugged and kissed and laughed greedily.

The second evening, Warren made dinner: he'd gone out to buy the very best fresh fish available in the city, and some vegetables at an open-air market, and two bottles of French wine, and some crusty rolls at a French bakery. Annie was troubled, that he should spend so much money. But he merely laughed, saying that this was their honeymoon, wasn't it?—and they must celebrate.

The dinner was excellent. Annie believed it was excellent—she said so, repeatedly—but in fact she hardly tasted it.

She was watching her lover, studying him; she could not help wondering at the miracle that had come into her life. *He was exactly as she remembered.* Perhaps his hair was a little thinner. She noticed that now. And his manner was at times highly excitable, almost frantic. He perspired easily. The cats made him nervous, so Annie put them both in the bathroom, where they yowled and scratched against the door. "I've never understood pets, the politics of owning pets," Warren said, smiling self-consciously. "I just can't see it, you know—living intimately with animals—even if it's to combat loneliness. But your cats are beautiful creatures," he said quickly. "The long-haired one especially—beautiful, like you. Like you." The sweet gravity with which he spoke reminded Annie sharply of the Warren of ten years ago, who had discussed philosophical and political subjects with such earnestness, and at such length, refusing to acknowledge his listeners' wandering attention. He had done them all the honor, Annie saw now, of presuming them to be his equals.

Dinner began at seven and lasted until after ten. They finished both bottles of wine and opened another, a gift bottle someone had brought Annie last fall; they held hands, talked and talked and talked, always circling back to their undergraduate years, to their friends and acquaintances and professors, to the rooms they had rented, the places they had frequented, the old, enormous, drafty library—which had been replaced by a new one, Annie told Warren, all glass and steel; did he know? He didn't know. He hadn't been back, he said, since the day of commencement.

And then there were the ten years to be accounted for.

Well, her life was—it was a fairly ordinary life, she believed. Rich, varied, adventurous—though not too adventurous—not *too* adventurous, like the lives of certain people she had known; young men and a few young women who had cracked up, died of overdoses or by more deliberate means—but—but she hadn't known many such people, of course. Hadn't known them well. "My own life has been rather conventional," she said. Warren stared at her lovingly. He did not blink, did not register any emotion at all, when she said this. Perhaps he was not even listening.

Annie went on to say, haltingly, that she hadn't married—hadn't wanted to marry—had had no interest in marriage at all. Her relationship with Tony had not lasted; Tony was too shallow, didn't know what he wanted to do with his life, they had quarreled over some trivial subject and parted and lost contact with each other . . . the last she had heard, he was in California. Doing what?—she didn't know.

Warren shook his head slowly. He didn't know either, and didn't care. "That son of a bitch never appreciated you," he said softly.

But Tony no longer mattered, Annie said. She never thought of him. Never. Nine years had passed—a small lifetime—so much had happened to her—so many people had drifted into her life, had become temporarily entangled with her—though not *too* entangled, she said quickly; she had always been, well, rather detached—like Warren himself, she had always kept a certain intellectual distance between herself and the world. . . . After graduation she had gone to England and Europe for a year, had wandered around, with Tony, and then they had quarreled and there had been other friends—did he remember Janice?—yes, he would remember her, they had been in some of the same classes—one of Annie's closest, dearest friends—and then Annie had returned to the States, had studied for a master's degree in art history at the University of Michigan—had liked—*loved*—Ann Arbor; had come close to marrying a man there but at the last minute decided against him—decided against marriage itself. She had made a few close friends in Ann Arbor and still kept in touch with them. The girls especially: a very nice girl named Fern Enright to whom she still wrote, though not so often, of course, as she should write. (It was so easy, wasn't it, to lose touch?—all along the way? One stage of life and then another and another, always people attached to each of these stages who are irreplaceable and dear yet somehow flimsy, precarious: so easily lost. Did Warren agree? Yes?)

Well, she had liked Ann Arbor very much. At least at first. Of course there were unhappy, desperate people there, really suicidal people, in the mid-sixties, and she had had to keep herself clear of them. Such fools, Annie said, her mouth twisting as she recalled certain incidents and then dismissed them, hoping Warren would not question her. He merely smiled, to show his interest; he asked no questions.

She was friendly with a few people but kept herself detached from others, as always: all her life she'd been rather alone. Not lonely but *alone.* She had been a serious student in graduate school—quite different from her undergraduate behavior—and had done a lengthy study of the art of Isabel Bishop, a fine painter. Was Warren familiar with Isabel Bishop's work? No? Well, she was a fine American artist, one of the outstanding "urban realists" of the thirties—not so well known as she should be, Annie believed—of course not a *great* artist, that could not be claimed, but an excellent one. At the same time, Annie said, as if anticipating a query from Warren—who was, in fact, simply smiling at her—her aesthetic principles were really more international, more "modernist"— she sympathized with the American Scene painters and their loving, meticulous work—their noble attempt to create a distinctly American tradition, but imaginatively she was more deeply engaged, perhaps, by—by the others—by Abstract Expressionism, still—though it was now denounced, and though people liked to say they were now bored by Pollock, she still felt a genuine excitement standing before his canvases—And—and, well, she said with a slightly annoyed smile, since Warren was not responding at all, after Ann Arbor she had tried to paint for a while without luck and had done a little part-time teaching— at a small college—and—and that hadn't worked out, the administration was terribly intolerant—narrow-minded—so she had quit and come here and had been working at a gallery downtown—a promising job, it had seemed—the Hunter Gallery dealt with some fine work—a promising job that had turned sour, since Annie had been used simply as a receptionist and clerk and secretary and clean-up girl—bossed around, treated patronizingly—and paid very little for the surprisingly long hours she worked. So she had quit. Had quit a few weeks ago. And—

But Warren was not listening. Had not been listening.

He stared at her forearm and touched it lightly with his finger.

"What's this, Annie?" he said. "Did you hurt yourself?"

Annie glanced at the scar and moved her arm away. "It's nothing. An accident."

"An accident. How?"

"I said an accident," Annie snapped.

Warren blinked. He mumbled an apology—he had not meant to be rude. Of course it was none of his business.

Annie said nothing and poured more wine into their glasses. Might as well finish the bottle. Their third. She looked at him and smiled, forced herself to smile, and he smiled at once, eagerly. He was drunk: but as a child might be drunk, innocent and disheveled. She loved him. She had called him to her, and he had come. Out of the past he had come in obedience to her. In obedience to love. She loved him, loved him. Certainly. Obviously. Otherwise why was he here, why were they drinking together, why was she smiling at him . . . ?

Begin with Warren, then, she thought. *Begin with Warren and work your way upward to God.*

In the morning they made love again, and again it was not quite right. Warren was breathless, clumsy, exasperated. He labored above her with his eyes shut tight as if in terror of their flying apart. "I love you, love you," he said almost angrily.

"I love *you,*" Annie wept.

She rose from the sweaty sheets and went into the bathroom to shower and he remained there, dozing. In her bed. His head damp on her pillow.

She would never be alone again.

That day she was oddly exhausted. It tired her to talk to Warren, as if they had been laboring together to comprehend something for hours, for days, and had failed, and yet could not stop. He was sweet—she adored him—and yet why didn't he shave, why didn't he shower?—why did he stay so close? He showed no inclination to leave the apartment. He turned on the radio and moved the dial slowly from side to side, listening to a station for a few minutes, then moving on. At all times there was a guileless half-smile on his face like something crudely sketched on a blank sheet of paper.

The telephone rang and Annie spoke hurriedly and apologetically, explaining she was busy. Warren's eyebrows rose; he listened closely to what she said, but never asked her, afterward, who had called. When she asked him if he would like to go out—to the Art Institute, to a movie, to visit friends of hers, he did not seem very interested.

"I'm content here," he said, smiling. "It's paradise, here."

"But—wouldn't you like some fresh air?"

"I'm perfectly content here, Annie."

She went out to buy groceries. She had to get out of the apartment.

Walking along Annie rehearsed a conversation: *Aren't you a doctor, Warren? What has happened? Didn't you go to medical school?—Aren't you a genius? What is happening—? Why are you here?* Her legs felt long and awkward as stilts. Her head rang with words. It was raining and she had rushed out with no umbrella or raincoat, wearing only a thin cotton shirt and blue jeans and sneakers so worn that her smallest toes peeped through. She began to cry again and her tears mixed with the rain.

"I love him," she said. "I do love him. . . . I must love him."

She walked a half-mile to the park. Something was wrong, gravely wrong, but it must be articulated before she could deal with it. From the few vague things Warren had said about his present life, she judged that he had no work—hadn't finished medical school—perhaps he hadn't even gone to medical school?—she didn't dare ask. She didn't want to hurt his feelings; and she had the idea that he wasn't quite the Warren she recalled—his thinking processes had atrophied somewhat. But probably that was her imagination. He had always been shy, clumsy, not very good with conversation, at times almost mute: poor Warren!

"Love, love, love ..."

She struck her hands together, half-fisted, prayerlike.

Skirting the playground area, which was deserted this afternoon, Annie happened to see a figure across the way—a man—moving slowly and sluggishly in the direction of the woods. In a streaked trenchcoat, head bowed. He did not turn, did not notice her. She strode by. On an ordinary day the park was filled with young mothers and hordes of children, white and black, and a few couples, and straggling indeterminate figures, mostly male, who walked along the wide graveled paths in utter isolation, like creatures blundering through a single, singular dream, which could not be shared with anyone else. In poor weather there were no young mothers, no children, but often the solitary people showed up—often, Annie was one of them—head bowed, heart pumping, mind racing with perpetual unanswerable shouts: *What do I do now? What now? Now? I had wanted a life so different*—Nearly six feet tall, slender but not slight, sharp-eyed, quick, her red hair falling straight to her shoulders, Annie must have seemed intimidating to anyone who saw her; at any rate, none of the other solitary wanderers ever approached her.

That day she went to a neighborhood library and, sitting on the floor by the shelves of art books, spent an hour or more looking through books—turning pages quickly, desperately—studying Van Gogh's drawings and Cézanne's landscapes and crude, touching woodcuts by anonymous Germans of the late medieval period—then paging quickly again, as if she were looking for something specific, though she could not have said what it was. Her legs ached; she must leave; Warren was waiting for her; she had not yet done the grocery shopping. . . . Then, by accident, she discovered what she must have been seeking: her breath was drawn sharply inward when she came upon the watercolors of Nolde, beautiful, indefinable, utterly perfect. *Here,* she thought simply.

At six the library closed and she returned to the apartment and saw that there was no one there—no one. "Warren?" she called. Her voice lifted in astonishment. "Warren?"

She set the bag of groceries down. "Warren. . . ?"

The apartment was empty. Even the cats were gone. She called them—called them in a voice that wailed absurdly. The bathroom window was open, and there was no screen; Warren must have opened the window deliberately so that the cats could get out, along the ledge, down the fire escape. They had both been strays, at times she had disliked the nuisance of having them in so small a place, but she had been very fond of them.

Annie was leaning out the window, calling the cats, when she felt a hand on her back.

"I thought maybe, you know, they stopped you on the street, made you come to the station for questioning. I thought maybe something had gone wrong. Something serious."

"No. No, Warren."

"—because you were gone so long."

"No."

"You were gone for hours," he said accusingly. "You must not love me, you must have been lying."

"I love you, Warren."

"They didn't arrest you? They didn't trace the car and take you to the station and interrogate you and force you to betray me?—Because they can do anything they want, anything. And you're a woman. They could have hurt you and forced you to betray me and then let you come back here—to put me off my guard."

Annie shook her head. "I didn't—there was no one—Nothing happened."

"But you must not love me" he said. "Otherwise you wouldn't have stayed away so long."

He took off his glasses and rubbed his eyes and made a

tired, exasperated noise. Annie had to go to him, had to put her arms around him and kiss him. Still he was hurt, sullen; he did not respond.

"You're not much different from *her,*" he muttered.

"Who do you mean, Warren?" Annie asked carefully.

He shrugged his shoulders. ". . . leave the house to go shopping stay away for hours . . . days . . . invent all kinds of insulting excuses . . . any fool could interpret their true meaning. What if I got hungry? I'm normal, a normal human being, I need to eat like anyone else . . . what if there's no food in the house and I get hungry? She stayed away for days. She thought she could hide. Pathetic bitch," he said softly.

Annie stood beside him, unable to move. She wanted to walk away but could not. If she embraced him more enthusiastically, if she brushed the messy strands of hair out of his eyes, and kissed him, everything might be restored; but she could not move.

"Who are you talking about, Warren?" she said.

"My son would have been three years old," he said suddenly. "What day is this? Where's a calendar?—Yes, see, it's the fourteenth today, he would have been three years old on the fifteenth, I have an excellent memory for dates and he was born on the fifteenth of August—but—but—"

He began to cry. His glasses fell into his lap, then to the floor. He cried, his face screwed up like a baby's, and Annie stood above him staring, blank, frozen.

"—my son—she tried to—they all tried to—sneaking behind my back, planting evidence against me—eavesdropping—spying—at the police station she uncovered herself—the slut—they saw her for what she was—and the burns on the baby—*she* did it—she lied—her family lied—Is she in touch with you, Annie, was she someone we both knew?—from college? Were you talking on the telephone with her, Annie, is that why you were gone so long?"

"No, no."

"Are you telling the truth, Annie, or—"

"I'm telling the truth, Warren."

He looked up at her. Not so young now, and yet curiously childlike: his skin was grayish, drawn, his brown eyes were bloodshot and opaque as marbles. Annie wondered if he could see her. He was nearly blind without his glasses.

"Annie," he whispered, taking her cold hand, "Annie . . . you're so beautiful, so beautiful. . . . I remember from years ago, how beautiful you were, you are, I love you so much and I need you, you won't betray me, will you? . . . So beautiful," he said, blinking up at her. "Tony didn't appreciate you. The bastard. That one week, you thought you were pregnant, do you remember? . . . and he was drunk for three days straight and wouldn't leave my room, said he was holing up there, wouldn't come to the telephone when you called, the bastard . . . wouldn't let me study in peace . . . none of you let me study in peace . . . but I didn't mind, I liked you all . . . envied you. . . . I loved *you*, Annie Quirt," he said dramatically, gazing up at her with those glistening myopic eyes, "and I will love you the rest of my life."

"I'm in trouble. I'm in bad trouble."

"But I can't talk now, Annie. You know that."

"Is anyone in the office with you?"

"I said I can't talk now. —Do you want money?"

"I'm in trouble, I don't know what to do—I don't know what to do—"

There was no reply. Annie wondered, in a panic, if he had already hung up.

"Look," she said, "I haven't bothered you, have I?—I haven't telephoned you—it's been a long time, hasn't it? You told me to call you, practically begged me to call—"

"I didn't *beg* you to call, Annie, you or anyone else."

"—there's someone here with me, he's sleeping now, he sleeps all day, he's been here two weeks now and—and I can't—I'm afraid—I don't know what—"

"Do you want money? I can't hear you very well."

"—I don't want to call the police, I don't want to turn him in—I'm afraid—I can't think what to do—I—"

"Do you want money? I'll send you a money order. All right? All right?"

"—money? I—"

"I'll send you a money order, Annie. Good-bye."

"But John—"

"Last time it was five hundred dollars and this time, dear, it's going to be only two hundred fifty. That should about discharge it, Annie, right? Good-bye."

"Wait—I need—"

"Good-bye."

The playground was deserted; since morning rain had fallen steadily and there were puddles beneath the swings, beneath the monkey bars, at the bottom of the slide. Annie crossed the playground, hands in the pockets of her raincoat. She was bareheaded. She thought her plastic scarf was in the pocket of her coat, but it wasn't there. So she was bareheaded in the rain and, after a while, she did not notice.

There was no wind. The rain fell quietly, steadily. From time to time Annie shivered. Her feet were wet; the cheap canvas tennis shoes had soaked through.

I can stay here as long as I want, she thought. *There's no one here.*

Impulsively she climbed the slide, taking the steps two at a time. She was a big powerful handsome girl. Well loved. Enviable. People glanced at her, and then looked again. Stared. She could handle her life as she wished. She was capable of anything. At the top of the slide she paused, hands on the railings. She surveyed the shabby little playground with its asphalt paving, and as much of the park as she could see—the duck pond riddled with rain, the trash containers filled to the very top, overflowing, the paths in all directions empty. A memory of Warren flashed to her, not the Warren who slept open-mouthed in her bed—at this very moment he was sleeping—but the Warren of a decade ago. He had been walking quickly along Salina Street one day, shoulders hunched slightly, head bowed, a rather ludicrous figure in his khaki jacket, his ill-fitting cheap trousers, his tattered shoes—walking along without watching where he went, so that he bumped into Annie as she came out of a store: bumped into her, mumbled something, and hurried away without seeming to recognize her. She had turned to watch him, sneering. He had half run away, not looking back.

Now she stood at the top of the slide, gripping the wet railings. She could not recall having climbed the slide, and she did not know why she had climbed it. But it seemed as good a place as any on this rainy afternoon.

Evan Hunter's first mainstream novel, The Blackboard Jungle, *was a huge critical and commercial success (it was a bestseller in 1954), and paved the way for such encore performances as* A Matter of Conviction, Strangers When We Meet, Last Summer, Sons, *and the recent* Love, Dad *and* Lizzie. *Under his Ed McBain pseudonym, he is well known as the creator of what has been widely praised as the finest of all police procedural series, the saga of the 87th Precinct. Hunter has published numerous mystery and detective short stories over the past thirty-five years, some of the best of which appear in his collections* The Jungle Kids *(1956) and* The McBain Brief *(1982), the latter as by Ed McBain. "The Interview," a marriage of the literary story and the crime story, is among his most accomplished short pieces.*

THE INTERVIEW
Evan HunteR

Sir, ever since the Sardinian accident, you have refused to grant any interviews. . . .

I had no desire to join the circus.

Yet you are not normally a man who shuns publicity.

Not normally, no. The matter on Sardinia, however, was blown up out of all proportion, and I saw no reason for adding fuel to the fire. I am a creator of motion pictures, *not* of sensational news stories for the press.

There are some "creators of motion pictures" who might have welcomed the sort of publicity the Sardinian . . .

Not I.

Yet you will admit the accident helped the gross of the film.

I am not responsible for the morbid curiosity of the American public.

Were you responsible for what happened in Sardinia?

On Sardinia. It's an island.

On Sardinia, if you will.

I was responsible only for directing a motion picture. Whatever else happened, happened.

You were there when it happened, however. . . .

I was there.

So certainly . . .

I choose not to discuss it.

The actors and technicians present at the time have had a great deal to say about the accident. Isn't there anything you'd like to refute or amend? Wouldn't you like to set the record straight?

The record is the film. My films are my record. Everything else is meaningless. Actors are beasts of burden and technicians are domestic servants, and refuting or amending anything either might care to utter would be a senseless waste of time.

Would you like to elaborate on that?

On what?

On the notion that actors . . .

It is not a notion, it is a simple fact. I have never met an intelligent actor. Well, let me correct that. I enjoyed working with only one actor in my entire career, and I still have a great deal of respect for him—or at least as much respect as I can possibly muster for anyone who pursues a profession that requires him to apply makeup to his face.

Did you use this actor in the picture you filmed on Sardinia?

No.

Why not? Given your respect for him . . .

I had no desire to donate fifty percent of the gross to his already swollen bank account.

Is that what he asked for?

At the time. It may have gone up to seventy-five percent by now, I'm sure I don't know. I have no intention of ever giving a plowhorse or a team of oxen fifty percent of the gross of a motion picture *I* created.

If we understand you correctly . . .

You probably don't.

Why do you say that?

Only because I have never been quoted accurately in any publication, and I have no reason to believe your magazine will prove to be an exception.

Then why did you agree to the interview?

Because I would like to discuss my new project. I have a meeting tonight with a New York playwright who will be delivering the final draft of a screenplay upon which we have labored long and hard. I have every expectation that it will now meet my requirements. In which case, looking ahead to the future, this interview should appear in print shortly before the film is completed and ready for release. At least, I hope the timetable works out that way.

May we know who the playwright is?

I thought you were here to talk to *me*.

Well, yes, but . . .

It has been my observation that when Otto Preminger or Alfred Hitchcock or David Lean or even some of the fancy young *nouvelle vague* people give interviews, they rarely talk about anyone but themselves. That may be the one good notion any of them has ever contributed to the industry.

You sound as if you don't admire too many directors.

I admire some.

Would you care to name them?

I have admiration for Griffith, DeMille, Eisenstein, several others.

Why these men in particular?

They're all dead.

Are there no living directors you admire?

None.

None? It seems odd that a man known for his generosity would be so chary with praise for other acknowledged film artists.

Yes.

Yes, what?

Yes, it would seem odd, a distinct contradiction of personality. The fact remains that I consider every living director a threat, a challenge, and a competitor. There are only so many motion picture screens in the world, and there are thousands of films competing to fill those screens. If the latest Hitchcock thriller has them standing on line outside Radio City, the chances are they *won't* be standing on line outside *my* film up the street. The theory that an outstanding box-office hit helps *all* movies is sheer rubbish. The outstanding hit helps only itself. The other films suffer because no one wants to see them; they want to see only the big one, the champion, the one that has the line outside on the sidewalk. I try to make certain that all of my films generate the kind of excitement necessary to sustain a line on the sidewalk. And I resent the success of any film but my own.

Yet you have had some notable failures.

Failures are never notable. Besides, I do not consider any of my films failures.

Are we talking now about artistic failures or box-office failures?

I have never made an artistic failure. Some of my films were mildly disappointing at the box office. But not very many of them.

When the Sardinian film was ready to open last June ...

July. It opened on the Fourth of July.

Yes, but before it opened, when ...

That would have been June, yes. July is normally preceded by June.

There was speculation that the studio would not permit its showing.

Rubbish.

The rumors were unfounded? That the studio would suppress the film?

The film opened, didn't it? And was a tremendous success, I might add.

Some observers maintain that the success of the film was due only to the publicity given the Sardinian accident. Would you agree to that?

I'll ask *you* a question, young man. Suppose the accident on Sardinia had been related to a film called *The Beach Girl Meets Hell's Angels,* or some such piece of trash? Do you think the attendant publicity would have insured the success of *that* film?

Perhaps not. But given your name and the stellar quality of it . . .

You can stop after my name. Stars have nothing to do with any of my pictures. I could put a trained seal in one of my films, and people would come to see it. I could put *you* in a film, and people would come to see it.

Don't you believe that films are a collaborative effort?

Certainly not. I tell the script writer what I want, and he writes it. I tell the set designer what to give me, and he gives it to me. I tell the cameraman where to aim his camera and what lens to use. I tell the actors where to move and how to speak their lines. Does that sound collaborative to you? Besides, I resent the word "effort."

Why?

Because the word implies endeavor without success. You've tried to do something and you've failed. None of my films are "efforts." The word "effort" is like the word "ambitious." They both spell failure. Haven't you seen book jackets that proudly announce "This is So-and-So's most ambitious effort to date"? What does that mean to you? To me, it means the poor bastard has set his sights too high. And failed.

Are you afraid of failure?

I cannot abide it.

Do you believe the Sardinian film was a success? Artistically?

I told you earlier . . .

Yes, but many critics felt the editing of the film was erratic. That the sequences filmed before the drowning were inserted piecemeal into . . .

To begin with, whenever critics begin talking about editing or camera angles or dolly shots or anything technical, I instantly fall asleep. They haven't the faintest notion of what filmmaking is all about, and their pretentious chatter about the art may impress maiden ladies in Flushing Meadows, but it quite leaves me cold. In reality, *none* of them know what's going on either behind the camera or up there on the screen. Do you know what a film critic's sole requirement is? That he has seen a lot of movies, period. To my way of thinking, *that* qualifies him as an expert on popcorn, not on celluloid.

In any event, you were rather limited, were you not, in editing the final portion of the film?

Limited in what way?

In terms of the footage you needed to make the film a complete entity?

The film *was* a complete entity. Obviously, I could not include footage that did not exist. The girl drowned. That was a simple fact. We did not shoot the remainder of the film as originally planned; we *could* not. But the necessary script revisions were made on the spot—or rather in Rome. I flew to Rome to consult with an Italian screenwriter, who did the work I required.

He did not receive credit on the film.

He *asked* that his name be removed from the picture. I acceded to his wishes.

But not without a struggle.

There was no struggle.

It was reported that you struck him.

Nonsense.

On the Via Veneto.

The most violent thing I've ever done on the Via Veneto was to sip a Campari-soda outside Doney's.

Yet the newspapers . . .

The Roman press is notoriously inaccurate. In fact, there isn't a single good newspaper in all Italy.

But, sir, there was some dispute with the screen writer, wasn't there? Surely, the stories about it couldn't all have been . . .

We had some words.

About what?

Oh my, we *must* pursue this deadly dull rot, mustn't we? All right, all right. It was *his* allegation that when he accepted the job, he had no idea the publicity surrounding the girl's death would achieve such hideous proportions. He claimed he did not wish his good Italian name—the little opportunist had written only one film prior to my hiring him, and that an Italian Western starring a second-rate American television actor—did not wish his name associated with a project that had even a *cloud* of suspicion hanging over it. Those were his exact words. Actually, quite the opposite was true. Which is why I resisted his idiotic ploy.

Quite the opposite? What do you mean?

Rather than trying to *avoid* the unfortunate publicity, I felt he was trying to capitalize on it. His move was really completely transparent, the pathetic little bastard. I finally let him have his way. I should have thought he'd be proud to have his name on one of my pictures. As an illuminating sidelight, I might add he did *not* return the five thousand dollars a week I'd paid for the typing he did. Apparently, my *money* did not have a similar "cloud of suspicion" hanging over it.

"Typing," did you say?

Typing. The ideas for changing the script to accommodate the ... to allow for a more plausible resolution were all mine.

A resolution to accommodate the drowning?

To explain the absence of the girl in the remainder of the film. I'm reluctant to discuss this, because it has a ghoulish quality I frankly find distasteful. The girl *did*, after all, drown; she *did* die. But that was a simple fact, and we must not lose sight of another simple fact. However cold-blooded this may sound, and I am well aware that it may be an unpopular observation, there had already been an expenditure of three million dollars on that film. Now I'm sure you know that leading players *have* taken ill, *have* suffered heart attacks, *have* died during the filming of other pictures. To my knowledge, such events have never caused a picture to halt production, and neither do I know of a single instance in which a film was entirely scrapped, solely because of the death of one of the leading players. Yet this was the very pressure being brought to bear on me immediately following the drowning, and indeed up to the time of the film's release.

Then the studio did *try to suppress the film?*

Well . . . at first, they only wanted to stop production. I refused. Later, when they saw the rough cut—this was when all the publicity had reached its peak—they sent in a team of strong-armed executive producers, and production chiefs, and what-have-you, all know-nothings with windy titles, who asked me to suppress the film. I told them exactly where to go. And then later on, when the film had been edited and scored, the same thing happened. I finally threatened suit. My contract called for a large percentage of the gross of that film, and I had no intention of allowing it to crumble unseen in the can.

You did not feel it was a breach of good taste to exhibit the film?

Certainly not. The girl met with an accident. The accident was no one's fault. She drowned. If a stunt man had died riding a horse over a cliff, would there have been all that brouhaha about releasing the film? I should say not.

But you must agree the circumstances surrounding the drowning . . .

The drowning was entirely accidental. We were shooting in shallow water.

The reports on the depth of the water vary from ten feet to forty feet. Neither of which might be considered shallow.

The water was no higher than her waist. And she was a tall girl. Five feet seven, I believe. Or eight. I'm not sure which.

Then how did she drown, sir?

I have no idea.

You were there, were you not?

I was on the camera barge, yes.

Then what happened?

I suppose we must set this to rest once and for all, mustn't we? I would much rather discuss the present and/or the future, but apparently we cannot do that until we've dealt *ad nausem* with the past.

As you wish, sir.

I wish the accident had never happened, sir, that is what *I* wish. I also wish I would not be pestered interminably about it. The Italian inquest determined that the drowning was entirely accidental. What was good enough for the Italian courts is damn well good enough for me. But there is no satisfying the American appetite for scandal, is there? Behind each accident or incident, however innocuous, however innocent, the American public *must* insist upon a plot, a conspiracy, a cabal. Nothing is permitted to be exactly what it appears to be. Mystery, intrigue must surround everything. Nonsense. Do you think any of us *wanted* that girl to drown? I've already told you how much money we'd spent on the picture before the accident. I would estimate now that the delay in completion, the cost of revisions, the necessity for bringing in a second girl to resolve the love story added at least a million dollars to the proposed budget. No one wanted the drowning. If for business reasons *alone*, no one wanted it.

Yet it happened.
It happened.
How?
The exact sequence of events is still unclear to me.
Your assistant director . . .
Yes.
Testified at the inquest . . .
Yes, yes.
That the girl pleaded not to go into the water.
The water was unusually cold that morning. There was nothing we could do about *that*. It was a simple fact. The light was perfect, we had our setup, and we were prepared to shoot. Actors are like children, you know. If I had allowed her to balk at entering the water, the next thing I knew she'd have balked at walking across a lawn.

The writer of the original screenplay claims that the scene you were shooting that morning . . .
Where the girl swims in to the dock? What about it?
He claims he did not write that scene. He claims it was not in the original script.

Well, let him take that up with the Writers Guild.

Was it in the original script?

I have no idea. If there were no innovations during the shooting of a film ... really, does anyone expect me to follow a script precisely? What then is my function as director? To shout "louder" or "softer" to an actor? Let the writers direct their own scripts, in that case. I assure you they would not get very far.

Was the scene an innovation? The scene in the water?

It might have been. I can't recall. If it was not in the original shooting script, as our Hollywood hack claims, then I suppose it *was* an innovation. By definition, yes, it would have been an innovation, isn't that so?

When was it added to the script?

I don't recall. I will sometimes get ideas for scenes the night before I shoot them. In which case, I will call in the technicians involved and describe the setup I will need the next day, and I will have it in the morning. If there is additional dialogue involved, I'll see to it that the actors and the script girl have the necessary pages, and I'll ask the actors to study them overnight. If there is no additional dialogue ...

Was there any dialogue in this scene?

No. The girl was merely required to swim in to the dock from a speedboat.

What do you do in such a case? In an added scene where there's no dialogue?

Oh, I'll usually take the actor aside and sketch in the scene for him. The gist of it. This was a particularly simple scene. She had only to dive over the side of the boat and swim in to the dock.

In shallow water?

Well, not so shallow that she was in any danger of hitting the bottom, if that's what you mean.

Then perhaps the estimates of the water's depth ...

The water's depth was no problem for anyone who knew how to swim.

Did the girl know how to swim?

Of course she did. You certainly don't think I'd have allowed her to play a scene in water . . .

I merely wondered if she was a good swimmer or . . .

Adequate. She was neither Eleanor Holm nor Esther Williams, but the part didn't call for an Olympic champion, you know. She was an adequate swimmer.

When did you explain the gist of the scene to her?

That morning, I believe. If memory serves me . . . yes, I believe the idea came to me the night before, and I called in the people involved and told them what I would need the following morning. Which is when I explained the scene to her. At least, that's usually the way it works; I assume it worked the same way concerning this particular scene.

You explained that she would have to dive over the side of the boat and swim in to the dock?

Which is all she had to do.

Did she agree to do this?

Why, of course. She was an inexperienced little thing; this was her first film. Of course, she agreed. There was never any question of her *not* agreeing. She'd been modeling miniskirts or what-have-you for a teenage fashion magazine when I discovered her. This was an enormous opportunity for her, this film. Look at the people I surrounded her with! Do you know what we had to pay her leading man? Never mind. It still irritates me.

Is it true he threatened to walk off the picture after the girl drowned?

He has said so in countless publications across the length and breadth of the world. I'm surprised he hasn't erected a billboard on the moon, but I imagine he's petitioning NASA for the privilege this very moment.

But did he threaten to walk off?

He did. I could not allow it, of course. Neither would his contract allow it. An actor will sometimes be deluded into believing he is something more than a beast of the field. Even with today's largely independent production structure, the studio serves as a powerful steamroller flattening out life's annoying little bumps for any second-rate bit player who's ever seen his own huge face grinning down idiotically from a screen. The *real* head sometimes gets as big as the fantasy head up there. Walk off the picture? I'd have sued his socks from under him.

Why did he threaten to walk off?

We'd had difficulty from the start. I think he was searching for an excuse, and seized upon the girl's drowning as a ripe opportunity.

What sort of difficulty?

I do not believe I need comment on the reputation of the gentleman involved. It has been adequately publicized, even in the most austere family publications.

Is it true, then, that a romance was developing between him and the girl?

I have never yet worked on a film in which a romance did not develop between the girl and her leading man. That is a simple fact of motion-picture production.

Was it a simple fact of this motion picture?

Unfortunately, yes.

Why do you say "unfortunately"?

The girl had a brilliant career ahead of her. I hated to see her in a position that . . . I hated to see her in such a vulnerable position.

Vulnerable?

The Italian press would have enjoyed nothing better than to link her romantically with someone of his reputation. I warned her against this repeatedly. We'd spent quite a lot of money grooming this girl, you know. Stardom may happen overnight, but it takes many *days* of preparation for that overnight event.

Did she heed your warnings?

She was very young.

Does that mean to say . . . ?

Nineteen, very young.

There were, of course, news stories of a developing romance between them. Despite your efforts.

Yes, despite them. Well.

Yes?

The young are susceptible. And yet, I warned her. Until the very end, I warned her. The night before she drowned, there was a large party at the hotel, given in my honor. We had seen the rushes on the shooting we'd done the day before, and we were all quite pleased, and I, of course, was more than ever certain that the girl was going to be a tremendous smash. That I had found someone, developed someone, who would most certainly become one of the screen's enduring personalities. No question about it. She had ... she had a luminous quality that ... it's impossible to explain this to a layman. There are people, however, who are bland, colorless, insipid, until you photograph them. And suddenly, the screen is illuminated with a life force that is positively blinding. She had that quality. And so I told her again, that night of the party, I took her aside, and we were drinking quietly, and I reminded her of what she had been, an unknown model for a juvenile fashion magazine, and of what she would most certainly become once this film was released, and I begged her not to throw this away on a silly flirtation with her leading man, a man of his reputation. The press was there, you know, this was quite an occasion—I had met the host on the Riviera, oh, years, ago, when I was doing another film, and this was something of a reunion. Well. Well, I suppose none of it matters quite, does it? She's dead. She drowned the next day.

What happened? At the party?

They managed to get some photographs of her. There is a long covered walk at the hotel, leading to the tower apartments that overlook the dock. The *papparazzi* got some pictures of the two of them in a somewhat, shall we say, compromising attitude. I tried to get the cameras, I struggled with one of the photographers. ...

Were these the photographs that were later published? After the accident?

Yes, yes. I knew even then, of course. When I failed to get those cameras, I knew her career was ruined. I knew that everything I'd done, all the careful work, the preparation—and all for *her*, you know, all to make the girl a *star*, a person in her own right—all of it was wasted. I took her to her room. I scolded her severely, and reminded her that makeup call was for six A.M.

What happened the next morning?

She came out to the barge at eight o'clock, made up and in costume. She was wearing a bikini, with a robe over it. It was quite a chilly day.

Was she behaving strangely?

Strangely? I don't know what you mean. She seemed thoroughly chastised, as well she might have. She sat alone and talked to no one. But aside from that, she seemed perfectly all right.

No animosity between you?

No, no. A bit of alienation perhaps. I had, after all, been furious with her the night before and had soundly reprimanded her. But I *am* a professional, you know, and I *did* have a scene to shoot. As I recall, I was quite courteous and friendly. When I saw she was chilled, in fact, I offered her my Thermos.

Your Thermos?

Yes. Tea. A Thermos of tea. I like my tea strong, almost to the point of bitterness. On location, I can never get anyone to brew it to my taste, and so I do it myself, carry the Thermos with me. That's what I offered her. The Thermos of tea I had brewed in my room before going out to the barge.

And did she accept it?

Gratefully. She was shivering. There was quite a sharp wind, the beginning of the mistral, I would imagine. She sat drinking the tea while I explained the scene to her. We were alone in the stern; everyone else was up forward, bustling about, getting ready for the shot.

Did she mention anything about the night before?

Not a word. Nor did I expect her to. She only complained that the tea was too bitter. I saw to it that she drank every drop.

Why?

Why? I've already told you. It was uncommonly cold that day. I didn't want to risk her coming down with anything.

*Sir . . . was there any other reason for offering her the tea?
For making certain that she drank every drop?*

What do you mean?

*I'm only reiterating now what some of the people on the
barge have already said.*

Yes, and what's that?

*That the girl was drunk when she reported for work, that
you tried to sober her up, and that she was still drunk when she
went into the water.*

Nonsense. No one drinks on my sets. Even if I'd worked
with W. C. Fields, I would not have permitted him to drink.
And I respected him highly. For an actor, he was a sensitive and
decent man.

*Yet rumors persist that the girl was drunk when she climbed
from the camera barge into the speedboat.*

She was cold sober. I would just love to know how such
rumors start. The girl finished her tea and was sitting *alone* with
me for more than three hours. We were having some color difficulty with the speedboat; I didn't like the way the green bow
was registering, and I asked that it be repainted. As a result,
preparation for the shot took longer than we'd expected. I was
afraid it might cloud up and we'd have to move indoors to the
cover set. The point is, however, that in all that time not a single soul came anywhere near us. So how in God's name would
anyone know whether the girl was drunk or not? Which she
wasn't, I can definitely assure you.

They say, sir . . .

They, they, who the hell are *they?*

*The others on the barge. They say that when she went
forward to climb down into the speedboat, she seemed unsure of
her footing. They say she appeared glassy-eyed . . .*

Rubbish.

*. . . that when she asked if the shooting might be post-
poned . . .*

All rubbish.

. . . her voice was weak, somehow without force.

I can tell you definitely and without reservation, and I can tell you as the single human being who was with that girl from the moment she stepped onto the barge until the moment she climbed into the speedboat some three and a half hours later that she was at all times alert, responsive, and in complete control of her faculties. She did not want to go into the water because it was cold. But that was a simple fact, and I could not control the temperature of the ocean or the air. Nor could I reasonably postpone shooting when we were in danger of losing our light, and when we finally had everything including the damn speedboat ready to roll.

So she went into the water. As instructed.

Yes. She was supposed to swim a short distance underwater, and then surface. That was the way I'd planned the scene. She went into the water, the cameras were rolling, we . . . none of us quite realized at first that she was taking an uncommonly long time to surface. By the time it dawned upon us, it was too late. *He*, of course, immediately jumped into the water after her. . . .

He?

Her leading man, his heroic move, his hairy-chested *star* gesture. She was dead when he reached her.

What caused her to drown? A cramp? Undertow? What?

I haven't the foggiest idea. Accidents happen. What more can I say? This was a particularly unfortunate one, and I regret it. But the past is the past, and if one continues to dwell upon it, one can easily lose sight of the present. I tend not to ruminate. Rumination is only stagnation. I plan ahead, and in that way the future never comes as a shock. It's comforting to know, for example, that by the time this appears in print, I will be editing and scoring a film I have not yet begun to shoot. There is verity and substance to routine that varies only slightly. It provides a reality that is all too often lacking in the motion-picture industry.

This new film, sir . . .

I thought you'd never ask.

What is it about?

I never discuss the plot or theme of a movie. If I were able to do justice to a story by capsulizing it into three or four paragraphs, why would I then have to spend long months filming it? The synopsis, as such, was invented by Hollywood executives who need so-called "story analysts" to provide simple translations because they themselves are incapable of reading anything more difficult than "Run, Spot, run."

What can you tell us about your new film, sir?

I can tell you that it is set in Yugoslavia, and that I will take full cinematic advantage of the rugged coastal terrain there. I can tell you that it is a love story of unsurpassing beauty, and that I have found an unusually talented girl to play the lead. She has never made a film before; she was working with a little theater group in La Cienaga when I discovered her, quite by chance. A friend of mine asked me to look in on an original the group was doing, thought there might be film possibilities in it, and so forth. The play was a hopeless botch, but the girl was a revelation. I had her tested immediately, and the results were staggering. What happens before the cameras is all that matters, you know, which is why some of our important stage personalities have never been able to make a successful transition to films. This girl has a vibrancy that causes one to forget completely that there are mechanical appliances such as projectors or screens involved. It is incredible; it is almost uncanny. It is as though her life force transcends the medium itself, sidesteps it so to speak; she achieves direct uninvolved communication at a response level I would never have thought existed. I've been working with her for, oh, easily six months now, and she's remarkably receptive, a rare combination of intelligence and incandescent beauty. I would be foolish to make any sort of prediction about her future, considering the present climate of Hollywood, and the uncertain footing of the entire industry. But if this girl continues to listen and to learn, if she is willing to work as hard in the months ahead as she has already worked, then given the proper vehicle and the proper guidance—both of which I fully intend to supply—I cannot but foresee a brilliant career for her.

Is there anything you would care to say, sir, about the future of the industry in general?

I never deal in generalities, only specifics. I feel that so long as there are men dedicated to the art of making good motion pictures—and I'm not talking now about pornography posing as art, or pathological disorders posing as humor—as long as there are men willing to make the sacrifices necessary to bring quality films to the public, the industry will survive. I intend to survive along with it. In fact, to be more specific, I intend to endure.

Thank you, sir.

Norman Mailer is generally acknowledged, even by his detractors, as being the most significant and probably the most talented living American writer. His service in the U.S. Army from 1944–46 was the basis of his first novel, The Naked and the Dead *(1948), published when he was just twenty-five and hailed by critics far and wide as the finest novel of World War II. He followed this with such other novels as* The Deer Park *and* An American Dream; *and with such nonfiction works as* The Armies of the Night *(1968), a description of the anti-Vietnam War marches for which he received the National Book Award and a shared Pulizer Prize. (He was the recipient of another Pulitzer, in the category of fiction, for* Executioner's Song, *his brutal and brilliant study of the life and death of convicted murderer Gary Gilmore.) "The Killer," a relatively early (midfifties) and almost completely unknown short story, has all the power in microcosm of Mailer's first crime novel, the bestselling* Tough Guys Don't Dance *(1984).*

THE KILLER
Norman Mailer

"Now," he said to me, "do you think you're going to bear up under the discipline of parole?"

"Yessir," I said.

He had white hair even though he was not more than fifty-two. His face was red. He had blue eyes. He was red, white, and blue. It was a fact I noticed before. They had this coloring. Maybe that was why they identified with the nation.

"In effect you're swearing that you won't take a drink for eight months."

"I know, sir, but I haven't had a drink inside for four years." Which was a lie. Three times I had come in with my cellmate on part of a bottle. The first time I was sick. The second time we had a fight, a quiet fight which I lost. He banged my head on the floor. Without noise. The third time we had sex. Democratic sex. We did each other.

"You understand that parole is not freedom."

"Yessir."

They asked these questions. They always asked the same questions, and they always got the same answers. It had nothing to do with what you said. It had nothing to do with how you shaved or how you combed your hair because you combed your hair the way everybody else did, and the day you went up to the Board you shaved twice. Maybe it had to do with how many shaving cuts you had, but I didn't have any. I had taken care, wow. Suppose it had to do with the way you moved. If two of the three men on the parole board liked the way you moved, you were all right, provided they didn't like the way you moved too much. Sex. No matter who I'm with, man or woman, I always get a feeling off them. At least I used to. I always could tell if they were moving inside or moving away, and I could tell if anything was going on inside. If we ever touched, I could tell better. Once I was in a streetcar and a girl sat down next to me. She was a full barrel. A very fat girl. Pretty face. I don't like fat. Very fat people have no quick. They can always stop. They can stop from doing a lot of things.

This girl and me had a future however. Her hip touched. I could feel what I did to her. From side of my leg, through my pants, and her dress, through some kind of corset, cheap plastic corset, something bad, through that, through her panties, right into her, some current went out of me, and I could feel it in her, opening up future. She didn't do a thing, didn't move. Fixed.

Well, five minutes, before I got off at my stop. In those minutes I was occupied by a project with that girl where we projected five years. I knew what I could do to her. I say without exaggeration I could take her weight down from one hundred eighty to one-eighteen in a year and it would have been a pleasure because all that fat was stored-up sugar she was saving. For somebody. She was stingy, congealed like lard, but I had the current to melt that. I knew it would not be hard to pick her up. If I did, the rest would happen. I would spend a year with her. It is difficult to pick up a fat girl, but I would have used shock treatment. For example, I would have coughed, and dropped an oyster on her skirt. I think it is revolting to do something like that, but it would have worked with this fat girl because disgust would have woke her up. That's the kind of dirt sex is, in the mind of somebody fat and soft and clammy. Sex to them is spit and mucus. It would have given me the opportunity to wipe it off. I could trust my fingers to give a touch of something. The point to the entire operation (people watching in the streetcar, me standing with my handkerchief, apologizing) would be that my fingers would be doing two things at once, proper and respectful in the part of my hand everybody else could see, flame through the handkerchief on her lap. I would have begun right there. For the least I would get her name. At the end of the five minutes I turned to take a look at her, and under that fat face, in the pretty face which could be very attractive, I could see there was a dumb look in her eyes that nothing was going to improve. That stopped me. Putting in a year on a girl like that would be bad unless she was all for me at the end. Stupidity is for nothing, not even itself. I detest stupidity in women—it sets me off. So I got off the car. Didn't even look at the girl. After she gets married to somebody fat and stupid like herself she will hate any man who looks like me because of that five minutes. Her plastic corset must have had a drug-store smell after I got off the trolley car. Think of plastic trying to smell.

I tell this as an example. On the outside it used to be that I never sat down next to anybody that I didn't feel them even when we didn't touch and two or three times a week, or even a day, I would be close to the possibilities of somebody like the fat girl. I know about certain things. I know with all policemen, detectives, correction officers, turnkeys, hacks, parole-board officials that sex is the problem with them. Smartest cellmate I had said one time like a philosopher, "Why, man, a judge will forgive any crime he is incapable of committing himself." My friend put it right. Sex is a bitch. With police. They can't keep their hands off. They do, but then it builds tension. For some it's bad. They can get ready to kill. That's why you comb your hair. Why you must look neat. You have to be clean. Above sex. Then a cop can like you. They ask you those questions knowing how you will answer. Often they know you are lying. For example they know that you will take a drink in the next six months. What is important is not that you are lying, but the kind of lie they hear in your voice. Are you afraid of them? Are you afraid they will see down into your lying throat? Then you are OK. They will pass you. If you are afraid of them, you're a good risk. But if you think they are stupid, faintest trace of such a thought in yourself, it comes through. Always one of them will be sensitive to condescension. It gets them ready to kill. A policeman never forgives you when you get him ready to kill. Obviously he can't do it, especially in a room performing official duty with a stenographer at the side. But the adrenaline goes through him. It is bad to take a flush of adrenaline for nothing. All that murder and nowhere to go. For example when you're standing up talking to a parole board it's important the way you stand, how tight your pants are. Good to be slim, trim, shipshape, built the way I am, provided you are modest. Do not project your groin forward or your hips back. It is best if your pants are not tight-fit. Younger juvenile delinquents actually make this sort of mistake. It is not that they are crazy so much as egotistical. They think older men will like them so much they will give them parole in order to look them up. A mistake. Once read in the newspapers about a Russian soldier who picked up a German baby and said, "It's beautiful," but then he got angry because he remembered the baby's father had been shooting his children, so he killed the baby. That's a cop. If you strut, even in good taste and subtle, they will start to get a glow where it is verboten, and they will like you, they will get a little rosy until they sense it goes nowhere, and wow the sex turns. Gets ready to kill you. If cops have an adrenaline wash for their trouble, you are remembered badly. It is much better to be slim, trim, shipshape, and a little peaked-looking, so they can see you as a thrifty son, which is the way they must have seen me because they gave parole that day, and I was out of there in a week. Out of prison. Out of the can. I think I would have died another year. Liver sickness or go berserk.

Now you may ask can police be so dumb as to let me go on an armed-robbery sentence, six years unserved out of ten? Well, they saw me as thrifty. I was careful that day with voice and posture. But how can police be so stupid as to think in categories like thrifty? That's easy, I can answer. Police are pent up, they're apes, they're bulls. Bulls think in categories.

2

Well, I've been feeling small for four years now. Prison is a bitch for people like me. It cuts your—I don't want to use doubtful language. It's a habit you build up inside. Some do use language that way. Some lifers. Spades. People who don't give a damn. They're playing prison as if it is their life, the only one they are going to have. But I am conservative in temperament. I comb my hair every morning, I comb it the same way. Minor matter you may say, but it isn't for me. I like to comb my hair when I feel like it. Animal of the woods. I have the suspicion— some would call it superstition—that combing my hair can spoil some good ideas. I would never say this to a hack but why is it not possible that some ideas live in your hair, the way the hair curls. I have very wavy hair when it is left to itself. Whenever I get a haircut, I have the feeling I'm losing possibilities I never got around to taking care of. Put it this way: when I comb my hair, it changes my mood. So naturally I prefer to comb it when I want to. In prison forget that. Comb your hair the same time same way every day. Look the same. If you're smart, keep your mood the same way. No ups. Nor downs. Don't be friendly. Don't be sullen. Don't offer company. Don't keep too quiet. If you stay safe, in the middle, and are the same thing every day you get a good report. The reason I get parole first time out, six years off a ten-year sentence is that I was a model prisoner which means just this: you are the same thing every day. Authorities like you if you are dependable. Be almost boring. I think what it may be about is that any man in authority finds his sleep important to him. People in authority can't stand the night. If you wear a uniform and you go to bed to sleep and a certain prisoner never bothers your dreams, you'll say a good word for him when it comes time to making out reports.

Of course you are not popular. Necessarily. My bunky shakes my hand when I get this good news, but I can see he is not happy in every way. So I complain about details. I am not to possess liquor at home, nor am I to frequent any bar even once, even at Christmas. Moreover, I am not to eat in any restaurant which serves liquor.

"What if you don't drink? But just eat there?"

"I'm not to go into any premises having a liquor license."

"A restaurant that don't serve liquor is a tearoom or a hash house."

"Crazy," I say. I don't like such expressions, but this is perfect to express my sentiments.

"Well, good luck."

It is possible we are thinking of the same things, which is the three times he got a bottle into the cell and we drank it together. The first time sick, second time we had a fight, third time sex. I remember I almost yelled in pain when my rocks got off, because they wouldn't stop. I was afraid I'd hurt myself. It had been so long. It seemed each time I took liquor something started in me that was different from my normal personality. By normal I mean normal in prison, no more. You wouldn't want a personality like that on the outside any more than you would want to smell like a laundry bag. But so far as inside personality went, I couldn't take liquor and keep the same. So if I started drinking on the secret when outside, I was in trouble. Because my style of personality would try to go back to what it was before, and too many eyes would be on me. My parole officer, people in the neighborhood. The parole board was getting me a job. They just about picked out the room where you lived. They would hear about it even if I didn't get into a rumble when I was drunk. If I kept a bottle in my room, I would have to hide it good. The parole officer has been known to come around and pay a friendly visit which is to say a sneak visit. Who could enjoy the idea of him sniffing the air in my room to see was there liquor on the breeze? If they caught me drinking in the eight months, back I would be sent to here. A gamble, this parole. But I was glad to take it, I needed out. Very much. Because there was a monotony in me. It had been coming in day after day. I didn't have the feeling of a current in me anymore, of anything going. I had the feeling if I sat down next to a girl like the fat girl now, and our legs touched, she would move away 'cause there was a blank in me which would pass into her. Something repulsive. There was something bad in me, something very dull. It wasn't in my body, it wasn't even in my mind, it was somewhere. I'm not religious, but it was somewhere. I mean I didn't know if I could keep control or not. Still, I couldn't have done it the other way. Eight more months. I might have flipped. Talking back to a hack, a fight. I'd have lost good time. There is only one nightmare in prison. It's that you don't get out, that you never get out because each time you come close the tension has built up in you so that you have to let it break out, and then your bad time is increased. So it's like being on the wrong escalator.

"Take it slow, take it easy," said my bunky. "Eight months goes by if you get yourself some sun."

"Yeah, I'm going to sleep in the sun," I said. "I'm going to drink it."

"Get a good burn your first day out, ha-ha. Burn the prison crap out of your pores."

Maybe the sun would burn the dullness away. That's what I was thinking.